THE

STORY

BEHIND

THE STORY

THE

STORY

BEHIND

THE STORY

26

Writers
and How They Work

EDITED BY Peter Turchi AND Andrea Barrett

WITH AN INTRODUCTION BY Richard Russo

 W. W. Norton & Company New York London

Manufacturing by The Haddon Craftsmen, Inc.

Book design by Chris Welch

Production manager: Anna Oler

Library of Congress Cataloging-in-Publication Data

The story behind the story : 26 writers and how they work / edited by Peter Turchi and

Andrea Barrett ; with an introduction by Richard Russo.— 1st ed.

p. cm.

ISBN 0-393-32532-6 (pbk.)

1. Short stories, American. 2. Short story—Authorship. I. Turchi, Peter, date.

II. Barrett, Andrea.

PS648.S5S766 2004

813'.0108—dc22

2003020045

W. W. Norton & Company, Inc., 500 Fifth Avenue, New York, N.Y. 10110

www.wwnorton.com

W. W. Norton & Company Ltd., Castle House, 75/76 Wells Street, London W1T 3QT

1 2 3 4 5 6 7 8 9 0

This book is dedicated to all the writers at Warren Wilson College.

CONTENTS

INTRODUCTION

Richard Russo

WRITING HAS ALWAYS been a romantic profession, linked in the popular imagination to drinking and myriad other forms of hard living, most of which are preferable to work, or at least the kind of work the majority of people are stuck doing over a lifetime. Writers will occasionally point out that writing is work too, but for the most part people don't believe us, and it's not a point we feel comfortable pressing, because most of us have had jobs as bartenders and cabdrivers and construction workers and teachers, and for us writing is a far more rewarding activity than mixing margaritas, driving back and forth to the airport, lifting heavy steel girders or grading lite papers; what we fear more than death or dismemberment is a life filled with nothing but activities such as these.

While writing novels and stories for a living isn't the scam that many people imagine, still, compared to the kind of work that puts bread and beer on the table without enriching the soul, it's pretty close. People who are not writers sense this, and they wonder if we'd mind sharing our secrets. They've got a zillion questions for us, but most of what they want to know boils down to this: did we learn this stuff, or were we born this way? Which is another way of asking whether we're basically the same as they are, or a different order of being. If we're a different order of being, then it's futile for them to try being like us. That would be like a cat trying to become a dog. The aspiration is certainly understandable, if futile. On the other hand, if we're basically the same as they are, then where does inspiration come from? Why does it come to us and not them? Did they miss a memo? Did we save our copy? The unsatisfactory truth of the matter—and most readers suspect this—is that we're both the same *and* different. The book you hold in your hand will help explain why and how this is so, and provide a window on the creative process.

IF WRITERS ARE not a wholly different order of being, possessed of special abilities that common folk can't hope to aspire to, then we should be able to teach others what we do and how we do it. But already we're on thin ice. It's a rare personal appearance where I'm not asked if writing can be taught, often by someone who has heard a famous writer say it can't. Writers who maintain that writing can *not* be taught and readers who believe them share a bond that can be very satisfying to both. The writer gets to pretend, maybe even believe, he's special and the reader gets to be special too, though in a different way. He, at least, knows the Truth—that writing is "a gift"—and this reader can therefore claim to live an undeceived life. It's sort of like the relationship of a fundamentalist true believer to his God: by accepting the truth of his own fallen nature, the born-again believer can at least take comfort in the fact that his faith has raised him above the common nonbeliever. It's your basic three-tier system—God first, then the few who have been blessed with genuine faith and understanding, then everybody else. The true believer's comfort derives from being closer to the top than to the bottom.

It's all horseshit, of course. Writers aren't gods, and saying you can't teach people to write is as silly as saying you can't teach them to play the violin. Of course you can. I myself have taught more than I can count, and so have the other authors included in this book, all of whom are on the faculty of the Warren Wilson College MFA Program for Writers, in Swannanoa, North Carolina, the finest program of its kind in the country. When I say we've taught people how to write, I suppose what I mean is that we've helped them to learn, we've supervised a part of their apprenticeship, we've read what they wrote and offered advice. We've shared our own experience of writing. Later, in the books these students published, they thanked us for our help, maybe even said they couldn't have done it without us. That's almost never true, as is evidenced by the fact that people were writing excellent stories and novels long before there were writing programs, but what's equally true, and more to the point, is that all artists need mentors, just as they need the company of other apprentices with whom to share their triumphs and travails. Good teachers and the company of other good students save the artist time, the one thing we're all destined to run out of.

Okay, I admit it. I'm playing a kind of semantic game here. Writers who claim that writing can't be taught generally mean that *great* writing can't be taught, or that genius can't be taught. The only thing that really *can* be taught, they maintain, is competence, and competence, for a serious artist, simply isn't enough. With this I agree, and so, I suspect, would every writer in this volume. Salieri never would have been Mozart, even with Mozart for a teacher, first because he wasn't sufficiently talented—when it comes to art, you can learn all the rules and still never be any good—and second because there were lots of things that Mozart couldn't teach because he didn't understand these things himself. But the more important point is this: artists seldom progress in a predictable, linear fashion. Most talented writers actually start getting good before they're entirely competent, which means that what can and can't be taught are proceeding along parallel tracks, and dwelling on what can't be taught isn't terribly productive, especially when there's so much work to do.

Far better to concentrate on what can be taught and shared: craft and experience. Most "how to" writing books, as well as the curricula of good writing programs, focus on craft. To write a good story, you have to understand how characters are developed, how conflict will deepen our understanding of these characters and impel them into drama. Just as important, you have to understand how point of view affects the story and how tone (the author's attitude toward the story he's telling) must at all times be clear without ever being stated. You have to know what goes in scene, what goes in narration, as well as when and how to slow time down, when to speed it up. You have to know what belongs in dialogue and what doesn't. These are a few of the building blocks of stories, and they can all be taught—every single one of them—and until they've been mastered, there's absolutely nothing to be gained by worrying about what *can't* be taught.

The veteran writer's experience, though, is nearly as invaluable to an apprentice writer as the elements of craft, and that's where this book comes in. It contains not just twenty-six well-crafted stories that apprentice writers can learn from, but also a discussion of the experience of writing them. Nonwriters may be struck by similarities of artistic experience revealed by the writers of these stories, by how often, for instance, they did not know where their stories were headed, by how surprised they were to discover a truth, a knowledge, they did not know was in them, as well as by similar strategies these writers used to coax their stories along, to trick them into revealing themselves. Apprentice writers, on the other hand, are more likely to be surprised by just how varied the tactics and habits of experienced writers can be. Clearly, we've not discovered one truth, or one Zen "way." That there is no wrong method (or right method, for that matter) for writing stories is made clear by Stephen Dobyns's recollection of how he came to write his first book of stories. His description of the exercise he used to teach himself (already an accomplished poet and novelist) how to write a short story left me slack-jawed with amazement. I wouldn't have believed a good story (much less a whole book of them) could possibly emerge from such an arbitrary, screwball methodology, but it did, and Stephen's story is, in fact, one of my favorites. That's one of the things you'll notice about this book. It doesn't say, "Do this," or "Do it this way," or "Never make the mistake of doing this." It simply says, "Here's what I did. Here's where I went wrong. Here's what I discovered. Next time, in a different situation—and the situation *will* be different—I might do it all differently, and I'll have good reasons then too."

For quite different reasons, nonwriters and writers alike are intrigued by the question of autobiography. How much of what's in the story really happened? How much did you make up? Every good writer places a premium on imagination, which is why we're sometimes reluctant to admit that a particularly vivid detail in a story was not invented, and why we shy away from providing an inventory of what actually happened. On the other hand, we're nowhere without the real world, nowhere without its gifts. Tracy Daugherty speaks for many of us when he writes: "It wouldn't be particularly helpful to list what is and isn't true in 'City Codes' . . . it's all true except for the parts I made up." What Antonya Nelson's imaginative contribution to her story was can be inferred from her essay, but she's anxious for us to understand that the story wouldn't have come into being were it not for a real-life "gift" from a student who tried to write the story herself, failed, and finally said here, you can have it. Steven Schwartz gives us a fascinating account of the problems that can ensue when real life is too generous, by giving the writer a story that has too many perfect narrative elements, too many answers and not enough questions. On the other hand, when we're given too little, we have to go out and find what we need. Jim Shepard, confronting what he refers to as "that horrifyingly narrow bandwidth we call autobiographical experience," explains how an artist's imagination can be triggered by research, by a thirst for knowledge of the world beyond the writer's experience, wisdom echoed by Charles Baxter, whose essay explains how his own obsession with Ezra Pound led to the writing of the strangest story of his career, even as it required him to break every rule of story writing he believed in (and taught).

This book also brings home the fact that our struggles with our material are as individual as we are, as individual as the motives that impelled us to write stories in the first place. Compare, for instance, Peter Turchi and Robert Boswell. The two men, it's worth noting, are roughly the same age and are friends who studied with the same writers at the University of Arizona. Yet in temperament, in habit of mind, they couldn't be more different. What surprised me most about Pete's essay was how much he remembered about the writing of his story. I no sooner write a story than I begin to forget the details of the struggle: what I knew, what I didn't, what came first, what came later, what was hard, what was easy. Pete seems to have forgotten very little, and his recollection and analysis are diary-like in their precision, providing a detailed and revealing description of his own creative process. Boswell's essay is just as revealing, but in a completely different fashion. If Boz remembers anything about the particular difficulties of writing his story, he doesn't feel compelled to share it. He's able to explain the story only by telling a second story, just as riveting, about two boys who tell stories. We're suddenly three layers deep in narrative, which Boswell admits is the way he seeks understanding. "I have grown to understand narrative as a form of contemplation," he writes, "a complex and contradictory way of thinking."

I was also particularly intrigued by how many of these essays dealt with "cross-fertilization," how figuring out the solution to a problem in one story paid a dividend in others. Joan Silber writes tellingly about the familiar experience of discovering in the ending to one story the beginning of another, and then another. For Margot Livesey, the dividend was even greater, in that the story she wrote for this collection provided the spark she needed for her marvelous novel *Eva Moves the Furniture,* which had had her stumped for a long time. In fact, this volume has a fair amount to say about these "sparks," these gifts of grace that the ancients personified as muses. For Kevin McIlvoy's story, the muse was music. "I do not revise in order to discover how the voice behaves, but how it breathes," he says, continuing to explain that his task was to locate "the many musics inside the music of a certain voice." For Susan Neville the spark was visual, a photograph she came across in a yearbook while she was looking for the right narrator for her story. "Once I had her face in front of me," she reports, "the narrative came easily." For Andrea Barrett, the key to her story was language itself—"the rhythm, the syntax, the infolded meanings of a certain phrase— through which so much else can be generated."

And finally there are in this collection glimpses of what I can only describe as joy. C. J. Hribal's essay reveals the pure delight of creating characters who are as real as anyone the writer knows, who continue to haunt the writer's imagination long after their stories are, we had thought, done. For David Haynes the joy is in "the wildness, silliness and absurdity that pushes against the neatness and discretion we are taught to value." Robert Cohen reports, with some embarrassment, "literally cackling" as he wrote "The Varieties of Romantic Experience." He took this as "a bad sign," but I didn't. Reading the story, I cackled right along with him, though I was very glad for his brave confession and understood completely his fear that his delight might be seen as immodesty, or worse, derangement. Truth is, I cackled all through the writing of my novel *Straight Man,* and for me that was a four-year spell of giggles. We're allowed to enjoy ourselves, we writers. In fact, if there's a single secret we're reluctant to share with nonwriters, it may be this: Damn, it's fun.

THE

STORY

BEHIND

THE STORY

Antonya Nelson

STRIKE ANYWHERE

T HIS WAS THE next time after what was supposed to be the last time. The father parked at the curb before the White Front, and the boy found himself making a prayer. It was Sunday, after all, and this was what his mother did when faced with his father's stubborn refusal to do what he said he'd do. Or not do what he said he'd not do. *Please God,* and God knew the rest.

"Don't move a muscle, buddy, you hear?"

The boy nodded. Afraid to look at his father—his father could find accusation in any expression turned his direction—he sat small on the truck bench seat. His father had inclinations like a dog, like a bear: he pounced on motion, a little witlessly. Just as the truck door creaked open, the bar's sign flashed on. His father climbing out of the vehicle grunted as if answering the neon light, "I'm coming." A vivid imprint of the beckoning white letters burned into the boy's mind.

"Not one inch," his father reminded him, face looming at the window before locking the truck door, slamming it, and crossing the sidewalk. He slapped the wallet in his back pocket, cinched his hat, drew breath to make himself tall, and disappeared through the dark entryway of the bar.

The boy's name was Ivan and he was eight years old. He had been sent on this errand to prevent just this sort of thing from happening. His father had quit drinking three months ago. Today they had gone to the Sunshine Station on the highway for lighter fluid and stick matches. His mother was home with the other three children waiting to ignite the barbecue. It was five o'clock on a Sunday in May in Portersburg, Montana. The snow had melted and the grass had popped up, bright green and bent, as if it'd been simply blanketed all winter, waiting. The boy's mouth watered for venison; they'd thawed a few steaks to celebrate spring, to congratulate his father's sobriety. His mother had fixed cowboy beans and his big sister made marshmallow whipped cream maraschino cherry fruit salad. Soft white dinner rolls you could squeeze into doughy spheres the size of eyeballs and poke all at once between your teeth. The meal shimmered like a mirage, like a hunger.

Main Street bustled in the welcome warmth of the day. Finally, it was time to step out. People dawdled on the sidewalk rather than plowing against a frigid wind. They had removed their coats so that you could tell who was who, the men from the women, the strangers from the locals. At Ivan's house his mother had pulled the plastic from the windows this morning, a ripping unzipping. Every winter the family grew accustomed to looking through the blurry insulating wrap. Then spring arrived, and the house, like the people, shed a layer, stood naked and clear.

They lived next door to the police station and jail. With the windows open you could eavesdrop on the dispatch radio, the funny codes the police used to mean one sort of mishap or another. "Nine one one," Ivan's sister Leanne said, whenever she spotted their father's truck rolling home late and slow. "That's a big ten-four, you can just call us at one eight hundred asshole, twenty-four seven."

What, Ivan wondered, had made his father come to the White Front today? He felt both responsible for his father's bad decision and completely irrelevant to it. A few years ago the grocery was located downtown, a mere three blocks from their house. If it hadn't moved to the highway—wider aisles, more parking, bakery, and ATM—then Leanne would have been sent on foot for the forgotten supplies. Perhaps Ivan himself. The whole town might be said to have conspired in his father's fall, guilty cause of this effect. Or not. The truck cab was neither too cold nor too hot; that simple fact could have been the one that had decided his father. Gentle spring weather. It would be safe to leave his son sitting in it for however long necessary.

INSIDE THE BAR Dwight took his stool. He hadn't been to the White Front since February but of course nothing had changed. No seasons here. There was payday, and happy hour, and closing time. There was the first sip, the free round, and the flung-back shot that was a flat-out mistake. On the wall, the Hall of Fame. Your picture, a gold star pressed reverently on the glass if you happened to be dead. No matter how long you abandoned this place, it was waiting when you returned. Welcome to Miller Time.

"Dwight," said the bartender.

"Frozene," said Dwight, admiring himself in the mirror under the stuffed jackalope, beside the landscape painted on a handsaw. The Coors waterfall fell. "Jack and a Bud back."

Frozene nodded, polishing with her damp cloth diaper the worn wood before her new customer. Frozene's adopted parents had owned the White Front; she'd lived here all her life. At the other end of the bar sat the young wife of the jeweler. Mrs. Donoglio, the second. Her husband's shop of sapphires was just down the block. An old man with a dowager's hump, he looked through his eyepiece at you when you entered his business, a giant wet oyster of a glance, suspicious and unctuous at once. Along with setting stones, Mr.

Donoglio fixed watches. Fine motor, his skills were. His first wife had died a few years ago, alone upstairs, while downstairs he catered to the town's meager tourist population. This new wife had come from Missoula, a college girl, bored here, a religious drinker and smoker always with her nose in a book.

"Hey, miss merry sunshine," Dwight called to her. She shared only one trait with his own wife: they both thought they were better than him. However, this one's sullenness cheered him, set him in heckling mode. She waited a second before looking up, holding her place on the page with a finger.

"Don't be telling me to turn that frown upside down," she warned.

"Sourpuss," Dwight said. Habitually she laid a twenty on the bar and drank gin and tonic until there were only a couple of damp bills left for a tip. She lived a twenty-dollar day; think what she might save, Dwight thought. After, she walked back to the jewelry store where she made her home upstairs, in the same bed, Dwight supposed, where the first wife had died. This scrawny female, profane and sarcastic, wearing Wranglers like a man, hair cut by her own hand, ready to swear at you and your cowpoke ideas, she seemed to think she was the first educated drinker the bar had ever served. Oh, by the way, Dwight could say, there was such and such the famous writer here once, also from Missoula, who set his famous poem, a moment of it, anyway, in the jailhouse beside Dwight's very own home, right up the hill. He could send that snooty girl, the sapphire king's young second wife, to the copy of the poem that hung in the back of the bar, typed up and yellow, signed by the poet himself. Now who's smart, Dwight could say, now who's God's gift.

"What?" she demanded.

Whoops. Drinking, he often found himself inside out, thoughts transformed into words, urges into action. "Can't a fellow be glad to see you?"

"Unlikely," she said. "Extremely."

"I'm an unlikely type," he allowed, magnanimous as could be. Alcohol, its proximity and promise, spread wings in his chest.

"You and that freak," she said, indicating the customer who'd just entered. This was the crazy man with his piggybacked pets, the dog, the cat, the mouse, each member of the food chain sitting smack on the back of his enemy. The mouse was never the same mouse for long. The freak was notorious from last summer, when the tourists had fawned over him. Nobody local—that is, nobody who had to deal with him day in, day out—made eye contact. His eyes were the intense heat-seeking ones of barely contained insanity. They wanted more than to see. Now he asked for and received a beer and a bowl.

"*Here* you go," he said, loud enough for others to listen in, dipping his fingers tenderly in his drink to let his creatures lick it off. "Who sits on Mr. Mouse? you might ask," he asked the air. "Fleas! I say!"

Dwight raised his eyebrows at the college snot, colluding gamely. It was good to know that the two of them, while drinking in the daylight hours in the afternoon of the lord, had not stooped to animal tricks.

The jeweler's wife pushed herself ungracefully from her barstool and headed for the women's room, where she'd sneer at the sign that told her *No more paper products? Wipe your ass with a spotted owl!* But then Dwight saw what had happened to her since February: she'd gotten big with child. When she returned she scowled at his appraisal of her.

"That's right," she said. "So just spare me the lecture. You and that frigging pharmacist. 'Madam, I hope you realize that Valium and prenatal vitamins are not a winning combination?' Oh, *really*? Go ahead, call the SPCA, you can report a twofer, me and the mouse-cat-dog sandwich over there."

The freak looked hurt but the bartender, like all wise bartenders, was keeping strictly out of it. Between her and the customers was a definite barrier: the literal bar itself, and her authority to cut them off. The Confederate flags hanging everywhere like a promise of loaded weaponry and a willingness to use it. Plus her simple, relentless sobriety; Frozene, legend had it, had been traded as an infant for a bottle of beer. One beer for one baby, her new parents the bartenders making the exchange. Just cockeyed enough to be true. Besides Frozene and Dwight and the jeweler's wife and the freak show, three Mexican construction workers sat at a far table speaking Spanish, ignoring all the whites, nutty or not. There was no one to whom Dwight could voice an appeal.

"I didn't know you were in a family way," he said.

"Oh, the *family* way," said the jeweler's wife, slapping open her book and glaring into its pages.

OUT IN THE truck, Ivan cracked the passenger window. The air smelled of mown grass. His stomach rumbled. He rustled the grocery sack idly, lighter fluid and matches. If only they hadn't needed these. *Strike anywhere,* the box instructed. Ivan opened the package and was pleased to see the plenitude, the rows of patriotic little sticks, white, red, and a blue dot like a berry on each of a hundred tips. He removed one of the ranks and stuck it in his mouth, first exploring the bland square end between his teeth as it turned, then reversing the match.

He chewed thoughtlessly. The match tasted like something he'd only smelled before, a curious crossover sensation. He had a missing tooth—"Canine incisor," his sister Leanne had informed him—and the matchstick slipped into the space in a soothing fashion, his gum tender yet pleasantly satisfied by the square plug of wood. Eventually, he pulled the denuded stick from between his lips. He could not tell one end from the other, now. His mouth felt oddly dry. He removed another match from the box and set to work. Time could pass this way, he thought. You needed a way to pass time. After his father had entered the bar, the man with the three pets had followed. Ivan liked this man, the way he would stop on the street and let you stroke his animals. They were tame. The kitty rode on the dog's back. The mouse sat atop the kitty. Ivan, all the children, were cheered by the way they got along. "The lion shall sleep with the sheep," the man claimed. "Heaven is liketh that, a peaceable kingdom." The man's eyes reminded Ivan of horse eyes, big and brown, lacking the common tiny pupil that most humans possessed. What would you see, without those little black pinpoints?

"Ivan!" a pack of girls called, banging on the hood. His oldest sister's friends, they adored teasing him, rubbing his head, wiggling his ribs. They clustered around, wearing what his sister wore, belly buttons one and all on display, henna tattoos wandering their wrists, hair washed and stylishly wild just for a saunter down Main. They were seeking other boys, in other trucks.

"You hungry, Mr. I?" one asked, grinning, showing her mouth of metal, tiny rubber bands blue and white, the high school colors.

"You want a cigarette to go with that match?"

"Maybe a bottle rocket?"

"You see that guy?" the girl named Kimmy inquired, hushed, watching the White Front door as if the man with his pets might pop right back out. "Well, my mom and me took one of his mice. We found it in the Trust Donut Shop. We knew it was his 'cause it was so tame and all, like on downers. Now it lives in my mom's dollhouse, that one with the lights?"

"Your mom lets it go poop in her dollhouse?"

"Oh hell no. She's got him in little mouse diapers. Diapers and a dress. But he won't wear the hat."

"Whatsup with this?" Margot leaned over to ask Ivan, bent at a severe right angle at the waist, swinging her rear and chewing a tiny piece of gum at his window. He smelled cinnamon, Big Red. She was the prettiest, the girl her friends had designated royalty. Ivan could see down her tank top, a mole, a pimple, her small pale breasts. "You get to come downtown, but not Leanne?"

"Where's Leanne?" the others asked, a vague refrain to accompany their skittery glances. They were following the traffic, endlessly running their fingers through their hair, over their hips, touching the corners of their shiny, shiny lips. They studied their reflections in the rearview, in the store windows, in each other's eyes. They pulled their shirts down, then stretched their bare arms to make their navels wink into view. For belts, they wore slim silver chains.

Ivan smiled around his match. His sister's friends used his father's truck the way moths used a streetlight, just fluttering.

"You think that weirdo misses his mouse?" Margot asked Ivan before she sauntered away, snapping her gum. But Ivan wondered if the mouse missed his man.

D W I G H T ,   O N   H I S third set of drinks, genuinely curious, asked the bartender if it was legal to serve a pregnant woman.

"Is it legal to serve a sanctimonious hypocrite?" said the jeweler's wife, face still in her book. She might have fooled some people, but Dwight had noticed the pages weren't turning. "You and Mr. Science at the pharmacy, him in his lab coat and his bulletproof glass with the little speak-hole."

"Live and let live," said the wise Frozene.

"Then we agree," said Dwight. "But see, my problem is, she's not letting that wee thing live. I mean, you've heard tell of the deformed infants, you seen that shit on the Discovery Channel."

"Discover this," the girl said, blowing a fat raspberry. Dwight laughed. He loved the ones who sassed back. Why, he asked himself, why did he love them? His wife didn't sass; she wept. Pathetic. She prayed and wrote in her diary and she used to talk to her sister on the phone, but nowadays he noticed she was talking to their oldest girl, Leanne. When Dwight found himself driven to strike his wife, she never struck back. From the beginning, he'd understood she was not ideal for someone like him. This one at the bar would have given him a run for his money. Resistance was sexy; maybe she and the jeweler

had some knock-down, drag-outs. The thought made Dwight reconsider the old guy with his monocle.

"Listen up," he said, "you've got your warnings on every bottle of
liquor in here, just look at 'em." Dwight pointed at his own Bud and
its pregnant woman clause. "Warning!" he shouted down to the jeweler's wife.

"Fuck! Off!" she shouted right back, which raised Frozene's
watchful brow. Briefly Dwight pictured the husband dashing around
that old iron bed, revving for this hellcat, his one magnified eye
swimming after her. Dwight laughed again. He loved liquor; the past
three months without it felt to him like a humiliation, a sentence he
had served for bending to his wife's will. And now his reward was a
barbecue. Ice cream and cake. Getting through those months had not
made him proud. It had been one dreary day at a time, lined up
behind him like empty boxes, a train of hollow testament to his wife's
saintliness and his own pussy-whippedness. He closed his eyes to visit
the full rosy bloom inside his head, the fiery flaring heat. You either
quit drinking or you ended up in the Hall of Fame with Shreve and
Helmar and Evert and Tiger and Tex and all the rest, each and every
one raising a glass for the camera, their tiny gold stars applied later,
when it was over. *Rehab is for quitters,* Dwight's favorite bumper
sticker said.

The Mexicans took themselves to the Keno machines to make
some hopeless wishes with their wrinkled dollar bills. On the huge
television hanging ominously over the room played the country
music station, complete with captions for the hearing-impaired.
Through the bar's front door drifted three slaphappy schoolteachers,
spouseless and silly. The jeweler's wife didn't look up, the freak bent
to confide into his dog's ear, and when the new people had settled,
called their orders out, and started talking among themselves, Dwight
rose to say howdy.

"Easy," warned Frozene, and Dwight reassured her with an innocent hand.

"Let me just ask you all something, you mind?" he began. They looked up gamely, one of the women he recognized as Leanne's teacher, and who, he discerned, recognized him. Not necessarily favorably. "You see that young lady over yonder?" Now the woman's smile trembled, her sensing, before her companions, that they were being enticed into a drama where they did not belong. Dwight insisted, "You see her? That smart girl reading a book and sucking on a long tall drink?" The jeweler's wife, Dwight realized, was closer to his daughter's age than his own, a fact that derailed him briefly. "Well," he went on, finishing what he'd started, "guess what?"

Because he obviously wasn't going anywhere until they guessed what, one of the schoolteachers cleared her throat, took a breath, and said, "What?"

"Pregnant!" Dwight declared. "That's what. Just as knocked up as she could be, drowning her little one in liquor. Now just what in the hell you think of that?"

They stared, sighing, this threesome of educators who'd rendezvoused for a giddy margarita at the tail end of the semester, who came to the White Front maybe once or twice a year, escaping the monotonous industry of responsibility, who, frankly, couldn't count the jeweler's wife among their concerns, and who finally politely, fearfully, ventured the opinion that the bartender had: none of their business. Dwight looked shocked, though he wasn't. Teachers. They'd confirmed a certain suspicion of his.

"Hey Hortense," Dwight said when he returned to his stool. "Isn't that your name?" It was the ugliest name he could think of. The jeweler's wife didn't even look up. Just transferred a burning cigarette to her left hand and raised the third finger of her right, nailbitten, both hands utterly ringless despite her husband's profession.

Smiling, Dwight glanced languidly in the direction of the freak's table. There, he finally made out that the man was dangling the mouse by its tail before the cat's whiskers. Back and forth the gray thing swung, its front fingery paws twitching together as if steepled in prayer, the freak gazing on as if to hypnotize himself. But why, you had to wonder, didn't the cat snatch at the creature?

IVAN WAS MAKING a house with matchsticks on the truck's dusty dashboard. The girls had moved on, glossy hair, languid hips, tottery platform shoes, rowdy voices, their bright shirts each bearing a message: *Hard Rock Café, Angel, Mischief.* The sun had fallen but the evening was light, temperate. A woman pushing a baby carriage had just walked by. At first Ivan thought she was speaking to him, her mouth uttering sentences in his direction, catching him, he thought, as he ate his matches. But then he had realized, as she passed, that it was the baby she spoke to in front of her in his stroller, the little guy waving his hands, cross-eyed, trying in vain to catch his own waving bare feet.

The rule was that Ivan could only use the naked matches to shape his house. Their square stems were like tiny one-bys. If he bit down, they threatened to give, like crisp carrots. Once he softened the wood beneath the tip, the red and blue substance melted quickly in his mouth. The taste was neither good nor bad, the flavor one that Ivan had grown accustomed to. He was reminded of the Fourth of July, the sizzle of sparklers. His house needed twenty-nine matches; he had completed the walls and windows and roof and was working on the chimney when he noticed the man.

Beside the White Front, in the dark entryway of the defunct wedding dress shop, a shadowy shape suddenly began moving. Inside the old shop windows remained the damaged mannequins whose rusty satin gowns still hung on their amputated figures, handless some, headless others. Fake eyelashes clung like daddy longlegs on the remaining pink plastic cheeks. The moving shadow emerging from between the dress windows assumed a human form, pale face first and then animate body, shocking, like a broken-down groom stepping out of the ruined wedding party. The dolls smiled but not the man.

Ivan watched wide-eyed as the man came forward, lurching, wavering, like a marionette manipulated by a child, one moment upright, the next heaping limp on the sidewalk, where a high school couple had to veer around his flung, booted foot.

"Totally trashed," noted the boy in the couple, and the girl fanned the air before her nose.

Then Ivan recognized the loose-limbed figure as Kermit Boyer, one of a few drunk men who haunted Portersburg, the quiet one who slept in a horse stable just outside town. Kermit gathered himself delicately from the pavement, collapsed skeleton in his flexible rubble. Ivan was tempted to aid him, to fetch the white cards that had snowed from his pocket which Kermit seemed not to have noticed. He gained his knees and then his feet, swaying there. He closed his eyes very slowly and then focused on Ivan through the windshield, lining up his gaze like a pair of floating compass needles. He aimed himself for Ivan's father's truck. The match in Ivan's mouth went wildly into and out of the empty socket. Kermit reached the truck's hood and melted onto it, sliding along the fender, grabbing on to the side mirror of the passenger door like a handle. His fingers were brown, crazy with scratches and scabs. His face was like a large rotten apple.

"Little boy," said Kermit Boyer, rapping with his free hand against the glass.

Ivan scooted to his father's side of the truck, beneath the steering wheel. His fingers trembled on the horn, ready to alert the people in the street, who would turn then and rescue him from his nightmare, this desperate drunken figure. When his father came home drunk, his mother hurried the children upstairs to their rooms. His father was not a bad man, she would explain. Only Leanne had the nerve to yell at him. "Drunk jerk!" she would shout from the top of the steps, and his father would yell right back up at her. "Hussy slut!"

Ivan, like his mother, suffered those words. *Please God,* the two of them whispered.

"*Please,*" his father often sneered, "is the beg word."

In the locked truck, in the oncoming dark, Ivan's fear paralyzed him, Kermit's appearance, its suddenness, its ugly publicness, a person crawling like an animal on the sidewalk, draped like dirty laundry on his father's vehicle . . .

"Little boy," Kermit Boyer repeated, his fingertips now inside the passenger window, chapped lips at the crack. A missing tooth, Ivan noticed, canine incisor like his own, whiskers, loose jowls, eyes loopy. "Little boy, don't do that," he said, his breath powerfully upon Ivan, a wave of sour ferment. "Don't eat the matches, boy," he said. "Good lord, son, that's *poison!*"

The stick in Ivan's mouth stopped. And then Kermit abruptly disappeared, dropped like a felled deer, unstrung puppet, onto the cooling pavement beside the truck.

I OFTEN MAKE CAVALIER statements concerning issues with the assumption that my students will automatically agree, the assertion having in its favor the weight of legend, received wisdom. Creative Writing Lore: we are partaking in Workshop-speak. Such was the case when I told my student Henry that though I thought irony essential in fiction, the irony in his beloved O. Henry stories was "easy" irony. As opposed to "deep" irony. The watch chain and the hairbrushes: sappy, I said dismissively. The makings of a children's book.

Henry the student was supposed to nod agreeably, and he even *sounded* agreeable when he replied because he is British, and carries that polite and proper intonation wherever he goes and concerning whatever he says. But he didn't agree. In fact, he said, he *much* preferred those stories that "hung suspended in the mind like a well-formed box." The structure that formed his "box," as he went on to explain, seemed to be plot- rather than character-related, an exoskeleton that contained the characters and their instrumental ironic peccadilloes. "The story rather tells itself," he concluded. He cited Graham Greene as a heavier-weight supplement to O. Henry.

One does like a story that tells itself. A few years later another student came to office hours to cry about a short story she was trying to write. The rough draft was a long handwritten ungrammatical cliché-ridden horror-movie sort of tale that ended with the sentence "And then she woke up and realized it was all a dream."

"A nightmare," I said, and meant. In fact, the whole thing *had* been a dream, the student's, and she wasn't crying because she thought I wouldn't like her story but because she herself recognized the lameness of her project. She really wanted to tell a story about this dream she'd had. Her dream had been instructive to her. It was about the rivalry between her brother and husband. In it, she had been literally torn asunder. Telling me about it (under questioning), she realized that her older brother had cared for her the first seventeen years of her life (they were orphans), and that she'd been married the next seventeen. This current year marked the point at which she would have been with her husband longer than her brother. It was a funny cusp.

Creative writing instruction often seems like therapy. I even have a couch in my office. I stock Kleenex. My undergraduate desperately wanted to impart the strong emotional content of her dream. At the same time, she wanted to write a story that resembled the kind of story you hear around the fireplace or at the bar, the story that is worth telling aloud, that guarantees an audience's attention and admiration, that, like jokes, inspires another in its wake. She said that her family was always telling stories, the men, she corrected herself, were always telling stories, and if you wanted to enter into the circle of their social gathering, you had to have a good story to tell. As an example, she told me her brother's story. It was the story of a boy who, left in a car outside a bar where his foster parent drinks, begins to eat matches. A drunk who has passed out on the sidewalk outside the bar, witnessing the ingestion of the matches, pulls himself to his feet and staggers to the car in order to warn the boy of the danger of eating matches.

"That's a great story," I told my student. One story had led to another; this one was dangling like a shapely Christmas ornament in my head already.

"You can have it," she said. "It's my brother's, and when I told him I had to write a story for your class, he said that I could have it. I couldn't write it, so you can have it. You write it."

The fact that my student and her brother understood stories as something like objects to hand over made me think of Henry and his well-formed box. And so I wrote "Strike Anywhere." Inspired by students and unlike any other story I've written.

Margot Livesey

THE FLOWERS OF THE FOREST

THE SUMMER I was ten my parents moved to a small village in the borders of Scotland. On the way down from Edinburgh I sat in the back of the car reading *Robinson Crusoe,* and once the bustle of moving had died down I felt much like Crusoe before Friday arrived. Six weeks stretched before me until school began. I did my best to fill the long empty days by exploring the countryside, but even the most exciting discoveries—a cave, a telephone-box in the middle of a cornfield—without companionship lacked lustre.

One afternoon, when I was bicycling along the main street of the village, a young woman came trotting towards me on a chestnut horse. Half the books I read were about riding, and every Christmas and birthday I asked my parents for a pony. As soon as horse and rider were past, I turned and pedalled after them. They led me down a lane of cottages to a farm.

I got off my bike and crouched beside it, pretending to adjust the brakes. In surreptitious glances I saw the rider negotiate the gate into the farmyard. A man emerged from one of the barns. He took hold of the reins and she bent down in the saddle to speak to him.

After that I visited the farm almost daily. I would sit on the wall surrounding the yard and watch the hens scratch in the dirt. Among them moved a woman with hair the colour of marmalade. She was always carrying something: a pail of water, a shovel. Much less frequently the man I had seen on the first day appeared. He strode swiftly through the yard accompanied by two collies. Whenever I saw him coming, I ducked out of sight, afraid he would think I was trespassing.

One morning as I perched on the wall the woman came over. Up close her skin was weather-beaten to a colour only a few shades lighter than her orange hair; her eyes were the pale blue of forget-me-nots. I was sure she was going to send me away, but instead she asked if I wanted to help feed the hens. I slid down off the wall and followed her.

She told me that her name was Chrissie; the man was her brother, Selby. They had inherited the farm from their parents and had lived there all their lives. "When I was your age," she said, "I had to be up at five every morning to milk the cows before I went to school." Next day when I climbed onto the wall, she simply waved at me to join her, and from then on it was settled that I could come and go as I pleased.

Chrissie never introduced me to Selby, but she must have told him who I was. He acknowledged my presence with the faintest of nods. Sometimes he spoke: "For Christ's sake, close the gate," he would say, or "Bugger this rain." He was more weather-beaten than Chrissie, and his eyes were a keener blue. During the war he had been in the RAF, and it was easy to imagine him scanning the skies for enemy planes.

One afternoon I was gazing after him when a voice said, "Hello. You must be Ruth."

I turned to find the horsewoman smiling down at me. Her lips were full and very red. She was unusually tall, taller than Chrissie, almost as tall as Selby. "I'm Irene," she said, "like the song." She sang the first line, "Now sometimes I live in the country." And asked if I would like to meet Ginger.

As we walked to the field, Irene told me that she had gone to the school I was about to attend. Now she worked for a dentist in the local town. She lived with her parents in a bungalow just up the road from the farm. On my trips back and forth I had noticed one house with a hedge so neat that it could have served as a table. I asked if that was hers.

Irene nodded. "My dad's a maniac with the clippers."

We leaned on the gate of the field and Ginger trotted over. His coat glistened like a newly hulled chestnut. "Isn't he beautiful?" said Irene. "I board him at the farm."

She produced two lumps of sugar from her pocket and stretched out her hand. Delicately Ginger bent to take his reward. "What do you think of Selby?" Irene asked.

"How do you mean?"

"Well, don't you think he's good-looking?"

The question made me giggle. "I don't know."

"Take my word for it," said Irene, "he's mouth-watering. If it weren't for Chrissie, he'd have been married years ago."

CHRISSIE HAD PREDICTED that once school began I would forget about the farm, but even after a couple of months I still felt out of step with the girls in my class. I did not understand their jokes about boys, their winks and nudges. It was a relief to go down to the farm where I knew just what to do.

The day after Halloween there was no sign of Chrissie when I climbed over the wall. I went to make sure that the ducks were shut in for the night, then set off round the henhouses. This was the second collection of the day and I would be lucky to find a dozen eggs. Most of the hundred and fifty hens were well past their prime.

Chrissie joked that the farm was a retirement home for superannu-ated animals. No animal was ever sent away and often she returned from auctions with live-stock that had been destined for the abattoir. Only the sheep, which Selby took care of, were handled in a business-like manner.

I made my way round the large henhouse. Then I went on to the stable, where one or two of the more adventurous hens sometimes laid. Ginger had not yet been brought in for the night and the door stood open wide. As I crossed the threshold, there was a gasp.

"Ruth," said Chrissie, "you startled me."

She was standing just inside the doorway, her hand raised. At first I had no idea what she was doing. Then I realised she was peering into the mirror of a compact. I felt like an intruder. "I was gathering the eggs," I stammered.

"I thought I had something in my eye." She gave her reflection a final glance and closed the compact. "I'm going to fetch Ginger. I don't think Irene's been down all week. He's awfully fidgety." Although Chrissie fed Ginger during the week, Irene was meant to come down and exercise him.

"Maybe she's busy," I offered.

"She lives five minutes away. How busy can she be?" Without waiting for an answer, Chrissie hurried out of the stable. On several occasions I had heard her say that cruelty to animals was the ultimate sin; she was even reluctant to put down poison for the numerous rats who lived in the granary.

A single egg, still warm, lay under the manger. I put it in the pail and headed for the smaller henhouse. By the time I finished, it was almost fully dark. I left the pail near the gate and shouted goodbye to Chrissie. A faint reply came from the direction of the byre.

As I was climbing over the wall of the yard, the door of the farmhouse opened. I recognised the familiar silhouette of Selby; his companion at first remained hidden in the shadows. Then the person stepped forward and I saw that it was Irene.

"Goodnight, Selby," I called. "Goodnight, Irene." I took pleasure in quoting the song.

I found my bike and wiped the dew from the saddle. As I pedalled up the hill, I thought about Chrissie looking in the mirror. I had often seen Irene, and even my mother, pouting over their reflections, but never before Chrissie. In her flannel shirts and corduroy trousers, she had seemed beyond such vanity.

THE FOLLOWING DAY my homework was especially difficult. I had to translate a piece of Latin about a flock of geese which had saved Rome from the barbarians by cackling loudly. I looked forward to telling Chrissie the story, but by the time I reached the farm she had already gone back to the house to make the tea.

I fetched a pail and started on the large henhouse. Almost all the hens were asleep with their heads tucked under their wings; they clucked peevishly as I slipped my hand into their nests. I decided, after one pecked me, to skip the other henhouse. With the vague hope of running into Chrissie, I carried the pail over to the house. As I rounded the corner, the light from the living-room window fell onto the cobblestones. I heard the sound of voices. I tiptoed forward until I could see Chrissie and Selby sitting at the table.

"Irene didn't come again this evening," Chrissie said. "I don't know what's the matter with her. Ginger could starve for all she cares."

She had her back to the window, but Selby was in full view. I watched his lips and eyebrows tighten into two thin, parallel lines. "Irene pays you to feed the horse," he said. "If she doesn't come every night, that's her business. Anyway it's better than hanging around all the time, like that brat."

"Ruth doesn't hang around. She helps me, and goodness knows, I could use a hand."

Selby held out his cup for more tea. "A farm is a dangerous place for a child."

"Don't be daft," said Chrissie. "When we were bairns, we poked our noses into everything. No harm came to us."

Her voice was light and teasing, but Selby only frowned harder. "Maybe so, but she's different. She's always snooping, always watching."

"Watching? What's there to watch?"

Selby said something I did not catch. I took a cautious step closer to the window. The pail clinked and a dark shape lunged towards me, snarling. I dropped the pail and screamed.

Chrissie flung open the back door. "Get down," she shouted to the collies. "Are you all right, Ruth?"

"Yes, but I dropped the eggs."

"Don't worry. It was an accident. There can't have been very many." She gave me a reassuring pat.

The dogs were lapping up the broken eggs with wolfish greed. I wanted only to leave. "I'm sorry about the eggs," I said. "I'm really sorry." Before Chrissie could reply, I hurried away to retrieve my bicycle.

THAT SATURDAY I did not dare to go to the farm. Chrissie was at an auction and I was afraid that if I met Selby he would forbid me to come again. Instead I went down to the meadow by the river and loitered along the bank, swishing a stick through the reeds. I found a dead fish lying tail up in the mud and two empty whiskey bottles. As I bent to examine the bottles, there was a burst of cawing from the far side of the meadow. A dozen rooks swirled noisily into the air, and Irene emerged from the copse of pine trees. She was on foot, leading Ginger. I dropped the stick and ran to meet her.

She did not see me until I called her name. Then she looked up, mouth agape. "What are you doing here?"

"Nothing. Why aren't you riding?"

"I don't feel like it. Do you want a go?"

I nodded, so pleased that I could not speak. She had never offered me a ride before. We went over to a fallen willow tree that lay in the middle of the meadow. Standing on its trunk I could just get my foot into the stirrup. Irene boosted me into the saddle. We began to walk. I tried to sit in the way I had read about, simultaneously upright and relaxed, but it was hard to relax on top of a moving mountain. We were almost at the gate of the meadow when I heard whistling.

Glancing over my shoulder, I saw Selby walking away from the copse in the opposite direction. He was whistling a song that Chrissie sometimes sang: "The Flowers of the Forest." I had asked her why it sounded so sad, and she had explained that the song came from long ago; it was a lament for the Scottish soldiers killed at the Battle of Flodden.

ALL WEEK I thought about riding Ginger. On Friday night I fell asleep praying fervently for fine weather. Irene had promised to give me a proper lesson, and she did not like to go out in the rain. When I woke, however, the sky was overcast, and as I cycled to the farm the first drops began to fall. I arrived to find Irene closing the gate.

"Hello, Ruth," she said. "What a dreary day."

"It's only a drizzle." I climbed over the wall as usual.

Irene shook her head sceptically. I saw that beneath her red plastic raincoat she was wearing a skirt. "Aren't we going to ride?" I asked. I felt hugely disappointed.

"In this weather? You must be joking. Is Selby around?"

"How would I know?"

I wanted to beg Irene to change her mind, but just then Chrissie came out of the smaller henhouse with a hen under one arm. "I haven't seen you for a while," she said to Irene.

"It's been raining every evening. Anyway I came down to feed Ginger."

"It's not feeding he needs," Chrissie said. "But exercise. You shouldn't ask me to give him oats if you're not going to ride him. I've already put him in the lower meadow."

"I haven't time to take him out today," Irene said quickly. "I'll give him a good workout tomorrow."

"Tomorrow," echoed Chrissie. She sounded like my mother when I tried to postpone cleaning my room.

Irene did not answer. She turned on her heel, opened the gate and, without bothering to close it, walked away. I stared after her in amazement.

Chrissie too seemed taken aback. "Surely she didn't come just to say she wasn't coming," she said.

"I think she wanted to see Selby," I offered.

Chrissie's face puckered as if she had taken a bite of something sour: a lemon or a sloe. She stood frowning until the hen she was holding roused her with a squawk. Then she looked at me. "A pity you're not bigger," she said. "Or I'm not younger. We're neither of us up to Ginger."

"I'll be bigger soon. Irene's teaching me to ride."

"That's good," she said, and retreated to the henhouse.

BY EARLY DECEMBER the days were so short that darkness fell before we were dismissed from school. My mother would not let me go out in the evenings, and a week passed before I returned to the farm. On Saturday I set off as soon as I had finished breakfast. I was on my way to clean out the duck-house when I met Irene. She was wearing jodhpurs. "I'm taking Ginger down to the meadow," she said abruptly. "Do you want to come?" I forgot about the ducks and fell in beside her.

In the meadow I stood on the fallen willow tree. Irene trotted a short distance, then kicked Ginger into a gallop. I'd never seen her do more than canter before; now she leaned low over Ginger's neck, lashing him forward. His muscles rippled and his hooves drummed on the frozen ground. I wanted to applaud. I turned, following their progress round and round the tree. But as I watched, Irene's heels kicking, the crop coming down again and again, my exhilaration faded. This was not pleasure but something else. If I could have left without crossing their path, I would have run back to the farm.

When at last they trotted over to the willow tree, Ginger's flanks were wet and the whites of his eyes showed wild. Irene too was sweating; her hair clung to her forehead and her cheeks were brilliant.

She dismounted. "Now it's your turn." As she clipped on the leading-rein, I saw that her hands were trembling.

I tugged at my boots. "Maybe we should wait a little. Ginger seems tired."

"That's why I rode him," said Irene. "So he wouldn't be too frisky for you."

She held out the stirrup. Reluctantly I climbed into the saddle. Irene adjusted the stirrups and, I was still figuring out how to hold my hands, led him away from the tree. As soon as we reached open ground, she let out the leading rein. "Make him trot," she called, urging him forward with the rein.

I did not want to. I was already having trouble keeping my balance. "Please don't," I said.

Irene snapped the crop. "Come on. You'll never learn like this."

Ginger broke into a trot. Almost immediately I lost a stirrup and fell forward onto his neck. I clung to his mane while he bumped along. The next thing I knew, Irene was holding the bridle and Ginger had come to a halt.

"Oh, Ruth," she said when I was safely on the ground. "If only you weren't so young."

Now I was the one trembling; still I did not want to give up on learning to ride. In my books the girls sometimes needed months of lessons. If Irene hadn't been so fierce, I would have been fine. "I'll do better next time," I said. "I promise."

I gazed up at Irene, trying to impress her with my sincerity, but she did not seem to hear me. "I just don't know what to do." She rested her head against Ginger's neck, and I saw her eyes fill with tears.

MY PARENTS AND I went to Edinburgh for the Christmas holidays. When I returned to the farm in January the ground was covered with snow. Chrissie greeted me with the news that the first lambs had been born. She led me to the byre, where three ewes and five lambs nestled in the deep straw. I knelt to stroke the lamb nearest the fence. It butted my hand in search of milk and I laughed with pleasure. Its wool was soft as thistledown.

"Don't touch it too much," said Chrissie. "The ewe won't feed it if it doesn't smell right."

Hastily I withdrew my hand.

As we walked to the granary, Chrissie thanked me for the chocolates I had left on her doorstep before I went away. I blushed. Chocolates were a boring present but I had been at my wits' end. I had given my mother a scarf and Irene bath salts but neither of these had seemed suitable for Chrissie. I asked what she had done for Christmas.

"Nothing special. The animals need to be fed and watered whatever day it is. Selby and I went to the Thistle for Christmas dinner."

"The Thistle Hotel," I exclaimed. My parents had taken me there as a birthday treat and the evening had made a deep impression. I tried to imagine Chrissie and Selby seated among the men in suits and the women in evening dresses, but I could only picture them as I knew them, in their flannel shirts and trousers. It occurred to me that I had never seen either of them outside the farm. Although they lived on the edge of the village, they were as isolated as if they dwelled on Crusoe's island.

At the granary there was the usual scurrying of rats. Chrissie took off her gloves to measure out the oats. As I held the sack open, I saw that her hands were badly chapped and I recalled the day I had caught her powdering her nose. Maybe I should have given her a jar of Nivea, I thought.

WHEN IRENE APPEARED that Saturday, she was pale and quiet. Instead of her jodhpurs and tightly cut jacket, she wore jeans and a blue anorak. Ginger too seemed subdued. The furious ride of a few weeks before might have taken place in another life. Today, although it was too icy to bicycle, I had no trouble keeping up with them. We plodded down the lane and back.

As we drew near the farm, Selby crossed the lane, dogs at his heels, going into the yard. "There's Selby," I remarked. He must have heard us, Ginger's hooves echoed loudly on the tarmac, but he gave no sign of noticing our presence. Nor did Irene seem to notice him.

"Let's go up to the main road again," she said. "Ginger's been indoors all week."

We clip–clopped past the market garden and up the hill. When we reached her house, Irene scrambled down and thrust the reins into my hands. She was even paler than before. "Are you all right?" I said.

Irene stood gazing back towards the farm. She did not answer until I repeated my question. Then she gave a faint shake of the head. "No," she muttered. "I'm not all right."

"What's wrong?"

There was another long pause. I felt the reins tighten in my hands. Ginger's bridle jingled.

"I'm expecting." She turned to look at me. "Do you know what that means?"

"Yes." It was both true and untrue. At school I had overheard two girls talking about somebody expecting; they had snickered and made faces. And a few weeks ago my mother had made the same remark about her younger sister, saying it was wonderful news.

Irene was staring at me. She was waiting, I realised, for me to prove my knowledge. My head buzzed with confusion. Should I giggle?

Should I say it was wonderful? At last Irene raised her gloved hands in a small, helpless gesture.

"I need to lie down," she said. "Could you take Ginger back?" Without another word, she hurried towards the house.

My father had told me that the important thing with animals was not to let them know you were afraid. I marched beside Ginger singing, "I love to go a'wandering." We reached the farm by the fourth verse. He waited docilely for me to open the gate, and followed me into the yard. I was struggling to close the gate again when a voice called, "Leave it."

As Selby passed, one of the attendant collies bared its teeth and growled. Ginger shyed. A roll of barbed wire lay on the ground. Briefly he trampled it, then stepped clear.

"Hold your peace," said Selby to the dogs. In a moment he was gone.

I had not lost my grip on the reins, and Ginger, once we were alone, calmed down. I led him to the stable without further mishap, but as I paused to shoo a hen out of our path, I noticed on the snowy ground several drops of blood. I looked closely and saw a cut on one of his rear fetlocks. He must have caught himself on the barbed wire.

Chrissie had taught me how to staunch the bleeding of a hen's comb with cobwebs. When I had Ginger safely inside, I found a web and smoothed the grey mesh over the wound. Already the bleeding had almost ceased. I let myself out of the stable and went to find Chrissie.

She was at the trough, filling a water container. Without looking up from her task she asked if we had had a good ride.

"It was okay. We just went up and down the road. Irene felt ill. She said she's expecting. She went home and I brought Ginger back by myself. He was very good, except when the collie growled at him. Then he cut his leg."

Water gushed to the ground as the container overflowed. I jumped back. "Jesus," whispered Chrissie.

"I put cobwebs on the cut, like you taught me." I waited for her to praise me, but she walked away in silence.

DARKNESS STILL FELL soon after I got home from school but by Thursday I could wait no longer to see Chrissie and Ginger and the hens. "Just this once," I begged my mother. "I'll come right back."

I went first to visit Ginger. I had saved my apple core from lunch, but when I offered it to him he simply hung his head. I touched his nose and the skin felt hot, and dry as a tinderbox.

I left the stable to look for Chrissie. As I headed for the large hen-house, I saw light coming from the barn. A bulb had been rigged up above the bales of hay. Beneath it stood Selby, with his back to me. I crept forward. He was standing in front of two trestles across which rested two poles. From the poles dangled a lamb.

Something glinted in Selby's hand. He leaned forward and so quickly that I scarcely took in his movements he cut a circle round each of the ankles and the neck of the lamb. A thin red bracelet sprang up to mark each cut. I must have made some sound, for Selby glanced round and saw me. Then he sank the tip of the knife into the lamb's throat and sliced down the belly.

"What are you doing?" I murmured.

He had begun to cut down the inside of each leg. "I'm skinning a lamb," he said. "It died this afternoon. The ewe still has plenty of milk and when I tie this skin onto another lamb, she'll adopt it as her own."

He bent forward to examine his handiwork, and moved on to the third leg. "It's easy to deceive a sheep," he said. "If I put the skin on you, she'd think you were her lamb."

I stepped back. Selby laid aside the knife. His hands moved over the small body. Soon the carcass was naked.

He turned to face me, holding up the skin by the fore-legs. The smell of blood hung like smoke in the night air. For a moment it seemed as if Selby really might drape the skin around my shoulders. "So what do you think, my pretty one?" He took a step towards me. "Would I make a good father?"

I turned and ran. I rushed past the stable and the hen-house. I did not slow down, even when I stumbled on a cat and it fled, yowling, from beneath my feet.

ON SATURDAY THE sky was steely grey. Fresh snow had fallen during the night and the farmyard was still white and pristine. I longed to make new footprints but I was worried about meeting Selby. I stayed close to the wall, scooping the snow into snowballs, until Chrissie came out of the granary. Then I zig-zagged towards her.

"I hope you're warmly dressed," she said. She herself wore two jackets, one inside the other.

"I'm fine." I flapped my arms to show that I was roly-poly as a Michelin man.

She asked me to let out the ducks and I made my way to the duck-house. I always enjoyed this task because the ducks seemed so pleased to regain their freedom. They erupted in a noisy crowd and headed for the pond, skidding slightly in the snow.

Back in the yard Chrissie was carrying an armful of hay to the stable. I went ahead to open the door. Ginger was standing in the far corner. Except for an occasional shudder, he was motionless. On his lips were white flecks of foam. "He looks strange," I said to Chrissie.

She flung the hay into the manger. "I'm only paid to feed him," she said. "He belongs to Irene."

"Is she coming down today?"

"I doubt it. Madame seems to have better things to do these days than take care of her horse."

Before I could question her further, she was gone. The water in Ginger's bucket was frozen. I broke the ice with the heel of my boot and hurried after Chrissie.

Later, as I bicycled home, I thought of stopping at Irene's. I had not seen her since the day she had asked me to take Ginger back to the farm, and I wanted to tell her that I thought something was wrong with him. But then I heard the village clock strike one; my mother would kill me if I was late for lunch.

WHEN I ARRIVED at the farm the next day, I headed directly for the stable. Chrissie and Irene were standing in the doorway, talking in sharp voices. At the sight of me they fell silent. Chrissie nodded and walked off.

Ginger lay near the manger. His legs stuck out at odd angles. Where yesterday there had been a few flecks of foam on his lips, now there was a thick rim of froth. His eyes were as wide and frightened as they had been on the day when Irene whipped him into a gallop.

"I'm going to try to phone the vet again," said Irene. "Could you get the horse blankets from the byre and cover him?"

She hurried away. I fetched the blankets. In the doorway of the stable I hesitated. There was no question now of Ginger trampling me, and yet I was afraid. When at last I summoned up my courage and tiptoed towards him, I saw the tendons stretched like ropes beneath his skin. I spread the blankets carefully over him.

In a quarter of an hour Irene returned with the vet. He had come straight from church and was still in a suit. Irene and I stood watching as he knelt to examine Ginger. He pulled up the lids of Ginger's eyes and felt his neck and legs.

After only a couple of minutes the vet rose to his feet. "I'm sorry. I'm afraid it's too late."

"No," said Irene. "It can't be." She went and laid her hand on Ginger's back. "While there's life, there's hope."

The vet shook his head. "The horse has lock-jaw. There's nothing I can do but put him out of his misery."

When he was gone, Irene burst into tears. "It's all my fault," she sobbed.

I stood by helplessly saying, "Don't cry, Irene." Finally I walked her home. I did not feel like going back to the farm so I went home myself, but as the day wore on, I kept thinking of Ginger. It was almost dark when I announced to my mother that I was going to see how he was.

The farmyard was deserted. The cold had driven the animals inside, and everything was quiet and still. I walked slowly up to the stable. The door was open, and even before I reached it I heard the sound of ragged breathing. Ginger lay in the same position as before. I saw the glint of the whites of his eyes and of his teeth.

I did not hear Chrissie come up behind me until she spoke. "I know what you're thinking," she said. "I ought to have called the vet. Whatever went on with her and Selby, there's no excuse."

It was that time of evening when sight becomes uncertain. I could see Chrissie's face, but I could not make out her expression. She was looking at me, as if waiting for something. All I wanted was to make Ginger well again. "Isn't there anything we can do?" I pleaded.

"No. Lock-jaw is fatal."

"What causes it?"

"A scratch or a cut. People can get it too, from a rusty nail, or a tin can."

Guilt blossomed inside me. I stared at Ginger. It was I who had killed him, not Irene, not Chrissie. I had let him step on the barbed wire and because of that small cut, he was dying.

"Chrissie," I blurted out. Before I could say another word, Ginger uttered a deep groan. By a tremendous effort he raised his head. A shudder passed over his huge body and he sank back onto the straw.

I kept my eyes fixed on the dark mass, hoping, desperately, for another movement. None came. I turned to Chrissie. If only she would say something, but she was dry-eyed and her face was stony. Neither of us moved or spoke. Without Ginger's breathing the silence stretched on and on until it seemed that it could never be broken.

At last from the far side of the farmyard came a sound. Selby was whistling. Gradually the thin, sad notes took shape. I recognised "The Flowers of the Forest." And then beside me, entwined with Selby's whistling, I heard another sound. Chrissie was singing. She began softly, the words no more than a murmur, but line by line they grew clearer.

I've seen the smiling of Fortune beguiling,
I've felt all its favours, and found its decay:
Sweet was its blessing, kind its caressing,
But now 'tis fled, 'tis fled far away;
I've seen the forest adorned the foremost,
With flowers of the fairest, pleasant and gay,
Sae bonny was their blooming, their scent the air perfuming,
But now they are withered and a' wede away.

As Chrissie reached the last words, Selby too fell silent. Across the cold dark air, brother and sister, they seemed to signal to each other, to send a message no one else could understand.

I WROTE "THE FLOWERS of the Forest" at a time when I had been struggling unsuccessfully for several years with a novel, *Eva Moves the Furniture*. I couldn't find either a voice or a point of view for *Eva* that seemed able to contain the story I wanted to tell. At moments of despair I would break off to write stories, one of which was "The Flowers of the Forest." The story reminded me that I still wanted to write about Scotland where I had grown up and that I wanted to look over my shoulder not just at my own past but at that larger past which included the effect and aftermath of two world wars in a country that had for centuries suffered bitter defeats.

I began the story with a location, a small farm on the outskirts of a village and two William Trevor–like characters, a brother and sister who had inherited the farm and each other. I also began with an event that had made a huge impression on me as a child, the death from lock-jaw of a horse I used to ride. I remember late one winter afternoon tiptoeing into the stable where the horse was lying, stiff-legged, in the straw and just standing there, staring. I had always been afraid of Ginger and done my best to conceal my fear. Now I was afraid in a different way. As I stood there, listening to his breathing, I was aware that a battle was going on of which the end was already fully determined. In the dim light the only part of the horse I could see clearly were the whites of his eyes.

But a death does not a story make and I went looking for a plot. The symbiotic relationship between the brother and sister at once seemed to offer possibilities; what if they were not equally committed to their hard-working union? If something, someone threatened their symbiosis? Pondering that question gave me a clue as to who should tell the story. I realised that I needed not so much an unreliable but an innocent narrator, one who could wreak harm unwittingly and still tell us about it. And who after all but a child would want to spend her free time sloshing around in the mud, collecting hens' eggs?

So Ruth entered the story, lonely, longing to please, a keen observer but poor at understanding what she observes. She blunders through the story, inadvertently killing a horse and almost destroying the relationship between Chrissie and Selby. The trickiest parts of the story had to do with Irene's pregnancy. I was vividly aware that this was a familiar plot device and that I needed to put that familiarity to good use, that the suspense had to reside not so much in the pregnancy itself but in how it was revealed. Why would Irene tell Ruth and why would Ruth tell Chrissie? After much back and forth, I settled on that mysterious word "expecting" as the key to this series of exchanges, a way for Irene to tell Ruth without quite doing so and a way for Ruth to pass on the news without being fully aware of what she's doing. It is, I hope, strongly implied by the period detail that the story is set in the days before abortion became legal.

My struggles with "The Flowers of the Forest" taught me several writerly lessons that I desperately needed to learn. The most important of these is shamefully obvious. More than much of my previous work the success or failure of "The Flowers of the Forest" depended not so much on adjusting the events of the story (which is what editors and workshops most frequently suggest when a story is failing to resonate) but on the method of telling, those stubborn, black marks that go from one side of the page to another and on which we rely to convey our most intimate and secret thoughts. The familiar, far-fetched plot could work if the prose was sufficiently lustrous and precise and atmospheric. That was the voice I tried to give Ruth and which she later bequeathed to the narrator of *Eva Moves the Furniture*.

David Shields

A BRIEF SURVEY OF
IDEAL DESIRE

> Fathers and teachers, I ponder 'What is
> hell?' I maintain that it is the
> suffering of being unable to love.
>
> —DOSTOEVSKY

GALLEONS LADEN WITH jewelry and threatened by pirates sailed through treacherous seas in the gold-on-blue design of Walt's rabbit-feet pajamas. He would hold the strap attached to his rocking horse's ears and mouth, lifting himself onto the little leather saddle. One cracked green glass eye shone out of the right side of Silver's head. His mouth, once bright red and smiling, had chipped away to a tight-lipped, unpainted pout. His nose, too, was bruised, with gashes for nostrils. Silver had a brown mane, which, extending from the crown of his head nearly to his waist, was made up of Walt's grandmother's discarded wigs glued to the wood. Wrapping the reins around his fist, Walt would slip his feet into the square stirrups that hung from the horse's waist. Walt would bounce up and down to set Silver in motion, lean forward, press his lips to the back of his horse's rough neck, and exhort him to charge. When Silver pitched forward, Walt would scoot up toward the base of the horse's spine, and when Silver swung back, Walt would let go of the leather strap and lean back as far as he could. Walt would make the rocking horse lurch crazily toward the far wall by squeezing his knees into the wood and jerking his legs forward. Then he'd twist his hips and bounce until it felt warm under him, bump up against the smooth surface of the seat until his whole body tingled. He'd buck back and forth so it hurt, in a way, and he wouldn't know what to do with this ache.

From age eleven until age fifteen Walt did little else but play basketball all afternoon and evening, and when it grew too dark to see the rim, he played by the light of the street lamp. He played on school teams, on temple teams, in pickup games, for hours alone, with friends, against friends, with people he'd never seen before and never saw again, with middle-aged men wearing college sweatshirts who liked to keep their hands on his ass as they guarded him, with friends' younger brothers who couldn't believe how good he was, with UCLA Bruins keeping in shape during the summer who told him he might make it, with coaches who told him the future of their jobs rested on his performance, with the owners of a pornographic bookstore who asked him if he wanted to appear in an art film, with his father, who asked him whatever happened to the concept of teamwork. He wore leather weights around his ankles, taking them off only in bed, so his legs would be strong and he would be able to jump as high as his black teammates could. He read every available book on technique, every biography of the stars. He jumped rope: inside, around the block, up stairs, walking the dog. He played on asphalt, in playgrounds, in gyms, in the street, in the backyard, in his mind, in rain, in winds that ruled the ball, beneath the dead dry heat of burning sun.

Walt ascended two flights of cement stairs, then knocked on the door, which had an engraving of Venus straddling an aqueduct. A large blond lady, wearing high heels made of glass, opened the door. "Hello," she said, aspirating heavily, "and welcome to A Touch of Venus." She handed him a glass of white wine and a poorly typed page, which was encased in plastic and which said:

A TOUCH OF VENUS—THE MOST IN MASSAGE

1. The Basic. Masseuse fully clothed. No oils, no scents. 1 drink. Access to billiard table. Very relaxing. Fifteen minutes. $20.

2. The Rub-Down. Masseuse clothed. Oils, no scents. 2 drinks. Access to billiard table, whirlpool, shower massage. Highly sensitizing. Twenty minutes. $30.

3. The Total Massage. Masseuse clothed in under-wear. Oils, scents. 3 drinks. Access to billiard table, whirlpool, shower massage, screening room, jacuzzi. Extremely refreshing. Thirty minutes. $50.

4. A Little Bit of Heaven. Masseuse topless. Asian oils, Parisian scents. Unlimited drinks. Access to bil-liard table, whirlpool, shower massage, screening room, jacuzzi, lemon creme facial. Quite exciting. Forty-five minutes. $75.

5. Ecstasy. Masseuse topless and bottomless. Asian oils, Parisian scents. Unlimited drinks. Access to bil-liard table, whirlpool, shower massage, screening room, jacuzzi, sauna, lemon creme facial. Hot towel wrap. Champagne bubble bath. Discount card for return visits. Fulfilling. One hour. $100.

Walt was astonished that so many of the details with which he had conjured up this scenario proved to be accurate: black leather couches, thick red carpet, low lighting, disco music, shiny wood pan-eling, coffee tables on which were spread recent copies of *Penthouse*. "So," his hostess said, "what'll it be—Ecstasy, A Little Bit of Heaven, Total Massage . . ." Her voice trailed off. It seemed clear that anything short of ecstasy was mere flirtation. "Ecstasy," Walt said. He paid her with money he'd saved from his job as a stock boy at a clothing store, and she took him on a tour of the building, which used to be the fire department, she said, before it was converted. Walt thought back to a time when big, happy men were polishing trucks and waiting around to be heroes. She held him by the arm and told him to relax as they walked through the lounge, in which the other masseuses were watching a faded color film of four people fucking, then gave him a white bathrobe and a key to a locker and told him to change into (the phrase was meant to be excruciatingly erotic, and it was) "something more comfortable." The sauna, the whirlpool, the shower massage (whatever that was), the Jacuzzi, the champagne bubble bath, all this stuff was in the basement of the ex-firehouse; Walt was instructed to slide down the golden pole and amuse himself for a while and come upstairs when he was ready. He was ready right then, of course—he hadn't paid a hundred dollars to take a bath by himself— and as he climbed into the sauna and sat on the wooden bench, he tried and failed to imagine anything worse than being in the basement of a converted fire station on Sunday morning. He consoled himself with the thought that before he left, at least he would have sinned. When he went upstairs, he sat in a director's chair, watching the movie and thumbing through magazines, and one by one the employees offered themselves to him. His hostess asked him to play pool with her, a short redhead sat next to him and watched the movie for a couple of minutes, and a skinny woman with black hair wrapped high around her head like tangled snakes brought him a drink. He was supposed to give a little ticket that he held in his hand to the woman of his dreams, but instead he got up and gave the ticket to the only masseuse who was not in any way appealing or exciting or terrifying. She was shy and Walt had to force the ticket into her hand to get her to look up. She led him into a room and told him to take off his bathrobe. He lay face down on a table in the middle of the room and she rubbed him from head to toe. He stared at a large square mirror positioned on the floor in such a way that he could see her. Most of what she did tickled, so he thought about other things to keep from laughing. It wasn't arousing and after a while he flipped over on his back, sat up, and complained. She said this was a legitimate massage parlor and they didn't do that kind of thing here. "We'll be quiet," he assured her and offered her a fifty-dollar tip, but she said she wasn't for sale. He lunged toward her; she stepped back and hurried out the door before he could stop her. He ran out of the room and down the stairs to the locker room, changed into his clothes, then left by the back exit. The rest of the money in his wallet was gone. When he got outside and into the sunlight, Walt felt the way he had felt the year before upon leaving the theater after seeing a pornographic movie for the first time: sentimental, thrilled by the mundanity of cracks in the sidewalk and flowers, and repelled by the prospect of physical love.

Walter and Nina had remained in bed until three o'clock in the afternoon, which was twenty minutes after he was supposed to have boarded a Bonanza bus to Logan Airport, because Nina, wearing only a pair of warm socks and very warm mittens, wanted to squeeze the fat in his back with her wool hands and dig into his legs with her warm wool feet so that he would feel like he was being devoured by a ferocious little lion and return as quickly as possible and think of no one and nothing else while he was away. Every time Nina got even near him, he started sneezing, and he was one of those people who, rather than make a quick little ka-choo into a handkerchief, not only neglect to carry a handkerchief but feel compelled to blow coagulations of snot into the atmosphere, into their hands, drippy and yellow, onto whatever is around them at the moment. What was around Walter at the moment was Nina's bedsheet, which she had just washed and dried so that she and Walter would have a clean, white surface to slide around on their last night together. She was so disgusted by the way he shook the snot off his hands into the wastebasket and blew his nose with the cord to his bathrobe that she got out of bed, standing with her mittens on her hips and her socked feet on the floor next to the electric heater, and quoted back to him the analogy he always liked to make between the itch in the nose and desire, between phlegm on the floor and fulfillment. "It really empties you out, right?" she said. "Tell me, sweetheart, does it also make you feel sad?" Walter thought he was sneezing because he'd finally developed an allergy to Nina, whereas Nina, who had learned all about psychosomatic disorders when she was in analysis, assumed he was sneezing because he'd developed an allergy to his family, whereas the truth was that he had developed an allergy to the dust he'd encountered the night before, searching for his suitcase in the basement. While he stuffed the suitcase with what few articles of light clothing he still owned, she started the car, an old Peugeot the color of pool water, which her father had given her after the mechanic said he'd never be able to stop the ping in the motor; she drove ten miles faster than anyone else on cleared and sanded 95 North all the way to the airport. They made it in plenty of time. "I'll miss you. I love you," he said to reassure Nina, who had started glowering when he glanced at the cover of *Club International* magazine in the gift shop before doing whatever was the opposite of deplaning. "You love your free detachable calendar of Miss Cunt of the Month," she said and kissed him good-bye until he started sneezing again.

"I can see why you're a Miss Nude USA regional finalist," Walter imagined writing the woman whose ad was placed in the back of *Club*. "You have beautiful long silky blue-black hair, a perfect pout, and a gorgeous body. Please send me the color photos you mentioned of yourself in fur, leather, lingerie, garter belt, and heels. Thank you. Payment enclosed."

THE ENDING OF James Joyce's story "The Dead" was usually interpreted as Gabriel Conroy's unambiguous, transcendental identification with universal love and human mortality, but to Walter it seemed more plausible to read the last page or so as an overwritten passage that conveyed emotional deadness taking refuge in sentimentality. "Generous tears filled Gabriel's eyes. He had never felt like that himself towards any woman, but he knew that such a feeling must be love." Gabriel was thinking about the passion of his wife's ex-suitor, but the word "generous" appeared—to Walter, at least—to suggest Gabriel's confusion of self-pity with selfless love. Walter figured that if Joyce had meant the last sentence of the story to be truly beautiful, he certainly wouldn't have used "falling faintly" and "faintly falling" within four words of each other. This repetition created discord at the very climax of the rising hymn so that even as Gabriel believed he was liberating himself from egotism, his language for compassion was self-conscious and solipsistic. Neither in memory nor fantasy was he capable of imagining union, completion, or even shared intimacy. That was Walter's interpretation.

Behind the Story

"A BRIEF SURVEY OF Ideal Desire" represents a formal break-through (breakout? breakdown?) for me. Before writing this story, I wrote in a fairly traditional manner—two linear, realistic novels and dozens of conventionally plotted stories. Since writing the story approximately ten years ago, I've composed almost exclusively collage-books and collage-stories.

I'm not a big believer in Major Epiphanies, especially those that occur in the shower, but I had one, and it occurred in the shower. Working on a collection of interconnected stories, *A Handbook for Drowning,* I had the sudden intuition that I could take various fragments of things—aborted stories, outtakes from novels, journal entries, lit-crit—and build a story out of them. I really had no idea what the story would be about; I just knew I needed to see what it would look like to set certain shards in juxtaposition with other shards.

Now I have trouble working any other way, but I can't emphasize enough how strange it felt at the time, working in this modal mode. The initial hurdle (and much the most important one) was being willing to follow this inchoate intuition, yield to the prompting, not fight it off, not retreat to the tried-and-true. I thought the story probably had something to do with obsession; I wonder where I got that idea—rummaging through boxes of old papers, riffling through drawers and computer files, crawling around on my hands and knees on the living room floor, looking for bits and pieces I thought might cohere if I could just join them together.

Amy Hempel reports about Gordon Lish that "while watching a documentary on building ships in bottles, he noticed that the mechanism was much the same for a story as for the model ship. Once the builder got the ship with its collapsed masts into the bottle, he pulled a string to which all the masts were attached, and the whole super-structure went up. Lish says the story, too, is already contained. "To erect the superstructure you pull up the reins of your 'horses'—the motifs you have ridden from beginning to end." Never mind Lish's mixed metaphor; I find this an enormously useful analogy for how, in particular, a collage-story works, since, absent narrative, motif-riding is everything. As a collage-writer, I sometimes feel more like a film editor than a writer per se. The cut is crucial; the art lies in calculat-ing what you can imply and still get your masts to go up. (More mixed metaphor, but let's go with it . . .)

Scissoring and taping together paragraphs from previous projects, moving them around in endless combinations, completely rewriting some sections, jettisoning others, I found a clipped, hard-bitten tone entering the pieces. My work had never been sweet, but this seemed harsher, sharper, even a little hysterical. That tone is, in a sense, the plot of the story: by the end, the reader, feeling, I hope, the depth of Walt's solipsism, understands why the close-third-person narration (Walt judging himself from a very slight distance) is so acerbic. Antonya Nelson once said to me that she thought in any story that comes together, the writer had to get lucky, by which I took her to mean that at least one more drawer of meaning has to open up beneath the drawer you, the writer, thought you were opening. I thought I was writing a story about obsession. I was really writing a story about the hell of obsessive ego, as the epigraph attests.

The final and perhaps most difficult challenge of the story was to build thematic momentum, which happens, I think, through a series of phrases that I inserted into the story; these are, to me, the secret (now not so secret) nerve-centers of the story. "He wouldn't know what to do with this ache" defines the problem; "whatever happened to the concept of teamwork" underscores the problem; "repelled by the prospect of physical love" vivifies it; "Tell me, sweetheart, does it also make you feel sad?" prepares for the ending; and "That was Walter's interpretation" is meant to be the knockout punch.

It really was pretty revelatory and exciting for me to see how part of something I had originally written as an essay about James Joyce's "The Dead" could now be turned sideways and used as the final, bruising insight into a character's psyche. (I think of Walter as me and not me, my Narcissus-self, me on my worst day, circa 1991.) All literary possibilities opened up for me with this story. The way my mind thinks—everything is connected to everything else—suddenly seemed transportable into my writing. I could play all the roles I want to play (reporter, fantasist, autobiographer, essayist, critic). I could call on my strengths (meditation and analysis), hide my weaknesses (plot and plot), be as smart on the page as I wanted to be. I'd found a way to write that seemed true to how I am in the world.

Charles Baxter

THE OLD FASCIST IN RETIREMENT

"DO YOU KNOW that story about Nietzsche?" The voice rose to the old poet out of the darkness. "You know that story about Nietzsche, don't you, what he was doing just before his mind gave way?"

The old man nodded. Yes, everybody knows that story.

The voice continued as if it had not paid any attention to his response. Below the balcony where the old man was sitting, a vaporetto steamed southward on the far side of the canal, its engine making a two-note slur as it rocked on the waves. "You know that on the day Nietzsche lost his mind, he saw on the streets of Turin a cart horse being whipped. We can imagine, if we choose to, small droplets of blood clinging to the horse's flanks, to the smooth hairs. What we imagine is always our choice. Nietzsche rushed toward the horse and threw his arms around the beast's neck. Something broke in the philosopher's mind at that moment, some small crucial relay of synapses. Nietzsche collapsed to the ground. From that moment on he never uttered a completely lucid sentence."

Yes, the old man said. I know that story.

"I thought so," the voice said. "And what else do you remember?"

The voice faded back into the water: a clawed winged voice. He didn't know to whom it belonged. He could not see anyone sitting with him on the balcony overlooking the canal and the stone jetty. And yet the voice came and departed regularly as if he had given it a special status. The voice would have to be dealt with. He would have to speak to it. Sharp flagellant light whirled above the horizon. Specks of blood on a flogged horse. False dawn? If so, according to what authority?

IN HIS TIME, the old man had often seen paradise: jagged panes, lightning angles, the unformulated glory of smashed leaded glass. In Paris in 1924 he had watched a workman accidentally drop from a second-story scaffolding a windowpane, which had broken on the stones of the Quai Voltaire. The shattered glass on the sidewalk contained the geometrical shapes of paradise: transparent isosceles edges, razors: glass made beautiful by fracture and the accidents of force.

He had wanted his poems to be as beautiful as that broken glass. He wanted them to cut into the skin and evoke the bloodflow. That day, he had planted his cane in the gutter of the Quai Voltaire and studied those glass shards while the oblivious pedestrians made their dulled ways around him.

He knew his poetry had no pity and that all tenderness had been expunged from its light. There, in poetry, the light was as hard and as brutal as purity required. He had told everyone this and explained it patiently. He wanted to wean the world. He wanted humankind to grow up, to see the beauty of pitilessness and broken glass. The point was to damn fear and softness forever, not to give in to the temporary comforts.

He suspected that he had grown stupid trying to tell them.

IN THE ROOMS behind him his caretakers came and went, the women and the visitors, his society. He closed his eyes, and his mind, which had once been his ally and confederate, flashed up Chinese ideograms, which, when he tried to read them, denounced him. In Chinese, the lettering of heaven, he read that he had been a fool. He had left the spectrum of intelligence at one end, the genius end, and reentered it again at the other end, the fool end. There he was now, a fool, and he was damned if he would open up his mouth in public one more time.

Somehow he rose, put on his cape and scarf, and found himself out on the sidewalk, heading who-knows-where. By accident he had sneaked past the women and the visitors to his decrepit salon, and now here he was outside, the night air smelling of history, a damp and fishy smell. As he walked, his mossy gray hair rising like aging fire from his head, the citizens of Venice saluted him. They bowed. "Maestro," they said.

He walked long enough through the alleyways and past the shuttered vegetable markets to lose himself. He had stepped into a cobbled street he didn't recognize, with closed grocers' shops and a bleak café with a crackling blue neon sign. The usual cats prowled near the gutters, and the old man reached into his pockets for pieces of cheese and bread. The cats mewled and slithered around his ankles. At the end of the street was a fountain with a broken stone dish through whose cracks water dribbled; above it was a statue of a lion, one of its legs broken off.

None of this was familiar to him. He stopped for a breath and wrapped his burgundy wool scarf closer around his neck. Darkness here. He felt something on the back of his neck and looked up. Snow was falling in the dark, a rarity. Pennsylvania: those afternoon cloud snowstorms with sun burning in another part of the sky: light ridging the snow. Bright air descending.

white dust the prismatic light seeks
while Pomona rests under amethyst branches

He waited on the sidewalk for his eyesight to clear, to clarify. Seeing a single lamp, fire butter yellow, he walked toward it. It receded ahead of him. Laughter, which he took at once to be American tourist laughter, echoed on stone and green canal water. He kept his eyes on the pavement, but from the sound of it two Americans, a boy and a girl, passed him. Still laughing. Pain, which he had spent a lifetime studiously ignoring, rose from his ankle, inhabited his kneecap for a moment, then actually lifted his right leg at the hip. A pain step.

He stopped to breathe. His old hatreds returned to him, the old friends. Coming to the end of the street, he turned left into a dank blank alleyway where the four-story houses seemed to tilt toward him, and he heard the sound of a radio playing Mascagni accompanied by two women bickering about opera. A dog came up to the old man, barked, wagged its tail; the poet rolled the bread in his pocket into a ball and dropped it straight down into the dog's dark mouth.

As he patted the dog, he felt the anger against the young Americans achieving a level. Against such people, the bourgeoisie, he had thrown his poems like bricks. Obstreperous box dwellers, the bourgeoisie devoured and consumed, leaving behind their filth. The dog, sensing rage in the old man, turned its head away from his hand and trotted down the alley.

He watched the dog go

> *that after borrowing, after the eating and tearing*
> *hoc caverat mens provida Reguli*
> *dissentientis condicionibus*

For a moment his mind caught fire and burned, like an old warehouse. It was an animal pleasure to feel it burning.

He found himself walking into a peculiarly lit square where late-night strangers could be seen inside a café drinking apéritifs. Despite the snow of a few moments before, the old man felt revived by the small fire of his hatred. Seeing the long receding plane of the sidewalk, the unsettled lamps electrically sputtering, he let the wings of his mind extend; he unsheathed the claws; and as he crossed diagonally another futile-looking square, he saw two Jews pass by him without seeing him. They were speaking heavily accented Italian.

He had once had thoughts about Jews, lengthy serpentine thoughts, but there were no thoughts there anymore.

He leaned against a wall between two drainpipes, which in the darkness had a brittle and crustacean sheen. He had once tried to set everybody straight about the Jews. On the radio. Elsewhere. The trouble was, since the time when silence had swallowed him up—it now seemed to have been all his life but maybe it was only last year or even yesterday—a small suspicion had fallen. The canal water lapped ahead of him; he thought he saw a rat scuttling in front of him, smooth glossy creature, crawling headfirst cheerfully ratlike down toward the water. The old man smiled, observing the rat. Yes, a suspicion had fallen. The suspicion was that he himself was a Jew. Had always been a Jew. Had not been informed about it. Had been kept in the dark. *Nunc retrosum vela dare atque iterare cursus cogor relictos.* In the dark about being a Jew, and, a prank, had been brought around to give speeches against them. Now that he was living in the trash can, an old piece of human rubbish, it had come to him, and it had a woman's face. Not smooth: angles and jags. She came to him in the street here in this city on a crepuscular Sunday and she had said, Henceforth you are a Jew. And she had left him, all but the memory of her face. Five efficient lines, but he recognized her. She had touched him and he knew. Canst thou see?

"Do you know that story about Nietzsche?"

The voice rose out of the paving stones, without footsteps. Like a thief, he would have yellowish eyes. The old man could see the eyes without looking.

"Do you know what he was doing before his mind gave way?"

THE OLD MAN accelerated. Against the paving stones his cane tapped a Provençal poetry rhythm, a beat of three against two. He was entering a mostly darkened street with one tavern. Beyond it, out of season, was an ice cream pushcart, with tin sides—aluminum? chrome? he couldn't remember materials—reflecting the sidewalk lights, a white dress, and, distorted, the legs of a woman standing close by. But after all it was not deep winter. Approaching, he stood head down near the woman, hoping to breathe in that rare green scent of oak leaves that American women sometimes carried with them: the odor of innocence, the odor of what-if-everybody.

He inhaled the woman's presence and thought of American trees, oaks and elms. Like those trees, the woman stood like something antecedent to the human reign. With her was a young man, so American that he wore a cap with a visor in the streets of Venice.

"Yes?" The ice cream vendor looked down into his cart, wanting the old man's order. Simple: he wanted vanilla. But he could not say it, not in any of the several languages that he knew, not a single syllable. Each one of the syllables had left him, taken its leave. He looked at the ice cream vendor.

"Ah, Maestro!" The Italian smile of recognition. The vendor spread his hand over his cart: anything here is yours, Maestro. Any flavor for the great man, the illustrious poet.

Sound—crickets, locusts crawling from their discarded shells— broke and shattered and echoed in his throat. It was the trench warfare of sound and silence: and words filling him with nausea. The words were eyes, gazing at him, floating halfway between the street and the windows. The words were the splinters around which this infection had grown. They were beetles; they were eyeless statues. Under his tongue the words had at last fallen to pieces like dried mushrooms. So that now—and this was hell, the inability to perform the smallest acts—he was unable to say what flavor ice cream he preferred.

The woman with the aroma of the oak tree grasped his arm. "Hey," she said, "are you all right? What's the matter? Jerry, come here."

The old man shook his head and freed his arm. He would not let himself be pitied by a couple of normal Americans wandering around the streets of Venice after dark. He would rather be pitied by a walled garden of eyeless statues. These Americans spoke English with such flat vowels that the sounds seemed to have come out of a plow cutting through topsoil. The normal Americans were consulting. Drawn together, they whispered, glancing at the old man with expressions of predatory helpfulness.

He bent his head. It occurred to him that he had not known many normal Americans. Perhaps none.

"Il poeta," the ice cream vendor explained, obviously pleased to be in the old man's company. "The famous and renowned poet. Of your country." He raised his palm toward the old man as if he were blessing him. "Of your country, America."

"Why doesn't he say anything?" the American woman asked.

Struggling with his English, the vendor said, "He says nothing, signora. For many years now nothing." He handed the old man an ice cream cone. Vanilla: what he wanted: he took it and reached with his other hand into his pocket for coins. Nothing there, all the money removed by the women for the protection of himself. The vendor held up his hand again, this time like a traffic cop: no money, Maestro, not from you.

"Why doesn't he say anything?" the visored American asked, taking off his cap and scratching his hair.

"Not for years," the vendor said. Then, in a scandalized whisper, he said, "Arrested!"

"Arrested?" the woman repeated. "A poet under arrest? I never heard of a poet being arrested. They don't arrest poets in America. Besides, I never heard of him. He couldn't have been *that* bad!" She said this as if the old man were not only mute but also deaf. Giving him a last smile, she took her husband's crooked arm and led him off into foreign dark.

The old man bowed to the vendor. "Grazie," he said.

Sometimes he could say it.

"You spoke," the vendor said.

The old man nodded. Then, holding what was left of his ice cream, he took himself into the shadows, where he was comfortable.

SOMETHING ABOUT THE night in Venice: one never saw stars here: a relief. He hated the stars. Overhead only the universe of the earthly atmosphere—smoke, haze, and breath. Though he had struggled only for light

> *the hawk form wing gathering*
> *and the integers poured from gold cups*
> *Ratio: ash, elm, and the thick sap drying*

the light had abandoned him. He had been a terrorist for light. He had taken up with The Boss in the cause of light: of order and economic hierarchy and the shapely organization of the affairs of state. And the light had flayed them both. They had lifted The Boss up on the hook, in the light, stripping him down to the bloody cartilage in the public square.

As for the old man, after caging him, they had left him with his life in the nuthouse, so that he could cultivate a proper respect for hell. In the Victorian melodramas of his youth, the ones he had seen in

Chicago and Philadelphia, they had lit the villain with a green light, the light of vanity and envy. They had been quite intelligent in those days.

He had learned a mild respect for the green precincts of hell. He was now so old that he knew the gods had decided to let him live so that he could suffer properly, in a timely manner. He was now four hundred years old and would live at least for another two hundred years.

UNDER A STREETLIGHT he felt himself shriveling. He took two steps to the right and leaned against a wall, damp like all the other stonework and now snowy, and he bowed his head as one of his hands picked at the skin of his other hand. Was this the place? He had an idea that he was out here for a rendezvous with a woman who was almost as old as he was but who had not somehow aged, who was unaging and therefore beautiful. Above all she was deeply and terrifyingly symmetrical. Out of another window came another swell of music, this time Wagner, the dripping poison of *Parsifal*.

He had a headache. He could not remember when he had not had one. And—this was the strange quality to his headaches—they were both in his head and his hands. He plucked at his hands in order to get the headache out of them. His ideas were stuffed down inside his hands. It came from too much writing.

He waited for her, watching the occasional snow; he tried to clear the phlegm out of his throat but failed. In this side street only a few couples passed, smoking cigarettes, but not speaking. He thought of language with nostalgia, a country house, all its doors locked.

Possibility for a long poem: a poet—an American!—takes over the country of language and becomes its ruler but then is violently deposed and cannot return, even to speak. The dictator robbed of words who cannot dictate. *Dicto, dictare*. To take dictation. The old man felt a sweet nostalgia for terror. And a warmer nostalgia for cleanliness, the purifying light.

"Do you know that story about Nietzsche? in the streets of Turin . . ."

"Leave me alone," the old man muttered.

"No: listen. Listen to me. He raised his arms around the horse's neck. He embraced the horse. He hugged it."

The old man swayed from side to side.

"The bright specks of blood . . . Nietzsche Caesar . . . the flogged horse . . . and the last act, *the one that you of all people should be aware of,* Nietzsche's last act, of purest tenderness . . ."

The old man raised his hands to his face. But did not weep.

IN THE DARKNESS of his hands he saw the lost American order. He had thought of his native country as a semicomical circus, a joke-society where men and women ran around in public in their underwear. America was a place of tunnels, and, more recently, of mental hospitals where he had been, for rather too many years, detained. He had wanted to put his hands to America and shape it as a child shapes putty. For a time he thought he would succeed to the place of John Adams and Thomas Jefferson as a theorist of societal arrangements.

But something had gone wrong. He was still trying to understand where: in some location there had been fissures.

America had put its hands on *him* and shaped *him* like putty.

The fissures were in his own head. It occurred to him that he was Roderick Usher, an expatriate American like himself, and that the rotting palace consisted of his ideas: all the ideas, the ideas that had gone into the letters and speeches and reviews and essays and poems. False friends, they had moved away, one and all. Economics, history, poetics, politics, they had sprouted wings and flown. Now—and he saw this, too—in his old age he was mixing metaphors: the ideas could not be birds and houses at the same time.

He could remember his ideas but they felt meaningless to him. It was an odd sensation to remember meaningless ideas. It was a bit like trying to eat waxed fruit.

He took his hands away from his face and proceeded to march down the sidewalk, his cape swirling behind him and his cane once again tapping out one beat to the dactyl of his steps. Wherever one was in Venice (and he could not be sure, ever since he had eaten the ice cream cone, where he was), one could smell the decadence of history, the bloodletting of the Council of Ten and its secret police, the movement of prisoners across the bridges, the eastward flow of the filthy Adriatic. Commerce and trade and usury, Marco Polo and Shylock.

He came to a place where he already was. He leaned back against another wall. Not wanting to, he nevertheless breathed out, a small breath. He remembered lakes and trees of the American Midwest, perhaps the only blues and greens he had ever owned outright. He had traded them in for some European statues with which he had cluttered up his mind, and a few Chinese characters that no longer expressed what he meant to say. He was a victim of a wonderful joke perpetrated by the gods, in which the natural tendency of intelligence toward mania was perfectly expressed. He was known worldwide not as a poet but as a maniac.

Here, standing inside this labyrinth of cities, old and raging, both the Minotaur and Theseus, he saw his old beard and old hair and old eyes reflected in the glass of a shop window. He looked like an elderly human goat. He had looked like a goat for several years now. He had once looked like an intellectual hero and his friends the sculptors had done his head in bronze and stone and marble. Now he looked like a goat and young people he didn't know came to take his his photograph. Once as a joke they asked to see his hooves.

He accepted himself as a barbarian. If one was an American, one remained a barbarian, no matter how many books one read. Because finally they would not be American books and slowly and certainly one turned oneself into a museum of foreign acquisitions.

Finally this world was too corrupt for him to fix. He remembered the urge to save and purify as a deep and satisfying source of energy. The Industrial Revolution had been a mistake; profits won on a massive scale were a mistake; banking in its modern form was a mistake. They must see that. But he himself was the greatest mistake; and there was now no fixing him apart from the silence that he himself had entered as a retreat from the mafiosi of meaning.

He had seen the world despoiled. He had eyes. Had seen the masses falling ever further into rootlessness. Deprived of dignity, they had been sent off to war to fight for the bankers and brought back to be injured in industrial servitude. Everything clean in nature had been pulled down out of the light and besmirched, fouled. There had once been a realm of light. But the light and its masters were being extinguished. What had surprised him was that everyone knew it. Everyone welcomed this sputtering of the light. The arrival of the uncreating word, the shit of chaos, was an occasion for joy! He saw that first in the prison and then in the hospital.

The puzzle: all his life he had campaigned for light and purity. But somehow he had found himself on the wrong side. He had never mastered the techniques of intellectual terror. So that when they came, in their uniforms, to arrest him, they had used terror effectively against him.

HE FOUND HIMSELF walking again. He had managed to move away from the glass and was now approaching one of the larger canals. For ten seconds snow fell, then stopped. It was an abstract snow, an idea of snow. In the canal ahead of him, a gondolier was watching him with a sleepy but still attentive look.

The old man gazed at him. The gondolier had the face of Titian's Pietro Aretino, though without the beard. Often in Venice he saw these time-spiral tricks. One walked out of a museum or gallery and saw a face from a painting by Tintoretto transferred to a waiter serving tea in the public square.

The gondolier, Pietro Aretino, helped the old man into the boat. The old man felt the gondolier's hands and realized with pleasure that the gondolier had no ideas in his hands; if he had any ideas, they would be in his head.

He asked the old man where he wanted to go. The old man pointed forward.

From the pier behind him he heard the yellow voice calling out about Nietzsche and the carthorse. Then the voice began to recite Nietzsche's poem about the pigeons in St. Mark's Square.

Die Tauben von San Marco seh ich wieder:
Still ist der Platz, Vormittag ruht darauf.

Again I see the pigeons of St. Mark: the square lies still, in—what?— slumbering morning mood . . . ? He felt a wave of nausea and forced the words down into his hands.

The waves lapped patiently against the boat in a patter of Vivaldian sixteenth notes. In the dark, heading nowhere through this tiny crooked canal that smelled of cheese and laundry, the old man closed his eyes and let darkness drop on darkness. He thought, for the barest moment, of paradise. This time it was pleasingly empty. Uninhabited by humankind and the messier forms of the vegetable realm, it manifested itself inside his eyelids as a single horizon line making a division of brilliant unclouded sky above and warmed earth below, green but not with grass, the green of a primordial element. A horizon line, blue sky, a sun. And no people at all.

He held his eyes closed for another moment while he wished in the innermost core cell of his heart for the obliteration of all human life.

When he opened his eyes again, he saw that the gondola was heading into some sort of fog, a halation effect surrounding the few lights from windows that he was still able to see. Reaching down to scratch an itch that had manifested itself on his knee, his hand dropped by accident into the water. The water felt green and cold, topped by an oily foam. The water had flowed toward him all the way from Byzantium. But at this moment it felt alien. None of the water was his.

He opened his eyes wider. The halation effect increased. The gondolier was taking him down a patchwork of ever-narrowing one-way canals. But then it brought him into the Grand Canal, past a palace with Moorish windows, and the old man thought he saw the Palazzo Barbaro where Milly Theale had died of that odd and delicate disease Henry James had thoughtfully given her in *The Wings of the Dove*. But no: they were not in that part of the Grand Canal at all. They were not approaching, as he had thought, the Accademia Bridge. As the halation increased around all of the lights—an effect of his cataracts, he thought—he could not be sure where they were, or even that they were making a progress down the Grand Canal at all.

Geography, in this city, anywhere, had become too much for him.

Location had given way to age. He was so old and so out-of-date everywhere that it didn't matter where he was.

Out of the haze of the misted lights hung on the piers and attached to the walls of the calles, he saw a woman standing in the distance, waiting for him. Without asking himself who it was, he knew. Dressed as she was always dressed, in darkness, her face radiating out of the cobalt-blue Persian silk scarves with which she surrounded her face, she saw him and stepped toward him. Of course she would say nothing: had never said anything: could not. It was for her he had grown silent. His muteness was intended as a response to hers, the last courtship of old age. Her gaze clear, she waited for him, as she waited every night, on this darkened pier.

The old man turned around to examine the gondolier's face. It was the same face every evening. It knew everything.

She was old and yet beautiful: unaging and terrifyingly symmetrical.

As he did every evening at this time, he thought of himself passing over another day and becoming eternal. But if he ever died—and he was not sure, now, that he ever would—he would die as a good and a bad American.

Slowly, with patient infirmity, the old man grasped the fringed cushion underneath him and brought himself to his feet. Standing in the gondola, his eyes fixed on the woman, the old man held himself erect, unappeased, and waited to arrive before her.

Behind the Story

I HAVE CHOSEN to discuss my story "The Old Fascist in Retirement" (from *A Relative Stranger*) for two reasons: first, because I am proud of it, and second, because any writing workshop would probably hammer it to bits.

This story violates most of the narrative norms that I have spent a lifetime teaching to my own students. It has almost no plot. Its action is minimal. It is discursive rather than dramatic. There is only one major character in it (the second major character is a hallucination), and this major character's outward appearance is described only minimally. The story refers to a set of external and apparently historical circumstances that it does not bother to explain. Its verbal texture is jagged and somewhat reader-unfriendly. My imagination's usual native realm, the Midwest, is absent from it, as are all warm-and-fuzzy feelings. The conflict, if there is one, is hard to figure out. The main character is not likable and does not engage in dialogue with others. There is no central epiphany, or: so many epiphanies crowd the story that they constitute a glut.

Clearly, this is no way to write a story. And yet I had to write it this way, and many years later, I am still relieved that I did.

The story's inspiration and main character is none other than the American poet Ezra Pound, treated here with some poetic license, in his last years, in Venice during the 1960s. Pound, whatever his deficiencies, was certainly a broken genius, and in order to give him his due, I felt I had to pitch the story at the level of culture and ideas, as if he had thought these thoughts in this way. But why write about Pound? Who cares about Pound?

It isn't only that Pound as a poet was a broken genius; he was also, arguably, a traitor and an anti-Semite before and during World War Two, and *he was the only writer of note in American culture during the last hundred years who came close to being executed by the government for treason*. During the war, he made broadcasts for Radio Rome. The texts of these broadcasts are available for leisurely reading, and they are still horrifying. We may be familiar with what Hitler did to Germany's writers and what Stalin did to the Soviet Union's writers, but Americans need to be reminded, again and again, of what we almost did to Pound. He only escaped hanging through a scheme by his friends to have him declared insane and installed in St. Elizabeth's Hospital.

In any case, that is why the story exists: it has a historical referent, though if the reader does not know about Pound in the first place, s/he is unlikely to get the bare facts out of "The Old Fascist in Retirement." You have to know a little about Ezra Pound if the story is going to work at all—if it is going to take you into the mind of an American fascist. That dependence on your knowledge is the risk the story takes, its particular gamble. The story is slightly anti-democratic; not everyone is invited into it. In this respect, the story has a touch of Pound's own fascism built into its own construction. It expects that you know enough, and care enough, about recent cultural history to read it—and these are not readerly requirements in my other fiction. As a consequence, "The Old Fascist in Retirement" has stylistic halitosis: it gives off the stale rotten breath of Modernism. I liked evoking that rottenness, though I had not done anything of the sort before I wrote this story and have not done it since and would not. This is a one-time-only story. Sometimes I can't believe I did it.

But I also believe that fiction can be understood to include stories like "The Old Fascist in Retirement." Much recent fiction— DeLillo's, David Foster Wallace's, Elizabeth Hardwick's, Renata Adler's—can and does comment on culture, on the political and social elements that we have inherited, live in, and breathe. I needed a break from what I usually did as a writer. And of course we are dealing here with my own obsessions with Ezra Pound—man, writer, and American. I had a relative who admired Pound's writing and would read it aloud after dinner. Finally, it may be worth noting that I am writing this essay now at a critical time of American cultural history, when civil liberties may possibly be in jeopardy as a response to terror, a central topic in the story.

Everyone needs a model, and my model here was a Lars Gustafsson story about Nietzsche immediately before his mental breakdown. This story, "Out of the Pain," is collected in his marvelous book *Stories of Happy People* (New Directions). Gustafsson's brief paragraphs, abrupt transitions, and brilliancies of thought-thinking-as-Nietzsche gave me the shivers. Gustafsson managed to get a sense of historical apocalypse into a five-page story; his tale is a miracle of compression and freedom possible only in fiction. Therefore my story begins with Nietzsche, a tip of my writer's hat to Lars Gustafsson. A writer is a reader, Henry James said, who has been moved to emulation.

There were other sources and inspirations for this story, including Donald Hall's memoir about Pound in old age, which contains the anecdote of the ice cream cone. I had also read somewhere an observation by Eugenio Montale that Pound was like one of those rich Americans like William Randolph Hearst who goes to Europe and buys up statues and paintings and takes them home. Pound's book *The Cantos,* said Montale, was a collection of all the statues and paintings that Pound had bought. But this did not mean, Montale went on to say, that Pound had become a civilized man—instead, Montale argued, Pound had become a cultured barbarian. It didn't matter how many statues he purchased; he would always remain a barbarian.

In one of his last interviews, Alfred Hitchcock had said that he remembered a green spotlight shining on the villain in the stage melodramas he had gone to see in London as a boy. That went into the story. Also his observation that for him paradise would be an empty field with a clear sky and no people. That, too, went into the story.

The story is full of peculiar punctuation: sentences with two or three colons, suggesting explanations that never arrive on the scene; proliferating semicolons; sentence fragments; even verse fragments, made up by me, and pasted in with Latin verse by Horace. The sentences are meant to look like sentences you've never seen before. They are full of textured coloration. The verse in German toward the end, however, is actually by Nietzsche. In the story, metaphors become as solid as "real" objects, and hallucinations, like the woman at the story's end, who is the poet's muse, drift in and out as if they were ongoing parts of the character's mental life.

The story also contains a memory of Thomas Mann's hero Adrian Leverkühn in *Doctor Faustus,* particularly the line (which I simply stole, with a change from "German" to "American") that when Leverkühn finally dies, he will die, he believes, "both as a good and a bad German." The damned composer of that novel also fantasizes the end of all human life, as my old fascist does.

My old fascist loves light and purity and then tries to bring purity to human affairs. That is his biggest, his elemental, his criminal, mistake.

The story does have a structure: its protagonist starts on a balcony, goes down to ground-level, walks through Venice, and at last arrives at a canal, where a gondolier takes him across the water, both the literal water of the canals, and the waters of Lethe, the waters of forgetfulness following death. Each image of a literal object creates a cascade of historical and personal associations, but not everything is explained in an expository way, simply because our central character would not have to explain everything that he knows to himself. The protagonist walks forward in space but backward in time. In this sense the story is in the tradition of all stories that follow a character's associative thoughts while s/he takes a walk, as in Thoreau's "Walking" or Robert Walser's "A Walk."

I cared about Ezra Pound, but finally what I cared most about was immersing my reader in a dream, in which broken parts and pieces of culture fly by like materials sent into the air by a tornado. The tornado is the old poet's mind, and there is ice cream in it, and Mascagni and Wagner, and memories of snow, and beautiful women, and faces in paintings by Titian, and gondoliers, and a dying character in Henry James's novel, and Jews; and there goes Nietzsche, and here's the Bridge of Sighs, and over there is what Hofmannstahl said in his "Lord Chandos Letter" about words as mushrooms, and here, finally, is a headache that you feel in your hands.

It may not be your world, or our world, but it is *a* world that I wanted to bring to life. To breathe, as it were, the breath of life back into something that had almost disappeared, something unusually difficult and complex. I knew quite a few readers would not like it, and that I would have to break many of the usual rules. So be it.

Robert Cohen

〰️

THE VARIETIES OF
ROMANTIC EXPERIENCE:
AN INTRODUCTION

GOOD MORNING. IT appears we have quite a turnout. This is an elective course, as you know from the catalogue, and as such it is forced to compete with several other offerings by our department, a great many of which are, as you've no doubt heard, scandalously shopworn and dull, and so may I take a moment to say that I am personally gratified to see so many of you enrolled here in Psych 308. So many new faces. I look forward to getting to know you ea—

Yes, there are seats I believe in the last few rows, if the people, if the people there would kindly hold up a hand to indicate a vacancy beside them, yes, there, thank you . . .

Very well then. No doubt some of you have been attracted by the title listed in the catalogue, a title that is, as many of you surely know, a play on that estimable work by William James, *The Varieties of Religious Experience,* a subject very close indeed to the one at hand. I assume that is why you are here. Because as you see, I am neither a brilliant nor a charismatic lecturer. I am merely an average one. An average-looking specimen of what to most of you must seem to be an average middle age, teaching at an average educational institution attended by, you'll forgive me, average students. Are there enough syllabi going around? Good. You will note right away that I subscribe to many of the informal, consensually determined rules of academic conduct and dress. I favor tweeds and denims and the occasional tie. My syntax is formal. My watch is cheap. You may well catch me in odd moments—and there will be, I assure you, no shortage of them—fiddling with this watch of mine in a nervous, abstracted way, or staring pensively out the window into the parking lot, with its perfect grid of white, dutiful lines, in a manner that suggests deep thought. You may well wonder what is the nature of these deep thoughts of mine. Am I parsing out some arcane bit of theory? Reflecting on the dualities of consciousness? Or am I simply meandering through the maze of some private sexual fantasy, as, statistics tell us, so many of us do so much of the time? Yes, there will be much to wonder about, once we get started. Much to discuss. Admittedly you may find me somewhat more forthcoming than the average tenured professor—more "upfront," as you undergraduates like to say—but that, I submit, is in the nature of my researches, and in the nature of the field itself. One must develop in our work a certain ruthlessness in regard to truths, be they truths of behavior or personality, be they quote unquote private or public. The fact is, *There are no private truths in our world.* If you learn nothing else this semester, I trust you will learn that.

I ask, by the way, that all assignments be neatly typed. I have no teaching assistant this term. I had one last spring, a very able one at that. Perhaps some of you met her. Her name was Emily. Emily Crane.

I say *was* though of course she, Emily, Emily Crane, isn't dead. Still, I think of her as a *was,* not the *is* she surely still must be. This is one of the most common and predictable tricks of the unconscious, to suggest to us the opposite of the real, to avoid the truth when the truth will cause us pain. We will discuss such matters in the weeks ahead. We will discuss the lessons, the often hard and painful lessons, of the wounded psyche in its search for wholeness. We will seek to gain insight and understanding into our worst humiliations, not because there is implicit value in such knowledge—this is perhaps open to debate—but because as a practical matter we are conditioned more deeply by our failures than our successes, and it is vital to gain insight into what conditions us, in order that we may operate more freely.

Many of you have been led to believe just the opposite. You have been fed by the media a vulgar caricature of our profession, one that claims we are all imprinted at an early age by forces of such deterministic magnitude that we are forever thereafter obliged to repeat the same few patterns, perform endless variations on the same thin script. This is an attractive idea, of course. Like all such mystical notions, it frees us from the burden of choice and responsibility, and lays the blame instead at the feet of our parents and culture. We can surrender the struggle for well-being and console ourselves with the idea that it was never in fact available to us.

But this is nonsense. Opportunities for transformation are as plentiful as the stars, as the paintings in a museum, as you yourselves. Look around you. It's September, and I know you can all feel, as I do, the rushing of the blood that comes in with the first Canadian winds. If one breathes deeply enough one can almost feel oneself swell, become larger, less imperfect. I quite love September. I look forward to it all summer, I savor it while it's here, I mourn it when it's gone. I experience this as a personal love, but of course this is sheer narcissism—the lonely ego seeking an escape into vastness.

Those of you who have had sexual intercourse know approximately what I mean. One feels oneself changing temperature, contours; one feels an immanence; and finally one feels oneself arrive, if you will, in a larger, more generous space. One feels a good many other things too, of course, if one is fortunate.

I myself was fortunate, very fortunate, when the teaching assistantships were designated last year, and I was paired with Emily, Emily Crane. Allow me to remind you, ladies and gentlemen, that your teaching assistants should never be taken for granted. They work hard in the service of distant ideals, and are rewarded by and large with long nights, headaches, and minimal pay. One must treat them well at all times—even, or perhaps especially, when they fail to treat you well in return. One must listen; one must attend. Certainly I tried to pay attention to Emily, to her various needs, and so forth. Her singularities. These are after all what make us interesting, our singularities. Our little tics. Emily, for example, had a most irregular way of groaning to herself in moments of stress. They were very odd, involuntary, delirious little groans, and they would emerge from her at the most unexpected times. She'd groan in the car, parallel parking, or at the grocery, squeezing limes. In bed, she'd groan as she plumped the pillows, she'd groan getting under the sheets, she'd groan as she pulled off her nightshirt, she'd groan all the way through foreplay and up to the point of penetration, and then, then she'd fall weirdly silent, as if the presence of this new element, my penis, required of her a greater discretion than its absence. I found it disconcerting, at first. My wife, Lisa, whom we will discuss later in the term—you'll find copies of her letters and diaries on Reserve at the library—used to make a fair bit of noise during lovemaking, so when Emily fell quiet I had the suspicion, common among males of a sensitive nature, that I was failing to please her. Apparently this was not the case, though one can never be sure. My own ego, overnourished by a doting mother—see the attached handout, "Individuation and Its Discontents: A Case Study"—is all too readily at work in such instances. But now, thinking back on Emily, Emily Crane, I find myself wondering what were, what *are,* the mechanisms that govern her responses. I wonder approximately how many small ways my perception, clouded by defenses, failed her.

Of course she failed me too. Emily was, *is,* a highly moody and capricious young woman, capable of acting out her aggressions in a variety of childish, wholly inappropriate ways. The night of the dean's birthday party last April, for example. We arrived separately of course, with our respective partners—I with Lisa, who abhorred parties, and Emily with Evan Searle, a first-year graduate student from the Deep South. Evan was tall, taller than I am, and thin, thinner than I am, a remarkably amiable and intelligent young man in every way, and so perhaps it's ungenerous of me to feel that if there were the merest bit of justice in the world he'd have long ago been the victim of a random, brutal accident. But back to the party. It was tiresome, as these things normally are, with much of the comradely backslapping that alcohol often inspires among people who don't particularly like each other. As you will no doubt observe over time, our faculty is not a close one. It is riddled with cliques and factions, with gossips and schemers and gross incompetents, and if there is anything that unites us at all, other than our dislike for teaching undergraduates, it is our dislike for the dean and his interminable parties.

This one appeared to be adhering to the typical flat trajectory. Standing between us and the liquor table was Arthur Paplow, the last Behaviorist, who subjected us to the latest in his ongoing series of full-bore ideological rants. Then Frida Nattanson—some of you may have had Frida last year for Psych 202—came over, Frida who back in her distant, now quite inconceivable youth made something of a reputation for herself by spilling a drink on Anna Freud at a party not unlike this one—anyway, Frida, in her shy, mumbly way, launched into a rather tragic litany detailing the various ongoing health issues of her wretched cat Sparky. Then Earl Stevens, our boy wonder, strode up and tried to enlist us in one of his terribly earnest games of Twister, a game cut short when our distinguished emeritus, Ludwig Stramm, fell into his customary stupor in the middle of the room, and had to be circumnavigated on tiptoe, as no one had the courage to wake him. All this time, understand, I was watching Emily Crane out of the corner of my eye.

May I have the first slide please?

I have not spoken of her looks, but you will observe that she wasn't beautiful, in the classic sense of that term, not beautiful by any means. She had a hormonal condition that kept her very thin, too thin really—note the bony shoulders—and made her skin too somewhat warmer than most people's, so that she dressed in loose, floppy cotton dresses without sleeves—dresses that reveal, if you look closely, a little more of Emily than she seemed to realize. Her face was long and her mouth quite small, and this smallness of the mouth limited the range of her expressions somewhat, so that one had to know her fairly well, as I thought I did, to read her. I saw her nodding absently along with some story Evan Searle was telling to the dean's secretary. I could see that she was bored, restless, and hoping to leave early. But with whom?

I had come to the party with Lisa, who was after all my wife. We had been married for close to sixteen years. This must sound like a long time to you. And yet, when you are no longer quite so bound up in your youth, you may experience Time in a different way. You may see a diminishment in the particularities, the textures, of lived Time that may well come as a relief. One could argue that this diminishment I speak of is really an intensification or heightening, closer to the Eastern notion of Time as an eternal present, an unbounded horizon. I'm not qualified to judge. I only know that Time is not the burden we think it is. It is in fact a very light, mutable thing.

Speaking of burdens, let us return to the salient fact here, my marriage to Lisa, a commitment central to my life. I had no intention of leaving Lisa for Emily. I knew it and Emily knew it. Moreover she claimed to be perfectly satisfied with this state of affairs. She knew the score, she liked to say. I was twice her age and married, to say nothing of being her thesis adviser, and it required no special sophistication to regard what we were doing together as the predictable embodiment of an academic cliché. Of course this did nothing to diminish our excitement. Far from it. Indeed, one might argue that in our media-saturated age, eroticism is incomplete without its corresponding mirror in one popular cultural cliché or another. Has it become a cliché then, to engage in oral sex on one's office carpet, five minutes before one's three-thirty seminar in Advanced Cognition? Of course it has. And is it a cliché to find oneself, during a recess in the Admissions Committee meeting, licking the hot, unshaven armpit of a twenty-four-year-old Phi Beta Kappa? Of course it is. Ladies and gentlemen, allow me to say that I wish such clichés on all of you. Let me say too that if they have already come your way, you will have ample opportunity to make use of them, either in class discussion or in one of the three written papers I will ask of you this term.

To continue our inquiry, then, into the events of the party: Sometime later, close to midnight, I saw Emily disengage herself from Evan Searle and wander off by herself in the direction of the kitchen. It so happened we had not been alone together in some time. Emily was busy studying for orals, and claimed to have an infection of some sort that rendered her unfit for sex. It was difficult to imagine any germ so virulent, but never mind. I did not press the point, even when the days became a week, the week ripened and then withered into a month. Oh, I called a few times, to be sure, merely to check on her health. In truth she sounded rather wan. Several times I had the distinct impression that I had woken her up, or perhaps interrupted some strenuous bit of exercise. Afterwards I would sit in my study, pour myself a finger of scotch—sometimes a whole handful—and stew in the darkness, utterly miserable, thinking of Emily, Emily Crane. The lunatic's visions of horror, wrote the great William James, are all drawn from the material of daily fact. All my daily facts had been reduced to this. I sat there alone, in a darkened room cluttered with books, a darkened mind cluttered with Emily. Emily with Evan Searle. Emily with Earl Stevens. Emily with the director of off-campus housing. Emily with delivery boys, meter maids, movie stars. Emily with everyone and everyone with Emily and nowhere a place for me.

But perhaps I have strayed from our topic.

We were still at the party, as I recall. Emily had gone into the kitchen, and I had followed. The kitchen was gleaming, immaculate, empty of people. For that matter it was empty of food. The dean, famous for his thrifty way with a budget, had hired a rather puritanical catering crew whose specialty, if you could call it that, was crustless cucumber and avocado sandwiches. Apparently Emily had not had her fill. The refrigerator was open and she had bent down to rummage through its sparse contents. She did not hear me approach. I stopped midstep, content to watch her at work—her pale bare shoulders, her tangled coif, her air of concentrated appetite. At that moment, class, it struck me with a profound and singular force: I loved Emily Crane, loved her in a way that both included and transcended desire, loved her in a way that brought all the blockish, unruly, and disreputable passions of the self into perfect, lasting proportion. Feeling as I did, it seemed incumbent upon me to let Emily know, that we might validate together this breakthrough into a higher, headier plane of affection. And so I stepped forward.

Perhaps I should say I *lurched* forward. Apparently I'd had a bit more to drink than was strictly necessary. Apparently I'd had *quite* a bit more to drink than was strictly necessary. I'm certain a good many of you know how that feels, don't you, when you get good and ripped, and that very pleasant little brass band begins its evening concert in your head, and the baton begins to wave, and the timpani begin to roll, and one feels oneself swell into a kind of living crescendo. There's nothing quite like it. It's different than the rush one experiences on very good marijuana, say, or opiated hashish. It lacks the vague, speedy flavor of the hallucinogens. No, if it can be compared to anything I'd say it's closer, in my opinion, to fine cocaine.

Do you young people still do cocaine? It's lovely, isn't it? Emily and I liked to snort it off a moon rock she'd bought from the Museum of Natural History in New York. The dear girl was absurdly superstitious about it. We *had* to be in the bathtub, Mahler *had* to be on the stereo, the bill we used *had* to be a fresh twenty, et cetera et cetera. As you can see, she displayed a marked predilection for controlled behavior, did Emily. Alas, my own predilections run in rather the opposite direction.

As I said, I lurched forward. Emily crouched before the white infertile landscape of the dean's refrigerator, unsuspecting. All I wished to do, you see, was press my lips against the fuzzy layer of down that ran like an untended lawn across the chiseled topography of her shoulder. That was all. There must have been some form of internal miscommunication, however, some sort of synaptic firing among the brain receptors that went awry, because what proceeded to happen was something quite different. What proceeded to happen was that I stumbled over some warped, wayward tile of linoleum, and went hurtling into Emily, and the point of my chin cracked hard against the top of her head, which sent her flying into the refrigerator. I might mention too that at some point in the proceedings my pants were no longer fastened at the waist but had slipped to a spot a good deal closer to my ankles, revealing a rather horrific erection I'm at a loss to account for. Where do they come from, these erections? Does anyone know? Why do they come upon one during bus rides, for instance, but not on the train? It's a subject worthy of exploration. Some of you may well decide to undertake it, in fact, for your first paper.

Emily, for her part, began to scream. One could hardly blame her, of course: I'd caught her off guard; I'd clumsily assaulted her; I'd invaded her space, as she liked to say. I'd done everything wrong, everything. She stood there, crimson-faced, fingering the teeth marks in her skirt, her mouth—

Sorry?

Oh yes, I seem to have bitten her skirt. Did I leave that out? An odd involuntary response, but there you have it. I still have a piece of it somewhere. A light, summery cotton material, as I remember.

Sometimes I'll pick it up and pop it in my mouth again, and the effect, if I may make so grand a claim, is not unlike Proust and his madeleine, conjuring up Emily in great rushing tides of sensory detail. *Remembrance of Flings Past,* if you will. Yes, a wonderful souvenir, that bit of skirt, to say nothing of its usefulness and durability as a masturbatory aid. But I am getting ahead of myself.

Emily was screaming. That was unfortunate, of course, but not unreasonable. The disconcerting part was that even *after* she had turned around, one lip fattening and starting to bleed; even *after* she had seen that it was only me, that it had obviously all been an accident, only an accident, one that had caused me too a great deal of pain; even *after* I had begun to stammer out a lengthy and perhaps in retrospect a not entirely coherent apology; even *after,* class, even *after—Emily continued to scream.* In fact she screamed louder. It was a scream without words, without inflection, as insensate and maddening as a siren. It appeared to come from some hot, awful, violent place inside Emily that I had not as yet explored . . . a place that I'll confess intrigued me. For a moment I had the completely insupportable idea that it bore some relation to her muteness during the love act, a place of inverted pleasures and projected pain, a place where all of Emily's emotional dysfunctions had sought out a refuge. Ladies and gentlemen, can you blame me for my interest in this young woman? She was fascinating, neurotic, convoluted, thoroughly extraordinary. No, I don't believe I can be blamed, not in this case, not with Emily Crane. My intentions were innocent ones, therapeutic ones. I wish to establish this point, my essential innocence, right here at the outset, because I will in all likelihood be making reference to it as the semester goes on.

There will be—did I mention?—a midterm and a final.

Of course they all came running at once, the entire faculty, including spouses, secretaries, and administrators, all came at once to the kitchen to see what had happened. For all they knew there had been a murder, a fire. How could they have known it was only a brief, botched kiss?

In time she began to calm down. Emily Crane, she calmed down. The vein at her temple softened and receded, her hands unclenched, her color assumed a normal shade. For the benefit of the onlookers she attempted a shrug of casualness, but her shoulders remained tight, unnaturally so, where I'd tried to kiss them, so that she appeared to have frozen midway through some strange, inelegant dance step. She opened her mouth to speak but nothing came out. Frida, cooing, stroked Emily's forehead. The room hushed. Emily looked at me softly, inquiringly, as she used to look at me during our Special Topics seminar only a year ago, her brow creased, her head cocked at a steep angle, her eyes wide and damp, and when she opened her mouth again I heard a whole robed choir of ardent angels rising to their feet.

"You're disgusting," she said. This in a loud and brittle voice. The sort of voice, class, one should never use on one's lover—and yet in the end one always does, it seems.

My tenured colleagues slipped away at once, grateful for the chance to escape and preoccupied, no doubt, with scandals of their own. But the untenured faculty looked on greedily, their faces lit by the kind of ghoulish pleasure with which small children attend the dismemberment of insects. They'd be dining out on this for weeks. Already I could hear the first rough whispers, the first conspiratorial murmurs. Emily, if she heard them, paid no mind; she stood proud, like a high priestess conducting a ritual sacrifice, slitting the throat of our love on the party's altar. "You're disgusting," she said again, perhaps for the benefit of Herr Stramm, who had missed it the first time. And then she wheeled, grabbed Evan Searle by the elbow, and commenced what I judged to be a rather theatrical exit.

Excuse me, but there are, I believe, a few minutes left.

Emily, Emily Crane, left this university soon afterward. I cannot tell you where she went because no one will tell me. It was the end of the term and I was left without a teaching assistant, left to grade 117 undergraduate papers, which I read, quite alone, on the floor of the unfurnished apartment that Lisa insisted I sublet the week after the dean's party. No doubt in a few weeks I will be grading your papers on that same floor. Sometimes it is all I can do to rise from that floor. Sometimes it is all I can do.

"There are persons," wrote the great William James, "whose existence is little more than a series of zig-zags, as now one tendency and now another gets the upper hand. Their spirit wars with their flesh, they wish for incompatibles, wayward impulses interrupt their most deliberate plans, and their lives are one long drama of repentance and of effort to repair misdemeanors and mistakes."

Who are these persons, you ask? You see one of them before you. If you take a moment and look to your left and your right, you will see two more. And by the time you are older, and not so very much older at that, you will begin to see him or her in the places you have not as yet been looking: in the reflection of a glass, say, or an intimate's stare, or a barren refrigerator. Ultimately, you see, the private will win out. The axis of reality, James tells us, runs solely through the private, egotistic places—they are strung upon it like so many beads. We are all in this together, ladies and gentlemen, in a way that would be horrible were it not so comic, but in a way that manages to be quite horrible anyway. We are all students of desire. We arrive at class eager as puppies, earnest, clumsy, groping for love. That is what brought you here this morning. You have caught the scent of possibility. You have begun to gnaw at your leashes, and they have begun to fray, and soon, soon, you will go scampering off in search of new ones.

Very well then. We are out of time. Next week, according to the syllabus, we will turn our attention to Janice, Janice Rodolfo, who left me for the captain of the golf squad in my junior year of high school. Among other issues, we will explore the theoretical implications of submissive behavior—mine—and analyze the phenomenon known as "dry humping" for its content of latent aggression. Until then, I ask only that you keep up with your reading and, of course, your journal, which I intend to review periodically. I ask that you keep your writing neat.

Are there any questions?

No?

I thought I saw a hand up . . . there, in the back row, the young lady with the red blouse, with the—

I thought I saw your hand.

Perhaps I have already answered your question. Or perhaps you're somewhat shy. There's something inhibiting, isn't there, about a forum such as this, all these narrow desks in their rigid lines. If I had my way in things, if it were up to me, this class would not be a lecture at all, but a succession of individual consultations in some small, comfortable room. A room like my office, for instance, on the third floor of this building, to the left of the stairs. Room 323. If it were up to me, young lady, you would ask your questions there. You would put down your pen and take off your shoes. There would be music, something chastened and reflective, to facilitate our inquiries. In the end we might choose not to speak at all, but merely to give in to a flickering candle, attending to the gyrations of the light, to the dance of its shadow up the wall, and to the small elusive effects of our own breath . . .

Yes?

Right, right, by all means, mustn't run over. It's only . . .

I thought, I thought there was . . .

I thought I saw her hand.

I WROTE THIS STORY one swampy afternoon in Houston, Texas, literally cackling, I'm sorry to report, much of the way. All writers will recognize this to be a bad sign. But I was in an odd state of mind at the time. It was 1990. I'd just moved down from New York to teach fiction writing at the local university. I had never taught fiction writing before; the sound of my own voice, jabbering its way indirectly and unimpeded, like some Beckett tramp, towards so many half-formed, ad hoc, or dubious truths, was still new to me, and vaguely mysterious, if not borderline farcical and scary. A lot of things were. I had never lived in the South before, never been so far from everyone I knew. I'd never had neighbors so friendly, so Christian, so eager to ply me with beer and show me their guns. The guy next door was on leave from the rodeo with a fractured leg; he stood out in his yard every afternoon like a seedy, unbalanced scarecrow, lassoing buckets. I watched him from my borrowed desk, sipping coffee from my borrowed mug. My whole existence felt borrowed, provisional, on loan from some threadbare branch library in Purgatory. I was not altogether in control of myself. I was not sure I *had* a self. In leaving New York, the needle of my life had skipped its groove, and gone skating wildly across the record. And it was only September. The school year, my whole new vocation, had just started, and already the whole thing seemed absurd.

I came home from teaching that first week, hot and bothered, and looked over the new Guidelines on Sexual Harassment which the administration had distributed to faculty mailboxes. That's what got me going, the lunacy of applying institutional language—an institutional life, such as I was about to embark upon—to the unshapely moanings of the human heart. All at once it was absolutely necessary to find a gun of my own to show off, and do a little damage. So I turned on my Selectric and let fly, went ballistic, egged on by the steady, maddening hum of the motor and that now-bygone rat-a-tat-tat of the keys, spraying out my rage, my confusion, my entrapment, my longing, all the meanness and me-ness I could no longer quite bear to keep to myself.

A passage I came across about this same time, from the great Natalia Ginzburg, nicely captures the effect of such bad moods as mine upon the creative imagination:

"Our personal happiness or unhappiness," she writes, "our *terrestrial* condition, has a great importance for the things we write. When we are happy our imagination is stronger. Suffering makes the imagination weak and lazy . . . it is difficult for us to turn our eyes away from our own life and our own state, from the thirst and restlessness that pervade us . . . A particular sympathy grows up between us and the characters that we invent . . . a sympathy that is tender and almost maternal, warm and damp with tears, intimately physical and stifling."

And so it was with me. I had no story to tell that day, no song to sing but self. But the Guidelines on Sexual Harassment had tapped a source of pressure, and that found its expression in a voice, which found its way to a conceit. The tone that emerged in the first line seemed somehow inevitable—high, quavering, lost in the maze of self-justification, and relentlessly, ludicrously, helplessly confessional. I had no idea what would happen, only that the lecture would proceed, and things would spiral rapidly downward, as things do, and that the language itself would find its way towards whatever situations had made it necessary. It was all about indulging this weird, giddy impulse one gets as a teacher and as a writer both, to shatter the plane of distance like a hammer, to say something unexpected and true. This compulsion to forge a philosophy out of experience, and express it. And how does one find truth in experience? Through defeat, disaster, humiliation. And are these the province of tragedy or comedy?

The answer seemed self-evident. When disaster happens to you, it's tragic. When it happens to someone else, it's comic. So make it happen to someone else . . .

A particular sympathy . . . intimately physical and stifling . . . I remember literally rubbing my damp hands together like Snidely Whiplash when the narrator began to veer off into an account of his adventures with cocaine. No wonder actors like to play the bad guy. It's all about the deliciousness of letting go. My narrator and I were in this together: I was the lasso and he was the bucket. Or was it vice versa? Codependents, we watched each other give voice to our wayward, feverish spewing, and even our guilt about indulging ourselves this way, rather than rein us in, pushed us forward. It was as if the only way to get somewhere serious was to go too far, plunge right over the top into silliness. My usual compass for making story decisions was no use to me; I had to navigate solely through voice, intuition, and nervous energy. Perhaps this is both why and how I came to write the story all at once, in a single draft, which had never happened to me before and alas, has never happened since either. (I've heard of aborigines still squatting by an overgrown runway in New Zealand, where a foreign aid plane once touched down, many years before, full of rice, Cheerios, and candy bars). Perhaps too, to be clear-eyed about it now, writing it in one long sitting accounts for a certain one-note quality to the monologue, a stubborn this-joke's-going-on-a-bit-too-long, which at the time seemed perfectly justifiable—a reflection of the narrator's plight, the nightmare of a self that won't quit—but perhaps not so essential for the reader, in all truth, as for the character.

When it was done, I ran over to a colleague's house and gave it to her to read with the usual fervent and defensive preface, only worse—"I just wrote this and I know it's weird and transparently stupid and all I need you to do is tell me if I should throw it out right away or try to salvage some tiny fragment of this mess for the future," et cetera. She called me the next day and said, "I really have no idea what to say about this."

This too all you knowing writers out there will recognize to be a bad sign. But I took it—that is, decided to take it—for encouragement. Because I had no idea what to say about it either.

Tracy Daugherty

~

CITY CODES

1.

"It DOESN'T PENCIL out," said the priest—the lawyer/developer/priest from the Portland Archdiocese. Father Matt. "We knock one unit off our sixty-unit plan, we'll lose our profit margin. Not that we'll profit. We're strictly nonprofit, of course. But in the next ten years we'll have to recoup our building costs, our maintenance outlays . . . otherwise, it's not feasible for us to proceed. In which case, Pizza Hut, Taco Bell—that's what you'll get next door instead of us." By *us* he meant God-fearing Good Guys. Nice Neighbors.

I was thinking, Pizza Hut. Hm. One squatty story instead of a four-story apartment house packed with Catholic college boys leering into my stepdaughter's bedroom window. I was raised Catholic. I know what those bastards are like.

I thought, Taco Bell. I could abide that.

"No, sorry." Father Matt shook his graying head. As a concerned neighbor, living by the lot where the Fellowship Commons would rise, I had joined other concerned neighbors in asking Father Matt to reconsider the project's density. We were sitting around a table at City Hall, after work. The table smelled of coffee though none appeared to be available. I was late; Haley was waiting for me at the Boys and Girls Club, where she went after school each day. "I can't accommodate you. It just doesn't, you know, pencil out."

I had a pretty good idea what he could do with his pencil.

————

"WHY ARE YOU sticky?" Haley sat up against her pillow. As I straightened her sheet, she reached to tap my collarbone. She pulled away quickly.

"My heart-scar isn't healing so well," I said. "You know the vitamins you take at breakfast? My doctor says if I cut one in half each night—a Vitamin E gel—and spread the juice on my chest, in six months or so, the scar might vanish."

"*Pill*-guts?"

"Yep."

"What was the matter with your heart?"

"It was all blocked up."

She curled her blankie under her chin. She'd had it since she was two—before I came into her life—and now, six years later, its frayed edges looked like fettuccini. "My daddy?"

"Yes?"

"He says his heart is broken."

Oh my. "How often does he tell you this, honey?"

"Pretty much often."

"Haley, you know, adults sometimes—"

"You were friends with my daddy?"

"For a while, yes."

"If you weren't having mating with my mommy, you and my daddy would probably still play together, right?"

Pizza! Tacos! Prayer! *Any* damn thing but this! "Maybe."

"My favorite game is 'Mercy,'" and for ten minutes she told me about the fun she had twisting her daddy's arm until he screamed, in mock pain, "Mercy!" Finally, a yawn. "Terry?"

"What is it, sweetie?"

"You got pill-guts all over Blankie."

"Here, let me rub it off. Lights out now."

Downstairs, I locked all the doors. Before heading to bed, I stopped at the bathroom mirror. Bumps and ridges right between my ribs, like a badly sown field of crops. Gone in six months? Well. In another six months, if the Good Father had his way, we'd never know that Sarah Levin's historic home had sat next door. I patted myself with a towel.

In bed, Jean was reading part of the Cascadia Land Development Code, downloaded from the internet: "Section 18A: Neighborhood Compatibility." She looked up at me. "Are we still going to fight this thing?"

"Father Matt?"

"I think we can get him on scale, the solar maps—that baby'll *bury* us in shade—and the fact that he's asking for seventeen different exemptions from the code. Plus he's got no parking or lighting plan. And the latest city stats show student enrollment dropping." She waved a sheet of paper. "This building is just a moneymaker. It's not a community service, no matter how they dress it up." From the beginning of the process—meeting with the neighborhood association, writing testimony for our upcoming appearance before the City Planning Commission—she'd been galvanized not just by the potential destruction of the Levin place and our loss of privacy (Haley's bedroom would be especially exposed to the new building) but by the fact that the couple who'd sold us our house, two years ago, *knew* this development was in the works, and hadn't told us. We'd learned this from the neighbors. Some of them suggested we sue the Wards for lack of full disclosure, but we weren't the suing types, nor could we afford a lawsuit. Besides, we just wanted to be done with the Wards.

When our real estate agent first showed us the house, Jean and I weren't married yet. Mr. Ward, a retired Navy man, in his early seventies or thereabouts, followed us closely as we toured each room, asking who we were, what we did (our agent told us, later, he was way out of line). He was tall and fit with a mildly rounded belly, like the curve of an old computer screen. He towered over me, but seemed hapless. Days later, though, I learned from a colleague at the university, a man who was active in the Catholic community, that Don Ward had been asking about Jean and me at mass. I imagined him shouting, "Living in sin? No sale!" and Jean and I got jittery.

As it turned out, sin didn't interest the state of Oregon or Bright Realty, and the deal went through just fine. "God bless you," Mrs. Ward, a frail, parchment-skinned woman, told us repeatedly the day we moved in our boxes. Her stuff was already gone—all but the framed, glass-sealed paintings of the Virgin Mary which hung in every room. The Virgin sleeping, blessing others, weeping, cradling her child. As we worked, Mrs. Ward gingerly removed these scenes from the walls, wrapped them in tissue, and placed them into U-Haul boxes. "God bless you," she said, passing through the kitchen as I unpacked my margarita glasses with their green, cactus-shaped stems. "God bless you," she whispered to Jean, slipping by the bathroom as Jean arranged her Tampax and contraceptives in the cabinet. "That woman creeps me out," Jean said once Mrs. Ward had gone. I agreed, though the old altar boy in me was touched by her care of the Holy Mother. Jean was Jewish and would have none of it—though she softened when a neighbor told us the Wards had raised nine kids in this house. "*Nine?* It's a wonder the woman can walk."

This bit of bio, we figured, explained the pass-through between the kitchen and the dining room, a space with a shelf, cut among upper and lower cabinets, where plates could be set. The space had been boarded up—scarred, splintery plywood—blocking the kitchen from the dinner table. Removing the plywood, and opening things up, was one of our first priorities. "Clearly, the woman was walling herself off from her children," Jean said. "And from Sailor Boy, too," I added. For a week or so we felt tenderness for poor Mrs. Ward, who, we surmised, had barely held her sanity in this house. If the Virgin had helped her survive, then God bless the Virgin.

Then we discovered what the Wards hadn't told us. Though Don had no financial interest in the Fellowship Commons, he was a local Catholic leader, and had helped persuade the Archdiocese to invest in the real estate. Initially, the rest of the neighbors understood that the church would renovate the Levin place, one of the oldest homes in our town—we're sixty miles south of Portland—and one of the few nineteenth-century structures in western Oregon designed by a woman ("*And* a Jew," Jean noted). The house had been vacant for years, but was listed on the Historic Register. The neighborhood was quite fond of it. "It could be rezoned and fixed up to make a nice coffee shop or cyber-café," Don Ward told his friends.

Then Father Matt started waving his pencil.

I slid into bed next to Jean. "We're sure the historic designation doesn't protect the Levin house?"

She shuffled her papers. "Oregon seems to consider property rights a kind of holy writ. If the owner—which, in this case, is the Archdiocese now—doesn't want the place protected, then not even a listing on the Register can save it."

I tugged the pages from her hands, pulled her close. "You're sticky," she said.

"Sorry. Haley was affectionate tonight. Well, not quite. She touched me briefly."

"She'll warm up eventually."

"You think she thinks she's betraying her dad if she's cuddly with me?"

She didn't answer. Instead, she licked two fingers and lightly stroked my nipples. "Still numb?" she asked softly.

The gesture, and the question, almost made me cry. Before my surgery, eight months ago, Jean had been delighted at how sensitive I was. "I've never met a man who got so aroused there!" Post-op, this pleasure had apparently been snatched from us.

She flattened her palm across my sticky ridges. Mercy! What had I become? "Is there some kind of list I can get *my* name on, to preserve what's left of me?"

"You think Haley's asleep by now?"

"Yeah, she was beat."

"Then I've got your list right here," Jean said, rolling on top of me.

———

WHAT WERE THOSE *people thinking?*

A dozen times a day Jean and I batted this question around as we erased traces of the Wards from the house and made it *our* home. We opened up the pass-through; pulled up the carpet in the living room, exposing a gorgeous oak floor; took down a gray, accordion-style divider in the entry between the foyer and the den; removed wallpaper, repainted.

In the front garden the Wards had placed a small grotto. A three-foot statue of Mary had occupied it; the Wards had taken her with them, leaving the structure empty. On a whim one Saturday morning in mid-February, as we were shopping for trellises at a nursery, Jean bought a stone chicken head, a novelty garden item, and we set it in the grotto. We referred to it as the Chicken Virgin, and joked about scrambling eggs for the Last Supper. I felt little guilty stabs, making these cracks, but knew it was part of the necessary ritual of claiming ownership. We meant nothing personal against the Wards, I told myself. We held no ill will toward the Catholic church.

One afternoon, right before leaving to get Haley at the Boys and Girls Club, I was uprooting part of the old garden with a shovel, tilling the soil, when the Wards drove up. Though they'd informed the post office of their new address, a few letters still came for them each month. We'd called and told them this. Now Don handed me a stack of mailing labels, and asked if we'd kindly forward the letters to him.

He frowned at my handiwork. I thought Mrs. Ward might cry. "We loved this garden," Don said tersely.

I wiped the sweat from my forehead. A mild breeze gave me a chill, now that I'd stopped digging. My chest was numb. "We plan to enjoy it, too." I wasn't feeling very charitable. That very morning, in a meeting at City Hall, Father Matt had threatened the neighborhood again. "This is classic Nimbyism," he'd said. "If you continue to protest our development plans, I might be forced, as I've said, to sell the lot to commercial interests, and you'll be dealing with fast food chains, something much less pleasant than us." Then he accused me (as a lost sheep) of acting out of anti-Catholic bias. "Absolutely not!" I exploded, aware that I was probably overreacting because of my chicken-jokes. "This is about neighborhood compatibility, pure and simple. Historic preservation. It's about who owns our community's future, the people who actually live here or some out-of-town developer who just so happens to have religious affiliations."

Father Matt glared at me. In my mind I heard him saying, *Your wife's a Jew, isn't that right? Like that Manischewitz-soaked old Levin woman?* I inhaled slowly and tried to relax. "You talk about fast food as a bad neighbor, but I don't think it's very neighborly of you, Father, to draw up a plan, failing to consult with us, then threatening us when we don't go along with it."

"All right," he said, gathering his papers into a calfskin briefcase. "I'll see you next week, in front of the Planning Commission."

Also that day, letters had appeared in our local paper, arguing both sides of the proposal. Among the project's supporters, who accused the neighbors of narrow self-interest and rejected the Levin house's historic importance—"it's just a ratty old shack"—were the Wards. Their letter pointed out that Cascadia was a growing university town, in need of more student housing, and that unlike most absentee landlords, the Archdiocese would be a thoughtful and conscientious caretaker.

Now the couple stood beside me, shocked by the stone fowl and my methodical disembowelment of their landscaping. I stabbed the shovel into the dirt. "How's the new place?" I asked, in a tone that was not very friendly, I admit.

"Oh fine, just fine," said Mrs. Ward. She wore a blue scarf and thick tinted glasses. The flesh on her cheeks looked as thin as the petals of the Siberian iris Jean hoped to plant here someday. "We loved this house but, you know, it was just too much for us to take care of with the kids all gone. The new condo isn't special or anything, but it's manageable. Better for us now."

Don cleared his throat and glanced next door at the Levin place. The shingles sagged. "Tell the truth," he said to me, straining for a jolly tone. "Won't it be good to have that old eyesore gone?"

His wife placed her hand on his arm as if to pull him away from me.

"Don, do you realize how amazing it is that that house, built in 1880, anticipates Frank Lloyd Wright and the Craftsman movement? What a visionary Sarah Levin was?"

"Father Matt is really a very good man."

"I'm sure he is. But in his dealings with us, he's been less than forthright and cooperative. He doesn't care about this town," I said, drawing energy from this morning's leftover anger. "Student enrollment is backsliding here. We don't *need* more housing."

"That's debatable."

"Father Matt only cares about wheeling and dealing—and hiding his business affairs behind the façade of 'good works.'"

Mrs. Ward flinched and tried, once more, to tug her husband's arm.

"Well now, you're quite the revolutionary, aren't you?" Don said. The old Navy man, I guessed, suspicious of anyone younger than he was.

"Just putting together testimony, based on the city codes. I'm simply exercising my legal rights as a citizen, Don." I reached for the shovel. "Like, for example, I had a legal right to know that developers were going to raze the house next door and slap up a four-story behemoth less than twenty yards from my stepdaughter's bedroom. Don't you think I had a right to know that?"

"Listen to me, now—"

"Come on, Don," Mrs. Ward urged him.

"We didn't know—"

"That doesn't wash," I said.

"Well, all right, but we weren't sure which plan—"

"You just wanted your money and you wanted out. Not very saintly of you, Don."

"Your realtor should have checked, she should have—"

"No," I said. "*You* should have."

"Don, let's go." I believe the woman *did* muster the stamina to move him. He half stumbled backwards on the walk. "We're old people," he said weakly. "Our kids used to play in this garden—"

"Don." Mrs. Ward took him by the shoulders and nodded toward their car. From across the street she glanced at me. "God bless you," she said.

"WHAT'S ZIOMISM?" HALEY asked me in the car, on our way back from Boys and Girls.

"Zionism? Where'd you hear that word?"

She showed me a pamphlet she'd gotten from the local synagogue for Young Judea Summer Camp. "I want to go, but my daddy says they'll turn me into a raving Ziomist."

Bill, Jean's ex, was raised Protestant, and it had always been an open sore in their marriage that he only half-assedly supported Jean's efforts to expose Haley to Judaism. Jean wasn't devout, but she loved the holiday rituals, the culture, and wanted Haley to treasure them, too.

I wasn't sure how to answer Haley's question. "Well, as I understand it—and I'm not an expert, okay, not by a long shot—it's a movement among Israelis, and other Jews around the world, to expand Israel's borders."

"You mean, make it bigger?"

"Make it bigger, yes."

"What's wrong with that?"

"Have you heard of Palestinians?"

"Mm-hm."

"They claim some of the same land Israel does."

"I know that. I've learned that, okay?"

"Good. Well, lots of people, including many Jews, feel that Israel *shouldn't* expand. It should just stay where it is—and the Palestinians should accept them, too—so everyone can live in peace." I didn't know how historically or politically accurate I was being. I'd probably just butchered all the facts, and—who knows?—scarred her for life.

"My daddy says his heart will be brokender than it already is if I turn to Mom's people and be a raving Ziomist."

"I have to say, honey . . ." I'd very carefully never spoken against Bill, never criticized him or questioned his authority in front of Haley. "I don't think your daddy should tell you things like that."

"Why not?"

"It's not fair to your mom. Plus it's too much of a burden on you for him to ask you to carry his emotional weight."

"Huh?"

"He can wrestle his own problems, okay?" Was I saying the right thing? Or claiming parental ownership?

I remembered, then, the day, two and a half years ago, when Jean and I told Haley we were together. She'd giggled nervously, and appeared not to register what we said. Later, at lunch in her favorite Mexican restaurant, she picked up a lightweight fork. "This one's for you," she told me, and bent the fork in half.

"DON'T *use* HER like that!" Jean yelled into the kitchen phone. "She's not your mother. Or your girlfriend."

I had just come in from dumping the trash. I rubbed my hands, locked the door behind me. Whenever the air was especially chilly, I became keenly aware of the dead spots in my chest and thigh, where the surgeon had "harvested" a vein for the bypass. He had told me I might never get feeling back in certain nerves, which had been disturbed by the procedure.

"She's talking to my daddy," Haley said casually, glancing up from the floor where she'd spread her multiplication problems. Her cat purred beside her. "She's mad about the Ziomism thing."

"Oh."

"You shouldn't have told her."

"Told her what, sweetie?"

"Told her what my daddy said about his heart."

"Well, *I'm* her mother!" Jean said, lowering her voice and retreating into a corner away from us. "She's not your private property!"

Haley aimed a purple pencil at me. "You really shouldn't have."

2.

Of course it's not Haley who's waiting for me to die. Jean hopes I'll live a long and healthy life, but fears otherwise, a dread that seized her in our earliest days together, before either of us knew I had heart trouble. It's related to her father's death, of leukemia, when she was nineteen and he was fifty-eight. She was traveling when he died so she didn't get to tell him goodbye. Her psychiatrist-brother in L.A. tells her she suffers "lack of closure," distilled into guilt, so now she feels responsible for her dad's departure.

One afternoon, as we lay in bed together, sipping margaritas, I placed my palm on her chest and she began to cry. "I think I'm grieving for my father," she said, surprised.

I don't know how one intimacy ripples into others, but Jean was very clear that day that love and grief are strongly twinned for her, bound up not only in memories of her father, but in love's structure: life's irresistible attraction for other life, the urgency, the energy, then the surprisingly swift falling-off after life has done its work. Just as someone, knowing she's about to leave a place, can feel homesick before she's even moved, Jean, after love, feels wistful already for her body and mine. She's mourning our loss in advance.

We fell in love when we were both in our early forties, and her melancholy is magnified, I suspect, by the fact that we *old people*—old enough to know better, at least—felt happier, sillier, more erotic than we ever had before. Time seemed pliable, warped—all the sweeter for being *short*. We felt we'd discovered our youth for the first time, just as we should have been letting go of it, gracefully.

From the beginning, she worried about my slightest cough, skin blemish, or exhaustion at night. I'd kid her about her displaced hypochondria. Once, she came right out and admitted she feared she'd lose me early. I joked about her romantic streak: her favorite movie was *Truly, Madly, Deeply,* the story of a young widow whose love for her husband is so intense, his ghost returns each night to schmooze with her. M. F. K. Fisher, Jean's favorite writer, suffered early widowhood.

When Jean and I bought the house from the Wards, Haley was six. We fixed her room up to look almost exactly like her room at her daddy's house, ten blocks away. Our house was in a neighborhood of run-down student rentals, once-proud bungalows that had been steadily trashed over five decades. The Wards had stayed put for thirty-seven years—nine kids!—and though we hated the remnants of their taste (*what were those people thinking?*), we were grateful they'd left intact the Craftsman-style wooden trim, and had maintained the place beautifully. Two blocks away was the campus where Jean and I taught literature. Convenience, old-fashioned élan, plenty of room . . . we felt lucky, but still, Jean walked around waiting for judgment to fall. I wondered if the sorrow she felt, dissolving her family—though she'd clearly been miserable in her marriage—had mixed with her father-guilt to crush her joy. We were two of our circles' straightest arrows, not religious, but generally fair-minded, traditionally moral. Unlikely partners for an affair. Yet here we were. Transgressors, against society and all of society's gods. Surely we wouldn't—*shouldn't*—get away with this.

When Jean first heard the Levin place might be wrecked, she took it as a sign that her fears were on-target. The Angel of Doom as a backhoe. It didn't help that, purely by coincidence, we learned the news last year on Passover. "That's right, get the Jews," she muttered, reading the city's notice.

My attempts to laugh away her worries had ended about sixteen months after we'd moved into the house. One night, during love, I doubled over with chest pains. She drove me to the emergency room. Doctors told me I'd narrowly missed "keeling over, kaput." Two days later, a cardiac surgeon opened me up, like our kitchen pass-through, and did a double bypass.

My primary-care man informed me I'd "exhibited no risk factors." I was as unlikely to develop ticker trouble as I was to start an affair.

In any case, all my jokes have stopped. Jean and I linger with each other now, squeezing as much as we can out of life. I've tried to reduce my daily stress, but our town is small, and I can't help regularly running into Bill.

One day, he and I arrived at the same time at Boys and Girls to pick up Haley. Jean had told me Haley was going to spend the night with us; Bill understood differently. She handled the moment better than we did. She looked at us, shrugged, then went on playing with her pals in the parking lot. "It's *my* night," Bill said, genuinely anguished, missing his girl. He scratched his sandy hair. "Okay," I said, and told Haley goodbye.

I drove away, damp with sweat. Earlier that day, I'd shampooed the carpet at home (we hadn't tossed it yet); now, I was convinced Haley's kitten had probably licked up the cleaning fluid. I should have locked her in a back room until the carpet dried. No doubt I'd return to find her dead. Haley would be inconsolable.

I passed a restored apartment house where a former student of mine had suffered a fire, a year or two ago, in which her dog had died. Still thinking of Haley and Bill, I felt responsible for the dog, now, too. I should have been a better teacher, more at ease in front of groups; if I'd been a better teacher, damn it, *somehow* that dog would still be alive. God forgive me.

At home, I found Haley's kitten sitting happily, healthily, on a windowsill, staring at the broken windows of the Levin place.

3.

Haley had been pissy all week, upset about her homework, picky at dinner. One night, when we'd told her she'd had enough TV, she paced the den, the heels of her sandals slapping the hardwood floor. "Bored bored bored," she said.

"Why don't you sit in the window," I suggested, "and draw the old Levin place?"

"Why?"

"It might be gone pretty soon. If that happens, your drawing will be one of the few records the city will have left of it."

"I don't want to."

We went back and forth until I wore her down. She got out her gel pens and sullenly scratched a few lines on a sketchpad: the broken rain spout, unhinged doors, tilted window frames. "Done."

"Terrific."

"It's stupid."

"No no, sweetie, this is wonderful, this is—"

"I mean the house." She grabbed her blankie and started upstairs for her room. "It's not even *worth* drawing."

THE DAY BEFORE show time in front of the Planning Commission, Haley was with her dad. Jean and I came home from classes, made love in the late afternoon. Sex was more relaxed, of course, with Haley out of the house. "I'm afraid she can sense it, from three rooms away, if we even kiss," I'd told Jean one night. "She's way beyond her years—"

"No. She's *right at* her years," she said. "That's the problem."

She ran her hands along my chest. I tried and tried to feel something. Finally, I turned my wet eyes toward the wall. In the day's wavering shadows, tinged by the last of the sun's red light, I could make out a faint square in the plaster—though we'd painted—where one of the Virgins had hung. Jean's brown hair splayed across my belly. She clung to my hips. "Neighborhood compatibility," I whispered, and we laughed.

For a while we lay half asleep, then, "Time to get ready," Jean whispered. "Okay, I'm awake," I said, feeling my arm for my pulse. We showered, dressed, fed the cat, then drove downtown to Barton's, a musty restaurant full of leaden foods and blue-haired organ music. Its claim to fame was that Hillary Clinton had stepped out of a limo here during her husband's '96 campaign. For ten minutes she shook diners' hands. God knows what she was doing in Cascadia. Maybe her publicist thought a photo op in a small-town eatery would wrap up Oregon's ag votes. For me, the restaurant was notorious for the fact that its former owner, a man my age, had gone face-down one afternoon into a bowl of four-alarm chili, dead of a heart attack.

On our own, Jean and I would never have set foot in the place, but our neighborhood association wanted to meet here tonight—it was quiet, rarely crowded. The students in town preferred Taco Bell, out by the interstate.

Rex Smithers, the association president, a retired car dealer, asked the six of us who showed to read our prepared testimonies. We'd have five minutes each in front of the Planning Commission, he said. We made revisions, cutting the fat, making sure our points didn't overlap. Rex passed out a list of words. "Spice your speeches with these," he said. "They're positive, attention-getting—the kind of thing I've heard the commission really responds to."

I glanced at the sheet:

continuity

stability

> identity (sense of history, place, culture)
> character
> style
> community
> quality
> livability
> human scale
> home

Mentally, I added "chicken-head."

"We don't want to be negative," Rex said, "overly emotional, or sacrilegious—"

"You better believe that padre'll have a crack legal team with him," said Andy Nelson, a dentist who lived two doors east of us. "That is, if he's stopped diddling little boys long enough to *put together* a team."

"Andy," Rex said, blushing. "That's precisely the kind of talk we have to squelch."

"I know, I know. A joke."

"Please."

"I *know*."

"He doesn't need a legal team," Jean said. "He's a lawyer himself, and very articulate. Don't underestimate him."

She and I excused ourselves early and were discussing where we could eat when we spotted the Wards in a booth. They were sitting with a thin woman in a blue scarf, just like the one Mrs. Ward wore. Great platters of buttery mashed potatoes, chicken-fried steaks, creamy, heart-clogging pies on the side—*what are those people thinking?*

Are *all* locally owned places, with historic ties to the city, worth preserving? I wondered.

We tried to slip past, but Don spied us, though he pretended he hadn't. As we approached the table, determined not to hide—now that we'd been caught—the thin woman, facing away from us, removed her scarf and touched a large, grainy scar on the side of her head. It appeared to flake a little. "I'll never get better," she said mournfully. Then she noticed us and swiftly tied the scarf back into place. For a minute none of us moved. I remembered Don's words: *We're old people.* Finally, Jean touched Mrs. Ward's wool sleeve. "Good luck tomorrow night," she said, and though we all knew she didn't mean it, the gesture startled us back to civility. "Thank you," Mrs. Ward said, and patted Jean's hand.

4.

The meeting took place in a conference room in the city's new fire station, a two-story red brick building with fully automated doors for wheelchair access, banks of computer monitors behind the receptionists' desks, and vintage photos of horse-drawn wagons on the walls. A list of fire-safety tips—"Hot Topics"—wilted in a wall bin labeled TAKE ONE! The station sat catty-corner to a Hollywood Video. Frat boys squealed their tires, pulling out of the lot, sneaking soft-core DVDs back to their tents, no doubt, or the underpasses they were forced to huddle under, since—according to Father Matt— cheap housing was so scarce in our mean little burg.

The commissioners looked well fed: shirts strained under too-small blazers, most of which were orange or black, the colors of the university's athletic teams. Probably these guys all ate at Barton's.

Father Matt and his supporters had dark smudges on their foreheads. "What happened to them?" Jean said, staring openly. Then it hit me: Ash Wednesday. The old words came rushing back. *The faithful must do penance. Remember, unto dust shall ye return.* The group sat stiffly, hands folded, staring intently at the commissioners, their pale flesh marked by the palms' residue. I knew, right then, we were sunk. The priestly robes, the solemn, graveyard air, the moral authority. We didn't stand a chance.

Haley squirmed in her seat. Bill had promised to babysit, but had canceled an hour ago. "Hot date," he'd said, grinning shyly at Jean as he stood with Haley under our dim yellow porch light. He'd come without calling.

"Bill, you promised," Jean said, fiddling with her earrings. I wrestled my necktie behind her. "We're in a hurry. We can't—"

"You want me to be happy, don't you?" he answered, sounding hurt—and boyishly eager about the date. *I* was happy for him. In any case, he knew Jean wouldn't hash this out with him in front of Haley. "I'll take her tomorrow night." He bent to kiss his daughter, and she looped her arms around his neck. I had to try again with my tie.

"All right, honey, it's going to be a really long meeting," Jean said once he'd driven away. She held Haley's face so she'd listen. "You'll need plenty to do so you can sit quietly. Bring some books and your gel pens and your Walkman, okay . . . don't forget your headphones . . ."

We scrambled to gather Haley's stuff as well as our testimonies, paper-clipped inside manila folders. The cat leaped on the table and rubbed my arm; I dropped the folders and several loose pages from Haley's sketchbook. Hastily, Jean and I pulled things together. "Come on, gals, let's go, let's go!" I said.

Now we sat in the firehouse trying to ignore the stares of our opponents, and cool air from a large open window. I felt for my pulse. Behind me, a man muttered, "Politics. It's the wet bar of soap at the bottom of a bathtub." I recognized a local sandwich shop owner. She was telling a woman beside her, "Last year I had to sell thirty thousand turkey subs to be able to afford to bring my building up to code!"

The meeting came to order. Haley sighed loudly, bobbing her head to Pink or Sting or Smashmouth. I touched her knee to settle her down. She moved her leg away. From across an aisle, Mrs. Ward gave us a tight smile. Nine kids? *Any advice?* I tried to signal back, nodding at her. Don wore his Navy uniform, which mostly still fit him. The sleeves were short. The elaborate gold buttons wobbled with each swift breath he took. "For God's sakes," Jean whispered, rolling her eyes.

The commission's Chair reminded us that "this body's judgment will be based solely on the Land Development Code and the city's Comprehensive Plan. We all know there are high emotions on both sides of this issue, we've all seen the letters in the paper, but I caution each of you to restrict your testimony to the pertinent clauses of the CP and the LDC. No personal smears, no charges of bias, religious, political, or otherwise. Is that clear?"

Haley, slipping off her headphones, said, "Yep." Jean shushed her.

City staffers presented their report, confirming that the Archdiocese was requesting over a dozen exemptions to the code, including smaller parking accommodations, less restrictive lighting requirements, and freedom from providing open space on the lot. The Levin House was noted on the state's Historic Register, and was considered an important example of early Oregon architecture. Nevertheless, staff recommended approval of the project, as it matched the CP's vision for higher inner-core density to avoid outlying sprawl.

Next, Father Matt. He straightened his white collar, straightened a hank of loose gray hair so his ash was prominent. From his calfskin case he pulled a sheaf of notes. He spoke eloquently about the New Urbanism, the city's need for affordable housing, the church's desire to help the community. He fended off the commissioners' questions with the air of someone annoyingly swatting flies. This was a man used to getting what he wanted. Who could say no to a priest? I imagined twisting his arm until he yelled, *Mercy!* "We will not be asking our tenants' sexual orientations. Under state law, we're not allowed to discriminate." Will you ask them not to ogle my wife's daughter? "Yes, we'll have on-site managers to make sure tenants respect the neighborhood . . ."

His ashen supporters testified next, most stressing that church ownership of the property would benefit the area. "They make it sound like a bunch of heathens live there, in need of conversion," Jean said to me. Some groused about a "small group of elite home-owners blocking progress." A few insisted there was no issue here: property rights were property rights, and no one, including the government, should tell an owner what to do with his land. They complained about having to appear before a city board at all. "Isn't democracy splendid? They want their damn rights, but don't feel they have to earn them by dirtying themselves with the process," Jean said determinedly. Her cheeks were red.

Person after person rose to speak, marching up the center aisle to sit at an oak table in front of the commissioners' dais. Haley slid off her chair and crawled beneath her mother's feet. She fumbled her Walkman. Jean told her to sit up, behave. Don and his wife moved slowly to the front, her tiny hand on his arm. "Oh great, now we'll hear from the *patriot,*" Jean whispered. Don said only, "Father Matt is a good man. He has my support." His voice shook. Mrs. Ward echoed her husband, and gave the commissioners God's blessing. As she stepped to her seat, I had an urge to wash the poor woman's forehead.

Right before Jean stood, the Chair apologized to the opposition. He was going to limit our testimony to *three* minutes each, not five, as the meeting was dragging on, and otherwise we'd be here till midnight. Groans of "Unfair!" but he rapped his gavel and silenced the room.

Haley stared beatifically at her mother as Jean assumed her seat up front. Jean's earrings gleamed in the light of a video camera recording the proceedings. Her voice was firm, just a smidgen of reined-in anger (including, I thought, her fury at Bill). "Thank you for this opportunity to address you," she began, her cheeks still flushed. "We all agree that inner-core density is desirable, but only when there is a demonstrated public need, which, I'll argue, there isn't in this case. The Comprehensive Plan also includes provisions for preserving the historical character of our neighborhoods and for ensuring neighborhood compatibility." If poise and persuasion alone could do the trick, and she'd had a shot at her father's doctors, she might have preserved the old man, I thought. Absolutely, I wanted her there when *my* time came. "The applicant's proposal flagrantly disregards these priorities. Specifically, it skirts the codes enforcing compatible scale, step-down rules . . . and I have some solar maps here . . ."

"She's good," Haley said, entranced. "Really *good,* isn't she?" Her hand strayed absently onto my leg. A warm ripple went through me. I glanced down at her fingers, and noticed on my shirt, just to the left of my tie, a dark Vitamin E stain. I tried to cover it with my coat, jostling Haley a bit. She took her hand away. I couldn't hide the mark. *Why on this night?* I thought, recalling the words of the Passover Seder . . . maybe if I rubbed ash into it . . .

"The city codes are clear," Jean concluded.

As I approached the oak table, feeling less like a revolutionary than the quivering mess I became on the first day of classes each year, facing a strange and questioning group, I tried maneuvering my tie with my elbow over the sticky spot. No use. The table smelled, oddly, of peppermint tea. I stated my name and address. The city officials stared down at me. *What are they thinking?*

I opened my manila folder. It occurred to me that I'd timed my testimony at exactly five minutes. I didn't know how to cram it into three. I shuffled the pages. My hands trembled. Glaring video lights. "Thank you . . . for this . . ."

My skin went cold. My chest felt funny. *Oh Lord,* I thought. *Unto dust—*

But it wasn't a pain or a flame or a squeeze. My nipples! Hell yes! My nipples had lifted their little heads! Anxiety, chill . . . the old nerves stirring! God bless them!

I grinned, idiotically, at the portly commissioners. They studied my stain. " . . . this opportunity . . . to be with you . . . I mean, *speak* with you . . ."

I sneaked a peek back at Jean, smiling broadly. She looked stricken.

Haley, gripping her headphones, glared at me: *How could you embarrass me like this?*

"My wife and I . . . have always wanted a home . . . in a historic . . ." I returned to my folder. The pages had fallen out of sequence now and my hands were too shaky to put them in order. In the earlier confusion, and our haste to leave the house, had I locked the front door? Had I left our home open, exposed to intruders?

Tucked among my papers, Haley's sketch of the Levin place. It must have slipped in when the cat brushed my arm. Ham-fisted, I held it high. The page rattled. My throat had gone dry. "My daughter," I croaked. "My daughter loves this place. Please don't tear it down."

Snickering, behind me. Titters here and there. I turned; the inside of my shirt snagged on a sticky ridge.

A sea of ashes. Father Matt stopped moving his pencil on a scratchpad long enough to glance up at me and beam triumphantly. The Wards bowed their heads, respectfully ignoring my distress.

Jean's face shifted from pink-cheeked dismay, like the day she'd grieved for her father, to pale confusion, settling finally into a sad, soft smile, as if to say, *You did your best, it doesn't matter, it's okay.*

It's more than okay, I thought. *Wait'll we get home.*

Haley wagged her head—not in disgust, I realized, but as if we'd shared a stupid joke, then she grinned at me, at her sketch, and gave me a quick thumbs-up. I returned the gesture and waved her drawing so she, and all the room, could see. I heard the Chair rapping the end of my time, felt my nipples hard against my shirt, and smiled at my clean-faced gals.

Behind the Story

EXPLICIT AUTOBIOGRAPHY RARELY makes it into my fiction. It's not that I find my life uninteresting; it's that I'm disappointed by the flattening involved in faithfully recording experience. Maybe I'm merely revealing my limitations as a writer, but I don't think that's all. When a painter studies her beloved's face, then goes to fix his features on the canvas, the likeness, no matter how finely detailed, is inevitably a falling-off from life. To say the obvious—but aren't artists always wrestling the obvious?—the painting of the beloved is *not* the beloved, any more than a photograph, digitized image, or written description of him can replace him. These renderings are silent and inert. That's what I mean by "flattening."

"The interest of [any] construction . . . is to be located in the space between the new entity . . . and the 'real.' This is, I think, the relation of art to world," Donald Barthelme said. "I suggest that art is always a meditation upon external reality rather than a representation of external reality or a jackleg attempt to 'be' external reality."★ His observation explains, for me, why factual self-expression is almost always the least absorbing aspect of a short story or novel.

With "City Codes," however, I recognized that certain raw elements of my experience formed the rudiments of a story. Notice I didn't say, "What happened to me made a good story." It didn't. In this case, what happened to me was like what *usually* happens to me—rapid-fire events mixed with random impressions and a faulty

★ Donald Barthelme. "Not-Knowing" in *Not-Knowing: The Essays and Interviews*, edited by Kim Herzinger (New York: Random House, 1997): 23.

memory to make the blur I call my days. But within this blur, a few specific contours emerged that suggested a story to me.

It wouldn't be particularly useful to list what is and isn't true in "City Codes." Suffice to say, it's all true except for the parts I made up. But I *can* talk helpfully, I hope, about those contours that built the story, and that make crafting any tale much more complex than simply writing what you know.

First, my experience in this instance—fighting a noxious development next to my house—had a limited scope, with a fixed beginning and end: the city's public hearings process, in which the building's developers presented their case, and citizens had a chance to protest it. Second, for my wife and me, this public ordeal was linked in time with a crucial private drama: my recovery from heart surgery. Not every writer is as galvanized as I am by the intersection of public and private energies, but as Grace Paley once said, "I don't have a story until I have *two* stories." Think of musical counterpoint, the magical subplots in Shakespeare, or the marvelous vitality of Dickens's secondary characters. Think, again, of paintings—in most cases, even in abstractions, the foreground needs a background to play against, to provide contrast and depth. The heat of a story is usually generated by friction. Rubbing two sticks together. I have a tendency to strike *too many* sparks—a weakness that may be evident in "City Codes."

Finally, to avoid self-indulgence, every writer needs some emotional distance from a story's *stuff*—a way of standing back and observing it dispassionately, to judge its effects on the reader. To paraphrase Wordsworth, strong emotions need to be recollected in tranquillity, otherwise you risk simply weeping, making private jokes, or throwing a tantrum on the page, to the reader's great boredom. In the case of "City Codes," the town I live in provided me with an automatic distancing opportunity. Corvallis, Oregon, has been fictionalized before, in Bernard Malamud's novel *A New Life* (1961). Sometimes, in writing a first draft, I'll plug in names as fillers, so I can keep working without losing momentum; afterwards, I'll change them. In his novel,

Malamud called Corvallis "Cascadia"; as a purely private pleasure, I stuck that name into my first draft, fully intending to alter it in the final version. S. Levin is *A New Life*'s main character; I borrowed the name and gave it to a character who is dead as the story begins. Levin is a Jewish name, so a possible new layering appeared that had nothing to do with my own experience. After seizing this unforeseen opening, I saw other values in keeping the names, ways to tweak the story line, to use religious/cultural tension as characterization. I wasn't rewriting Malamud the way Richard Ford or Rick Moody have echoed Sherwood Anderson, or the way Raymond Carver riffed on Ernest Hemingway, but in similar fashion, I was reaching beyond myself, however humbly, for the heart of the American literary tradition. In the end, it wasn't what I'd lived through, but the sense that I'd entered a conversation with fiction that enabled me to pull the story together (*if* it comes together, which remains an open question for me).

Probably none of this matters to the reader, nor should it. But I can't emphasize strongly enough that whatever happened to us *stops* the moment we start to write about it. At that point, *writing* is what's happening to us, a process with its own needs, demands, and surprises entirely separate from whatever may have generated it. Among the definitions attached to "craft" in Webster's Dictionary (Second Edition) are "art," "skill," "guile," "trade," "device." These, more than self-expression and autobiographical details, are the elements of storytelling. The word "craft" connotes for me the old European artisans' guilds—glassblowers, cobblers—with their dedication to tradition and their immersion in minute details; it also recalls the tacky yarn-and-glue projects that Cub Scout leaders or desperate mothers splay across kitchen tables to mollify screaming kids; finally, it conjures deviousness, trickiness, traps about to spring. Together, these notions form the essence of writing stories. The first two engage the hand, the third, the mind. Stories may begin with facts, or with self-expression, but neither shapes their final form. Fiction is a making, mind to hand to another mind—the mind of the reader— who will make it all again.

Karen Brennan

~

SACHA'S DOG

THERE IS A little dog that belongs to Sacha and we see it here and there walking the streets like a human being with a destination. More often than not it is in search of Sacha who is getting drunk and then falling asleep someplace. Sacha's dog, who is golden-haired and as small as a cat with a pointed face and ears like mittens, is no familiar breed, even as a mutt it is not familiar. The dogs here are different from the dogs in other places mainly because they have been allowed to roam the urban streets for centuries and one senses they have evolved in ways that please them as opposed to ways which please the human population. They strike us as a bit uncanny, these dogs, as if they were scaling the edges of their species, about to transform themselves into some other creature.

This dog, the dog of Sacha, does not strictly speaking belong to Sacha; that is to say, Sacha didn't purchase this dog or find the dog and then decide to feed it. This dog, like most of the dogs in the city, is entirely self-reliant in the matter of food and entertainment. It loves Sacha, this is clear, and when Sacha is off on a long drunk the dog is disconsolate for a while, wandering anxiously trying to ascertain Sacha's whereabouts.

Tonight Sacha is at the cantina dancing with a woman with long hair. He does not know her name and thinks he will probably not ask because she is obviously a gringa and communication becomes so frustrating. Also, he is very drunk. He has been drinking margaritas and beer for three days and also smoking a little pot, and he is happy to dance to the salsa band and shut his eyes and groove with the music. The dog, who is nameless to humans at least, has no idea where Sacha is, but at this moment decides to try the cantina where the doorman, recognizing the dog, steps politely aside to allow it entrance. When it spots Sacha on the dance floor with the long-haired woman it gives a sharp yelp which Sacha recognizes as the signal for him to call it a night.

On the way home, Sacha is so drunk he stops every once in a while to get his bearings by holding on to a wall or the side of some building. Also, he takes a piss in the street. The dog is very long-suffering during all of this and only nudges Sacha once when it appears he might fall asleep in a doorway against a green door. At his own door, which is black, he fumbles with his key and then with the lock; he drops his keys once and they fall into a grating. Then he has to pull up the grating and rummage in a pile of leaves with his bad eyes at night. This is where the dog proves invaluable, ferreting out the keys in the pile of leaves and holding them out to Sacha with its teeth. Soon they are inside, the dog curled in a corner of the room on the cool tiles and Sacha lying horizontally across the bed with his clothes on.

Why does the dog love Sacha? Does Sacha play catch with the dog? Does he enter the dog in beauty contests? Does he send the dog to school or buy the dog doggie treats or make sure the dog has a nice flea collar? None of the above. Nor is he especially affectionate with the dog in other, simpler ways: he hardly ever scratches the dog on the neck nor does he feed the dog scraps. But the dog loves Sacha in the neurotic, overbearing way that most people love their pets. It worries about Sacha, worries that he might get into a bar fight and lose all his teeth like Antonio, and worries that he will forget to feed himself. Many of his companions—the other *perros* of the city—tolerate this rather unconventional attitude in their friend, but to them it is strange to want to mingle so intimately with another species unless there is a payoff of some kind. But Sacha's dog is an altruist and expects no recompense for its trouble. The reward is in the deed itself, the feeling of peace it gives.

I am a satisfied dog, that's all I can say about it, he tells his friend, the white dog with the spiraled tail. I do what I can for Sacha and I think without me he'd actually be pretty lost. I'm grateful I have this chance. Here he pauses with a degree of smugness unbecoming in a dog. And so the white dog merely nods and smiles a little insincerely, because none of this makes sense to him and he secretly thinks this dog, his old friend, is possibly unbalanced.

NOW SACHA IS lying on the bed crosswise with his clothes on. The dog would prefer Sacha to be under the covers with his shoes lined up neatly against the wall, but what can it do? It only has so much influence, especially when Sacha is drunk. It is content to have gotten this far with Sacha after his three-day binge. When there's a knock at the door and some shouting at the stoop, the dog doesn't think twice about it, he feels sure that Sacha is unconscious enough that he will not be disturbed. The knocking continues, louder, as if somebody began by pounding the door with his fists, and wound up by pounding it with an implement of some kind. The dog gives a long sigh and goes to nudge Sacha awake. But Sacha is presently having a dream about the woman with the long hair who is riding a horse in the mist and he is the cowboy with the lasso on a sand dune and then he is at his mother's house and she is feeding him ice cream, and then he is at the beach with his childhood friend, Jose the bell ringer, and they are throwing stones into the sea. Sacha has never actually seen the sea, but in his dream it is green with little specks of orange shot through it and covered with rolling waves that look like the white scalloped hems of his sisters' communion dresses. He is experiencing great happiness being at the sea with Jose and suddenly in the moment of throwing a flat purple stone, he realizes he is dreaming and turns to Jose so they can laugh together about this miracle of meeting in a dream. Then Jose throws a stone at Sacha's head and he wakes up with the dog thumping his tail in his eye and to the sounds of people hammering at his door and shouting his name and many profanities.

THE PEOPLE WHO are visiting Sacha are his friend Tonio and some others who happened to be passing by at this hour. Don't you have any beer, Sacha, you son of a bitch, what's wrong with you? There are two men counting Tonio and one woman and the woman, Rosa, is wearing cutoff blue jeans and a Guatemalan vest with nothing underneath. Sacha can see her small breasts, the nipples dark brown and protruding at the tips. It excites Sacha to glimpse them through the gaps under her arms and he gives Tonio a knowing look when the woman's back is turned. The friend winks and says loudly, Rosa, Sacha thinks you're hot stuff. I didn't say that, says Sacha, but he is laughing, embarrassed, and he opens his refrigerator and says again, I don't have beer, maybe some rum. Rum is okay, says Tonio. Rum is good. Do you have Coke? No, says Sacha, I have milk and I have juice. Let's have the juice, says Rosa. She is lying on Sacha's bed now with her hands behind her head. You are so drunk aren't you, Sacha? I'm still pretty drunk, Sacha admits, I've been drinking for days. Then the other man, who hasn't said anything until now, says, What kind of juice? I thought you said this guy would fix us up. Do you have any weed? Maybe I have a little weed, maybe just a joint, but I don't have much weed, I don't even know if I can find it, says Sacha. Now Tonio is plugging in the Christmas lights around Sacha's window. Let's have some atmosphere, what do you say, Sacha? This place is a shithole, says the other man. What is your name? My name is Sacha, says Sacha to the man he doesn't know. Fuck off, what do you want with my name, *cabrón*? says the man. Sacha looks closely at the man for the first time. The man has very small eyes in a mean face and he is wearing a T-shirt that says *LA Lakers* on it. Come on, Charlie, be nice, says Rosa languidly from the bed. Sacha is a friend of Tonio and this makes him a friend of mine. Charlie kicks something on the floor and the dog gives a howl. Fucking dog, says Charlie. Leave the dog alone, Charlie, says Sacha. Find the weed, man, says Charlie, I'm sick of this shit. I don't know if I can find it, says Sacha. Maybe it's under your pillow, says Rosa, and she rolls over on the bed and the vest rides up her back and Sacha notices her flesh above her belt and how smooth it is, and the smooth backs of her legs. He is still so drunk and on top of being drunk, tired, and he cannot stop staring at Rosa, her skin is like the ocean in his dreams with orange glints of light and when he is thinking this he is simultaneously having a fantasy of what it would be like to have Rosa in his bed without her clothes on and how he would like touch her dark nipples and the flesh on her back, which is when Charlie knocks him on the side of his head with something hard like a rock, it can't be his hand, and he falls over, which is when Tonio says, Take it easy, Charlie, slow down, man. Sacha is on the floor with his eyes closed and the dog of Sacha is licking his face. Fucking dog, says Charlie, the guy was lusting after Rosa, that's why, I saw the way the son of a bitch looked at her, man, don't tell me take it easy, man, *cabrón*. And Rosa from her place on the bed, still languid, starts to laugh and says she thinks she found the weed in Sacha's pillowcase and sure enough she is holding up what looks like a joint. Is she your girlfriend? asks Sacha from the floor. His eyes are opened now and he is thinking that if Rosa is Charlie's girl-friend he can understand why he hit him with whatever it was. But

Tonio says, No, man, Rosa is Charlie's sister. Oh, well, then, says Sacha, because he can understand that too, and he says, Look, man, to Charlie, but Charlie is on the bed lighting up the joint with Rosa and Sacha can hear the hissing sound of the joint being inhaled and held in the lungs and then the hissing sound of the smoke being exhaled. Sacha, why don't you get up from the floor and have some of this weed? says Rosa. She is laughing because she can see that Sacha is too drunk and hurt to get up and it suddenly strikes her funny that he is on the floor with a certain look on his face of resignation. Sacha, she says, up, up! And she is laughing so hard she starts to cough. Charlie is quiet now and he is taking many hits of the joint and inhaling and exhaling very fast and when the joint is down to a roach he says in a deep growling voice, a muffled voice buried under the weight of marijuana, Sacha is a dead man. There is at that point a stunned silence in the room, even Rosa stops laughing and looks nervously at Tonio, who is sitting over by the window drinking rum and has been especially quiet all this time but now he finds his voice. What do you mean, man, what're you talking about? This weed is shit, says Charlie by way of explanation, I think it's poisoned, I feel like shit, I bet it's laced with PCP or some shit. No, Charlie, how could it be laced with PCP? Nobody laces with PCP anymore, Charlie, you know that. This fucker's been tampering with the fucking pot and I'm going to fucking kill him, says Charlie. No, says Rosa finally, Charlie, don't be crazy, sit down over by me, Charlie, relax and take it easy, because Charlie is now standing over Sacha and Sacha sees his little eyes in his mean face, eyes that are so small they are inscrutable really in a face which is actually a fat face with little pockmarks on the cheeks and large nostrils. Sacha looks briefly into the nostrils and they are dark inside and he can see the little hairs in the nostrils quiver and he closes his eyes. How stupid to notice someone's nostrils right before death, he is thinking.

Meanwhile the dog has decided to howl. It goes over by the window, by Tonio, and starts in, it throws its head back and lets out the howling sound, and Rosa is delighted by this. How adorable! she says. Listen to the adorable dog! What's the dog's name, Sacha? And Sacha opens his eyes and there are Charlie's nostrils in the same place but Charlie himself seems to have fazed out slightly, his eyes are a little out of focus and he seems not to be paying attention anymore, even though he continues to stand over Sacha in a menacing way. The dog's name? says Sacha, and he frowns to himself because it doesn't occur to him until this minute that the dog might require a name, the dog who has been his faithful friend, who has stuck by him, even now the dog is probably howling to save his, Sacha's, life. I don't know its name, says Sacha finally. You don't know its name? says Rosa in disbelief. You don't know its name? she says again. How long have you had the dog? I don't know how long, says Sacha, maybe three or four years. Male or female? says Rosa. What? says Sacha, because this is another thing that Sacha has no idea about. The truth is he never had any curiosity about the gender of the dog until this minute and he closes his eyes again and tries to remember the dog in various contexts and tries to recall if he ever noticed balls or a penis on the dog and since he couldn't call forth an image of this sort, he says to Rosa, I think it's a girl. What do you mean, you think? You don't know if this dog that you've had for three or four years is a girl or boy? It's a girl, says Sacha, I'm sure of it. But then he thinks that if it were a girl it would have had babies by now and Sacha knows for a fact that the dog hasn't had any babies. There's only one way to settle it, says Rosa, and she rises from the bed and tugs a bit at her vest, which has this time begun to ride up in the front, though Sacha doesn't see since he is still on the floor between the legs of Charlie, who continues to look down on him in an out-of-focus way. Then Rosa is going over to the dog, who all this time has been howling at various pitches, and she grabs its forearms and tries to turn it over. Leave the dog alone, please, says Sacha because now there are a series of hard little yelps which Sacha has never heard coming from the dog. What's up? says Charlie. What's up with the dog? And he steps over Sacha and goes to where Rosa is trying to turn the dog over. Need some help, baby? he says to Rosa who is struggling with the resisting dog, kneeling on one of its legs and trying to wrestle it onto its back. Then Charlie's hand goes up and there's something in it, Sacha from his position on the floor can't see quite what it is, and he shouts, No, and at the same time Tonio tries to grab Charlie's hand but it is too late. The hand with whatever is in it crashes on the dog's rib cage and the dog gives a long shudder and Rosa screams, What the fuck, Charlie, you fucker. And she beats him with her hands and Tonio says, We better get going. He walks over to where Sacha is still lying on the floor, this time with his hands covering his eyes, and says, Sorry, man, and then Sacha hears the door opening in back of Rosa's terrible screaming. Rosa must be the last to go, and she must still be hitting Charlie because behind her screams Sacha hears the soft thudding of her fists on his shoulders.

Then the door closes and it is silent, except for a thin noise coming from the dog, and Sacha rises uneasily to his knees and crawls to where the dog lies with its eyes closed, taking deep breaths of air and shuddering uncontrollably in between and making that thin noise. The dog is dying, thinks Sacha, and there is nothing I can do about it. What can I do about it? he says out loud to the dying dog. And the dog is in too much pain to have a corresponding thought. I'm sorry, says Sacha finally, and he puts his hand on the dog's face. Until this minute he never noticed what a valiant jaw the dog has, even though now it is clamped tightly in pain. Sacha pulls himself to his feet and runs the tap water in the sink. Then he takes out a saucer and fills it and, without bothering to turn off the tap, he puts the bowl over by the dog's head. He goes to his own bed and rips off the blanket and covers the dog with the blanket, wrapping the blanket more or less around the shuddering dog, only not too tightly because he can see it is injured in its chest. Then he kneels on the floor next to the dog and listens to the little breaths of the dog coming faster and then slower, and the thin noise fading out and then coming on again.

And so it goes deep into the night with the dog breathing and the water running into the sink, and after a while Sacha doesn't know if it's the water or the dog he's hearing. It seems to him he hears the dog in the sound of the water and the water in the sound of the dog, and eventually he drifts off to sleep with his head next to where the dog is breathing its last breaths and he continues his dream about the ocean.

Y OU SHOULD KNOW I'm not a dog person. That is to say, I'm not a *pet* person. I like dogs (and even cats and birds) and, from the distance that spares me the responsibility for their care, feeding, and walks, I appreciate their spunkiness, their general affability. Thus, I can understand why people love them, as I do not. On the other hand, I have often referred to myself as a kind of "friendly dog," a designation which is meant to be self-deprecating, invoked in moments when I fear I am perceived as likable enough, but harmless, unable to deeply affect anything. Perhaps this is why—this solipsism of self-identification—dogs keep cropping up in my fictions. Otherwise, it is baffling to me, this cropping-up-of-dogs in the stories of one who is not a dog person.

"Sacha's Dog," which is a story about a particular dog who meets a tragic end, originated in my real-life observation of the dogs in San Miguel de Allende, Mexico, where I had been spending a good deal of time. In this small city of pedestrians, I'd noticed that a hefty population of dogs walked the streets like any of us, purposefully and seemingly with destinations in mind. They walked singly or in pairs, not especially interested in us human passersby, having, it seemed to me, other things on their minds. I was interested in telling a story about such a purposeful dog and wondered what it would be like if such a dog were in charge of a man, instead of, as I say in the story, vice versa.

It is always risky business to tell a story that involves a dog. Dogs are sentimental, even sacred, subjects. When I've read this story to audiences, the death of Sacha's dog has provoked more outrage than, perhaps, the death of Sacha himself might have. So one of my challenges was to tell a story that draws on the natural sympathies we have for helpless, well-meaning creatures, but finally overcomes these sympathies in a way that would take the story out of the arena of whimsy and sentimentality and into the arena of the more profoundly, humanly tragic.

I recognize that I tread a thin line in this story—just as, arguably for the dog person, there is a thin line separating humanness from dogness. Suffice it to say that I did not want to write about the loss of a *pet,* so much as the loss of a loved one who had agency and will as well as good-heartedness, and whose loss occurred, as many losses do, as a consequence of human carelessness or failure of attention.

The brutish force which is the literal cause of Sacha's dog's death, personified in the figure of Charlie, is an impersonal force, an agent of the accidental and also, in the context of this story, an emblem of social change. That Sacha recognizes his love for the dog only after it is too late is, it seems to me, a common enough human failing, one that intensifies all our losses and makes them just that much more unbearable. Still, in the face of the unbearable, Sacha continues his dream—his life—as we all do at such times, inevitably, and with a regret that presumably fades with time. This predilection to continue on with our lives, arising from the inability to solve our losses, is what I'd hoped to offer as the tragic paradox in the story.

The narrative voice I use here—a kind of Mexicanized English—allowed me to tell the story from the point of view of a narrator who is close to the cultural conditions of Sacha and his dog. In any Mexican tourist town, the underclass local person, like Sacha, finds himself disenfranchised—beleaguered by cultural invaders on the one hand and his own persistent poverty on the other. The forces of the "invader" (Charlie in his *LA Lakers* T-shirt) are ultimately destructive to the impoverished Mexican, who finds himself caught between two cultures and a member of neither. I wanted to suggest this social tragedy, the real story of a real loss, as well as to convey the personal account of Sacha's loss. So it seemed crucial that the narrative voice not be a construction of the Anglo diction of the tourist, which would distance the reader and condescend to Sacha.

But even though my narrator allowed me to tell the story the way I wanted to and as respectfully as I tried to do it, I recognize certain problems in taking on a voice and culture not my own. I might be accused, not without reason, of exploiting those like Sacha for my own artistic purposes. In this sense, I worry that I am, perhaps, no better than any tourist who spends her summers in Mexico and comes home laden with trinkets.

In another, more frivolous sense, dog people may now accuse me of exploiting dogginess. Like Machiavelli, I suppose the fiction writer will always accord herself such princely treacheries, this being the nature of fiction-writing, itself an expression of compulsive acts of the imagination. In my further defense, I would like to add that when I last spent time in San Miguel, I was *heartbroken* to discover that the wonderful, promenading dogs had mysteriously vanished. Dog catchers, I was told. The tourists complained, I was told. I miss those dogs.

Christopher McIlroy

ICE-T

IN THE SECONDS before his tires hit the black ice, Bob Weiss apprehended that the reservation experiment had gone bust, a false start—after the school year ended, he would leave. Nearly unconscious with drink, he didn't slow down. The undersized pickup left the road without hesitation. It was January, the edge of Crow Indian country in southern Montana. The pickup snapped off a swath of bare branches before overturning beside a frozen pond.

A scant half hour later two of Bob's students, juniors at Arrow Creek High, spotted the headlights staring walleyed into the trees. They stopped their rusted Impala, dragged the cold, inert form from the wreck, hightailed it into the rez town of Arrow Creek, and dumped it on the living room couch of another teacher. Bob was O.K. He slept the weekend.

Bob's students immediately dropped the "W" from his name, in honor of his driving exploit. Then, from "Bob Ice," the rapper boys with the backward Bulls caps dubbed him "Ice-T," from a used CD they'd picked up in the swap shop in Billings. Some of the girls preferred "Encino Man," after the revived frozen Stone-Ager, star of a video they rented from the Arrow Creek Lunch and Trading Post.

Bob looked the part of a Montana mountain man, tall, angular, and bearded, though balding. But he was from Ohio. He walked stooped and was given to rudely sudden intimacies. For instance, the first Monday after the accident he told his class, "They said I was passed out, but I was awake the whole time, looking through that hole in the windshield at the cold stars. I knew I was freezing. You'd expect to see stuff like the face of Jesus, but I was with this French whore. I've never been to France, you understand, this is in my head. She's saying in her accent, 'Ro-bear, tonight we make baby. I take my basal temperature, my body is ripe.' And we're going at it, and she's talking about the baby, his curly hair and big chin. It's all an act, a whore's thing, but extra creative, and personal. For me."

The kids had the impression of peering into the Visible Man. They didn't necessarily like what they saw, but they liked him for being weird enough to show it to them.

Bob taught vocational agriculture, his second year after fifteen with USDA. Enrollment for his specialty was near zero, so he'd diversified into woodworking and auto shop, both popular. Crows didn't want to farm, he'd concluded.

The following weeks he replaced the truck and drank even more incautiously, keeling over onto the floor of his triplex with a thud that alerted his neighbors. In class he'd be still drunk. It was said he drank with the kids. Indisputably, he bought Mortal Kombat and allowed them to play at his home all hours, so the next day they'd be as hollow-eyed as he. The principal warned him, but in midyear, for the rez, it was tough finding teachers without criminal records or certifiable mental disabilities.

Bob couldn't think past the end of the semester, to what he'd do next. USDA had fired him for prolonged drunkenness following the breakup of his second marriage. While earning his teaching certifi-

cate he'd worked a series of jobs. Most memorably, he'd cooked for
Ramada Inn until a buffet luncheon when he'd composed a salad of
whole, unpeeled oranges garnished with unshelled boiled eggs. Diners examined it in wonder but without sampling. Then he'd stacked
apple cores like Lincoln logs around a pâté.

Bob met Carolita Salgado at a Billings bar. He bought into the
idea that being Mexican made her hot. She wore men's Levi's with
the button fly, the bulge of her tummy parting the denim flaps like
labia. Yet she volunteered that she was a Seventh-Day Adventist, that
the liquid in her highball glass was straight ginger ale, and that the
bar's dense smokiness inflamed her eyes.

Bob took her to an all-night coffee shop. Summers in a rustic cottage on Lake Erie, when he was a boy, had given him a sense of
home, and that made him a lucky man, Bob said. He had no children. Carolita's two belonged to that "old life," she said, jerking her
head as if at something over her shoulder.

That night she wouldn't let him touch her, but over the next few
weeks Bob forced himself into athletic sexual feats for which she
complimented him. She quit her job with the phone company and
moved onto the rez. Next to his flyweight Isuzu, her white '71
Chevy pickup looked more at home, huge, slightly crushed in, like a
lunging animal.

Carolita volunteered in the classroom as a general gofer, circulat-
ing in the barnlike shop amid the table saw's whine and the sharp
reports of the impact wrench. She said she was thirty-eight, nine
years younger than Bob, but with her hair dyed jet-black she could
have been in her late twenties. She also dyed a blond-and-brown
streak down the middle, which some girls imitated. To the boys, she
was a chunk of raw sex set down to thaw in the big cat cage. They
circled, biding their time, practically rubbing their heads against her.
Her demeanor was proper, brittle, scarcely smiling. Yet Bob couldn't
control his voice. "This is how you stay in school when you're flunk-
ing everything else?" he yelled at Alex Old Bull, who wore a T-shirt

with rain on the front and lightning in back. Alex had leaned behind Carolita's neck and whispered in her ear.

"Just jivin', Ice. Sorry." The boys nodded and went back to work. Unafraid, they had no heart for shaming him.

In fact, with Bob, Carolita was more often romantic than sexual, as if they were still courting. She didn't approve of their sex without marriage. If he didn't drink so much, she said, he could afford to take her on a helicopter ride. "You put away that habit of poisoning your body, and your mind goes more places. Being up there . . ." she said. Her eyes closed, mouth tightened into a line, forehead clenched. She didn't nag, but that yearning was a hollow place, scary if left unfilled. Besides, Bob liked the transaction, a high for a high. After a month on the wagon, he drove her to a helicopter pad in Billings, April 2.

The weather and view were magnificent, but it wasn't much of a social afternoon. As they flew over the vibrantly sallow skin of the earth, furred by woods, cracked with gullies, the uplift of mountains patched with snow and shadow, Carolita prayed and cried. She wasn't frightened, but rather something private she tried to convey with her wet face turned up to him.

They became engaged.

Bob heard of a paleontologist who would take kids fossil hunting, so he organized a field trip at the beginning of May. Hell, he thought, you invent your own job in this place. Maybe some kids would grow up to be paleontologists. The high school, junior high, and elementary combined for the event, two busloads rattling and swerving twenty-five miles on a narrow gravel road into the badlands. Finbacks knifed into the sky, cliffs dropped off sheer. Dry coulees spilled boulders onto a suddenly red outcrop of sandstone. Several acres appeared to have been blasted by a giant blowtorch, ash heaps littered with sugary crystals and rocks forged into nearly recognizable shapes, a melted camera, a horseshoe. The kids were wondrously excited, yelling to each other as they scooped up ancient sea life and even dinosaur gizzard stones. Atop a ridge, a teenager gave a great cry and whirled a flat stone, like a discus, into space—not approved procedure, but funny enough.

Carolita had made lunches for all. Across the primeval landscape kids were eating her sandwiches. Bob felt staunch with a sense of possibility. Adhering to the paleontologist's lecture on the way over, he helped the youngsters discover fossils. A ten-year-old, disconsolate that he'd found no gizzard stones, collected three of the strange rounded pebbles, so ordinary but for the glassy, luminescent polish. He knew Bob. "This was really in a dinosaur's guts, Ice-T? Ho," he breathed. Bob said he used to imagine what kind of dinosaur that people would be. His grandmother was fat with a little head, so he called her brontosaurus. "You're Ice-T-Rex, man," the boy said. He tagged after Bob the rest of the trip. Bob was tempted to hold his hand. Walking back to the bus, he said to Carolita, "I could live with these kids."

But already Carolita was slipping. Twice Bob had come home to find her rocking out to devil-worship heavy metal, and when he asked if those were Seventh-Day Adventist hymns she poked him in the belly and armpit, flirtatiously, but it hurt.

The week after the field trip she started taking off in the big white pickup. He said what the hell and she jabbered as if she were on something, about a movie with a talking butt, about people with really big gobs of fat that moved independently of the rest of them.

Then she was gone two days and nights. Bob cruised the parking lot of every Billings bar, drove up and down residential streets scanning driveways and open garages. Late Sunday afternoon she pranced in, purse balanced on her wrist and eyes staring out of her head. "I left some stuff here," she said and disappeared into the bedroom. Bob ran out and deflated one of the Chevy's tires. When he stood up, she was pointing a pistol. Bang! The Isuzu's left front tire popped. Bang! The left rear. The gun swung to Bob's head, and he dove just before it fired again. From under the Chevy bed he saw high heels heading fore and he crawled aft. He heard another shot and shattering glass.

The BIA cop from across the street called her off, cuffed her, and took her in.

After her arrest Bob set fire to the vacant lot behind the triplex. The flames leaped as high as the windows before kids smothered them with blankets and hoses.

"I was burning her picture," Bob explained to the principal. "The grass caught, and I said, 'Oh, what the hell.' " The principal said his contract would not be renewed, but Bob could say he'd resigned.

As part of his severance, Bob negotiated an extension that included building maintenance over the summer. For Fourth of July he drove a group of kids thirty miles up a twisty dirt road into the mountains, to an ice cave.

They stepped into the mouth, sliding immediately on the slick gelid floor. Lumps of ice reared like ghosts.

"Hohhhhh," exclaimed Leonard (Poochie) Runs Behind.

"Where Encino Man rises," said his girlfriend.

Despite the warning signs, Bob let them duck under the railing and explore the recesses hidden in darkness. Their voices fluttered past his head like bats. They seemed to be going far away from him.

Afterward, the kids still were stirred up, gathering wood for the fire back at the picnic grounds or huddled in an only slightly menacing knot around the boom box. Butterflies skipped through the pines. Bob poked sticks into the fire. The pot for corn was balanced at a rakish angle on two stones.

"Why are you quitting, Ice-T?" asked Poochie. Poochie had been famous for imitating two women arguing shrilly at Crow Fair, the performance including background powwow singing, until his voice had changed. He'd been suspended five weeks for bringing a .38 to school, then rallied and finished the year. But the guy who snitched, Poochie would kick his ass. Kick his *ass,* Poochie thought. He'd imagined ways of killing him. No one had found where Poochie had hidden the gun.

"How'd you like to be written up all the time?" Bob answered the question.

"That'd be about right," Poochie said.

"I spent more time with the principal than you did. No, I gave this job two years and it's not working out. A man reaches a point in life when he's got to make a change."

"What are you going to do?"

"I don't know," Bob said.

But Poochie was no longer listening. *A man reaches a point in life when he's got to make a change.* The words rang his head like a rock hitting him. Damn, he thought, he was going to shoot a guy? And then jail, and his dad was a low weak bastard but did his mom need her heart broken right now? Poochie looked down the slopes at the lodgepole trunks half lit, half in shade, and the white clouds springing up over the treetops, and the blue going on forever, and he broke a sweat. His chest felt caved in. Dump the gun, dump the sucker fast, he thought. Sink it in the creek, easy, done. Already his breath opened wider. Damn, damn. A message could come from anywhere, and this one had come from Ice-T, an old guy who had lived through a lot and was still in there kicking. Poochie was in awe of the man, he looked at him with such love that he could not speak.

Everyone was stuffed with hot dogs. After all his hassle boiling the corn, Bob Weiss thought, nobody wanted to eat it.

Behind the Story

THE PAST FEW years, the writing time I've had has been devoted to a novel, so what stories I've written tend toward the miniature.

With a miniature the essential challenge of the short story, the balance between economy and amplitude, is that much starker. Overdevelopment unbalances the effect, while the opposite cheats meaning.

"Ice-T" was written at a single sitting, not an astonishing feat considering its brevity, but a circumstance that factors spontaneity more heavily than is true of most of my stories. Virtually none of the story was planned, including its pivotal point-of-view shift at the end. I was writing an imaginative version of the real-life misadventures of someone I barely knew, as they occurred to me, and when I reached the last of them, the ending insisted itself. Only then did it seem I might have a story rather than a mere sequence.

So conscious problem-solving was largely absent from the process. Within the published version the initial draft is largely intact.

Two tinkerings seemed necessary to consider.

The first was to prepare for that abrupt point-of-view breach. It seemed the first step already was taken, that of distancing the narrator from the character at the beginning. Within a consistently close third person the story likely could not have sustained such a rupture. But with a brief exception, the opening paragraphs place the reader outside Bob Weiss's consciousness, allowing the reader a more flexible stance.

In a paragraph closely preceding Poochie's POV intrusion, I began shading the consciousness toward him, to invite what follows.

The return to Bob Weiss's point of view in the final sentence is necessary to confirm his obliviousness to the minor miracle he has wrought in Poochie's life. In fact, Bob's revelatory statement to Poochie is casually disingenuous, implying intention, control, where there was none. But I like these characters. Each deserves his state of grace, whether or not he's aware of it.

In retrospect, I think the crossed points of view serve another purpose, emphasizing the pervasive mutual misunderstandings that characterize relations between whites and Native people, even with goodwill on both sides. There's nothing to say these misreadings of each other can't be benign every now and then.

The second potential revision centered on the issue of amplitude. I believe that to be satisfied with the story the reader must at least intuit or even recognize the latent theme that culminates in the ending. While the foreground story relates Bob's disastrous affair with Carolita, this deeper theme is Bob's barely articulated desire for a child. In the exchange with Poochie his yearning is consummated— for an instant they are aligned as father and son—though of course he'll never know it. To me, Bob's consistent devotion to the kids, however misguided at times, earns him this outcome.

This theme is present almost from the beginning, though I wasn't writing it consciously. But it's faint, and one of my decisions was whether to emphasize it more at the end. I'd considered adding a disgruntled line after the uproar with Carolita—Now he'd never have a kid, Bob thought—but ultimately I didn't. I'm still not sure that was the right decision, but happily, by pairing these notes with the story I can have it both ways.

Joan Silber

MY SHAPE

BREASTS WERE HIGHLY valued when I was a teenager. Everyone knew that men became entirely helpless at the sight of cleavage, the compressed hills rising gloriously above a strapless gown. This fashion in bodies has dated, but it was fortunate for me. I came from a family of women with large breasts and by the time I was fourteen I had grown my own set. I sheathed them in satin brassieres that made them point forward in military cones. Torpedo tits they were called, by us girls too. It is true that in junior high the boys yelled dirty comments (they mooed like cows, they made milking gestures with their hands), but I believed that these immature oafs, as we called them, liked me.

What did I want before this? I took ballet lessons twice a week in the gym of my grammar school and loved the arabesques and the leaping and even the strictness of Miss Allaben drilling us in the six positions. When I saw ballet on TV, I dreamed of flying, of myself as a figure in a tulle skirt floating above an audience. My other hobby was attending services in churches and synagogues, all around Cincinnati, where we lived. My parents were a mixed marriage (Jewish and Catholic, a big deal then) and had solved the alleged difficulty of this by not following any religion. So I was a fascinated tourist in any house of worship, and would go anywhere I could get taken. The whole notion of *worship* knocked me out. I saw Jews kissing their fingers and touching them to the velvet cover of the Torah, I saw Catholics kneeling with their mouths open in practiced readiness for the Host, I saw Greek Orthodox placing their lips on icons as if they could not bear to pass them without this seal of adoration. I would emerge blinking into the daylight, shocked at my friends' laughter over what had gone on in there—the choirmaster's bad haircut, the tedium of the sermon, the utter ridiculousness of somebody's mother's hat. I listened, harder than anyone else, to words never said in daily conversation—beseech, transfigure, abounding, mercy. The rapped chest, the bowed head, the murmured Dear Lord. I could not get over people doing this together, the gestures of submission that went on within these walls. Then the congregation got up and walked outside.

Since no one—not my friends or family or even the clergy themselves—seemed to take this to heart the way I did, I had to keep quiet, like a spy with her encoded notes or a tippler sipping a flask in the ladies' room. I made up perky reasons for wanting to go each week, "just to see how people are really all alike." After a while, I heard myself making fun of it with the others, and I stopped going. All at once, suddenly, cold turkey. I turned my back on the whole thing.

So. Then I grew the mounded body that was to be my adult shape. Everyone seemed to be telling me that I might enjoy certain privileges if I played my cards right. Once that idea got unpacked, it was more complicated than I guessed—what these privileges were and where contempt hid in the granting of them and what had to be paid for them anyway. People think they know all about this now, but they don't, not exactly.

I wanted to be an actress. I was too silly and shallow to be any good at acting, but I could keep my composure onstage, which is something. I was given small parts in summer stock, the hooker or the stenographer or the cigarette girl in the nightclub scene. The summer after my first year of college, I worked in the Twin Pines Theatre. I slept with the bullying director, a fierce-browed man in his forties who had sex with a lot of us and didn't give anybody a bigger part for it. Sleeping your way to the top is a bit of a myth, in my experience.

I liked acting, at that age. You got to dwell on feelings, which were all I dwelt on then anyway, and turn them over, play them out. We had long discussions: would a child afraid of her father show the fear in public? would a man who was in love with a woman talk more loudly when she entered the room? Those who'd had real training (I was not one of them) spoke with scorn about actors who "indicated," who tried to display a response without actually feeling it. An audience could always tell. What was new to me here was the idea that insincerity was visible. I understood from this that in real life I was not getting away with as much as I thought.

But otherwise I was a little jerk. I was so hungry for glamour that I put a white streak in my brown hair, I wore short-shorts and wedge heels, I drank banana daiquiris until I threw up. I thought the director was going to find himself attracted to me again and we might have a legendary romance, although I could hardly talk to him. I didn't know anything.

One of the other women told me about a job on a cruise liner. If I could dance a little, which I was always saying I could, I might be one of the girls strutting around in sequins in the musical revues they put on to keep the passengers from jumping overboard in boredom. I could get to Europe, to the Caribbean. They didn't pay you much but you ate well.

The woman who told me this was the director's new cookie, and I was not sure what she was really saying to me and in what spirit.

We're artists, you're the showgirl, etc. But perhaps she did want to give me something.

And I worked on cruise ships for years. I went to Nassau and Jamaica and Venezuela and through the Greek islands. I worked in nightclubs in Miami too, walking around with a big feathered head-dress on and the edges of my buns hanging out the back of my satin outfit. I lived with a bartender who was irresistible when he wasn't a repetitious, unintelligent drunk, and with an older man I never liked. I was twenty-seven—getting old for this stuff—when I got work on a ship going through the Mediterranean, along the French Riviera and Monaco and Liguria.

It was a French ship and that was how I met my husband, who was the ship's purser. He was a soft-eyed man with a whimsical blond mustache, who looked wonderful in the white uniform of the cruise line; everyone on the ship had a crush on Jean-Pierre. He was really just a boy. He was older than I was by a year, and he had poise and good sense, but he was not very worldly. I seemed to dazzle him, which was certainly nice. And I fell for him, his genial flirting and his down-and-dirty ardor in bed.

There is an hour on any ship when twilight turns everything a bright and glowing blue and the horizon disappears, the sea and the sky are the same. The line between air and water is so apparently incidental that a largeness of vision comes over everyone; the ship floats on the sky, until night falls and everything is swallowed in the dark. I have memories of being very happy with Jean-Pierre while standing out on the lower deck in that blueness, before the ship's lights came on. He asked if I looked like my mother or my father, and if I was close to them (I certainly was not). He wanted to know if I could ever live away from my family and my country for good, if I had ever thought of such a thing, and I saw myself moving toward a destiny as interesting as any I could have wished.

I had very little to leave behind, when I went with him to live in St-Malo, the ancient walled city in Brittany where he had grown up.

Jean-Pierre acted utterly proud to have nabbed me. When he introduced me to people, he always repeated my name, *Ah-lice,* with a certain delighted pause before it, and his translations to me included goofy compliments no one had really said ("my cousin says you are the flower of America"). We were staying in an apartment that belonged to his uncle, two doors from a fish market whose scent I did not even mind. We married a month after he brought me there. It was a pretty town, high on a bluff, but it had been bombed badly in the war and not all of it had been built back. The rainy beaches were filled in summer with dogs and children running around on the sand. Signs insisted it was *strictement défendu* to bring unleashed dogs anywhere on the premises, and I was amused to see that none of its citizens paid attention.

His family was not unkind to me either, although I tried their patience with my meager French and seemed dopey to them in general. Their friendliness was to ask me about Mickey Mouse and Elvis Presley, and in the childishness of these questions my language skills got better. At the endlessly long family dinners on Sundays, I could yammer my answers.

I had a running joke with Jean-Pierre about all the idioms English speakers have for anything sexy or duplicitous—French kisses, French leave, Frenching the bed, French ticklers. We were pretty jolly, the two of us. When we went back on the ship together, I was full of rich confidence. I beamed at the corny banter of old men and their wives, I danced like a proverbial house on fire. I wrote letters to my family from our ports of call, Corsica, Sardinia, Malta. *Allo, chère maman,* I said, I'm having more fun than I can tell you. *Baisers* to everyone, from Alice the blushing bride.

After Easter, when we went back to St-Malo, the town was full of tourists from other parts of France, and I would chat with them across the tables in cafés. People there didn't do that, but I thought they should, and I got them going. In the winter, when Jean-Pierre was hired for another tour of duty, there was no job for me on his ship, and he said maybe I could just stay home without him this once. I had worked since I was nineteen, and this offer of leisure seemed wonderful to me.

But I went a little crazy, by myself like that. I was no longer a novelty to his family and they had conversations I could not follow. In the dank and icy months, I walked around in a heavy, dressy cape and told the children I had a gun underneath it; I told Jean-Pierre's mother she was so cheap that she fed us horsemeat; I tried to hitchhike to Rennes but I came back after fifty creepy kilometers on the road with a dead-silent truck driver. Once I got drunk and stood on a table in a café, singing "Blue Monday" and looking down at the patrons. By the time Jean-Pierre got back, I was mopey and fat; I had gained twenty pounds. I had become a thing the French really hate, a blowsy woman.

What could we do then? We fought, quite nastily. He seemed stuffy and spiteful, not like someone I knew at all. He said everyone had told him I was a selfish baby but he had said, oh, no, I was devoted to him. We made up and spent two days straight in bed (our desire never cut so deep as then). We went on excursions to Caen and to Mont St-Michel, which even I knew was a famous abbey, although I had stopped caring about churches. We walked across the causeway to get there, and that was the part I liked, walking into the sea. We gave parties for his friends and I made American foods—fried chicken, coleslaw, macaroni salad. The wives began to think I was a big, loose, amiable fool. Jean-Pierre got work in a shipping firm in St-Malo.

For my thirtieth birthday we went to Paris. I had never been there before, and much of it thrilled me—the cakelike elegance of the buildings, the determined verve of people in the streets—and me, Alice, walking through it with my handsome French husband. But I felt too, in the thick of those groomed and confident crowds, the discomfort outsiders often know in Paris, the dawning sense that this is not, really, for us at all—we will never be this stylish or this knowing.

I came back in an agony of thwarted hopes. I thought that all my prettiness, all the gifts I'd been so pleased to have, had gotten me nothing at all. What did I want so desperately? What in the world is *glamour,* what did I mean by that? A heightening of the ordinary, an entry into the club of splendor, a feast of endorsed sensations? Whatever it was, my anguish in wanting it was almost more than I could stand. Since that time I have come think that shallow people suffer more sharply, because they can't see outside their bad ideas. Dolly of silly notions that I was, I wept real tears.

I knew I couldn't stay there weeping. I wasn't bound or indentured, it was the twentieth century. But I wept like that for another year—a shrew to Jean-Pierre and a puzzle to the town. I had one affair, with a humorless older cousin of his, and Jean-Pierre had lovers. In the end, I took the train to Paris and got a cheap ticket on a charter flight, and I left—after weeks of ugliness with Jean-Pierre's family (I might have handled that part better). I went to New York to dance and sing in Broadway shows.

What was I thinking? That it was my last chance. I had never been to New York, and I didn't know how to go about any of it. I showed up for one audition and waited in an outer room crowded with women much younger than I was. In the studio, I could keep in step, when they had us copy a sequence of dance moves, but I was not really dancing. I could sing on key, but in a watery, underpowered warble. I sang "*Je Ne Regrette Rien,*" which made the casting people smile wryly.

This did not make me want any of this less. I thought I had never worked hard enough for anything before (this part was right). *Being in a show* seemed like the exalted professional use of the body, the gold spun from sweat. In *Variety* I saw an ad run by a man who coached performers for musical auditions—twenty years' experience, proven methods. I was so happy after I called him—I was taking charge of my life, as I meant to do. I walked back to the Y where I was staying and I celebrated by eating a steak at the coffee shop next door. I can remember chewing it happily, sitting alone at a table in private joy, putting little charred pink-brown bits of it on my fork with the baked potato, reading a *Vogue* magazine as I ate. I liked food in America.

I was late getting to the coach's the next day. The studio was on Tenth Avenue, farther west than I'd been before, and I had not realized how far this was from the subway.

"Should I bother with you?" he said when he opened the door. "What do you think?"

"Oh, yes," I said, tittering and dimpling. "Please."

He was a tall man who had probably once been handsome; he was gaunt and leathery now. His dance studio was on the sixth floor of an office building, and the room smelled of old wood and mildewed drapes. I had to display myself for him. That is, I had to strip down to a leotard (I did this in a corner, awkwardly sliding out of my skirt) and follow him in a few dance steps, then perform them again while he looked glumly at me. Next he sat down at the piano and asked me to sing "Three Blind Mice."

"You remember that one, right?"

I tried to carry it off as jauntily as I could. Then he had me sing "Frère Jacques," which I at least did with a decent accent.

"Not much of a singer, are you?" he said.

I shrugged cutely, but I was very miserable. "I can be a dancer," I said. "Don't you think?"

"Maybe. How much do you want it?" He glowered at me from over the piano, a scratched black upright with a hoarse tone.

I answered that question with so much fervor that he smiled, a thing he rarely did, as it turned out.

HIS NAME WAS Duncan Fischbach and I was to spend many hours in his studio. At first it was like any dance class—he demonstrated some steps, and we did them together, and then we linked a few of these sequences, which I was supposed to remember. "Listen to me, are you listening?" he said. "The word *oops* does not get you anywhere in this world, no matter how big a rack you've got on you."

I laughed a little. Women did not take umbrage in any club I'd worked in.

"I hate a giggler," he said. "Do it again till you get it right."

I did the steps again. He circled around me, checking. "Your balance is bad," he said. "Stand on your right foot and don't move until I tell you."

I stood for as long as I could, swerving and dipping and regaining my center. "You have to do better than that," he said.

I had to jump in place for fifteen minutes without losing the beat. I had to run around the room and change direction on a dime. I had to hold a number of positions for long spells of time—a split, a high kick, a stretch to my toes with my butt in the air. All of them were exposing, implicitly sexual positions, and I felt like a crude cartoon, twisting and straining, muscles trembling. Nonetheless I was proud of my discipline in the regimen this strange *maître* was drilling me in. I did get more limber.

At my age I had no chance of getting anywhere, Fischbach said, unless I practiced at least seven hours a day. Minimum. I could not do much in my closet of a room at the Y, so I paid to use Fischbach's studio in the evening hours. I was given a key, and I went into that room, with its old-gym smells, always afraid that he was going to appear, but he did not. My body grew lighter and trimmer. I was skipping meals to save money, as the savings I had brought with me ran lower. I had taken a vow to myself not to look for other work. I was so lonely my voice cracked from disuse when I spoke, but I was elated too in a starved and ghostly way.

Sometimes I went to shows (or halves of shows—I walked in at intermission, the one way to go for free.) Things had been changing in the theater; the hit shows of the decade were *Hair* and *Jesus Christ*

Superstar. They were okay, although I liked the older ones better—
Gypsy, Guys and Dolls, Oklahoma!—an earlier style of full-throated,
tip-tappy entertainment. Most musicals gave me pleasure, but it was
not a fan's love for them that made me knock myself out. I saw them
as a way to be in a parade of dazzling motion, to be a lovely dancing
version of myself, without the rawness of the clubs. The best of me (I
believed) was in that lineup, slim-legged and tight-waisted, too
delightful to keep under wraps. That parade, which is always passing
through this world, was what I was made for, I thought. I could not
bear to have it go by without me. It hurt me to think it might have
slipped by already, that I might be too old. I probably was too old.

Fischbach had other students. A few times I met women going in
or out, girls with pearly lipstick and pixie bangs. Never any men. I
couldn't tell what his own desires were, which gender he liked, or
whether he couldn't stand the thought of doing anything with anybody. There was no gallantry in him—the tools of his trade were
mockery and command—and he was uncharmed by femaleness in
general. He was a strong dancer himself, not miraculously light on his
feet but muscular and sure; his lines were always clear. He called me
an oaf, a potato, a slob, a blight, a hippopotamus.

He believed in tests for me, rehearsals of my resolve, as if the
strongest desire had to win, simple as that, in any instance. "Pop
quiz," he would say. "If a director asked you to stand on your head
with a dead fish in your mouth, what would you do? If someone
stepped on your hand in the middle of a number, how would you
act? If you were in California and had to get to a performance in
New York and no planes were flying, what would you do? If your
grandmother wanted you to stay at her bedside in California, what
would you tell her?" There were no trick answers, but the recitation
of responses was my practice in "mental clarity."

Sometimes I called France collect and talked to Jean-Pierre on the
phone. The life I'd had there seemed cushioned and soft, a child's
tented garden. When Jean-Pierre was friendly (sometimes he was

not), I would get off the phone and shed tears. I would sit in my room at the Y and have to talk myself back into doing my exercises. How had I, who had once been loved and had a home, thrown myself into this pit?

This could not go on forever. Fischbach had forbidden me to go near any audition until he said I was ready, but I had had thirty-six sessions with him. Week after week. On Labor Day weekend he was going away (did he have friends? it was hard to imagine) and he would do a special extra-long class with me before he left on Friday afternoon.

I was a little late, and he said, "I might have known. Do you have any idea at all what traffic is going to be like this afternoon? Any clue at all?"

"I'll dance fast," I murmured brightly.

This was the wrong joke to make, because it gave him the idea to have me do routines in double time. He hammered at the piano with his fingers angled like claws. I was beet-red and sweating heavily when we stopped.

"Now that you're warmed up . . ." he said.

He took up a wooden yardstick from the corner. For a second I believed that he was going to hit me with it. "You know the limbo?" he said. "Did the frogs limbo in your part of La Belle Frogland?"

He held the stick out stiffly, like a traffic gate. "Under," he said. "Lean back. Go with your pelvis first."

I had done this before, as a teenager in Cincinnati. "Oops," I said now, as I bent my knees and cakewalked under the ruler, my shoulders and head going last. It had been much jollier with a line of guffawing kids and calypso music on the hi-fi.

"Again," Fischbach said.

He lowered the stick. I wriggled under. The silence was not pleasant.

"Again," he said. The move meant thrusting my private parts at him—that was the whole comedy of this game—and for once I was not happy to be doing that. Fischbach kept his face impassive; he looked stony and perhaps a little bored.

"Again," he said.

I had to spread my knees wider to keep my footing.

"Again," he said.

I tried to angle one hip lower and twist my torso under the stick, which made me lose my balance. I righted myself by holding on to Fischbach's arm. "No," he said, and shook me away. I skidded and landed hard on my tailbone.

"You didn't last very long," he said.

"Yes, I did."

"Stay, don't move. I have floor work for you."

He walked to the far wall. "Okay," he said. "Come to me. On your hands and knees."

"What?"

"Just a little crawling. Fast as you can. It's a good workout. Don't argue."

I was going to argue, but then he told me not to. I thought I would just get it over quickly—I put my palms flat on the floor and I lunged and scuttled forward, like a swimmer in a race. My bare knees scraped the floor, but I kept thinking I was almost there. Soon, soon. This was a nightmare, but if I did what I had to properly, it would be finished.

"Very good," Fischbach said, when I had reached him. "Very nice. Don't get up, sweetheart."

I sat on the floor, cross-legged, waiting. *Sweetheart,* he said that?

"One last thing," he said. "Then you're ready." I actually nodded.

"Lick my shoe."

"What?"

"You need to do this. You pick. The right or the left."

He was wearing white canvas tennis shoes. I looked at his feet and I looked up at him. His face had almost no expression, but his eyes, in their hooded sockets, were fixed on me, to let me know that I had to do this. I respected (that is almost the right word) the clarity of his will. You might have thought we were both in the service of a great idea. For a moment I did think that. I lowered my head and I touched my tongue to the tip of his shoe, just once. The roughness left a dry spot on my tongue.

I was crying, of course, when I looked up at him. Not a mild flow of tears, but helpless, snotty sobs. Fischbach stayed poker-faced. He really did believe in some theory of severity and triumph, some grand dedication, but there was nothing at its center. He did not care whether I danced or not, or whether anyone did. There was no divine substance he was burning me down to.

While I was crying, I understood clearly that I was never going to be a dancer in any Broadway show. Not now, not later. I saw too that I didn't want it so much really. It was as if I suddenly remembered a thing that had been blocked by distraction and interruption. I sat on the floor in my soaked leotard and I was sick with disappointment to be someone who didn't want this.

My crying naturally disgusted Fischbach, although it could not have been a surprise to him, I could not have been the first to break down in his studio. (Unless I was the first he was able to push that far, a truly painful thought.)

"Okay, okay. We're done," he said.

He went over and rolled the casing down on the piano keys. I could see that he was trying to carry out these last moments with what he thought of as style. "Get your stuff together," he said. "I'm in a hurry. Don't dawdle like you do."

He got his dungaree jacket off the chair and put it on, tugging at the bottom of it and turning up the collar. "Are you listening?" he said. "Move it. Chop-chop. It's time." He seemed pathetic to me, bossing around a woman who was stretched out on the floor in a fit of weeping. Where could that ever get him? I didn't move—that was my one tiny piece of resistance—and he said, "I'm waiting." He stood over me for some minutes. At last he said, "Never mind. You can lock up when you leave." I left the door open, in fact, and I never mailed him the keys either.

A N D   S O   I went back to Jean-Pierre. He met my plane in Paris, and he looked wonderful to me, with his soft eyes and his cropped sandy hair, his topcoat flapping in the wind. He seemed very happy to see me, and he didn't rebuke me or ask me terrible questions, although later he was less kind. His family never treated me with any warmth after I came back.

Everyone did notice how slender and strong I was. I could not explain to them how I had stretched and kicked and plié'd and tied myself in knots in that stuffy studio, tearing and rebuilding the muscle fibers, pushing myself past the threshold of strain. Once I was back in Brittany, those hours in the studio seemed heroic—*I* seemed heroic, in my submission to the regimen, my single-pointed efforts. And for what? For a vision that was laughable even to me and had made me come back ashamed.

But I did come back a less silly woman. I did not plague Jean-Pierre about things he could do nothing about. And I tried to keep up my training. I would put on a record of *Wonderful Town!* and strut across the kitchen floor to Rosalind Russell. My niece and her friends, who saw me through the window, wanted me to teach them. I began to give lessons to little girls in "jazz dancing" and also tap, which they requested. I liked children and might have had them with Jean-Pierre if we had gotten along better. I could get my class looking like a line of Shirley Temples, all shuffling-off-to-Buffalo in their patent leather shoes, merry and mostly in step, and afterwards I helped them on with their little coats.

When the class got too big for any room in our house, I rented a room in the *mairie,* where the town's municipal offices were. It was quite a grand room, with molded plaster garlands along the ceiling and a nice parquet floor. It tickled me to have "The Pajama Game" pouring through its august spaces. Adults wanted to come too to the class, so I had an evening group of solid housewives and lithe young office workers and even a few men. I was a fad, perhaps, but people had fun.

I could not have lived on what I made from my dance classes, but they kept me afloat. Some girls came year after year, and their sisters too. Every fall I worried I wouldn't have students, but I always did. And I was allied with what Americans used to call physical culture. I went hiking in the valley of the Rance, I went to Paris for yoga weekends. Jean-Pierre laughed the first time he saw me in hiking boots; he said I looked like a Valkyrie in shorts.

I liked my muscles more than he did, and they weren't ungainly either. The littlest girls used to beg me to show them a *grande jetée*— and I could jump and land without much thud or bobble even in the later years. The classes were the best part of my week. When Jean-Pierre fell in love with someone else and we split up at last, I was not altogether at a loss. I had something I could do, an occupation. I could not, however, stay in the town.

I went to Paris, to brood and idle for a few weeks before I went home to the States. It was not a happy time. I was appalled to think my marriage really was broken forever and I was sorry for the messes we had made. I walked through the whole city of Paris, from Sacré-Coeur to Montparnasse, from the Chaillot Palace to the Jardin des Plantes, trying as hard I might (not hard enough) to keep from stuffing myself with food and drinking a whole bottle of wine every night. I chatted too much with waiters and ticket-takers and all the people in my yoga class.

We were doing the shoulder stand in yoga when I kicked someone behind me by mistake. He was a very polite Parisian in his late forties, who told me not to worry for a single second, it was good for his health to get clipped in the jaw now and then. I was not usually that clumsy. We whispered back and forth about how this was a more dangerous sport than soccer, but at least (he said) you didn't have violent yoga fans. After class he took me out for a very good lunch.

I liked him right away, most people did. He was a history teacher in a *lycée,* a widower with a grown son, with an interest in Zen Buddhism and Duke Ellington. I stayed in Paris because of him—Giles was his name—one week longer and then another week. People say Paris is expensive but you can get by if you know how. After it was plain that I was not going to leave the city anytime soon, I began to teach beginners' classes in the yoga studio. I was living with Giles by then in the 13th Arrondissement, in a tiny apartment with a rocky sofa bed and an armoire as big as a stable.

We had a simple, almost rustic life. In the evenings we stayed in, without TV or too much outside company; we read and we listened to music. On weekends we had *pique-niques* in the park when the weather was good, or we played long, companionable rounds of honeymoon bridge. You might have thought we were old people, except that the sex was frank and lively. Quite lively.

Sometimes in the early days I went with him to talks by one of his Buddhist teachers, although they never really seized my imagination. I did learn to meditate, and the followers were certainly a smart group. Giles never pressed any of his enthusiasms on me, except for a habit of buying me cheap Japanese sandals, which he insisted on liking. How could a person scold him? He was always able to consider the most outlandish idea without arguing and was unshocked by anything I told him.

Ten years after we first started living together, I went home to the States to visit. My family made a fuss and then ignored me. I had become one of those ex-pats who didn't know who David Letterman was and who held her knife and fork like a European. When I flew back to Paris a week early, I told everyone I was never leaving France again. Giles' son called me *la convertie.*

At the yoga school we always got a number of Americans in the classes, and I could see they envied my unfazed command of this city and its folkways. It amused me that I of all people had become some worldly personage with good bearing and a forthright gaze, like a type out of Henry James.

I might have turned out a lot worse. I tried not to be vain around the students, not to be some fluttery old bird in drawstring pants. I worried about Giles' health, which was not as strong as it might have been. Otherwise my complaints were truly minor. When Giles had a heart attack last summer, I came to know clearly what minor was.

I was not always good during his illness. In the hospital, I cried out when I saw the tubes clamped over his nostrils. On my visits, I held his hand and gazed at him, while everyone else chattered to him brightly. In my apartment I didn't want to answer the door or the phone. I wouldn't go outside at all, except to visit Giles. People came to check on me—Liane, the head of the yoga studio, and Giles' son and his wife. "Get up now," Liane said. "Get yourself dressed." What a nuisance I was to everyone, what trouble.

When Giles came home again I was better. I cleaned myself up, I cleaned the house. I nestled on the couch with him, we laughed at the TV news, I went out to shop. And I went back to teaching yoga, which helped me greatly. The difficulty of certain poses was especially useful. I had to concentrate and I had to be exact. Giles himself got lively again within a few weeks and claimed he felt the same as before. Better even.

In the months right after he was ill, when I'd begun working again, I began practicing a kind of Tibetan meditation called *tonglen*. In its later levels, you send relief and spaciousness, on your outtake of breath, to someone who has done you an injury. Naturally I picked Duncan Fischbach. I have never had another enemy. I'm sure no thought of me has crossed his mind for decades; I was one clumsy student among many for him. How our limits vexed him. He couldn't bear how little we could do. Broken athlete, he must be now, empty shell—who would need relief sent more than he would? I sit with my famous bust rising and falling as I breathe; he would laugh if he saw me. But I do think of him, in short spells and sometimes longer.

IN THE SUMMER of 1999 I was finishing a novel in a rented cottage in Mount Tremper, outside Woodstock, New York. There was a stream in the backyard, where I would swim with the dog in the mornings, and then I'd write all afternoon, and my friend and I would swim in a lake before supper. Those were very nice days. When I reached the novel's end in the middle of August, I still wanted the routine of those days, and so, with much less deliberation than usual, I took a chance on a hazy idea. A friend I'd known years before had told me a story about a dance coach who'd humiliated her. She mocked herself when she told the story, but I felt that I understood it.

What haunted me in her account was the teacher's repeated question, "How much do you want it?" An ecstasy of sacrifice was asked of her, for the sake of a fairly frivolous goal she had no hope of attaining. I was interested, not only in the odd sexuality of the scene, but in this confused desire to submit to a higher purpose. In my first notes, I had the idea that a religious impulse was embedded in this. I was mixing the received incident with my own preoccupations.

I knew the dance lesson scene was not going to stand on its own. I've always written somewhat novelistic stories that include chunks of the past. A writer friend said about one of the first ones I wrote, "And that woman's whole fucked-up life is in that story!" I took this as a compliment, which it was. In this story, I might have begun with the dance lessons and hearkened back to key incidents from earlier days. But I seemed to want to begin in childhood and move forward in a straight chronology, rather than shuttling back and forth. I wanted her whole life, as she'd led it that far, to bear down on that crucial scene. This was the first in a series of what I think of as biographical stories. I once gave a class at Warren Wilson on "Long Times in Short Stories"—I didn't know then how carried away I was going to get with this form.

Beloved examples of such stories are Flaubert's "The Simple Heart," Chekhov's "The Darling," and Natalia Ginzburg's "The Mother." The chronicle form is, of course, more common in novels, and I was going back (I later saw) to a scheme used in my first novel. In any case, the early pages of this story went easily. I didn't think it was going to take me so long to get Alice to that fatal dance class, although its placement two-thirds of the way in turned out to be right.

What was hardest and newest for me in this story was not the lurid scene between Alice and her dance coach, Duncan Fischbach, though this was difficult to write, but the open treatment of religious longing. I had wanted to write about this for some time, and many paragraphs laden with treacle and gravitas hit the cutting room floor in previous attempts. Once I had sketched in Fischbach and his flair for derision, I knew I wanted the ending to have Alice attempting *tonglen,* a meditation practice I'd heard explained by Pema Chodron, a teacher in the Tibetan Buddhist tradition, but I had resolved not to do this if it really sounded awful. I did the most rewriting on the ending. Much obsessive tinkering went on here, but what happened was not just that I got the sentences right, but that I was able to move the fiction into different territory.

It's tricky. Though I've made forays into Buddhism for years, my feelings about it are complicated, qualified, and not fixed. Earlier fiction writers could evoke a realm of religious feeling with a recognizable set of images, but a contemporary writer probably needs to be both more direct and more lightfooted, if that's possible.

This story led to other stories. I saw that what I really wanted to write about—and there was plenty to say on the topic—was sex and religion. I didn't mean by this their dual roles as sources of transport, the sort of thing that has a store near me calling itself Religious Sex or that powers the amazing imagery of St. Teresa of Avila. I was thinking of the ways in which they each tend to pick up for each other's failings, to take up one another's slack. I wrote six stories in this series, and all of them are about forms of devotion and forms of consolation.

I had the idea too that the stories might be linked so that a minor element in one was major in another. So the next story is Fischbach's and is narrated by him. And I had been thinking that summer about Gaspara Stampa, a sixteenth-century Venetian poet praised by Rilke for her "soaring, objectless" love, and later one of the stories went to her. The last story belongs to Giles, Alice's lover—the group is a ring.

Judith Grossman

I'M NOT THROUGH

T HE HEATER IN the club pool had broken. Lesley saw the notice, going in, but she swam anyway. All the lanes were open, and the water shone blue crystal in the light from the end-windows. At 72 degrees, it felt like a dive into that remembered pristine quarry-lake, outside Ithaca. Ten fast laps, then fifteen more at a quieter, rolling pace. On the last lap something kept brushing faintly over her right shoulder. When she stood up in the shallow end, water streamed off, leaving a long, straight black hair—not hers—wound over her arm.

Pristine, my ass. She peeled it away and draped it over the side. Some other doctors from West End Clinic swam at the club; Lesley knew a couple, also the internist who bragged about doing a daily mile at five-thirty a.m. But she was the only one from the dermatology practice. When she'd mentioned—not bragged about—the plan to work out three afternoons a week, a senior colleague said: "Not to deter you, but you might take a sample culture off the floor, first. I couldn't count the fungal infections we've seen out of there." Lesley did wear flip-flops, as now into the shower. And she ran the water hot, lifting one foot at a time free, to strip off her swimsuit. The drain in the gutter along the wall was circled by a foamy nest of more hairs. Who was it who imagined hell as a filthy country bathhouse (read, suburban) with spiders in the corners?

Smullyan was right. *No.* Rationally, Smullyan should know better than to suppose you could maintain health through isolation. Skin a perfect case in point. Take reasonable measures—wash hands after patient or toilet visit—and practice equanimity. To reduce bacterial/viral load, ideally have a strong married relationship, no outside sex. *Thank you, dear Keisuke.* But Smullyan had got divorced, just at the time she joined the practice, so she might have asked him how he thought going to the gym stacked up against having multiple sexual partners. Right now, though, she was going to take ten minutes in the sauna, bake away any residual gym-crud, and go home.

She opened the door. Out of the hot darkness inside, an unhappy, demanding voice sprang at her.

" . . . could've possibly *happened* at that Wellfleet House? And he *still* doesn't know, except she was fine when she came down there. Stayed only two nights, then told him she had to leave. Phoned him from her place, day after that, and told him she couldn't see him, quote unquote, *any more now.*"

"But he'd have *some* idea, Karen?"

Lesley's eyes adjusted to the dim light. Karen was sitting to the right of the door, cross-legged against the wood slats, eyes closed, a towel wrapped modestly round her lap. The other one reclined along the same bench. Both were women of her mother's age, but the reclining one showed off her nude odalisque figure, narrow up top with an oval head, neat oval breasts, and the rest of her rounded like a vase. If you had to become middle-aged (and you did), that'd be the way to go. But, like that pearlescent complexion, it came only as a genetic gift.

Lesley went to the opposite corner, lay down, and closed her own eyes, to be unintrusive. *Relax, these aren't your problems.*

"He did say she seemed bothered by Rosie's condition. The dog, you know?"

"But he's had that dog for years. Was she allergic?"

"No, I mean Rosie's *heart* condition. Golden retrievers don't live too long. He had her since graduation. Anyway, the pills quit working, she had congestive episodes."

"You're not saying he kept a *dying dog* in the *bedroom*—?"

Pause. "I don't actually know that—"

"Well . . ."

Lesley pressed her hands over her face: it'd be too sick to laugh.

"He asked her when she was leaving, and she said Rosie wasn't the reason. Dana does medical research, okay?—she deals with animals."

Dana. *Her* Dana?

"Last thing he got was a message on his machine: please don't call. Meanwhile he took Rosie to the vet last Saturday: she was just—suffering. Now that's over."

"I don't know. . . . The sweetest kind of boy gets the heartbreak."

"Of all my four, why him? Jeremy's the true believer. He waited a long time for this one. And when she visited I just thought she was perfect. Even now, he says he's not over her. When I see him, I almost wish I'd never had children."

"Don't say that, Karen—"

"I mean, what did I *do*?"

"You didn't do *anything*—"

"So, what *should* I have done?"

Lesley got up softly and left. When someone cries in a sauna, the tears must dry almost before they can be wiped off. To avoid seeing the two of them in the light, she quickly pulled out enough paper-towels to stand on, went to her locker, and got into her underwear, pantsuit, and shoes.

It had to be her Dana they were talking about, because Jeremy was the guy's name that Dana wanted her and Keisuke to meet earlier in

the summer. And when they all four did get together (June?) for dinner in Cambridge, she thought immediately—like Karen just now—
that this was serious. Someone who was clearly both sweet and sharp
enough for her. What was it he did? Some new kind of medical software, yes. A running joke between the two of them was that they'd
met at a martial arts dojo (Dana had been doing judo for years),
where they'd first had body-contact. No doubt that explained something else remarkable. Dana had never liked anybody touching her in
public, and even when they were roommates back at Cornell, sharing
everything, she couldn't deal with Lesley even fixing a loose clip in
her hair: all part of Dana's rules of privacy. But now, with Jeremy, she
seemed in constant physical connection—her fingertips on his sleeve,
his hand in hers, or pressed to her knee. Not for show, but as if she'd
discovered some newly compatible element.

Driving home afterwards, Keisuke admitted surprise. "To be can-
did, I thought Dana was rather the Ice Queen—or maybe she still
had a thing for you."

"Not!" said Lesley. "This is great for her, though."

Afterwards, an odd recognition came back to her from when they
were standing in the mirrored entrance to the restaurant: Jeremy, in
fact, looked a little like herself. Taller, obviously, but his coloring—
chestnut-brown hair, eyes too (though he wore rimless glasses rather
than contacts), and a light amber skin-tone—was undeniably similar
to hers. A trivial thing, and nothing she'd ever mention. After that
evening, she and Keisuke didn't get a chance to see them again for
the rest of the summer. One or other had been out of town, or busy,
every weekend through July and August. When Lesley had thought
of Dana, it was as a problem solved. *If only*.

But that was unfair. Lesley still held to the truth that Dana was her
gold standard among friends—had practically got her through college, as Keisuke had later got her through her internship and beyond.
She herself grew up in a family of jocks—her older sister had been a
high-school basketball champion, then cadet at West Point—and

nobody cared what Lesley did with her mind. Dana was her first experience of intellectual drive, of someone bent on mastery, intolerant of anything less. Lesley learned from that, even as she was enchanted by the angular symmetry of Dana's face, and her transparent skin that was blue at the temples and inner arms. How could a membrane so thin and fragile protect, or even contain, an entire person? From there, to the mysteries of dermatology.

When she got home Keisuke was making mustard chicken, rolling the pieces in crumbs. He'd already put together a warm red-cabbage salad, topped with parsley, pine nuts, and Valpresa feta, all in the brown-glazed earthenware bowl.

"Fantastic," she said, going to him. "*O dolce mani*—you've made the perfect supper."

"For me and you both." Quickly he set the chicken in its baking pan, and drizzled it with melted butter. Then he rinsed his hands, wiped off the drops, and turned round to gather in her kiss. It would be time later to ask what he thought about this news of Dana, and what to do.

When she did ask him, they were watching a *Sopranos* rerun. She caught the influence in his tone, as he said: "Go carefully, Lesley, if you say anything at all."

"Why carefully? I'm overdue for calling her, anyway."

"Because . . ." Keisuke had to think: that meant it was a question of tact. At the same time, Tony was deciding Pussy must die. "I mean, because she may be thinking more differently from you, than used to be the case. That research track's a whole other direction."

"Then I'll see what difference it makes."

Dana gave Lesley the choice of which downtown restaurant to eat at, P. F. Chang's or Pho Pasteur—the way it had been all last year, when they used to meet once or twice a month. Lesley had made her call simple enough—no mention of the Jeremy hiatus. And Dana's response was casual, as if they were reconnecting after some random little absence.

"Vietnam cuisine, then—Thursday, usual time."

Driving into town against the traffic, Lesley kept returning to Keisuke's comment about a divergence between them. What it meant, that she'd gone straight into practice two years back, while Dana, all set for cardiology, competed for and won the fellowship at Maurice Rachlin's lab, to work on synthetic blood substitutes.

"You want to wrangle rats—again?" she'd protested. Besides, Rachlin had a big reputation as hard-driving egomaniac, as high-stakes entrepreneurial type. Such people weren't generous mentors.

Dana put her questions aside. First, Rachlin's lab was known as very open to women, who were regularly listed as co-authors on his papers. Second, she had ego enough to cope; and most important, she was convinced the project was within a couple years of breaking through. So much work had already been done, pointing towards the viability either of modified bovine hemoglobin or some form of PFC emulsion, it would likely be a question of teasing out the winning formula. What success in this would mean to Rachlin was one thing: Dana saw only that it could be within reach, and that it was supremely worth doing. Unlimited supplies of a life-saving, universal donor fluid—for trauma victims, cardiac, and all major surgery patients, world-wide—who wouldn't want to make it happen?

"The military will be happy," Lesley commented.

"So let the military be happy, if civilians are served too. I mean, I know where the funding comes from."

Last winter, Dana invited her to visit the lab, after work. What instantly impressed her was how much money must have gone into this facility. It was all spacious, clean, well-lighted. Half of the equipment was so new Lesley didn't recognize it. No rusting, leaky refrigerators labeled "Biohazard" here. Even the familiar stuff, from centrifuges to computers on down, looked conspicuously state-of-the-art. Dana introduced her briefly to Maury Rachlin, who'd taken off his white coat for the day and looked every inch the doctor as potentate in his fitted pinstripe suit. He wore his grey hair Continental-style, brush-cut over his high dome of a head. Though he was scarcely taller than her, he put a firm hand on Dana's shoulder when he said, "As a friend of Dana's, I'm sure you know she's quite the rising star here."

That didn't surprise Lesley at all, but the possessive gesture told her more about the claims Rachlin enjoyed making on his juniors. She also took in Dana's little distancing remark, after he'd left, to the effect that some graduate students had nicknamed Maury "Dr. Moreau." Scanning the perimeter work-stations, she conceded that maybe forty percent of the researchers were women. Whatever that might mean.

When it came to the animal rooms, of course, the familiar stink of rats and disinfectant made her throat contract, as it had years before in Bio lab. Dana explained the row of current subjects, from which two-thirds of their blood volume had been removed earlier, via cannulas inserted in the femoral artery. It took two stages, ten minutes apart, to reduce the shock effect. Here was Number One, the limp control animal, with no resuscitation measures taken. An opulently handsome Indian graduate assistant reached into the cage with his stethoscope and routinely confirmed its death. Cause: hemorrhagic shock leading to heart failure.

Subject Two, hind leg also taped, was actively sipping from its water tube. "Reinfused with its own blood: obviously just fine," Dana commented, and moved on. "Okay, here's Number Three: received old-style lactate saline. Rehydration, not much more." Three lay stretched out, in rapid tremor, its paws working little grooves in the cage litter. "So much for old-style. Now—"

Four was resting contemplatively in its cage, nosing alternately its genital area and bandaged thigh. It had received a cocktail of perfluorocarbon agents, designed to carry oxygen into the body's cells. Sundeep would monitor its progress through the evening, and hook it up to a monitor before leaving. Expected survival time: anywhere up to a week, or more.

Dana moved on and tapped Five's cage. This was what they were currently betting on—a replacement formula cross-linking hemoglobin with soluble polymers for enhanced oxygen. Five looked about as good as its autotransfused colleague, wiping its whiskers under the water tube. It could be tracked for weeks, with checks for longer-term evidence of toxic damage. They were progressively reducing risks to the vulnerable areas: lungs, kidneys, vascular system. Impressive, Lesley had to say. If Dana was confident that they'd be authorized for patient trials by the time she completed the two-year fellowship period, that was good enough for her. When, after all, had Dana ever failed at something she'd set her heart on?

IN THE EVENINGS, Dana read at random in books she had kept from college. She was blessed or cursed with a measure of eidetic memory, and as she sat waiting, sipping the light beer in front of her, whole lines from the night before unrolled in her head. *The individual doesn't have what he strives for, and history is the struggle in which he acquires it. Or he has it, but still can't take possession of it, because something external . . . History is the struggle in which he overcomes these obstacles. . . .*

Dana couldn't look forward to seeing Lesley today. How to manage a time like this, when you were drifting away so fast from someone who'd been so necessary once? In another couple of years they'd be complete strangers. It shouldn't matter to her in the least that Lesley always showed up in new clothes, whereas she had on a dark-red shirt and navy jacket that she remembered wearing three winters ago at the last conference they'd attended together, and had also worn to Lesley's bridal shower early last year. New clothes, that was all part of Lesley's settling into a practice with cosmetic implications. Meeting the public, all that. And marriage of course, even if it was to Keisuke, for whom she'd nothing but respect. But she, Dana, could still wear things to rags before replacing them—it made no difference.

History is the struggle in which he overcomes these obstacles. She was reconsidering Maury, was he the ally, or an obstacle to be overcome? Both? When he announced it was time to move up to the next stage of testing, he'd put her in charge of the group working on dogs. And trained her himself for three weeks, this summer. A vote of confidence. Also, she recognized, his test of her mental toughness for the work. She must perform the de-barking procedures first. Then supervise putting the animals in restraints for the experiment, since you couldn't use any anesthetics. Dogs were expensive subjects, so she must re-use them as many times as possible, storing the drained blood for re-transfusion, to keep them going on weekly rotation. The animals peed when she came in the room—a fear reaction. They shivered in their restraints whenever she touched them. They jerked when she stuck them, because obviously it hurt. They couldn't bark, but they could look, and the jaws opened wide at her with a gasping sound, as their blood filled the tubing. You could feel its heat through the clear plastic. She and the assistants kept close track of signs of post-procedure distress: dehydration symptoms, cramps, rapid pulse, spasmodic breathing, cardiac arrest.

Resuscitation wasn't much more fun either.

Through the window she saw Lesley walking past, late. *Two currents that flow in opposite directions*—yes, now the rest of that page was coming back: *Wherever the individual's inner blossoming has not yet begun, wherever the individuality is still closed up, it is a matter of outer history. As soon, however, as this bursts into leaf, so to speak, inner history begins.*

Perhaps it could be true of Lesley, that nowadays she lived an inner history; but how would one know? That athlete's body-presence of hers was still instantly recognizable, as she swung through the door and turned to scan the room. Then she came and gave Dana a big, generous kiss. It was for sure that Kierkegaard couldn't have imagined a Lesley in the first place.

When they ordered food, Lesley wanted a double order of summer rolls on the table: she confessed a craving for the pale, elastic feel of the outside, combined with the filling of cold shrimp, crisp lettuce, and cilantro. "I don't know why I like them," she admitted. "Mainly the taste's in the dipping sauce, but I could eat them even without sauce—why?"

"It's the feel," Dana said, halfway into hers. "Biting through the combination of textures."

"Yes, weirdly addictive." Lesley stopped for a moment, then said casually, "I have an Israeli neighbor who showed me this translated Yemeni cookbook. It had a recipe, for young bulls' penises. I wonder if these rolls somehow remind me—"

"Refrigerated?" Dana whispered. "What perverted things are you thinking?" She didn't deliberately mean to catch Lesley's sly look, but it happened, and instantly they regressed into stifled laughter. Nobody else could do this to her—switch her back into someone she hadn't been for years. *Stop it now, Dana.* And she did pull herself together when the entrées arrived: stylishly plated fish with vegetables too brilliantly green and vermilion to be alive. The waiter asked, should he take off the half-eaten summer rolls. Dana said yes, but Lesley put a hand over hers. She was going to finish it, and she did, with a mock-fierce bravado.

Soon now, Dana knew the questions would be coming; but which first, the one about Jeremy, or about the lab? Lesley picked the lab. A wise choice.

"The lab," Dana repeated. "Yes. We're hoping we can make the case for patient trials sometime next spring."

"That's fast. Which means you must've moved on from the rats already."

"Right." She helped herself to another clump of rice, more sauce.

Lesley persisted. "So, dogs, I guess? The rough stuff, not for dinnertime?"

"Oh—pretty much what you saw six months ago. Similar procedures. When we get done, though, nobody'll turn down the benefits, except Jehovah's Witnesses. We'll just do it till we get it right." Dana was aware of her own defensive calm, and resented it. "So—what's your news, from the skin trade?"

That was well over the line, she knew. Whatever—Lesley would remember the argument they'd had when she picked dermatology in the first place. She'd put the matter straight: did Lesley really want to deal with an endless parade of teenagers with acne, middle-aged golfers with precancerous cells to scrape off, women demanding another face-peel? Professional status not far above cosmetology? Presumably, now, she'd learned to live with it.

Lesley didn't react. "I've been thinking about parasites," she said. "At this point there's a group I'm in touch with, on mites. The populations everyone has, like eyelash mites. Interests me, but it's long-term work. Not like your heroic measures."

Dana let the words "heroic measures" just sit there between them, a little return of serve, while the waiter cleared the table. She broke open a fortune cookie, and dropped the slip of paper without looking at it. They talked on for a while longer, until Dana sensed it coming. Any moment, Lesley was going to raise the Jeremy issue. And she did.

"Something happened, Dana, that I feel uncomfortable telling you about. But I'd feel worse if I didn't, you understand?"

Well, no, Dana didn't, but she put her hands in her pockets and listened to Lesley's recital of what she overheard in the sauna last week, from the beginning to the inevitable end of Rosie the dog.

"Well," she said, "I thank God that poor animal's out of its misery. Final-stage heart disease since April, at least."

"And Jeremy?"

"Jeremy. Well. I just realized that what I do is not acceptable to someone with a lot of feeling. No!" She stopped Lesley from interrupting. "Think about it: there's nothing you, or Keisuke, have to excuse to each other. It's all a brutal profession, that's why we stick with people like us. I can't always be making excuses."

"Nothing to excuse? Think again," Lesley said. "There's always *everything* to excuse."

"Example."

"Keisuke telling lies to his dying patients—some of them. Including lies about what certain treatments entail. Bad stuff. As for me, I guess you know as well as anyone what needs excusing. Plus, did you think *I* like what you're doing? No, who could? And by the way, I doubt Rachlin's project will succeed in under five, maybe ten years. But you're still Dana: I can wait it out."

"Jeremy's more severe than you."

"The question is, is he more severe than you are?" Lesley gave her a straight look, then without waiting for an answer picked up the check and began figuring.

At the corner, they kissed goodbye and Dana walked up to Park Street to catch the Red Line home. She passed a man leaning against the Common railing, pouring something with exquisite care from a brown-bagged container into a Coke bottle. Fortifying himself before going to the shelter tonight, she figured; and there was a dash of rain already blowing in the gritty wind down Tremont. So, Jeremy had let old Rosie go at last. If he'd only asked her, Dana could have told him when an animal's had enough of dragging the air in, out, in, out. She could've told him, whether he asked or not, about the savagery involved in forcing it to keep going on.

But, she argued back at herself, the whole point was that she *couldn't* tell him. No, because whatever she knew didn't apply. Didn't apply because there was a history in place between him and the dog. Eight, nine years together: what she recognized objectively as a history of attachment, though not of a kind she could afford to understand. What she *did* understand was a pure insult to all that.

She descended the steps underneath the Common, two flights below. Down beside the dark subway tracks, a mouse of the same color crept about eating invisible bits that people must have dropped off the platform. A way to live. Dana's left hand rested in her pocket, warming a folded-up piece of paper. It was an e-mail printout from Jeremy, the day before. She knew what it said—

> I never went to your lab's website, although I knew it
> must be there. (As you're aware, your Dr. Rachlin likes
> publicity.) It seemed to me a matter of respect for pri-
> vacy not to look in, but only to hear what you wanted to
> tell me. Now it's five weeks since you stopped seeing me.
> My body doesn't forget you, Dana, it never will. Rosie's
> gone. That was past time, I'll concede. So I went to the
> lab website. I know what you do there, more or less: it's
> much what I expected. Can see why you thought being with
> me an impossible thing. But you were with me, it was pos-
> sible & it happened. I'm still not through, Dana. If ever
> you decide you can bear the contradictions, please

—and was thinking how it might be answered, how to endure what was (yes?) possible

L AST YEAR, A perturbed member of an undergraduate class I was teaching asked my senior colleague, was this true what I'd said, that they couldn't write "just a love story" anymore? By the time the question got reported back to me, I couldn't remember what exactly I'd said—whether it was an unwise general proclamation (preferable) or a local peeve directed at the unlucky manuscript of that day. Certainly I do remain convinced by Vivian Gornick's brilliant argument against sexual love as story salvation, in "The End of the Novel of Love." And yet.

And yet, although in stories as I see and write them, death is forever the Mastercard, love (however coolly encoded as desire) is the accepted-everywhere Visa. Moreover, as an old woman now, I find an innocence of feeling coming back to me, at moments, that I barely recognized at first, it's been so many years lost. So in "I'm Not Through," the writer makes amends, and pays tribute to love—with difficulty, the costly way.

Part of that difficulty is reflected in the short length of the story, and the margin of distance allowed by the third-person point of view. I was working with mystery here, and the best I could do was to approach it by indirection, through evidence supplied by characters on the periphery. At first I thought that my chosen point-of-view character, Lesley, could mediate everything needed. She was adequate, I imagined, to showing enough of the barrier keeping the true lovers—Dana and Jeremy—apart. That barrier of course is the nature of Dana's professional work.

A word on that barrier: I'm more interested all the time now in the ways that work and institutions can complicate, indeed determine, the shape of human life and character. It can't ever be underestimated. We tend to think that these matters are pretty intractable, because of the dangers of "information dump" when the writer has to confront the inside scene of a given workplace. But the risk had to be taken, has to be taken. In the case of this story, where animal experiments were that scene, I depended on Chekhov's advice, that the writer is obliged only to present a problem, not to solve or to supply the "answer."

After a first draft, I had to recognize that avoiding close contact with Dana and Jeremy, my lovers, was really a failure of courage on my part. So the final third of the story shifts towards Dana's point of view—at a time, though, when she's still avoiding the issue at stake. My last realization was that Jeremy's voice, his truth, must be heard, if only by e-mail. (I'm writing this now by e-mail....)

Do I imagine that a love-story begins after this written story ends? In my new innocence I might hope so, but not knowing I can only let the tribute to love rest here.

Wilton Barnhardt

MRS. DIMBLEBY

A LICE SHIELDS WAS convinced, idling at the curb across from Lakeside Elementary, that she had made a botch of motherhood. Occasionally her reverie was startled by an acorn hitting the roof of the van or, more serenely, by golden sycamore and burnished oak leaves arraying themselves on her windshield. Every moral precept, every rule she had written for herself, every parenting principle was blowing away, falling free, like the leaves, skittering down the street.

"Maybe it was broke when I came in here," her six-year-old said of the lamp that went crash after a sofa-trampolining session.

We'll just see what your father has to say about that, was her response, the very thing she'd sworn never to do: to cast her gentle, warm husband as the deferred engine of retribution, to threaten daughter with father. And it was no way to role-model womanhood for Katie: Mommy's too weak to pop that backside so we'll just let Daddy do it. Of course, Daddy didn't pop that backside either. The backside that was doing its damnedest to get popped, nearly every day.

Most of the time Alice spent with her daughter was here, in their mini-van, shuttling Katie from home to school to daycare or to gymnastics. On Tuesday-Thursday, it was Mrs. Childers's duty to pick up her daughter Anna with Katie; on Wednesday (today) and Friday, Alice carpooled the girls, and on Monday, since Anna had dance lessons, it was just Alice and Katie, mother and daughter on their own. Quality time.

Katie had long adopted the suffix "-head" in her dirty talk—*pottyhead, peepeehead, toilethead,* etc.—but last Monday she'd gotten ahold of the word *bitch.*

"We've had enough bad words today, young lady."

"I've heard you say it."

"I don't think you have."

"Uh-huh, I heard you."

"Mommy's an adult and can say what she likes."

"Well, I'm a kid and I can say what I like too." Then, when that failed to elicit a response: "It's *not* a bad word because a dog is a bitch. That's what Janie Helen Johnson says. Janie Helen Johnson says it in front of *her* mother all the time."

"Well, you go say it in front of Mrs. Johnson, because you're not going to say it in front of me."

Silenced, Katie contented herself with breathing the word *bitch.* Alice glimpsed the rearview to see the forbidden word was soundlessly repeating on her daughter's lips.

God hears you saying that, Alice had told her.

The whole point of introducing Katie to God in recent years, the benign, undoctrinaire and hippie-dippie Sunday school at First Universalist (reached by an ever-so-long, ever-so-early drive across town), was to instill a little order and goodness, to introduce Katie to an omnipresent God of Love who cares. Not some puritan with a clipboard, looking earthward to dispense demerits.

There had been a previous God-incident at the Giddyup Corral, Katie's favorite place to eat, where Alice didn't like to go but went anyway to forestall Katie whining all through dinner. In addition to sizzling steak-slabs served by men in cowboy attire, the Giddyup Corral boasted an "endless Texas-size" salad bar—so far Katie liked salad—and a more lavish dessert bar, which Katie liked way too much. There was this poor woman in a wheelchair at the next table. Nothing unusual, no tubes or monitors or oxygen tanks, just an old lady in a wheelchair. And Katie, ignoring her salad, was stuffing herself with cupcakes, standing on her chair like someone else's brat, to stare and to stare at her.

"Stop staring," Alice whispered. "You know it's rude."

And: "Would *you* like to be stared at?"

And: "We're leaving in one second if you don't stop looking over there."

But Katie kept gawking, chewing with her mouth open in mesmerized fascination by the wheelchair, only turning to her mother to perform a dismissive down-the-nose sneer.

"All right, we're going," announced Alice, leaving the better part of her own longed-for chocolate pudding in the bowl.

She grabbed Katie's hand and pulled her along, and damn if she didn't ogle the woman every step of the way to the exit. "I did not raise you to be that rude!" Alice snapped, en route to the car. And then: *You won't think it's so funny if God puts YOU in a wheelchair one day . . .*

God not only counted dirty words, but He put people in wheelchairs. And whereas Katie never felt a hint of guilt for acting up, Alice felt guilty enough for two. While the other girls in her first grade were getting taller and losing the baby fat, Katie was getting chunkier. It was Alice's fault because they did not usually eat at home, but dined out on fatty restaurant fare, on second runs to the Giddyup Corral dessert bar. Alice was too beat after ten-hour days to go home and cook. And she dared not say anything to Katie about her getting fat since Alice harbored a phobia of starting her six-year-old down the path of eating disorders and bodily self-hatred.

184 • Wilton Barnhardt

With her husband on longer and longer sales trips for a telecom firm that was sinking ever deeper on the NASDAQ, Alice had gone back to work as well. She hated it, hated going back to work with all her might, didn't realize just how very much she hated working until she didn't have a choice but to do it. She was ashamed of that, ashamed to be weak and wanting to remain a throwback of a house-wife who stayed home and did her aerobics tape, gabbed on the phone, watched the better talk shows, finished the paper, saw to the garden, while keeping the house presentable. They needed backup money in case Babblecom went bust. Poor teetering Babblecom with the cute cartoon hyenas yakkety-yakking on those nationwide digital cellular TV commercials. Well, it wasn't so cute now, was it?

Alice's first week as a legal transcriber was unendurable. Cramped hands, a bad back, constipation, indigestion from the vending machine snacks. Her amused husband reminded her, "You know, honey, this is what men do from adulthood to the grave—going to work. At least you got a few years to be at home with Katie."

The law firm Alice worked for was self-congratulatorally progres-sive, letting the mothers out of bondage for an hour every afternoon to go pick up their children. Last year had been the Golden Age of their mini-van minutes: Alice and Katie had shared the drive from home to kindergarten, from kindergarten to daycare, from daycare to home, with spontaneous diversions to parks and friends' houses and shopping with Mommy, with all the titanic events of the day to relive in detail together . . . It didn't occur to Alice until it was gone how splendid that chatty confidential time had been.

Then Katie got to first grade and changed. She wanted to ride the bus to school with the big kids, and not be seen with Mommy. Mommy found herself constrained to Monday-Wednesday-Friday. There were no confidences like in the kindergarten days, just aggrieved sighs and rolls of eyes and shaking heads—all new, acquired behavior—and exhalations of disgust: "Oh Mom, that's just *so feeble*." Or whatever the word of the day was, circulated by her cadre of prissy girlfriends.

"Katie, do you even know what 'feeble' means?"

"Oh *Mother* . . ." she'd say in maximum exasperation. *Mother,* like she was an heir to some British manor.

Another conversational gambit, another time: "Honey, who are your best friends this year?"

"I sit by Janie Helen Johnson for break time and nap-nap."

Alice wondered if Janie Helen Johnson liked her daughter in equal measure. How long before the popular ones decided Katie was getting chubby and couldn't tag along? It used to be first grade was too young for those discernments, but no longer.

"Miz Hamilton *hates* me."

"No, she doesn't."

"She made me sit in the back."

"What'd you do bad?"

"Nothing." The following pause suggested otherwise. "I had to sit next to Shrati."

"I remember her from Parents' Day. The Indian girl with the beautiful hair."

More eye-rolling, head-shaking and sighing—the trifecta. "Oh Mom. *Nobody* likes her."

"Isn't she nice?"

"She's funny-looking and, I *told* you, nobody likes her."

Alice thought carefully. "Don't you think it must be lonely being Shrati?"

"I dunno."

"Don't you think it's sad when nobody likes you?"

Her daughter had lost interest in the conversation and was looking out the window, mouthing the forbidden *b*-word. Then, sensing she was being looked at, Katie had met her gaze directly: "*Whut?*"

Alice had stared right back. My daughter, she decided, is a moral vacuity. Where are the fond feelings, the easy, schmaltzy compassion that little girls are known for? My daughter could drown sacks of kittens, put down Black Beauty, Old Yeller and Bambi's mother. My little angel is going to grow up and be a vicious dictator's wife in some Latin American country, responsible for the deaths of thousands. And history will record that Alice Shields, her mother, was wholly responsible.

Just then, there was a knock at the passenger-side door. It was Anna Childers. Alice pressed the button that automatically slid open the mini-van door, and Anna scrambled inside: "Good afternoon, Mrs. Shields."

See, that was the cosmic joke: Anna Childers, dream daughter. Pretty, polite, considerate, courteous, with splendid manners, a little lady at seven who wanted to spend time cooking and talking with her mommy . . . and Beverly Childers was the least maternal, most callous, oblivious mother alive. Beverly did nothing to deserve this gem of a daughter, this envy of all mothers. In fact, she did her best to undermine Anna but Anna was too stubbornly sunny to acknowledge it. Alice recalled, two Wednesdays ago, Beverly turning in the seat to survey Anna with pained wonder:

"You wore that today? Oh honey, not the yellow stockings . . ."

Anna shrugged. "But I have dance lessons later on—"

"Yellow leotards make a girl's legs look fat!"

Alice marveled that Beverly was so free to criticize her daughter's looks—and clearly *someone* got her child fed, dressed and off for school each morning but it wasn't Beverly. Once, Anna and Katie were talking about odd and even numbers, and Beverly broke in:

"I don't know about numbers and it hasn't done me any harm! Anna, you're probably like your silly old mother, dumb as a brick about sums and subtraction! I let Elmer deal with that . . ."

Didn't even the most remedial encouragement of her daughter's studies ever leave her mouth? Did not a drop of women's lib filter down? By Alice's measure, Beverly comprised wholly uninteresting enthusiasms: tennis, the club, what was in fashion magazines, hair and nails, shopping. Elmer Childers was a lawyer, so they were rich and his wife's perky shallowness could be well funded—and soon, Beverly promised, the Childerses were moving to a "much nicer" neighborhood. Beverly maintained blithe indifference about what her daughter was up to, what was being discussed in school, at school boards and PTAs, in the popular culture, in city and state politics. Do you suppose she could name the vice president of the United States?

Mention of Elmer that afternoon had led to talk of the club and a new restaurant in town, and Beverly offering, "Alice, why don't you join us girls for lunch?"

And Alice did, but once was enough. "Us girls" meant the women from the club who "tennissed" at the same hour, went for a soak, a sauna, carefully reassembled themselves in the ladies' locker room and then went for a boozy downtown lunch. Alice had no idea why she was included that time—maybe a regular dropped out and Beverly, like her friends, shared a horror of silence, chasms opening up in the absence of small talk. Nor was it that Beverly was a snob or wished to cast Alice as the dowdy friend; such calculation was beyond Mrs. Childers, who was innocent of complexity or insecurity. There were petite plates of warmed spinach and arugula salads with bits of goat cheese and toasted pecans, slices of pear—a good six bites' worth—all for $11.95. And balsamic vinegar everywhere, in everything, on the table in plates to douse bread in, on the salad. Wasn't the place called Balsamic? She couldn't recall, though that sounded right.

Once Katie and Anna were all buckled and secure in the back, it was off to the hair salon.

"Well, how do I look this time?" said Beverly, slinging herself up to the front passenger seat in impeccable tennis whites. "I told Henri I wanted everything swept back—see? What do you think?"

"You look beautiful, Mom," Anna said with genuine worship.

On Wednesdays, Beverly Childers was at her hair appointment two blocks from the school. Once, she had telephoned and laughingly proposed that Alice swing by and pick her up because her car was in the shop; then the Wednesday after that for another excuse. And soon, somehow, it became Alice's duty to swing by for Beverly every Wednesday. Since her hair appointment followed the boozy lunch which followed tennis, Alice reckoned that she kept at least one tipsy socialite off the road.

Today Beverly droned on about the house and how difficult it was to sell. The Childerses' house was worth $75,000 more than the Shields' upper-middle-class home; homes like the Shieldses' were driving down the value of the Childerses' fancier home. Good, thought Alice. Beverly, who knew nothing at all about real estate, indulged herself on the subject at length while Alice tuned out, straining instead to hear what Anna and Katie were whispering about.

Anna: " . . . and that's the house right there."

Katie: "Nawww, really?"

Oh no, Mrs. Dimbleby's house. Alice figured that Mrs. Dimbleby's accident was a staple topic among kids of a certain age throughout the neighborhood.

Anna: "Right there in the driveway . . ."

Katie made a car noise and then a *squish* noise, and they both started giggling.

"That's enough back there," Alice said. All that did was alert Beverly to the fun. She pivoted in the front seat and breathlessly asked, "What are you girls whispering about?"

Katie said, "Mrs. Dimbleby."

Alice made a mental note not to take this route again.

Beverly lost her good humor. "That woman oughta be in jail for what she did."

Katie: "Tell the story, Mommy."

Alice stalled with, "When you're a big girl we'll talk about it—"

"But I'm a big girl *now.*"

They passed the Dimbleby residence with both Katie and Anna frozen in fixed stares to the window. Soon the curve on Myrtlewood Drive robbed them of their view. "It was in the driveway," Anna whispered, revving up the topic again.

It was not in the driveway, Alice reflected.

"Mom," Anna now said, tapping her mother on the shoulder. "You said she did it in the driveway."

"That's what I thought I heard," Beverly said, apparently having no problem discussing a child's untimely death with her seven-year-old. "I can't imagine how she sleeps at night or gets up in the morning . . . If I had done something like that—"

Katie: "Mommy, *whut*? Tell the whole story!"

"I don't think," Alice began, "this is an appropriate topic for children."

"Oh for heaven sakes," Beverly chirped, "they're getting it from their classmates—I'm sure they talk of little else but that little girl getting . . . In the bright light of day, as well. That woman can't say she didn't see where she was going."

Katie made the *squish* noise again and she and Anna couldn't stop giggling. Then Katie made a face if she were a run-over child, tongue hanging out, making a noise, and that convulsed Anna even more. Alice was going to raise her voice but to her side Beverly was smiling and vibrating with suppressed laughter. "Not you too," Alice muttered.

"Better that they laugh about it than have nightmares about it!" Beverly's explosive chuckle filled the front seat with bourbon breath.

"She didn't mean to do it," Alice insisted.

"You actually talked to her?"

Yes, Alice talked to her. The accident was in all the newspapers, local news, on the radio, Mrs. Dimbleby's horrified face was ubiquitous in the city media for forty-eight hours: the pale skin, the jet-black hair pulled back like a schoolmarm's, the dark glasses and the slack open mouth, waiting for words, for an explanation to come out. Alice knew her as a kindergarten grade-mother, so she had taken over a casserole after the accident, thinking other neighbors or friends would be there too, gathered family, but Mrs. Dimbleby was all alone. Mrs. Dimbleby had answered the door very long after the doorbell, squinting around for reporters or gawkers. She looked tired but not like she had been crying. It was a face Alice would never forget, and the tone of voice—lost, already out of the remaining world, no longer here. Tranquilizers, probably.

"They were so mum with the details," Beverly pursued. "I guessed that she just snapped—"

"It wasn't that *at all,*" Alice said, turning into the Childerses' driveway ready to be rid of them, even well-behaved Anna, who had become thoroughly corrupted by Katie.

"Oh don't tell me she didn't snap. She's like those women you hear about who drown their kids in bathtubs—"

"Beverly!" Alice all but shouted. "That's not how it was. She didn't 'snap.' She was trying . . ."

Oh, everyone was all ears now. All righty, everyone wanted this story told, Alice would tell it:

"It had nothing to do with the driveway. She was coming home one day, much as we are now, driving down Myrtlewood, and she saw her youngest daughter in the yard. The rakes were lying around and there was a nice big, tall leafpile in the street, all ready for the city to pick up. So she decided to give her daughter a laugh and drive straight into the leaves. Something crazy, just to break up the dreary day, the way you just want to do a thing for some reason all of a sudden."

Mrs. Dimbleby, who insisted that the Dixie cups of punch be lined up in five rows of six, like soldiers in formation, that the animal crackers went in one bowl and the chocolate chip cookies in another. The only spontaneous, reckless moment in her life likely occurred on that autumn afternoon, an impulse to be a silly mommy, the last spark of giddiness her heart would ever know, a slight step on the accelerator . . .

"Well, she picked up a little speed and the daughter looked up . . ." Here she was saying what Mrs. Dimbleby had explained dry-eyed, word for word. " . . . and she plowed into the leaves, sending them scattering, then there was a scream and a horrible—a horrible . . . bump. And her oldest daughter had been lying down in the leafpile."

All was quiet.

"They were playing some game," she finished haltingly. "Some hide-'n'-seek game after raking the leaves."

Alice checked the rearview; Anna was wide-eyed, picturing the worst of it. Alice now wished she hadn't told the story—what was she thinking telling it?

Beverly mumbled, "That poor daughter who was watching it all . . . How could she ever forgive her mother?"

How could she not, thought Alice.

"I think I'd turn around and kill myself if I'd done such a dumb thing! No one just drives into a leafpile."

"The younger daughter," Alice began, finding her voice, "came to understand it was an accident. And there was some therapy but the younger girl is going to be all right about it," she added quickly. That was completely fabricated, but Alice felt something hopeful had to be wrenched from the whole thing.

Alice checked again in the rearview. Katie was lifting a button of her blouse to chew on, though that had been forbidden, since she frequently pulled the buttons off her shirts in this fashion. And Anna . . . Anna's lower lip was quivering and she started to sniffle, then audibly weep. "Oh Anna, honey," Alice began.

The Childerses' departure was very quick. Beverly hopped out, then dove into the back, unhooked Anna from her booster seat and belt, patted and aimed her toward the house, not saying anything as she closed the car doors. But then she circled back around; Alice rolled down her window.

"Alice," Beverly said pleasantly enough, and the worse for that, "Anna is going to be taking ballroom in addition to ballet starting next Tuesday and that means, on three afternoons a week, she won't be coming straight home from school."

"I see. I didn't mean to upset Anna—"

"Oh she'll be just fine. But you do see there's no good reason, really, to continue carpooling in this arrangement, hm? But it's been lovely to visit these last few weeks and I do appreciate you picking me up from Henri's."

"Well, I—we—still could . . ."

But Beverly had closed the door and was striding into her lovely home. Alice checked the rearview again. Katie was still chewing on the button—

"Uh-oh," she said, another one coming off in her mouth.

Alice put the car in reverse and backed out of the driveway and drove down their street very slowly, barely giving the mini-van any gas. She looked at Katie in the rearview, before connecting with her own tired expression.

"Did the story make you sad too?" she asked Katie.

"I dunno."

"Just don't laugh about those kind of things, that's all."

"I can if I want to," Katie offered without much conviction. "You wouldn't do that to me," she stated, just checking, as they turned into the daycare parking lot.

"No, honey."

But who knows what idiotic thing Mommy will do? Maybe, in trying to keep her little girl from getting fat, she would cause a lifetime of bulimic binges and self-loathing, cause Katie to be like those girls who confess on afternoon talk shows about cutting their bodies with a razor blade in secret. Maybe Alice would live to see the day when she turned her daughter over to the police or committed her to a sanitarium; or maybe a lifetime of therapists waited to find false memories of molestation at daycare or at Sunday school, or *real* memories, for all Alice knew and could control. Maybe, like all the other mothers in town, she would have Katie pumped full of some behavioral drug by the time she was nine, or maybe Alice was laying the groundwork for heroin addiction, kleptomania, unwanted pregnancy—well, there were solutions to those things—but how about riding with the boy who drives drunk and kills her, all because Mommy said don't date that one. Or the motorcycle punk with the swastika tattoo Katie would let beat her. Or the AIDS she would catch from being too promiscuous because Mommy implied her body wasn't pretty. Or just being screwed up and hating Mommy for no good reason, estranged the rest of their lives. Or the suicide Katie could commit. Yep, getting run down in the mini-van would be the quickest, Alice thought, clutching the steering wheel for support, but, more likely, it'll be a slow finish, spread over our whole lifetime with me only sure of one thing, that I have no business doing this, no clue how to bequeath my little girl a life of joy and promise. The odds are against even the naturally maternal. A few happy passages but, by and large, heartache, regret, folly.

"Mommy," said Katie as they walked together to the double doors of Tiny Tots. "Do I *have* to have Anna at my birthday party?"

"I thought you liked Anna."

"Janie Helen Johnson doesn't like Anna. I want to have a big cake with two kinds of icing and lots of chocolate milk. And candy corn? Can we have candy corn? And my presents have been *feeble*. They have to be much much better'n last year's . . ."

To both of their surprise, Alice popped Katie on the backside, a resounding whop. It didn't really hurt but Katie spun around openmouthed, not sure whether to cry or have a tantrum, wondering what extravagant behavior was called for—

"Not a word," said her mother, with new resolve welling up from somewhere, some willful second wind, perhaps a gift from Mrs. Dimbleby. "Not a single word."

I GREW UP ON Ray Bradbury, sci-fi mags and comic books by the dozens, a ratty volume of O. Henry, *Alfred Hitchcock's Mystery Magazine* and *Boy's Life,* not to mention my grandparents' one short-story anthology, *World's Greatest Tales!,* featuring yellowing pages of Maupassant, Poe, Bierce, Lardner, Shirley Jackson, all of which contributed to my twelve-year-old sensibility that the short story wasn't much good unless it had a surprise ending, a sneaky twist at the end, like a *Twilight Zone* episode. Whereas my taste in novels is broad and tolerant (I sat my Oxford master's exams on *Finnegan's Wake!*), whereas any sort of Jamesian dawdle and Proustian self-indulgence is all right by me, it took me a long time to allow the short story the same latitude to stop being pure plot-driven entertainment and just exist for its own sake.

Shamefully, I am a latecomer to the very sort of story I've written here, the place where most writers sensibly start: the small slice-of-life scene, an incident or a moment explored, considered or maybe just brushed against. More importantly for my growth as a writer, I suppose, is that it is "small" in subject matter, family stuff, parents and kids, carpooling neighbors—small, that is, compared to the putative ambitions of a novel. Increasingly, I've come to see that all the high drama in the world rests in our day-to-day chores, our routines with our loved ones, if we're conscious, if we're observant.

Though the subject matter might be a departure, the storytelling probably is what I always try to do, I hope: capture the vivid inner life, the elaborateness of self, moments of guilt or pride, envy or worship, to follow the unexpected and perverse play of someone's mind.

Originally, having—god knows how—imagined the tragedy in the leafpile, I thought I would write it from Mrs. Dimbleby's point of view . . . but that became weary, like that second reprise of "You'll Never Walk Alone" in *Carousel*; no amount of finesse could take the Oprah-segment out of it, the nobly going forth from tragedy, the owning of her foolish accident with her head held high. Much better to let Mrs. Dimbleby be this unknowable, odd woman down the block whose infamy lay uneasily on that idyllic neighborhood, and better yet to have an outside observer with motherhood issues of her own.

I suppose the prime challenge of the tale for me was what *not* to include. Alice's husband, his role in the family dynamic? Alice's own childhood and her experience with her mother? Why not provide more reminiscences about when Katie was more angelic, more Mommy's little girl—why drop in now, when she's a total brat? I wrote paragraphs in every one of those directions, then took them out. A little voice kept saying, "This is about Alice's fears of being a bad mother, and her observation of changes in her amoral—or is it premoral?—little girl and her sense that this is her own failure," and so those other digressions fell away.

If the reader doesn't get a real sense of Katie, if she seems to exist only sparsely in dialogue—then good, that's how I wanted it, to reinforce her having become a stranger, unrecognizable to her own mother. Is there too much about shallow and selfish Beverly Childers? Why include the time Alice went along with her crew to Balsamic Restaurant? I cut that paragraph and then missed it and restored it. It seemed to reinforce Alice's isolation from the other women on her block, her age and roughly her income—it was a shorthand to shut her out of other social currents and get her back in that mini-van with her daughter, that insular, nearly codependent world in which there was no real peace.

As much of an outcast as she feels she is, Alice has nothing on the scorned pariah Mrs. Dimbleby, with whom, spiritually, Alice makes common cause. People, it always strikes me, live through the most amazing losses, deprivations, miseries, and somehow keep plodding forward. Katie getting a premiere pop on the backside is Alice saying, hey, I'm not going anywhere, I'm going to be around and in your development, kiddo, for the long haul, good or bad.

Ehud Havazelet

PILLAR OF FIRE

SOMETHING MADE HIM turn around. He had said his goodbyes and was halfway down the walk to his car when something made him stop. It couldn't have been the gravel, the way it popped and slid under his feet, and it couldn't have been the light in the trees ahead, the way the air shimmered the leaves. It couldn't have been these but he felt it was, as if for a sudden sickening moment he could feel the earth moving through space. He stumbled, then stopped. He turned around.

They were there still, on the elegantly sagging porch, among the plant hangers and chimes, his wife and this man, Oliver, one padded arm across her shoulders. They were watching him. In Maura's face David saw a flicker of concern—she must have known he would see it and he thought this was why he stumbled, what he had turned to see. But then Oliver lifted a beefy hand and called out "Safe travels," and David watched his wife look at the man, saw the raised eyes and dip of the shoulder, the happy, intimate surrender to the embrace. He found his keys this time and reached the car, gunned the engine, feeling a hollow pleasure at the sound the tires made, the spatter of pebbles he left behind.

He drove fast. He pulled onto the road fast and didn't slow down. He tapped the accelerator and the big car responded. He breathed the wind, felt the gears mesh deep in the engine, and told himself he was all right.

It was the sweater that got him. Not the fact that she had left him. Not the fact that she had left him for a potter—named Oliver, for God's sake—a potter who *looked* like an Oliver, all furry eyebrows and nodding concern, smug fingers praying in front of his face. You're angry, Oliver had said. You're in a lot of pain. They were in his artistic living room, books piled everywhere, bowls, knickknacks, curios, assorted cultural artifacts, African, Chinese, casually heaped in the corners. I can see it in your face, the potter had said, tilting his head to show he meant it, and David wanted to clock him. But that wasn't it. Not his tacky Berkshire chateau, with the wind chimes and hummingbird feeders and happy gargoyles. Not even that the potter seemed to enjoy David's company, inviting him for dinner. Couscous and salad, Oliver said, homemade bread. Stay and eat. We'd like you to. Sure, David had thought. We. And after dinner do *we* go upstairs with my wife?

Well, that wasn't what got him, though you'd think so.

It was the sweater, white and a thick lumpy blue in some pathetic amateur crosshatch. It sat on him like a wool sack. All their years together Maura had knitted—socks, scarves, mittens, whatever—without finishing anything. As far as David knew, she had never completed a single piece. There was a wicker basket in their living room full of abandoned efforts, it made him sick to look at, a little woolen graveyard in the corner by the TV. Then all he had to do was take one look at the sweater Oliver wore, the way it bunched in the shoulders and tented at the waist, to know it was Maura's, she'd finally goddamn finished one. And for some reason this was what stuck with him, came up in his throat to choke him.

He didn't know everything, he knew that. He thought he had made that clear. He wasn't perfect and he'd made mistakes. He knew that too. But here—here was craziness. David, she had said, this is Oliver. Like he was a neighbor in the building, some guy in the street—except he had his hand on her back at the time, except he stood there in the world's ugliest sweater, *his* goddamn ugly sweater, if anyone was interested, or that should have been his.

Seven years they had lived together. Maura was his wife—did that mean anything? They paid the mortgage on the co-op. They had a bedroom suite and a dining room suite, a stock portfolio, they owned this car. They ate Chinese twice a week, liked *every* Schwarzenegger movie, preferred MacNeil to Lehrer and thought the show had gone down—what were they doing, if not building a life? Didn't they have plans?—moving out of the city eventually, children, trips to South America, Europe, all over the place. When David looked into his future he saw Maura there, nothing else.

He had sat there, them on the couch, he in a chair covered with some itchy Indian rug, drinking tea that smelled like roots out of one of Oliver's mugs. I want to stay, Maura said, smiling at them both. I'm happy now.

Well, it was crazy. They sat there, three people drinking tea as if they were normal, as if the day was, but it wasn't, they weren't. It was insane. There was an order to things, David wanted to explain, but how do you explain anything to crazy people? You didn't just wake up one day with a wife and go to bed that night without one. You didn't make plans, live your life a certain way for thirty years just to have it disappear one afternoon at four o'clock because some bearded guy in the woods gave you tea and told you he felt your pain. Didn't anyone see that? There was an order to things. If you broke that up, what would be next? And what did she mean, "now"?

He careened down the middle of the blacktop, looking straight ahead, both hands holding the wheel. His throat hurt, his head ached like he was coming down with something, a rare and sudden disease.

He hoped he was. He hoped they found his body in the morning. Would serve her right. He took the curves at sixty-five, seventy, fishtailing, rear tires catching roadside brush. He pressed the accelerator, not caring, faster on the straightaways, glimpsing houses behind barriers of hedge and lawn, a man cutting his grass stopping to look as David roared by, gripping the wheel and leaning into the acceleration, feeling for the floor of the car through the pedal, until a wooden fence sprang up to fill his windshield and he slammed the brakes, sliding. The car fanned slowly behind him, came to rest at an angle to the fence. He could reach out and touch it if he tried. Ahead, a pasture sloped away to a white barn on a hill. Not five feet from him a Holstein, munching grass, lifted a massive indifferent face, its black eye, a huge wet marble, glistening dully in the light. David cursed the cow, the fence, the barn, floored the car in reverse, squinting through dust and rubble until he managed to turn it around.

He didn't understand what happened next. Five hundred yards from the highway he must have done something—swerved, slowed, who knew?—because suddenly in his rearview mirror there was a black muscle car, a Mustang maybe, honking and flashing its lights. "That's right, you sonofabitch," David muttered, saying it louder as he slowed and signaled he was entering the highway with the car still on him, high beams and horn going, white face hovering in his mirror, so close David wasn't sure if he felt a tap, screaming now, "That's *right,* you sonofabitch!" pulling over on the tight curve of the entrance ramp, some kind of flowering bush streaming up his hood. He stomped the brake, one wheel off the road, branches scraping his windshield, dust sifting through the open windows. He stuck his head out to call, "Die, you fucker!" as the driver, a kid with long hair and a baseball cap, lightly gave him the finger and disappeared behind grillwork and red taillights.

———

HE HAD HAD his affair first, Rhonda, an intern at the firm. He wished she were waiting for him now, in her two-room apartment near the park. He was still up-and-coming then, the partners' darling. The Crestview deal hadn't collapsed yet, he was twenty-nine and overseeing a fifty-million-dollar investment, and he knew he was watched, talked about. He felt like he was in a movie, the camera always on him.

Rhonda was fresh from the Virginia program, one of this year's eager crop, her cubicle right outside his office. Her first day he helped her hang a Hockney print and they couldn't get it straight, no matter what they did. They joked about how many thousands of dollars had gone into their architecture degrees, with the result that together they couldn't hang a picture. He made her laugh, and when she caught him looking at her she seemed to like it. That was all it took. He knew he could have her. She was beautiful and talented and smart and she carried herself with the seductive air of someone who knew she would get whatever she wanted. For a while, six weeks, maybe, this had included him.

David had thought it was love, because it changed everything. New vitality stunned him. He rose early to get to the gym, watched what he ate, made sweeping design modifications to the project without needing to consult anyone. He was witty with the partners, firm with the contractors, airy and patient with the interns and staff. He took up cooking, started reading again. His physical reflexes seemed to have improved, if that was possible. All day he was aware of Rhonda's whereabouts—as he showered in the mornings he could imagine her rising from bed and moving through her darkened rooms. At the office he could sense where she was, in the conference room, at the coffee machine, as if they were hooked up by radar. Their movements seemed charmed, synchronous, touched by some mysterious and happy significance. They talked about this, whether people's lives moved along a preordained path, if their meeting had been in the cards from the start. Rhonda told him he had looked strangely familiar, even that first day, and David told Rhonda—this was past midnight, in his office, take-out boxes and clothing scattered on the floor around them—that he felt drawn to her almost magnetically. She had a glow, he told her—he'd never seen anything like it—in her eyes, her hair, around her shoulders, and it was as if he walked in it all day. He could breathe it. It was something he had never felt before and he was certain it was love.

He was so certain, when he told Maura he believed she must have known, felt it on him, smelled it on his skin. It was a terrible thing to expect her to understand, but this wasn't about them—not ultimately, not in its deepest sense. He had come home after she was asleep, had woken her, the words rushing out as if by their own momentum—he couldn't lie anymore, it wasn't fair to anyone to lie, not about this, it was too big. What was happening to him was unusual, if it happened to you once in your life you were lucky. Could she try and see that?

But she had not known. When he told her, her jaw actually dropped open, her eyes stretched wide as if he had hit her in the face. She sat on the couch in her robe and nightgown, hair pushed sideways from sleep, and when she started to cry he felt desperate to do something, hold her, get her an aspirin, take it all back. He stood there—he realized then he still had his coat on—and said, "Can I do anything?"

Her laugh startled him. She looked up at him, her eyes wet, as if they'd been laughing a good long time. She shook her head as if this were a joke she'd remember and when she moved past him to the bathroom put a hand on his shirt. "Thanks," she said. "You've done enough for one night."

When she came out of the bathroom her hair was brushed and she held a glass of water. Her eyes were dry. He stood by the couch with his coat on—it was hard to move, hard to look at her—while she asked him a few questions. She held her jaw in a hand and looked at the floor as if she could barely stay awake.

"So this is the big one," she said.

"Yes."

"The one we all hear about. The lifesaver."

"I think so."

"Right," she said, rising, pulling her robe close and moving toward the bedroom. "You'll have to excuse me now. Those of us mortals untouched by bliss need our sleep."

She gave him a week to decide. When he told her nothing had changed—it had, he had lied; Rhonda had taken the news of his confession coldly, was even then moving subtly away—Maura had nodded once, as if a bargain between them had been sealed. "Okay," she said. "Are you staying for dinner? Frozen lasagna sound good?"

Over the next few weeks, brochures appeared around the apartment—skiing, woodworking, Outward Bound, pottery classes—and sometimes Maura wasn't home when he arrived. Twice there were notes taped to the refrigerator, saying she'd be gone for the weekend, back Sunday night, late.

HE GOT OUT of the car to check for damage, saw nothing obvious, not much he could tell from where it sat, tilted off the road, covered in branches. One of these whipped him in the arm when he tried to get in, so he whipped it back. Then the door closed on his shoulder, so he got out again and slammed it a few times, then kicked the tire until he hurt his foot and went up front to lean against the hood. A car or two passed on the ramp, people offering expressions curious or hostile, and David returned their looks blankly, as if to say he belonged here, just where he was, and had every intention of staying as long as he felt like it. He followed them with his eyes. He hoped someone else would give him the finger. He hoped someone would try it.

Ahead of him, over the highway threading west, what might turn into a fine sunset was taking shape, clouds stacked in thin wedges across the horizon, just tingeing red. Maura loved sunsets, David remembered. She liked to sit in front of the window and watch them. He wondered if she would be watching this one. He thought of her coming out onto Oliver's porch, drawing a shawl over her shoulders—she'd probably completed an entire wardrobe for them both—Oliver following with more dirt tea. He pictured her here with him, out for a picnic, roast chicken and a bottle of wine in a hamper in the trunk, pausing on their way just a moment for the view, watching, no need to talk.

And then he saw himself as he was, hours from home, alone and ridiculous with his car half off the road in an oleander bush, gazing at an empty sky. The pain was back in his throat and he moved angrily, as if to shake it off. He threw the car door open and climbed inside.

HE THOUGHT THE place was empty, maybe shut down. The big neon light was working—red letters flashing T & R—but there were no cars out front. Then to the side of the building he saw two trucks and through the window a waitress pouring coffee at the counter. He parked the car and got out.

The phone was in back, at the end of a short hallway between the bathrooms. It had a rotary dial, which confused him a moment—he hadn't seen one in years. He fumbled for change, surprised to notice his hands were still shaking, then remembered he didn't need any. A toilet flushed on the other side of the wall. He dialed the three numbers as a man opened the bathroom door, water still running behind him. David had to turn to one side to let him pass. A woman came on the line.

"Yes, hello," he said. "Is this 911?"

"Emergency services, sir. Can I help you?"

"I'm calling . . . I need to report an accident."

The man who had come out of the bathroom immediately struck

up a loud conversation at the counter. David had trouble hearing. "Excuse me?" he said.

"Is anyone hurt?"

"Yes. I think so. I'm not sure."

"Were you involved in this accident, sir?" the woman asked.

"No," David said, "I just saw the car."

"And you say someone is hurt?"

"I think so. I was driving by and this car was overturned, off the side of the road. I couldn't see. I think the driver is still inside."

"Did you make certain someone was inside?"

"No, I was already past it. It was upside down, off the road. That's why I'm calling."

She asked for the location and he told her. Behind him, somebody said, "Hey, it ain't jailbait if you *marry* it," and somebody answered, "Yes, it is, you dumb fuck," and they laughed. David leaned into the wall to hear better. Someone had written "Bobby" in green marker, then a number.

"Can you describe the vehicle?" the woman asked.

He told her. A black car, souped up, maybe a late-model Mustang. The kid inside had long hair and was wearing a baseball cap.

"You did see the driver, then, sir," the woman said.

"Before," David said. "He passed me on the entrance ramp, before. I saw him then."

There was a pause, as if she were considering the truth of what he told her.

"Will you send someone?" David asked.

He heard a breath through the line and he waited for her to say something, but she didn't. "Thank you," he said, and the line went dead.

David turned around, unsure what to do next, and as he did, the conversation in the diner stopped, as if they had been waiting for him. One of the men at the counter made movements with a hand, as if he were entering numbers in a calculator; the second man watched. The man who had passed him was leaning against the counter, a mug of coffee propped on his large stomach. He wore a black leather vest over a cowboy shirt, a straw cowboy hat pushed back on his head. He looked at David. The other two swiveled to look at him also, while the waitress stacked empty plates on the shelf leading into the kitchen. David stood there, feeling the change still in his hand. He felt they were waiting for him to do something. He turned back to the phone and lifted the receiver, reaching in his shirt pocket for a piece of paper. He dropped the change into the slot and dialed the number.

He had had some trouble getting the car back on the road. He had to pull a branch from one of the wheel wells, and he had to rock the car several times before he could regain the asphalt. Then he had to stop to remove some twigs that had lodged against the windshield, and as he drove, a sound, new to him, rumbled dimly from under the chassis. He decided to ignore it. He had to tell himself to unclench his teeth and twice had to take his hand off the steering wheel to flex it. He realized he was shaking. There was a sour taste in his mouth, adrenaline, he supposed, but maybe, on top of it all, he really was getting sick. He felt his forehead, and the side of his neck. He decided music was what he needed and turned on the radio as he cautiously entered the highway, but all he could find was country and a religious talk show, so he upended a cassette case on the seat near him and kept one eye on the speedometer as he threw the tapes around, looking for something he liked.

Leaning over this way, he had nearly missed it. But it caught at the edge of his vision, a single tire rotating slowly in the air off the side of the highway. He eased his car left, slowed until he saw another tire, this one still, then the whole car, a black Mustang overturned in the culvert, its wheels in the air and its windshield a starburst of shattered glass. Steam leaked from the engine. He turned nearly full around but couldn't see inside it as he passed.

After three rings the phone was answered and David opened his mouth to speak. Celestial music, complete with harp and birdsong, filled his ear. Answering machine. He waited until a soothing voice—Oliver's—said, simply, "Please."

He realized he had no idea what to say. Why had he called? Behind him, conversation was picking up again, he could hear the waitress joining in. He turned to the wall.

"Hi, it's me. It's David. Maura, listen, can I talk to you a minute? Anybody there?" He waited a few seconds. From behind him came laughter, a wolf call. "Look, I'm sorry to bother you, something's happened, I'm a little upset. There's been an accident, on the road. Not me, I'm fine, some kid in a car. He flipped it. I didn't see him flip it but I saw him, that's what's weird, I saw him not five minutes before . . ." Behind him the cowboy said, "You think I didn't *try*? *Two* of 'em? Believe me, Cochise, I tried," and the men laughed. David continued. "Look, I'm sorry I took off like that. I had to go. I just . . ."

A beep sounded in his ear and a metallic voice said, "Thank you." Feeling a flush come into his face, he fished for more change and quickly redialed the number. Behind him the cowboy said, "I don't know, Neptune or someplace. Wherever in the hell they come from." "They come from Uranus," another man said, to a burst of laughter. David tried pressing into the wall. He read Bobby's number three times while the phone rang.

After the music he said, "Maura, could we talk? Just me and you, just for a few minutes. I think we should, you know? Maybe we could talk some more." He twisted deeper into the corner, speaking lower. "The thing is, I really need to tell you some things, there's some things you really should hear." He checked his watch. "I'll be home in four or five hours, maybe you could call me, or we could talk in the morning . . ."

The beep sounded a second time and he hung up before he could be thanked again. He faced the diner. The three men were looking at the waitress, who was mopping the counter with a rag. She had a cigarette in her other hand and she spoke, moving the cigarette in the air for punctuation. "Well," she said, "and this is just me, mind. Okay—say it really *was* the end of the world, and you really *were* the last?" She paused for effect, pulled on the cigarette. "I guess that's when I finally learn to do without."

This was met with a roar of laughter, the loudest yet, even the cowboy, to whom David supposed the comment was addressed, laughing hard, his cup of coffee jiggling merrily on his stomach. Something was wrong with the light in this place, or maybe it was the air in here. The four of them by the counter made up a disturbing tableau, as if he had never seen one like it before. As if in walking to the phone he had crossed an invisible barrier, where the air was different, the light changed, and now he couldn't get back. He shook his head to rid it of this stray, useless notion, moved before they could again look up and see him standing there.

As he passed behind them David saw what the man at the counter was doing. He had one of those games, a triangle with wooden pegs, the object being to eliminate as many of the pegs as possible by jumping them. He worked quickly, dropping pegs on the counter, then sweeping them up and starting over. When the others laughed he joined in. David watched him leave four pegs, then two, then four again. Nobody looked up as David closed the door and went out into the evening.

IT WAS FULL dusk. The eastern sky was deep blue edged with purple, and beyond the highway, to the west, he could see a still band of sunlight low over the far hills. He stood a moment, breathing the cool air, then realized he didn't see his car. It took a few seconds to figure that he'd come out the wrong door, had somehow walked right past the door he had entered through, to the side lot, where two trucks sat, one idling contentedly with its running lights on. He crossed the gravel to his car.

There were two girls, one in the passenger seat with the door open—had he forgotten to lock it?—her feet out on the ground. She was leaning forward, examining his cassettes. At her feet lay a red plastic backpack. The other girl, maybe a year or two older, was stretched on her back on the hood of his car, looking at the sky. As he watched she made a tube of her hands and peered through it, scanning the horizon. They were twelve and fourteen, maybe younger.

He stopped again—would this insane day never end?—and looked around for another car that might be his. But there was a single car in the lot, his, obviously. He must have left the door open, these two had seen him do it and marched right in. He walked over.

"Can I help you?" he said.

The girl on the hood sat up to look at him. "Hey," she said. The younger girl smiled. In the back seat, he could see now, were two duffel bags and one of those old-fashioned cosmetics suitcases, round and powder blue.

"Can I help you?" David said again.

The girl on the hood said, "Hey, mister, you just missed a stupendous sunset. Superial. What would you give it, Ange?"

"Ten," the younger girl mumbled, her face lost in lank brown hair as she leaned over the cassettes.

"It wasn't *that* good. Nine point three, maybe nine point five, tops," the other girl said. She smiled at David and hooked a thumb at the girl in his car. "She's a romantic."

David didn't say anything.

"Cool car," the older girl said, and the younger girl looked up and repeated it. "Yeah, we like it."

His eyes were adjusted to the failing light now, he could see them more clearly. The girl on the hood was older than he'd thought; still, maybe fifteen at the most. She also had long hair that, when she turned to look at him, fell in two skeins that nearly covered her face. She was dressed in jeans and running shoes, both filthy, and a man's green army jacket. She had a silver ring through a nostril and another through an eyebrow. The other girl looked even younger than twelve.

She was plump and fresh-faced—even in this light he could see two red cheeks—and wore black high-top sneakers, a heavy sweater several sizes too large, and a baseball cap backwards. She smiled shyly at him.

"So," the older girl said. "How far you going?"

"Why? Why do you need to know that?" David asked, coming closer now, running his fingers on a series of wide scrapes along the body of the car.

"We thought we might ride with you awhile, you know, if that was cool."

David was at the side door now. He bent to peer in at their luggage. The younger girl had stacked the cassettes neatly in their holder; otherwise he could see nothing had changed. He stood up and looked at the girl on the hood.

"You broke into my car?"

She was off the hood in an instant, the car between them, hands up as if he were about to rush her. "We didn't," she said.

He looked at her a moment, then at the younger girl, still sitting in the car. She hadn't moved. An odd, sweet smell came off her, as if she'd been eating candy all day. "It was open, sir," this girl said, looking up. "We just sat in it to wait."

"You left the keys," the other girl said, keeping her distance. She reached in her jeans and came out with his keys. She tossed them at him. "Someone could have stolen it. We watched it for you."

He caught the keys, not believing what was happening. He ran both hands through his hair, stepped away from the door, and leaned against the car. He supposed he could have left them in his rush to get inside, though he had never done something like that before. The sensation that he was becoming ill returned, delivered on a surge of weariness. Maybe they would help him stay awake. "I'm not going far," he said, then, too tired to lie, added, "on this road." He moved to the driver's side. "I turn south a few miles ahead."

The older girl was around the car before he had finished talking. "That's cool," she said, nodding at him, motioning for the younger to climb in back. She got in and reached for the seat belt. "So do we."

HE LEARNED THEIR names. The older was Drew, the younger was Angie, though recently she had decided to be called Sandra, Drew said. They had left Toronto that morning, heading south. They were from Cleveland, originally, but that was history. Drew spoke rapidly, using her hands, looking from him to the highway, then back, talking all the while. Here was something, Drew said. Did he realize that, statistically, more people in this country were from a certain place than actually still in it? This was a proven fact. He could look it up. David glanced at her as he drove. Her expression was intimate, animated, as if he could not fail to be delighted by what she told him.

"I like this car," Drew said, touching the dashboard, the door panel. "I've seen cars, you know? This one's nice."

"You've been hitchhiking all day?" David asked.

"Yup." She found the makeup mirror on the flip side of the sun visor. She turned the light on and explored her face, pressing here and there, arranging her hair with her fingers. She smelled of smoke and unwashed clothing, of leaves. From the back seat, off the other girl, came that odd, sweet smell, cotton candy or caramel. Drew opened the glove compartment and looked inside. David was about to tell her that was private when she snapped it shut and sat back in her seat. "You can tell about people from their cars," she said. "Also their accessories, jewelry and tattoos and stuff. You see that big guy in the diner?" Drew said, pulling her legs up under her on the seat. "What was his name, Ange—Newt?"

"Tex," Angie said sleepily from the back. "And call me Sandra."

"Yeah," Drew said, "Newt. All Newt could talk about was marriage, you know? He'd been married, what, four times? Like who would marry him *once*?" She shook her head. She pulled her hair back and examined something on her scalp in the mirror. "He had a cousin, Louise, who was married at thirteen. This was in Tennessee, he said, and he had pictures of the wedding back in the sleeper. He offered to show us. He offered to put us up at a motel and buy us dinner." She flipped the visor up, apparently satisfied, and looked at David. "He was all over Sandra, kept putting his hand on her leg, you know, like, Oh, let's see, where'd I leave the gearshift this time? He said he'd take us to a Ramada Inn and buy us steak dinners, like we were cannibals or something. You mind if I smoke?"

She cracked the window and pulled a packet of cigarettes from her pocket. "Yes," David said, "I do."

She looked at him seriously, nodded twice, and put the cigarettes away. "Newt said he'd drive us all the way to San Francisco, wherever we wanted to go, right, Ange?" Drew said. There was no answer from the back seat. David pulled into the right lane and pressed the cruise control. "As if," Drew said quietly.

HE DROVE WEST, looking for the turnoff to the city. He'd driven this road, but only in daylight and not for many years before today. He searched for landmarks he might recognize from this afternoon, but it was useless in the dark. Nothing looked familiar. In the back seat the younger girl slept, the smell still coming off her. Sweet, but not like candy, he decided—thicker, more chemical. Drew, beside him, ate from a big paper bag of granola, which she twice offered him. She said it was good stuff, cleaned out your system. This guy she'd met in Buffalo, Sal—you'd think that was a girl's name but not in this case—Sal ate only granola and yeast extract and legumes, totally macro. Did David know legumes? Like beans, but with fiber. Good stuff. Sal said he expected to live till ninety, more if he cut out the smokes. She put her feet up on the dashboard as she ate, and he asked her not to do that, and a few minutes later she did it again, humming to herself, and he opened his mouth to say something, but decided to let it go.

The turnoff had to be around here somewhere. This day already seemed endless and he was exhausted, with several hours of driving ahead. He couldn't have missed it. He had to concentrate. He would find the turnoff, then talk to these girls, find out where they were headed. He would find a phone and call Maura again. Maybe she and Oliver were back, or maybe they were in the house, screening calls. He did this himself, standing by the answering machine as it recorded, deciding whether to answer. He would call, and by the calm tone of his voice he would let Maura know he was okay, she could pick up the phone. He thought of what he'd said earlier, that he needed to talk. He remembered the sense of urgency that had come over him in that moment—he really did need to talk to her, though what he had to say eluded him now. It would come to him, something reasonable and heartfelt and calm that would show he'd been thinking things over, that it was okay to answer the phone.

"So I hope you don't mind words," Drew was saying.

"Pardon?" David said.

"Words. You know, talking, verbilation. I talk a lot, have you noticed? Some people do. Angie doesn't talk much, so I talk for us both. She says I'm a people person, which is why I like to talk, but I don't know, I'm not that overly fond of people as a whole, are you? I think they're overrated, as a whole. That's why we tried Canada."

"Fewer people?"

"Not in Toronto. You'd be surprised."

David looked in the mirror at the sleeping girl. She had pulled her legs onto the seat and laid her head on the duffels. He wondered if it was warm enough back there. She couldn't be comfortable, but she seemed to be sleeping soundly.

"Why does she smell like that?" he said quietly.

"Angela?" Drew turned to look at her. She patted a high-topped foot. "That's diabetes, what it smells like when you're not on your medicine. Your body manufactures too much glucenase or fructone and it exudes right through your skin membrane. That's what that smell is."

"She has diabetes?"

"Yeah. Bummer, huh?"

"Why isn't she on her medicine?"

"We ran out," Drew said, pulling a string rucksack from the floor to her lap. "That's why we came back to the States. To get more. That and that people thing we were talking about."

"Is she all right?" David asked, again checking the sleeping girl in the mirror.

Drew was drinking from a bottle of water, which she wiped off with her sleeve and offered to him. "Yeah, she's fine for a day or two. She's just tired. We'll hit a clinic tomorrow. Where are we heading?"

"New York," David said, aware he had not thought he would be driving them that far. He was confused momentarily and took the bottle from Drew. He drank some out of politeness, and was surprised at how thirsty he was.

"Le grand tamale," Drew said, taking the bottle from him. She had a way of looking at you—smiling, eyebrows slightly raised in anticipation—even when you weren't talking, that David found disconcerting. "Cool. So, what do you do?"

Ahead the road was filled with lights, headlights pulsing at him from the opposite lane, red lights weaving in his own. The sound from the bottom of the car, a steady, dull rumble, worried him, and he knew he'd have to deal with it in the morning. The turnoff must be coming up soon, he knew, but in the meantime he was overtaken by weariness. It surged through his body and lodged between his shoulders in a blunt ache. He'd driven from New York that morning, nearly five hours each way; still, it felt as if he'd been driving much longer. Glancing in the rearview, he was met by a confused sensation, the landscape there floating unattached, streaming away from him, no relation to the ground he had just covered. He looked over at the girl next to him. She had put the bottle down and was looking at him expectantly. She gestured with her hands. "Wrong question?" she said.

"No," David answered. "No. I'm an architect. Or I've been an architect. I'll be one for a few more weeks."

She nodded sympathetically. "Lost your job, huh?"

He nodded.

"Life changes can be good," she said. "Remember Sal? He used to be a barber." From the back seat came a soft thick snoring, and Drew looked at Angela, then back at David, smiling. He smiled too.

"How long have you been on the road?" he asked.

"Couple of years."

"And you're all right?" he said. "How do you get by? She can't be more than twelve."

"Thirteen, actually," Drew said, pushing her hair back over her ears, then immediately shaking it loose. "We do okay."

"Even if she's sick? That must be hard on her."

"I take care of her. Better than what she left."

She was slumped against the door now, looking ahead with a blank, unmoving stare. David understood she had heard this lecture before.

"So what do you like best about traveling?" he said. The weariness had crept behind his eyes now, into his head, where it weighted like sand. He was afraid he might close his eyes a moment and miss the turnoff. He needed to talk. "You must have seen some interesting things."

"Oh, yes. Absolutely," Drew said, drawing her legs up under her again, liveliness back in her face. "We met a trucker with six fingers on each hand, this was just last week. The sixth was not really what I'd call a regulation finger. It just sort of lay there, like this." She held one finger over the other hand to demonstrate. "It didn't move or anything. It was awesome, though. Superial." He nodded, encouraged her to go on. "We saw a flood in Indiana last spring. Whole town underwater. We saw a rowboat go by the firehouse with three dogs in it, no people, just three dogs, two with their paws over the side, the other running from the front to the back, howling like crazy. You would've thought dogs could swim, but these dogs were scared." She stopped for a moment to see if he had anything to add, then continued. "Okay." She put both hands up near her face, as if she'd saved the best for last but couldn't hold it any longer. "We saw Waylon Jennings at a Howard Johnson's on the Garden State Parkway on August eleventh. We were just standing by the Coke machine and he came out of the men's room, hitching up his belt. No one saw him but us. I couldn't believe it. I said, 'Hey, Waylon,' and he waved at me and said, 'Mornin', missy.' Just like that."

She was looking at him with her raised eyebrows, as if this last piece of information couldn't fail to impress. He looked at her and had to laugh. "That's pretty good," he said.

"I know," she said, and laughed herself, a sound David hadn't heard from her before and which he enjoyed.

"And then of course there's the comet," Drew said.

"Comet?"

She looked at him, dumbfounded. "You know, the Halley's comet, out *there* somewhere?" She gestured through the windshield at the skies. "Where have *you* been?"

David remembered now. The comet was supposed to be approaching Earth's orbit this week, or was it leaving, he had heard about it on the news, seen a headline on someone's desk at work. People were talking about making a trip out of the city to avoid the lights, with blankets, a bottle of wine. Someone had a telescope. But it had not come as close as predicted, or wasn't as bright, something. He had been too upset and distracted to pay much attention. "Right," he said.

Drew was still looking at him, as if his ignorance defied belief. "I remember now," he said.

"I can tell you about comets," she said, searching in her drawstring bag and coming out with a tattered paperback. On its cover was a drawing of a family on a hillside, parents, a boy and girl, looking up in benign fascination as a burning fireball hurtled toward them from the heavens. It was called *Messenger from the Skies*. From the back seat came movement and he turned to see Angela waking, rubbing her eyes. "Oh, is she on the comet?" Angela said, as Drew riffled the pages of the book. "She's an expert."

"Have you seen it?" David asked.

The girl nodded, still sleepy.

" 'Comets have been visiting our atmosphere ever since the dawn of time,' " Drew read. " 'The history books are filled with accounts, and the earliest records of humankind are often concerned with the visitations of these otherworldly sojourners of the cosmic highway.' " She looked up at David, then back at her book. " 'Scientists estimate there may be as many as one hundred thousand comets journeying in mute orbit around our blue planet. Indeed, some speculate that, if not for the interference of terrestrial and solar light, we could look up at an entire sky filled with streaks of fire.' "

"I love that part," Angela said, leaning her arms over the seat.

"It's full of cool stuff," Drew said, closing the book. "They knew about comets in China, in Egypt even. They used to predict wars by them, famine, plagues, you name it. In 1910, Halley's comet came so close to earth we passed through its tail, which is full of radioactive gas, and thousands of people died, mostly in Europe."

"I didn't know that," David said.

"It's in the book," Drew told him.

They drove for a few moments in silence, the girls peering out the front, David willing his eyes open.

"Hey," Angela said from the back. "I bet we could see it tonight." She had her elbows draped over the seat, her head propped on her hands. Her face was flushed, from sleep or her illness David couldn't say. "We could find a field or a mountain where there'd be no lights. I bet we could."

"Hey," Drew said, looking at David, putting down the book. "What do you think?"

SOMEHOW HE HAD missed the turnoff. It was impossible, but he had. He was feeling absolutely groggy with weariness, couldn't remember the last time he had slept, and he had not argued when the girls had chosen an exit from the highway. They were on a hillside now, in some kind of park. They had left the car and were climbing through wet, uncut grass. There were lights from the highway and some town behind them, but if they looked ahead, to the south, the horizon was dark. The girls ran on before him, reached the crest of the hill. The younger one turned and gestured for him to hurry.

The night air was quiet, cool; it cleared his head a little. He could not remember another day like this one. Nothing in it made sense, and now, to top it off, he was lost. He should have checked a map, maybe found a hotel to catch an hour's rest, but it was too late now. He had missed the turnoff, would, at some point soon, be leaving the state entirely. He would drive the girls to Cleveland, that's all he could think of, offer them some money, drop them where they wanted to go. He supposed he would know what to do after that.

He heard the girls talking up ahead, felt his shoes soaking through in the wet grass. He could see them on the hilltop, moving from one side to the other, pointing, arguing about where to look. Drew was consulting her book; he heard her say she couldn't read the map. The night was so dark they were nearly silhouettes framed against a blank sky, a star here or there behind them.

He had a lot to do. He had not even told Maura about the letter from the partners telling him after the Crestview collapse he should expect no promotion, suggesting, in terms so bland and restrained it took an expert to decipher them, that it might be time for him to move on to other employment. He had that to deal with. He had a damaged car. He would call the police in the morning and see what happened to the kid in the Mustang. He would drive these girls home.

He looked around again. Below him, the lights of a small town spread out, road signs, gas stations, a string of houses on a far incline. But when he turned back to the hillside it was completely dark, nothing ahead of him but a couple of black trees and the girls moving back and forth in the grass. How he had gotten from his apartment in the city to here, wherever here was, in one day mystified him. Take a wrong turn, however slight, and you could be in an entirely new situation. Life hadn't always seemed this way to him. He had thought it was sequential, logical, you knew where you were because you knew how you got here, which was how you prepared for where you had to go next. Well, not today. All of that was out the window today.

It came to him what he wanted to tell Maura. He didn't know how to say it, and he doubted he would be able to, but he knew now what he would like to say. She had looked beautiful on the porch. It wasn't the sweater that got him, it was that. It was the look she had given Oliver, right before he had left, the way she had looked up at him and leaned into his arms. She was beautiful then. Even in the arms of another man she was beautiful. Not sexy beautiful or maternal beautiful, not beautiful like Rhonda, or like women in magazines. She was content, and from the way she looked at Oliver, David could tell she was where she wanted to be. That was it. She was beautiful in ways he could not explain, that had taken years to discover, that maybe nobody but he could even recognize. He didn't know. Whatever it was, he saw it, and he wanted to tell her he did. That was all.

Ahead the girls were excited. He could hear them calling. "There it is!" Drew said. "Oh, my God, take a look at that sucker!" Angela was excited too, and she turned down the hill to David, waving her arms. "Come on!" she said. "There it is!"

He walked toward them. He remembered something barely overheard on the news about the comet no longer being visible from the northeast past the first of the month, which was yesterday, something else about it being due south in the sky. The girls were looking east. He approached them. He had looked up at the sky many times before, and he knew what was there, a shimmering cold, a speckled absolute nullity. They told him to close his eyes. Angela came up and took his hand. There was nothing to see and he knew it, but he walked over to where the girls led him, let them direct his face upward. He waited, and then Drew said, "Okay. Get ready." He waited with his eyes closed, feeling the night air on his face, hearing the girls move beside him. "Wait till I tell you," Drew said. She had her hands on his face, Angela her hands on his arm. "No peeking," Drew said. He didn't peek. He waited until she moved her hands and told him. "Okay," she said. "Look."

IN 1974 I was nineteen, driving through a severe winter storm, coming back to the City after visiting a high school friend in Teaneck, New Jersey. I was in a silver 1962 Buick Invicta, a real bomber, worth somewhat less than the $300 I'd paid for it. It hemorrhaged oil, shuddered apoplectically between gears, and I ended up selling it for $50 in parts when a mechanic told me to give up, but I loved it. It was my first car (the family's first too) and, at nineteen, it betokened much—freedom, coming of age, unfocused ideas of sexual triumph.

On the toll ramp for the Lincoln Tunnel, I saw a shape through what was by then a blinding storm of sleety snow. A girl, hitchhiking, shivering with cold and wet. I pulled over and shoved the door open, and, as I should have expected, she motioned to the bushes behind her and her two friends, one male, one female, came running up to the car. She got in back and immediately lay down, the boy threw some duffel bags in after her and joined me up front, while the second girl got in back and cradled her head. The guy reached over and turned the heater up.

They were heading to Florida, had left Canada two days before. First it was fine, then the storm blew in and they'd been stuck in it for twenty-four hours, Buffalo to New York. The guy was about my age. I couldn't see the second girl well, but the one lying down was young, too young, I thought, to be out here. Her face was bright red and I could hear her breathing. A smell came off her, candy-sweet, and I asked the guy what it was. "That's her diabetes," he told me. "What it smells like when she's out of insulin."

I offered to let them stay in my dorm room, suggested they go to the student clinic, and in the morning, feeling guilty for not doing more, wrote them a check for $20, took the checkbook with me to class, and told them to eat as much of my stock of Chef Boy-ar-dee and Campbell's as they liked. When I came back all the cans were gone, plus a favorite shirt, but overall I felt I could have done more, though I had no idea what. I remember thinking, boy, if I ever start writing again, this'll be great.

1986's biggest dud was Halley's comet. I, with the rest of the world, geared up for a once-in-a-lifetime brush with the cosmos, a light show the whole planet could share. In Northern California, at least, there was nothing. I was writing by then, and somehow thought of the hitchhikers from college, whom I'd tried to paste onto several stories already. I threw the two ideas together, wrote one hapless draft where the college boy—me—has his unique angst confirmed after refusing to help the hitchhikers and then getting drunk at a comet party. In another, an unfulfilled Peninsula housewife stumbles across a powwow on the Stanford campus and is welcomed, gets caught up in the ritual, the food, the dance, and stands with her new fellows at night looking for the comet in the sky above. On her way home, feeling certain her life has changed, she picks up the hitchhikers, who rob her. Bad Raymond Carver.

I was flailing, flinging elements of a story together because their basis in my life moved me, hoping they'd stick somehow, cohere on their own into a meaningful shape. I was learning the hard way— probably the only way—that a story's form needs to be organic, the shape it takes, all the elements of craft—point of view, theme, voice, plot—having to emerge from what the story slowly tells you it needs, not from an infatuation born in experience, or a neat idea, or a thematic that is way too clever by half. Experience, which seems so enticing to a young writer, bursting with existential significance, is often exactly what is wrong with the material. Stories do speak to you, eventually, and not in some mystic, muse-driven way. If you watch and listen carefully, characters will develop needs, plots will be determined based on what the characters have done, or refuse to do, or fear they may have to do in the end, not on a predisposed trajectory of rising and inevitable and predictable action. Theme, toughest of all, will emerge too, because nothing in a story is ultimately accidental, if you look and listen well enough.

In 1997 I was trying to complete a related-short-story collection, centering on an unhappy New York family. I had two problems. I was struggling with a main character who grew more unappealing by the page. I kind of liked the guy but people I trusted told me he was a jerk. I had a sense that 300 pages of resolutely downward character development might not attract the throng of readers I hoped for. I'd written a story which seemed to reveal the nadir of his capabilities in which his angry, isolate nature manages to ruin his marriage. What next? I'd also decided to abandon the traditional order for the stories, resisting the chronological and its ready biographic appeal. I needed a theme, a form had to emerge from the material. If there was form here so far, I couldn't see it.

I thought of the old hitchhiker/comet story. By then we'd had another, more successful comet, Hale-Bopp, and I started writing. What I learned from "Pillar of Fire" helped me pull the book together, understand the main character's need, showed me the form I'd been blindly reaching for.

What I came to see, finally, was there were two stories here. The grafting I'd repeatedly tried to impose hadn't worked because it couldn't, as long as the imposition of form came from the outside. The comet in my earlier drafts, almost literally *deus ex machina,* appeared, trailing portent, to lineate all the story's undeveloped tensions. It lacked, finally, specificity. Anybody, a college kid crippled by self-consciousness, a housewife with unsounded depths and delusions, anybody, could stare at a comet and feel . . . something. Flannery O'Connor discusses how a story has to reveal the particular in light of the universal. It isn't enough to nudge us toward the momentous. Why now? Why here? Most important, why to this individual character, now, here?

"Pillar" was to be David's story. The whole first half of the book belonged to him. By this I mean that he tried to control the narrative, believed his beliefs and intentions could determine his fate. This contributed to his unappealing nature—Mr. Bulstrode from *Middlemarch* comes to mind. "Pillar" would be his tale of heroic reclamation, life returned to his terms—gather the errant wife home, ignore the wreck he's made, in fact, build on it. Like all narrators and most protagonists, he thought it was his story to tell. But from the start, things go wrong. From Oliver to the kid in the Mustang to the girls in the car, everything slips from his control. The old story's done; if "Pillar" works, a new one, beginning with the girls and the comet, may be starting.

Similarly, my fusion of two disparate stories into one might work if the hitchhiking girls were not another randomly evocative coincidence but transformative, part of the story's evolution beyond David's narrow hopes.

And the book itself may have discovered its form here, this story a fulcrum from a first half where the protagonist was resolutely, if at times unwillingly, destructive, to the possibility of a new, undiscovered way of living (which, being human, being David, he maneuvers with only partial success). The stories in this book, it is my hope, work by refracting one another, by raising more questions as they are successively read. Everyone can hope, can't they? What I hope emerges from "Pillar" is a sense of a greater landscape than a single character or point of view can apprehend, articulate, manage—Flannery O'Connor called this "mystery"—and the possibility of change that arises from a simple act of faith.

Stephen Dobyns

PART OF THE STORY

T HERE WERE DAYS when Lily Hendricks would look from the picture window of her mobile home for an hour or more, watching the clouds making round, hopeful shapes in the air. What was hopeful for Lily was anything ongoing: clouds moving west to east, birds keeping busy, progress being made. But mostly the western Michigan sky was overcast and life didn't care squat. Mostly life tried to pen you up within its chain-link fence. Lily had a little dog named Joyce that would bring her the box of Kleenex whenever Lily cried and the tears spilled onto her lap. The dog, half cocker, half beagle, would yip and wag her tail. Joyce was always upbeat. Lily had also tried teaching Joyce to fetch the bottle of Old Crow, but Joyce could only manage a pint bottle and Lily liked to buy her bourbon by the gallon.

Lily was sixty-three. She had had five children and she had given all five up for adoption. But that was long ago. In those days whenever she was with a new man and she asked herself should she or shouldn't she, the wildness always won. Maybe two of the children had had the same father, but Lily wouldn't put money on it. She hadn't played the field, she'd played the county. But that was history. Now she had Burt on Saturdays and Herbert on Wednesdays, and weeks would go by when neither of them could get it up. They were older men who liked their quiet and they did what they were told.

In the past year Lily had thought more about her five children than in the previous twenty-five. This was not a result of awakened conscience; they had tracked her down. Robbie had been first. He was forty-five and taught high school in Monroe, outside of Detroit. Lily felt proud that one of her children was a schoolteacher. He had phoned and she was a little cool until she realized that he didn't want money and he wasn't going to complain. Robbie's father was one of three possible men, all dead now. Maybe it had been that time she had done it in the hayfield, or maybe that time in the back seat of a Plymouth. She had asked Robbie, "What color's your hair?"

"Brown."

"Curly?"

"Straight."

"And your eyes?"

"Brown."

She had asked more questions. Maybe Robbie's father had been Jerry Lombardi, who died in Jackson, where he had been serving ten to fifteen for armed robbery. Somebody had stuck a knife in his back. When Lily heard the news, she thought that Jerry probably deserved it. He had always been a mean man, someone who'd cross the street just to kick a stray dog. She wanted to ask Robbie if he had a mean streak, but she didn't feel it was something she could discuss over the phone.

In that first conversation she had told Robbie about his four half-brothers and half-sisters. It was just chitchat as far as she was concerned. She would have told anybody. Now, however, she felt he had wormed the information out of her; he had asked questions and she'd been too truthful to lie. She had given him the dates of their births, more or less. She had used the same Catholic agency in Lansing with each adoption. She'd call up Sister Mary Agnes to tell her she had another little parcel on the way. Sometime later Sister Mary Agnes would give her a new name to remember in her prayers. Not that Lily did much praying, but it was more convenient to have a name to think about than Baby X.

If Robbie was the oldest at forty-five, Marjorie was the youngest at twenty-five. Five babies in twenty years. And lucky she was to have had only five. After the last, Lily had had her tubes tied.

Robbie had contacted them and one by one they called. They had hushed voices as if talking to somebody important. They didn't want anything, seemingly, except to hear her voice and let her know they were okay. But she knew that was only part of the story, and for months she had been expecting the next installment. "I'm waiting for the other shoe to drop," she told Burt and Herbert. "It's going to be the big one."

THE NEXT INSTALLMENT had come in spring, the middle of April. Robbie had called on a Sunday—one of those gray, bourbon-drinking Sundays. He said he'd been talking to his brothers and sisters, and they had decided to take a big step. They wanted to make her acquaintance. When would be a good time to visit?

"All of you?" asked Lily.

"That's right, all five. We want to meet our mom."

"Won't that be too much trouble for you?" asked Lily.

"Nope, we've been talking about it. I've met Gwen and Frank, but this would be a good time for all of us to get to know one another."

Lily wanted to ask why, but she kept silent. She didn't see why they wanted to meet her, and she didn't see why they wanted to meet each other. She wished them well; she hoped they had happy lives, but she didn't want to get to know them. They were mistakes, bloopers. The rubber had broken or the man hadn't used a rubber or she had stopped taking her pills or they had been in too much of a hurry. She had opened the door a crack, and one by one her children had snuck into the world. They were like ghosts, but they were living. She was glad they were living. She even liked it when they called. But she didn't want to meet them.

"I got a pretty tight schedule during the next few months," said Lily. The lie sounded so obvious that she felt bad about it. Twenty hours a week she worked at the Rex Diner and that was about it. Sometimes she played cards with a couple of the girls. Then on Saturdays and Wednesdays she had Burt and Herbert. She considered saying that she was off to Disneyland or Indianapolis, but the prospect of a whole string of lies exhausted her. It was not that she felt any allegiance to the truth. God knows she had cheated on too many men for the truth to be more than a stumbling block. But sometimes falsehood took more strength than she could summon up.

"What do you have to do?" asked Robbie patiently.

"Oh, it's nothing I can't get out of," said Lily. "You come whenever you want and I'll make the time. But there's no room in the trailer. You'll have to stay at the motel." Lily felt it was only right that they should stay where at least one of them had been conceived.

Robbie handled the arrangements. He was practical and efficient, which made Lily think he probably wasn't Jerry Lombardi's kid after all. Jerry was a fuckup. In the afternoons, Lily would sit staring at the clouds through her picture window and she would know that right at that very moment Robbie was pushing his plans forward. It frightened her. It was like what she had heard about soil erosion or the ice caps melting. Bit by bit it was going on even while you slept or brushed your teeth. There was nothing hopeful about such activity, nothing upbeat. The negatives were rushing to get a leg up on the positives and someday soon she would be knocked for a loop. Little Joyce would lay her furry head in Lily's lap and stare up into her eyes. Even the dog knew trouble was coming.

A week later Robbie called back. "We want to come in May," he said.

"Just don't make it on Mother's Day," said Lily. "I don't think I could stand it."

They settled on the Saturday after Mother's Day. Many phone calls were made. Robbie took care of the reservations at the motel. Lily thought of these five adults and their expectations. In her imaginings they had question marks instead of faces. Soon those question marks would be exchanged for specific features. Would they have her straight nose? Her brown eyes? She felt anxious and hopeful. She would give them pancakes for breakfast. She was afraid they wouldn't like her, that they would feel disappointment.

MOST LIKELY THE weekend would have been pleasant, even slightly dull, if events hadn't conspired to make it otherwise. Lily had known something would go wrong. She had even ticked off the possible disasters on her fingertips, but she had never thought of this one. She had never thought that Burt would cash in his chips right in her own bed. Kicked the bucket, bought the farm—whatever Lilly called it, the whole business took about ten seconds from beginning to end. Maybe it was a stroke, maybe a heart attack. In days to come, Lily would think of his death and want to blame Burt for the trouble he had caused, as if his death had been an act of petulance.

Burt was a retired hardware salesman, and he was soft. That was the problem. No exercise. Too many sweet things over a lifetime on the road. Jams and jellies. Thick butter. He felt hurt that he had to miss his Saturday just because Lily's children were coming to visit. He grew sullen and made remarks about how things should stay where you put them and not come back to plague you. So at last Lily said, "Then come Friday night, but you have to be gone by eight o'clock Saturday morning." Which, in a manner of speaking, he was.

And when Lily blamed Burt for dying, what she mostly blamed

was his appetite, that on this particular occasion he had wanted to have sex more than once. "Burt had a greedy streak," Lily would later tell the girls over cards without bothering to explain herself. Often Burt didn't want to have sex at all and they played gin rummy instead. But because Lily's children were coming, Burt must have felt a need to assert himself. He got himself all inspired again around seven-thirty that morning, and fifteen minutes later he was dead, lying naked on the sheet with his mouth open and his teeth still on the dresser. Lily had scrambled away and watched as Burt had seemed unable to catch his breath. He had choked and gasped, and his face reddened. Then he was gone.

"For crying out loud!" Lily stared at Burt, waiting for him to do something. He lay on his back with his arms flung out. After a minute she leaned forward and gently slapped his face. "Burt, Burt." Lily was so used to him doing exactly what she said that she felt some exasperation when he failed to respond.

Once she realized he was dead, she hurried to the phone. She could call the rescue squad or she could call the police. She glanced at her watch. It was eight o'clock. At eight-thirty her five children were due to arrive to have breakfast with their mom. She stood with the receiver in her hand. She thought of her children, the accidents of their births. Late nights in parked cars. Twice in the diner on the kitchen counter after closing. And here was Burt, the last of them, or at least the most recent, sprawled naked on her bed. The rescue squad would have to come from town. Most likely they would arrive at the same time as her children. She imagined Robbie and Frank and Gwen and Merton and Marjorie standing by the door watching Burt being removed from their mom's bedroom. What she saw on their faces was disappointment. Their mom was up to her old tricks again. Sixty-three years old and still having fun. Lily hung up the phone. Burt was in no hurry. He could wait. Lily returned to the bedroom to get dressed and make herself look pretty. Then she'd get started on the pancakes.

ROBBIE ARRIVED AT eight-thirty on the dot and brought Gwen with him. Robbie was a tall man wearing a blue plaid sport coat, and Lily could see something of her face in his, like looking at her own face through several inches of water. Gwen, who was forty-one, didn't favor her at all: a stout black-haired woman who would look like she was crying even when she was laughing. She wore a dark green suit with some lace at the collar and glasses with thick black frames. Little Joyce barked and barked. Lily kept nudging the dog with her foot and telling her to shush. She would have shut her in the bedroom if she hadn't been afraid that Joyce would take a bite out of Burt's nose. Lily had dressed Burt, even putting on his shoes and socks. There was an easy chair in the bedroom, and she had dragged him over to it. She had stuck a *Reader's Digest* in his lap, put in his teeth, and shut his mouth. She brushed his hair and set his reading glasses on his nose. Now he looked as if he had just happened to die in the bedroom. Maybe he had reached an exciting part of the story and popped his ticker. His death didn't look sex-related; it looked reading-related.

Gwen stood just inside the door with her arms folded, looking around the trailer. "This is really very nice," she said.

Robbie was trying to keep the dog from jumping up on his trousers. "Active little fellow," he said.

"It's a girl," said Lily, with a smile that hurt her cheeks. "Her name's Joyce. But come in. Have some coffee. It's almost ready." She had put on dark slacks and a beige turtleneck sweater. On a chain around her neck was a good luck medallion showing a rainbow in four colors and a little pot of gold.

"Do you have any decaf?" asked Robbie.

"I'll check," said Lily, who knew she didn't.

"It must be nice living in a mobile home," said Gwen. "Everything's always within reach."

Lily sat her two children down at the kitchen table. It was a red vinyl booth, just like the booths at the Rex Diner. Lily had even taken one of the diner's chrome napkin dispensers and a glass sugar shaker with a chrome screw top. "What about tea?" she asked her son. Both her children were glancing around while trying not to appear nosy. They kept making sideways looks.

"That would be fine," said Robbie. When he spoke, he leaned forward and opened his mouth more than was necessary. His teeth reminded Lily of a wolf in a story. The front ones were as big as postage stamps. They didn't look like her teeth, nor did they look like Jerry Lombardi's. She couldn't stop staring at her children. Her fascination with their faces almost frightened her.

Lily poured coffee for Gwen. Her daughter's mouth was puckered as if a drawstring had been pulled tight. She wore no makeup and her eyebrows were dark and shaggy. Lily herself plucked her eyebrows, and she liked to wear the brightest lipstick she could find. That morning she was wearing one called Passionate Appeal.

Joyce kept jumping up on Robbie's knees. "You can just whop her if you want," said Lily. "She's used to it." Then she thought of poor dead Burt and hoped he wouldn't topple onto the floor. She hadn't even had time to grieve yet. She put the kettle on the stove. "So you're from Toledo?" she asked Gwen.

"That's where my adopted parents lived," said Gwen, "and that's where I was raised."

Lily wondered if she heard a note of complaint in her voice. Gwen was an accountant. Numbers were her life, she said. It amazed Lily that all her children did things. She took down the flour and baking powder and began to prepare the pancake batter as Gwen talked about Toledo. There was more to it than met the eye, she said.

A few minutes later Lily heard the rumble of motors and glanced out the kitchen window. A Ford pickup had drawn up behind Robbie's Chevrolet, and a little green Toyota was right behind it. Two men and a woman got out. The woman would be Marjorie, her youngest. She had been riding in the Toyota with one of the men.

Marjorie was pretty, with strawberry-blond hair, but nervous-looking, and she fidgeted with her hands. The two men were Frank and Merton, but Lily didn't know who was who. For a second Lily felt she lacked the strength to open the door.

Frank was the taller one; he was thirty-six. Merton was pudgy and soft; he was thirty-two. Soon all five were crowded around the kitchen table. Lily was struck by how different they were from one another. If she had shoved a pencil blindly into the phone book she couldn't have found anyone more different. They were as different from one another as she was different from a Chinaman. Lily couldn't recall having sex with a Chinese gentleman, though she might have had she known one.

"I can't tell you how long I've hoped for this happy event," said Frank. He was a lay Baptist preacher in Marshall. He wore a dark brown suit and had elaborate sideburns that curved forward and ended in points. His face was long. It didn't seem thin so much as squished, as if something had squeezed his head at the ears. He wore black shoes and white socks.

"I've been waking up early every morning just from excitement," said Merton. He was a druggist in Flint and still unmarried. He kept fooling with red spots on his face. His hands seemed swollen and soft. He wore a baby-blue corduroy sport coat, a red plaid shirt, and no tie. His jeans were white.

"Sometimes I start to weep," said Marjorie, "and I don't know why. I've been dreaming of this moment all my life." She was a dental hygienist in Saginaw. There were tears in her eyes. She kept pushing her hands through her blond hair, which would rise up and float back down like a cloud. When she spoke, she never looked at the person she was speaking to until the very end of her sentence. She wore a light-green summer dress with a full skirt that rustled when she shifted in the booth.

The five of them had gotten acquainted over dinner the previous evening, but Lily could tell they were still strange to one another.

They kept looking at each other as if seeking resemblances. Lily stirred her pancake batter; it seemed the one safe thing. Gwen poured coffee and made tea for Robbie. Then she began hunting for dishes. She was short but efficient. Like her mother, she seemed to take comfort in activity.

Later Lily decided there was never really a specific moment when she felt it wasn't going to work. Rather, she had experienced an increasing dread. Her children's collective grievances were like a sixth person in the room. Lily could almost see his face: a real trouble-maker. She thought of Burt sitting in her bedroom getting stiffer and stiffer. She almost envied him.

"I can't tell you what a special occasion this is for me," said Lily. It seemed her only hope lay in falsehood. "Seeing you together is like having all my eggs in one nest." She cracked two eggs into the bowl and stirred vigorously.

Gwen gave a tight smile. Marjorie's eyes welled up. Robbie gave the dog a push. Frank lowered his head and nodded. Merton scratched his face and stared at the breadbox. Their neediness oppressed her.

"The pancakes will be ready in a jiffy," said Lily. The bacon was already sizzling on the grill. Once they started eating, they would be occupied. But what would they do after that?

Frank said grace and they bowed their heads. Her children's mouths filled with food seemed a reasonable alternative to silence. Chewing, after all, was akin to talking. They all sat crowded at the table and bumped one another with their elbows. Lily had real maple syrup. She kept sneaking furtive looks at her children and she felt them taking quick looks at her as well. It was barely nine o'clock. The day stretched ahead like an alp.

She was struck by how they chewed in similar ways: slowly and methodically. Frank ate with the tines of his fork pointed up. Robbie ate with the tines of his fork pointing down. Lily asked them about sports and Merton was talking about dart games. Marjorie said she played bingo at her church. Lily considered the passion that had sparked their lives into being and wondered where it was now. Robbie, Frank, and Gwen were all married, with children, which made Lily a grandmother. Even this surprised her. She imagined generations proceeding into the future just because Jerry Lombardi had gotten her drunk in the back seat of his old Plymouth. She found herself suddenly yearning for actions without consequences, simple routines like taking food orders or wiping off tables with a clean white rag. She remembered all those nights when some faceless man had had his way with her. She had thought of those actions as having clear beginnings, middles, and ends, but she had been mistaken. There weren't any ends. Never were, never would be. There was only a dull ongoingness, as if she had taken it into her head to walk all the way from Grand Rapids to Detroit. But even that journey would end, while this one didn't seem to. It was just one foot plopped in front of the other for the duration. She had had these children, and they had had children, and those children would have more children. Again she thought of Burt propped up with his *Reader's Digest*—the lucky devil.

Her children went on to talk about things they had recently read in the newspaper: troubles in Russia, troubles at home. Frank told about a circus elephant that had rampaged through a shopping center in Cleveland and had to be shot. Marjorie spoke of how Boy Scout leaders seemed to be getting in trouble almost everywhere. Lily felt touched by how they were trying to be conversational and civilized. They stumbled between one subject and the next while the subjects closest to their hearts remained lurking to the side. Lily wondered how long it would take them to speak their minds. If things got too far out of control, she thought, she could always walk into her bedroom and scream. Then they would find Burt and that'd be that. In the midst of Burt's death, her children wouldn't have the courage to ask their mother embarrassing questions about her life.

AFTER BREAKFAST WHEN the dishes were washed and put away, they moved into the small living room. Her three sons sat in a row on the sofa. They were crowded and leaned forward with their elbows on their knees. Whenever they did anything in the same way—scratched their noses or wrinkled their foreheads—Lily wondered if it was genetic. Marjorie sat in the easy chair and Gwen sat on the arm. It seemed affectionate but they weren't touching, Lily stood in the entrance to the kitchen.

Robbie glanced around at the others and cleared his throat. "We were wondering," he said, "if you could tell us anything about our fathers?"

Even as the question was articulated, Lily had an image of their fathers. Oh, she didn't know who they were exactly but she visualized a row of men who might have been their fathers: a rogue's gallery of male longing. The dim-witted and lustful. The mean-spirited and carnal. Lily doubted there was a high school graduate in the bunch. And their accumulated jail time approached triple digits. Think of the beer and whiskey these men had consumed, the cars crashed, the women beaten or bullied, the jobs lost. In her imagination the men peered at her, leering and moronic. They had wanted her and she had been unable to say no.

"Your fathers were all grand men," said Lily at last.

"Were they all different?" asked Frank. "I mean, are any of us full brothers or sisters?"

"Five fathers for five children," said Lily. "They were all different, yet they were men you'd be proud of."

"Can you tell us their names?" asked Merton.

Lily had been afraid of this. In her bedroom stood a tall book shelf packed with paperback romances: intimate tales to soothe her solitary hours. Now she called on them for inspiration.

"You have to ask yourself why we never married," she began. "Love was experienced and exchanged. Deep truths were shared.

These were men with families, with positions in the community. In their youth they made mistakes. They had married the wrong women. As the years passed they came to realize the error of their ways. It was then we met."

"And this happened five different times?" asked Merton.

"More than that, but only on five occasions was a child conceived. In fact, three times I had miscarriages. Somewhere your little heavenly half-siblings are circling the globe. But if you could have known your fathers, then how proud you'd be."

"You mean they're dead?" asked Gwen in a whisper.

"Every single one," Lily covered her eyes with her hand. She was thinking hard. In her mind's eye she saw the dark-haired, bare-chested men on the book jackets, the women whose torn gowns were kept in place only by the magnitude of their bosoms.

"What was my father like?" asked Robbie.

"The colonel," said Lily. "He disappeared during Tet. Missing in action. He had sent me a note from Saigon saying he was going underground. Without doubt, he was one of the bravest men I've ever met. They never found his body. Could be he's still in some dank jungle cell, chained to a post."

"And my father?" asked Frank. "What about him?"

"He raced cars. He was no stranger to Indianapolis. He was at home on a thousand tracks. Your father was one of the great ones. How ironic that he should be burned to death at a small county fair in Tennessee. He swerved to avoid a child who had strayed out onto the track. His wife was a strict Catholic and dead set against divorce."

"And mine?" asked Merton.

"The priest," said Lily. "The only one who wasn't married. He looked just like Cary Cooper."

The others pressed forward with their questions.

"Your father," Lily told Gwen, "was a state senator. One of the grand old men of Michigan politics. When we were together he was over seventy, still vigorous and full of life. Had he been a younger man we'd have married. He was eighty-five when he passed away. He knew you lived in Toledo. He kept his eye on you."

"I got a scholarship to the Brothers School," said Gwen.

"That was the senator's doing," said Lily.

"And your father," Lily told Marjorie, "was a navy stunt pilot. You remember that crash over the fairgrounds in Detroit twenty years ago? No matter. He was about to tell his wife he wanted a divorce. I've carried his picture in my heart. Compared to him, other men were flotsam in the wind."

Now her children were perking up. Their faces were developing lively expressions. Lily brought out the bottle of Old Crow, and Gwen got ice and glasses. Marjorie no longer wept and Frank no longer looked dour. Robbie sat a little straighter. Even Gwen began to smile. Merton stopped picking at the red spots on his face.

"But how did you happen to be with my father, the colonel?" asked Robbie.

"It was shortly after the Miss Michigan contest," said Lily. "He had seen me on television."

"You were Miss Michigan?" asked Robbie respectfully.

"No, no. Only a runner-up. The colonel called me at my parents' farm in Okemos. We agreed to meet at the state fair. One thing led to another and we ran away together. I've always been a sucker for a uniform. Then the colonel was sent overseas. After that, life was very hard. Of course I never inherited a penny."

"You must have met the senator shortly after that," suggested Gwen, pouring her mother a little Old Crow.

"He saved me. I was sitting on the lawn outside the capital weeping and he found me. Without him, it would have been the white slavers or worse. He had a shock of pure white hair that nearly reached his collar. And a white mustache as well. Can you blame me for going with him? He had a stretch limousine with a smoked glass partition. Even the chauffeur couldn't see us."

"You did it in the limousine?" asked Gwen.

"Not only was the senator impetuous," said Lily, "he was forceful. He wanted to take my mind off my troubles. He swept me away." Lily was beginning to enjoy herself, but then she thought of Burt, how he was becoming stiffer in death than he had ever been in life.

"My father must have come next," said Frank.

"The dentist," said Lily.

"You said he raced cars," said Frank.

"Yes, a dentist who raced cars. I was hitchhiking out of Lansing and he picked me up in his Jaguar. He drove like the wind, and he fixed my teeth as well."

Her children's eagerness propelled her forward. To Merton she told the story of the priest who had given her confession and how she had become his housekeeper. The first domesticity she had ever experienced. She had cooked him sweet things, but in the end his temptation had been too great and he had thrown his clerical collar to the floor. To Marjorie she described the amorous excesses of the stunt pilot and how they had once had sex parachuting over Sleeping Bear dune. "When we hit the sand, we were still coupled," said Lily. "His organ was black and blue for weeks."

Their willingness to believe drove her to further excesses. But as she spoke she remembered how it really had been, with high school dropouts pulling her down between parked cars. She visualized how the sleeves of their jean jackets had been cut off at the shoulders and how they wore little silver chains across the instep of their motorcycle boots. They kept packs of Luckies in the rolled-up sleeves of their T-shirts. They had flat bellies and freckles, and they chewed toothpicks. Although they had seemed tough and virile, they were lousy lovers. Had they stayed around, they would have been lousy fathers, slapping their children just as they had slapped her. With them in the house, none of her children would have found a profession. Robbie wouldn't have been a teacher, Gwen wouldn't have become an accountant.

Lily had a hunger that overswept her and she had squandered it on riffraff. It was only as an older woman that she had begun to exert some control over her male companions. There had been Burt and Herbert and others. If they weren't all kind, they were at least obedient.

But hadn't Burt been kind? He got her a new TV and had her refrigerator fixed. He talked to her about her life and told her she was a good woman even when he got nothing out of it. Again and again she had kicked him out, calling him a sorry brute and a worthless dead sausage. He had been a salesman from Illinois, a childless man who had wandered into western Michigan and taken a part-time job with the hardware store. "My biggest regret," he often told her, "was I never had kids." Now he was dead in the bedroom armchair with a *Reader's Digest* propped in his lap. And at that thought Lily, who had been laughing and joking with her children, burst into tears.

Her little dog Joyce was sitting beside her. When Lily began to cry, Joyce trotted out of the room. Lily didn't stop to think that Joyce was off to fetch the Kleenex and the Kleenex was in the bedroom.

"I've been a bad mother," said Lily, sobbing.

"No, no," said Marjorie.

"I have. I've been with men it was wrong to be with, and I've been irresponsible with my body."

"You were following your inner needs," said Merton.

"I've cheated and I've done what I shouldn't."

"But we're glad to be alive," said Frank. "We're grateful for that." Her five children stood in a semicircle around her. Their foreheads all wrinkled in the same way.

In was then that Joyce began her ferocious yapping. By the time Lily got her thinking in order and called to Joyce to stop, it was too late. Gwen had gone to see what the trouble was and screamed. Then she came running back to the living room. Little Joyce trotted after her with the box of Kleenex.

"There's a dead man in the bedroom!" Gwen said. "And he's reading the *Reader's Digest*!"

"How can you tell he's dead?" asked Merton.

Frank and Robbie went to look. The others stared at Lily.

She covered her eyes with her hand. Truth and falsehood stretched ahead like two roads. But truth was a dark and muddy track compared to which falsehood was all fresh macadam. "I've been a terrible liar," she said.

"But who is it?" asked Gwen.

Lily buried her face in a wad of Kleenex. "That man's your father," she said.

"You mean Gwen's father?" asked Merton.

"No," said Lily, with her face still in the Kleenex. "That's Burt. He's the father of all five of you."

There was silence. Lily looked over her wad of Kleenex and saw she was alone. From the bedroom she heard the hushed voices of her children. Little Joyce jumped on Lily's lap to have her neck scratched. Lily wondered if she could escape while her children were occupied. But where could she go? She had to see her story through to the end.

Robbie was the first to return. The others trailed after him. Their faces showed surprise, grief, and confusion. It gave them a family resemblance.

"But how?" said Robbie. "Are you sure he's our father? Who is he?"

"That's Burt," said Lily, "Burt Frost. He drove out to meet you. He lives just this side of Grand Rapids. The excitement was too much for him. All night he talked about you, talked about seeing your dear faces. He got wound up tighter and tighter. He died just before you arrived."

"He's the father of all five of us?" asked Marjorie. Her children began to sit down again.

"That's right. You're full brothers and sisters. Burt and I were lovers for forty-five years. His wife wouldn't give him a divorce. He was a salesman and she was a rich woman. She didn't want children and he

yearned for them. I wanted you to think you had grand and important fathers. Burt never did a mean thing in his life. He was gentle as
a kitten. When his wife died, he didn't get a penny. He moved here
from Illinois to be near me."

"But why didn't you get married?" asked Merton.

"By that time it seemed too much like locking the barn door after
the horse was gone," said Lily. "We were companionable, but we
didn't want to tie the knot."

Lily recounted the history of her sexual escapades, and it wasn't far
from the truth. She described how and where each of her children
had been conceived. But instead of Jerry Lombardi or Bobo Shaw or
Leftie Meatyard, she inserted Burt. She had loved only one man, and
she had been faithful. Now they were still together in their twilight
years, but the fire of sexual passion had cooled. They were companions over cards and the checker board. They discussed their children's
careers with pride.

"But he sounds like a wonderful man," said Marjorie.

"He was," said Lily. She was struck by the eagerness of their belief.
They had a mother, but they wanted a father too. And wouldn't Burt
do? Lily's story was leaky, but it would float. Outside, it began to rain.

All during their talk, one or another of her children would go into
the bedroom to take a look at their new dad.

"I was going to wait till you'd gone," said Lily, "then take him back
to his place. He's got a little house. It would embarrass him to be
found here. If Burt had a fault, it was his love of privacy."

"I'm like that myself," said Robbie.

"You favor him in more ways than one," said Lily.

"People are going to wonder why you kept him here so long," said
Frank. "You could get in trouble with the authorities."

"I figured I could take him home, then call the rescue squad," said
Lily, "but I just don't feel I could do it now."

"Maybe we could take him," said Robbie. "Is it far?"

"Not far at all," said Lily.

And so it was settled. There were loose ends but Lily snipped them off. There were doubts but Lily slowly rubbed them away. She drew a map to Burt's house. She made sandwiches for everybody. They drank more whiskey. Frank said Baptist prayers over Burt and they had a little service with all six of them crowded into the bedroom. They stared at Burt fondly. Lily felt how glad Burt would have been had he known. She found herself happy.

Around dusk, they put Burt into the back of Frank's Ford pickup, chair and all. They couldn't bend him; it was best to keep him seated. The rain had stopped and there was a red glow in the sky.

"We'll buy you a new chair, Ma," said Merton.

Robbie, Gwen, and Marjorie sat in the back of the pickup to keep Burt from toppling over. Merton followed in his Toyota. They were only going about ten miles. In the dim light Burt didn't look dead. He looked fatherly and alert. His new children sat at his feet as if Burt were telling them a story. And perhaps, in a way, he *was* telling them a story, because weren't they learning the story of their lives? What did it matter that it wasn't a true story? They would commit it to memory. They would embroider it and pass it along to their children and grandchildren. It would be a bright color in a dim world. And wasn't that more useful than a sentimental allegiance to a series of events called truth?

Lily stood by the window and watched. She held little Joyce in her arms so she could watch too. Lifting the dog's right paw, Lily moved it up and down. From outside it would seem that the little dog was waving goodbye.

W HEN I WAS in my late twenties and early thirties I wrote about ten short stories and disliked them all. They were bad. They barely rose above anecdote. They had punch-line endings. They were melodramatic. And so I stopped writing stories and concentrated my fiction-writing time on novels, doing three before I published my fourth when I was thirty-one. But some of my favorite fiction—other peoples—were short stories and so I continued to brood about how to write them.

Then one day I asked Ray Carver about how he had written a particular story—we had many conversations over a ten-year period. He said the first sentence had come into his mind and he just followed it. The sentence was something like: "He was vacuuming the living room rug when the telephone rang." Carver said, "It came into my head and so I tried to see what came next." In such a way had the story unwound itself.

When I write a novel, I outline it quite closely, and before I begin the first chapter I can easily have a hundred pages of notes. I know what I need to do in each chapter and how I want the book to end. There may be surprises along the way—characters and chapters I hadn't anticipated, or even cutting characters or chapters—but the outline gives me the curve of the story. I know when and how nearly all the important things happen. Writing stories, I had tried to do the same thing: I had outlined them. So I was struck by Carver's description of his method in that particular story—after the first sentence had occurred to him, the whole process had been a process of discovery. This was much closer to how I wrote poetry: having some little bit—a word, a phrase, a line, a sound, a rhythm, a metaphor or image—and then pursuing it, writing the poem in order to find out why I was writing the poem.

This was interesting but I did nothing with it. And I also wondered about that first sentence—wouldn't it have to be in some way significant? Yet Carver's sentence seemed quite banal, so what constituted significance?

Then in the early spring of 1993 or '94 I had a one-week visiting writer job at the University of Idaho in Moscow. I arrived with a head cold and was put into a motel at the edge of town. Though people were nice, it was clear I was going to be left alone for most of the time. I had to give a reading and I taught three classes. That was it. Maybe there were a couple of dinners, but mostly I was by myself. I had no car and because of the cold I didn't feel like wandering around.

So the second day I found myself thinking about short stories and what Carver had told me. In the evening I sat down with my portable computer and wrote sixty potential first sentences. Some were absurd—a man being hit by a falling pig as he crossed the street against the light—some were thoughtful, some sad. They could be anything but I also wanted them to have some intrinsic interest and most contained a name. For instance, "Frankie tripped over the throw rug when he entered his apartment on a Thursday evening with two six-packs of Budweiser under one arm and Woofie, his girlfriend's Maltese terrier, wedged under the other." There, I've just invented a sentence. It popped into my head. It goes absolutely nowhere. I don't know what happens next. But something might happen next. I only have to pursue it.

The sixty sentences had come one right after another. Then I went through them again, forcing each into a paragraph. Some went nowhere. Still, after two more hours I had about forty paragraphs. A few started to move toward situations I had heard about or experienced, but most were totally invented. My criteria were they had to be different from one another and had to have action and detail—

some sort of specific information. So to continue with Frankie and his problem. "The waxed floor was slick and his feet went out from under him. Dropping the beer, he nearly dropped the dog as well, but in the last second he snatched hold of Woofie's collar, swinging the dog in an arc and at last releasing him when he felt himself falling, so that Woofie was lofted across the room and landed smack on the tray of crackers and Brie which Abigail had put out an hour earlier to let the cheese soften. She stood across the room and watched the action. 'Can't you do anything right?' she asked, as the dog yelped and the crackers and cheese spilled onto the loveseat. 'You remind me of my father.'"

Again, the story of Frankie, Abigail, and Woofie has no future. It begins in the middle of an incident. But with Abigail's remarks a seed of a conflict is planted. The need for me in writing my paragraphs was not to judge, to see them only in terms of potential. So once I had the forty paragraphs, I went back and began to push each one forward until I had a page. By the next day I had thirty-five or so.

Well, as I pushed them, conflicts started to arise, characters began to develop, plots declared themselves. This meant engaging myself into an inquiry of cause and effect. If A happens, then what is B, and if B happens, what is C? Over the next few days I wrote quickly, until by the end of my week I had full or partial drafts of twenty-five stories. Certainly, they were rough, but I refused to judge them unless I felt the subject matter was too close to something I had written before. My main job was invention and following a progression of cause and effect. And what happened was a process I rather knew would happen because of my experience with poetry. At any time I—or anyone—have a whole lot of concerns: psychological, emotional, spiritual, philosophical, even physical. As I wrote, these concerns began to lodge themselves in the stories. They became part of the plots or governing metaphors, or they appeared in the details. They were everywhere. So each story—which had begun basically as meaningless—slowly became significant to me. They became enwrapped and energized by my own inner life. One always views the world through the opaque glass of one's own subjectivity. There is no way I can write something about the outer world and not have it become a metaphor for the inner world. Even when I write journalism, bits and pieces reflect my inner world. The stories also borrowed from my experiences and history, though only three or four contained a large amount of autobiographical detail, but they occurred in places and towns that I knew.

Not all of them worked. Some I couldn't finish, others seemed too small or unoriginal in their conclusions. After about a month, I had twenty stories. Some of my originating first sentences disappeared or entirely new first paragraphs were added. Then I worked on the stories for six or seven years. They went through dozens of revisions. I threw out five more and ended with fifteen, which appeared in my book *Eating Naked*. I mostly don't like contemporary short stories. Many of them have no conclusions. They have that bullshit premise that since life has no conclusions, then fiction should have no conclusions. Or they are somehow meta- or post-modernist. My model was always Chekhov—not to be like him but to have that emotional/psychological connection to the world, to use his narrative curve as a model. But I was also writing in the 1990s, so there might be echoes of Borges, Kundera, Cheever, Kafka, Munro, Trevor, all sorts of people. And I would think of Frank O'Connor's book on the short story: *The Lonely Voice*—not taking it as a model but as something to argue with. But I also knew that as a writer my major tool or gift is my imagination and I need to explore it in the same way that Lewis and Clark slogged across the United States.

The story "Part of the Story" occurred like the others. A sentence formed itself in my mind and I followed it. "There were days when Lily Hendricks would look from the picture window of her mobile home for an hour or more, watching the clouds making round, hopeful shapes in the air." The first sentence was a rougher version of that but my main question was what in the hell was she doing there and I wrote the story to find out. So it begins with an older woman who is depressed and drinking whiskey. I set the story in central Michigan because I had once lived in central Michigan and it has a lot of gray sky. As I wrote, it turned out that Lily Hendricks had five adult children by five different fathers and she had given all five up for adoption as babies. Now they have tracked her down and want to visit. At the time I was teaching at Syracuse University. I had two graduate students—women—who had both been adopted and were in the process of tracking down their biological parents. What would they find and what did they want to find? Our pasts are partly invented; they are distorted and changed by our subjectivity. I had talked to these women and had been interested in their concerns. And it had also made me wonder about the parents who would soon be discovered. All this worked its way into my story.

When I began "Part of the Story," I had no idea that the narrative would center on such events. I discovered it in the writing process, and then spent a long time making the story, measuring and weighing every word and piece of punctuation.

I haven't written any more stories since that experience, though I expect I will. In those years I had a job that easily paid the bills and I could give myself over to a literary labor from which I could expect no economic return. I prefer writing poetry to writing fiction and so I am already committed to spending large amounts of time on something from which there is no economic return. A book of poems can take three or four times the amount of time as a novel and the book of stories took as long as a book of poems. So at the moment I can't afford to write stories, especially if I also mean to write poems, while continuing to work on long fiction. In any case, I'll go on exploring the landscape of my imagination. As for Frankie, Abigail, and Woofie, they are poised in the midst of their small chaos on the threshold of a narrative. I give them to you. Tell me, what's the next sentence?

C. J. Hribal

MORTON AND LILLY,
DREDGE AND FILL

ORTON AND LILLY Brunner had been had, but they weren't going to admit that, not even to themselves. Morton and Lilly's house was on a spur of raised marshland behind the train tracks that unevenly bisected the south end of Black Otter Lake, then ran into town behind the loading docks for the canning factory, the toy factory, the feed mill, and the lumberyard. Theirs was a relatively new ranch in a subdivision built on ground too wet for housing. They had gotten in late on the development of the lakefront, and by the time they were ready to buy there was only marsh to build on. They built anyway. To compensate for the lack of drainage their contractor scotched the full basement, put in a half basement big enough for a sump pump, and extended the foundation an extra four yards, giving them a concrete pad out back for a deck, which the marsh was slowly reclaiming. What Morton and Lilly owned, then, besides some of the best mosquito breeding grounds in the county, was an expensive rectangular box parked on a slab of cracking concrete with a view of the Northwestern and Central train trestle. The railbed, like their yard, was raised to get it above the marsh. Fifty yards of cattails and marsh grass separated them from the raised railbed and it was another fifty to the weed-choked water. Scattered about were mounds of the leftover trucked-in fill for the berms and the dredged piles of lake muck that were now being settled by birch and staghorn sumac and whatever weeds had found a toehold. Porter Atwood sold them that view as a picturesque windbreak and perhaps a sound barrier to the twice-daily train. It used to be lake here, too, but that was choked off and filled in years ago: fertilizer runoff from nearby farms causing an explosion of algae and grass. What was now Morton and Lilly's back yard and their broken deck used to be navigable water. More mounds of colonized muck there. There was no pier on the little bay behind them—too shallow, too mushy. They had to walk over the mounds of fill to the train trestle or drive back to Roosevelt to see the water they've built so close to.

Morton has just returned from the beer shed at Veteran's Park, and is standing now on his crumbling slab of deck, the edges of it green with mold, clumps of chickweed erupting from the fissures that seem wider every spring. It's Homecoming Weekend down at Veteran's Park, and he's wishing he'd stayed there, drinking beer with his buddies and hitting on women he knew in high school. Rita Sabo especially, though she made it clear she wanted no part of him. He figured maybe for old times' sake. *I used to date your sister,* he told her, like that should be an argument in his favor. *Date.* He'd had to say date. That wasn't the half of it, what all they'd done, but he was trying to be polite. Didn't that count for anything? He was asking polite, it being public and all. He didn't know why he was wasting his time. Then he looked at Rita laughing as she sauntered away, her slim hips moving back and forth in her jeans, and he knew why. Everybody knew why. *I want me a piece of that,* he'd told his friend Byron Joe Gunther.

"Everybody wants a piece of that," Byron Joe had answered. "It's between the wantin' and the gettin', there's the rub, ainna?"

"So I'm *gettin'* a piece of that," said Morton.

"You and whose army?" answered Byron Joe.

Why do they call it Homecoming? Morton wonders. Who leaves? Nobody. And the ones that do never come back. It's the ones who don't leave who go every year. They ought to call it Homestaying Weekend. He thinks about this as he twists the top off another long-neck. If only he weren't married, he thinks. If only he hadn't been forced into marrying Lilly. He wouldn't have done it if she hadn't appealed to his better nature. He's a softie in matters of the heart. Always has been. She caught him in a weak, unthinking moment, and the rest, as they say, is history. God, but he loathes her.

The psychology of the large does not apply to him and Lilly. Their deck furniture consists of those metal scallop-backed chairs can-tilevered over a base of U-shaped tubing. The chairs are permanently tipped backwards, the leg tubing having succumbed over time to Morton's and Lilly's weight. No matter. Here in this enclave of ranch houses plunked down on fill and lake muck, their sump pump con-stantly going, wheezing out dribbles of water only to have it perco-late back into their basement, Morton and Lilly Brunner act like smaller people. There's a plastic fawn grazing on the weeds where it gets too wet to mow, and hummingbird feeders are attached to the picture windows behind their heads. Lilly is sitting like a potted plant in one of the chairs, its metal laboring to support her, and she's doing needlepoint under the bug lights. A bug zapper is glowing purple behind her, zitzing moths and mosquitoes into oblivion with great regularity. Lilly's needlepoint is of leprechauns dancing beneath a rainbow. She's working on the pot of gold coins now, which look, because she's miscounted her stitches, more like pennies left out on the railroad tracks than like coins of the realm.

That doesn't matter, either. Anything round in her needlepoints—bears, babies, hot-air balloons—all come out looking thin, malnour-ished. The balloons look like they're about to make a sudden descent through the bottom of the pillow, the babies look like those old-men infants common in fifteenth century paintings. It's as though she sees the world as thinner than it is, as though something vital—the world's largeness, perhaps?—were already squeezed out of it.

This extends to her clothing. She's a twenty-four on her good days, a twenty-six or a twenty-eight on her bad ones, which are frequent enough to seem permanent, but what she buys are twenty-twos that sit in her closet unused, or she squirms herself inside the too-small clothing so that it seems as though her arms are bursting from her blouse sleeves, her belly from her waistband, her thighs from her slacks. Morton sometimes will say she looks like a sausage cooked inside its own casing. Well, she says, maybe somebody should poke me, then, let them juices flow. She's hoping he wasn't just being mean, was being playful, too, but often as not he'll look away right then, and the message is clear: nobody, he thinks, would like to poke her, least of all her husband.

As she's gotten older she's gotten short of breath as well. So she sits a lot, and does needlepoint, and often puts that aside to look at the crane flies trying to find a way to make a safe landing on the bug lights. They're so skinny, those flies, she bets they're unkind to their kids. She and Morton have never had children. She's not sure if there's a regret in that or not. There used to be, but she thinks it's gone away now. If they had kids it would have been when Morton was . . . But she won't allow her thinking to go there. She remembers trying to get pregnant all those years. Once or twice it seemed like she was, but her doctor told her, no, it was just that as large as she was she shouldn't expect to be regular. The thought crossed her mind once that God was punishing her for having married Morton by getting him to believe she was pregnant, but she dismissed that notion. It required her to think of God as being ironic and mean, and she didn't want to believe that. It would mean God was too much like her husband.

If they had had kids they'd be in high school now. She's sorry now they didn't. She and Morton—Morton especially—did a lot of stupid things, and not getting pregnant was one of them. Though it's not the kids themselves she misses; it's the not having had them. Her friends with kids are almost through having them. They're talking about trips they'll make without the kids, things they'll do, places they'll see. She and Morton have always had that but they never went anywhere. She wonders, if they *had* gone anywhere, would it be different from having gone after your kids are grown, gone, she means, with the knowledge that you're going without your kids versus going never having had any? It probably is different. It's probably better.

Life can be so unfair. Even that Sabo woman was just about done raising hers, and for her friends it seems as though it's a part of every conversation: what the kids did, how they are, who they're dating now, what they're thinking now for after high school—a big rash of graduations this spring, and she and Morton went to a lot of parties; they were like an extra set of parents, only their kids didn't really exist, and Muffy, their miniature schnauzer, was just so dear but nobody saw her like they did and it was embarrassing to keep bringing up Muffy's antics when everybody else was discussing children so after a while she just kept quiet about it.

It just didn't seem fair, the way some women dropped children like they were bonbons and she and Morton . . . She tries to concentrate on the leprechaun's foot. His face bears a curiously sad expression for someone who's just discovered a pot of gold coins, even if they are a little lopsided. It must be the light. He'll look better once she takes him inside.

That Sabo woman. And her sister, whom Morton had . . . She doesn't want to think about that, either. That was a long time ago. She sets her needlepoint aside, looks over at Morton. He's drinking a Miller Lite and looking at the piles of dredge and fill that obscure their view of the lake. And he's been telling her about his run-in with Rita Sabo at Homecoming.

She should have been there. That woman wouldn't have dared bother Morton if she'd been there. She wouldn't have talked to Morton if she'd been there. That Sabo woman shut up around her. One thing that Sabo woman respected was a baleful glare. Her husband, too. It wasn't a one-way street. Nothing ever was with Morton, even if he said it was. He'd been drinking, too. No doubt he looked approachable. As big as he was now, women still found him attractive. They still came on to him. She knew that. When he was drinking he'd tell her things. She'd gotten used to this early in their marriage—his refusal to share intimacies with her (his refusal to be intimate with her) unless he was drunk. Then he told her everything. So he'd been drinking hardy this evening or he wouldn't be telling her any of this now. How that Sabo woman—she was in her cups pretty good, too, he reasoned—had just come up to him in the beer shed and started badgering him about her sister. That, anyway, is what Morton wants her to believe. Because no matter what she tells herself, the fact is Morton makes up things. He tells stories. He is like a nine-year-old boy in that way still. Catch him with his Mr. Doodly outside his pants, a wrench in one hand and an unconscious woman beneath him and he was as likely to say "she made me do it" as anything. His explanations rang false, always, and while she might believe that Sabo woman had started the conversation this evening, once Morton opened up his own mouth to say so she had to throw that belief in the trash with all the other ones she'd ever held or cherished about her Morton. Her Morton—that was good for a laugh. He had always considered himself on loan to her, and she knew that, marriage vows or no. And even now, some twenty years after they'd first said, *I do*, Morton didn't. It makes her angry, and when she picks up her needlepoint again she stabs the leprechaun's feet with quick flustered angry jabs that are the real cause of his dancing. If you look closely, the leprechaun isn't grinning at all. He is gritting his teeth. Which is what Lilly is doing now as Morton holds forth on how he had explained everything, once again, yet one more time again, not that it did any good, to that Sabo woman.

"And did she believe you?"

"She doesn't believe anybody. She could have seen it happening and she wouldn't believe it. Betty Sabo herself would have to come back from the dead and explain it to her for her to buy what I was saying to her."

"And what did you say?"

Morton finishes his beer and goes back inside for another Miller Lite. He throws the twist-off cap into the marsh. The empty he leaves by the picture window's sliding glass door. He won't pick up after himself if you put a gun to his head. "Same old same old. She don't listen. Never has."

"There was a boy drowned over by the subdivision yesterday." Lilly doesn't know why she offers this bit of information, only she's tired of Morton's lying and she wants to change the subject, and this seems to fit the bill. Never mind that Morton will find a way to get that conversational train back on track.

Morton has a long pull on his beer, sits on another green lawn chair that looks like a seashell. Its tubing creaks under his weight. "I heard about it. The story is he got himself tangled up and stayed under."

"I was there, Morton."

"What are you saying? You went over to the subdivision and checked it out?" He can imagine Lilly doing this. Being the vicarious mom, putting trembling fingers to her lips as she contemplates the body of her drowned imaginary son. The horror, the horror. He wants to belch.

"I'm saying I was there that other time. I'm saying I'm tired of you making up stories about what did and did not happen. I'm saying I'm tired of that Sabo woman staring at me every shift for six or eight hours straight like she knows something I'm supposed to know but don't because you won't ever tell me." There. At least the train on the tracks now is hers.

"There's nothing to tell. You seen it."

Lilly stabs at the leprechaun and wonders about what she has seen.

Twenty years ago, nearly—was it really that long ago? Seventeen, anyway. Then as now, Lilly and Morton and the Sabo sisters—there were two of them then—all worked at the Everfresh Canning Plant. Morton was a year-round employee, head of maintenance, and Lilly and her friend Lila and Rita Sabo all worked on the cook room floor. Betty Sabo worked over in labeling. Easy work, letting all those labels go by. A machine piddles two stripes of glue on the labels, the cans roll over them, and all you have to do is make sure the glue machines are cleaned and clog-free and full of glue and the labels are lining up straight. The women down at that end of the plant smoke cigarettes and chat as they watch the cans roll by them. They have plenty of time for foolishness. Plenty of time to seek out the younger, still boy-slender husbands of women who don't look so good, who might have a little weight problem, whose frames justify a little more meat on their bones. Only who understands that? Nobody, least of all their husbands. So their husbands chat up these silly women who have no real work to do. They spend time with them during their breaks, go out for beers with them after work, ignoring their own wives, who might like a fish dinner on a Friday night once in a while, too.

But no, there's no time for that. There's time for going out with the boys, and staying out till all hours, and never mind that some of the boys are women, no, never mind that, it's just, I'm sorry, honey, I'll be home late tonight, don't wait up, and don't worry, honey, we'll get around to a little evening out for ourselves one of these days, too.

Well, baloney. He wasn't fooling anyone. And she was going to prove it. One hot night when he said he had to work late she just waited until around midnight or so and took the other truck down to the plant to see. Sure enough, his truck was there and he was in it. In the truck's bed. With somebody. Her truck wheels crunching gravel, her lights off, they didn't hear her until she was right on top of them and she switched on the high beams. And then Morton swung his head round, jacklit like a deer, and then that head surfaced, that other head, Betty Sabo's head, and Morton, as though he could keep her from seeing what she'd already seen, smacked that head with the flat side of a wrench. She had seen that, all right. She had seen plenty.

They carried her inside the plant—Morton had keys—and they set her down next to the cooling tank. That was where Morton said the party had been. And there were still bottles scattered around and water splashed over the side of the cooling tank as though a great many people had been frolicking. They set her down there, where she could sleep it off, and the day crew would find her if she didn't wake up early enough to leave by the side door.

So how did she get into the cooling tank? And why would she drown herself? These were questions Lilly would always stumble over, and when she wasn't thinking about them, there was the drowned woman's sister looking at her reproachfully, as though she had had a hand in doing something about it, which wasn't the case at all. She didn't know how these things happened, and she didn't want to know why, so why was God punishing her? Why was God making her live with the shame of something she hadn't done? No charges were filed. Why should they be? It was an accident, however that woman found herself in that tank. That woman was a wreck, a disaster waiting to happen. She probably did a balance beam act once she woke up and fell in and was too damn drunk to realize she was drowning. So why was that woman's sister always looking at her like she'd done it? She hadn't done anything. And Morton neither. He came home pretty much right away after she did. He just had to tidy up, he said. So stop looking at me, Rita Sabo! Just quit your godawful staring! And Morton! With his stories! He couldn't go out for a paper without her thinking he was lying anymore. She was so furious. And now he was telling her that Sabo woman hit on him tonight. Well, maybe she had and maybe she hadn't.

They really should have had children. Everything would be different if they'd of had children.

"It was easier, you know, Morton, when Rita had that dazed look on her face. When all them kids of hers were little and she couldn't hardly breathe to keep up. But they're mostly grown now and she has time on her hands. She has time to think about things, Morton."

"So let her think. We didn't do anything."

"We didn't do anything? Of course *we* didn't do anything! It was you, you and her that did something. You didn't do anything. Maybe it slipped your mind how I found you?"

"You won't give that a rest, will you?"

"I should give it a rest? I should just forget what I saw in those high beams? You with that woman in the back of your pickup? You with your pants off and a wrench in your hands? You coldcocked her, Morton, like she was a heifer you didn't have any use for."

"Betty was fine when we left."

"When we left? No, when I left. I don't know how she was when you left."

"The same. She was the goddamn same!"

"She was propped up beside that tank when I went home."

"She was beside the tank when I left, too! Then I came back and there she was."

"So how'd she find her way inside? You think she walked into that tank and drowned?"

"How the hell should I know? You think I was her goddamn mother? I was her lover, dammit. Not her mother, her lover!"

"Stop shouting at me!"

But Morton can't stop. They'd been over this territory so many times in the days right after it happened, and then he'd shut up, and then the years of silence after, and always, always, always with Lilly holding this silent card on him, this trump card, like she knew what he'd done, like she'd been covering for him when she didn't know the first thing about anything. So now he is screaming at his wife, "I was her lover, okay? I was just her lover! Her goddamn lover!" until his wife is a quivering mass of jelly, and now she's weeping, hands over her eyes like she can't or doesn't want to see anything, blubbering, weeping, "Stop it, stop it! You don't know how much I loved you to put up with that much shame!"

Which is what stops him. He quiets himself. He had been about to heave his bottle into the field or smash it on the cement but he puts it down next to the needlepoint she'd dropped at her feet. That idiot leprechaun. Why is she crying? He puts his hand on her jellylike shoulder and pats her hair. Quietly he says, "Jesus, woman, sometimes you drive me crazy. I poked her a few times, that was all. Nothing else ever passed between us, I swear."

"And how is that supposed to make me feel?"

"I never loved nobody but you."

"You didn't love her?"

He crouches down as low as his belly will allow. "How could I? I was married to you."

Lilly snuffles. He is lying but in some way she feels better. Nurtured by her twin beliefs. That he is lying—how could he not have loved his lover? But he is right, too—they *were* married, and that carried you over or through a lot of things. He could have loved Betty some but not completely. One love, the married love, could ride you over the other kind. One was finer, higher, than what you did out of base need. One was permanent, one was temporary. She had tried his belief in the furnace of her soul, and it had not been found wanting. It was stronger for being in the fire. She is glad of that, whatever else he has done to cause her shame. Through her sniffling and her tears she crinkles her eyes at him. Morton, her husband.

And Morton, her husband, looks out over the fill and the dredge piles, at the twisted limbs of sumac that grow out of their crowns, and knows she has won another round. She is wearing him down, she is, and what Morton feels is just like Peter after a long night that supposedly ends up in relief. You say what you need to to get yourself off the hook.

"I'll get ready for bed now," Lilly says, getting up and gathering her things—her leprechaun with its grimace and misshapen coins, her basket of yarn, her tea. "You'll be coming soon to me, yes?" she asks, and Morton nods assent before she slips into the house, a triumphant woman, sure of her womanliness, sure her husband will come to her soon and they will do the things husbands and wives do to each other in the privacy of their own bedrooms. He slides the screen door closed behind her and waves as she goes round the corner, down the hall to where she'll be waiting for him, freshly washed, freshly perfumed, her immenseness glowing in a flimsy rag of chiffon she liked to call her peignoir.

And then Morton Brunner picks up the bottle he'd set by her feet and throws it as hard as he can towards the lake that he knows is there but for the goddamn life of him can not see.

I STARTED "MORTON and Lilly, Dredge and Fill" when I needed a break from *The Company Car,* the fat comic novel I was writing. A fifty-year marriage, with all its ups and downs, is at the center of *The Company Car,* and probably I was drawn to writing about Morton and Lilly and this darker side of a marriage, one with a secret at its center, because it was time to get some real darkness out of my system. Also, I had written about Morton and Lilly before, in the novella "War Babies," which appeared in *The Clouds in Memphis,* and I couldn't stop thinking about them, how they managed to hang together in a weird mix of loathing and longing and distrust and betrayal, and yes, even love.

The conclusion of "War Babies" slides into Rita Sabo's point of view, and in trying to come up with an explanation for how her sister died she imagines the scene of Betty's death. She even goes so far as to project herself into Lilly's point of view and consciousness for the climactic action and its aftermath. It seemed—and seems—absolutely right that the novella end there, with us inside Lilly's consciousness, which is actually housed inside Rita Sabo's, a babushka doll of point of view that creates empathy for both women, even though Rita believes Lilly is deeply implicated in Betty's death. But after I'd published that and was working on *The Company Car,* I kept thinking, Well, that's what Rita needs to believe, but what if she got it wrong? What if her explanation wasn't the right one? What if the truth was even more complex than that?

My intention, though, was not to come up with the "true story" of what happened the night Betty Sabo died, but rather to explore the nature of this relationship between Morton and Lilly. I had a sense of who Rita thought these characters were, but she was a biased observer. What were the insides of their lives like? Omniscience as a point of view choice made sense, perhaps with the point of view shifting from one of them to the other, but I didn't know where I wanted the scene to start, or in whose head I should begin. What I did know was that they had remained stagnant as a couple, trapped by their own past, with those events—Morton's betrayal of Lilly and Betty's death (whatever actually happened that night)—between them. I knew going in that structurally this would be an aftermath story, the past burbling up into a present-time conversation. I also had the sense that it would take place as a single scene in the present, but there would be a recent trigger (Morton or Lilly running into Rita at work or somewhere else) that would lead into the conversation and evoke thoughts of the past. What I didn't have was something to ground the action, "a place in space" where they could interact. I needed to see them somewhere: At work? After work, in a bar? Over dinner? Watching TV? Getting ready for bed?

As is often the case, a trip home to visit my parents provided me with serendipitous images. On Friday night I had to drive into town for milk and drove past the Homecoming celebration. I didn't stop in but recalled the one time, years before, that I had. That gave me the story's trigger—Morton's just come home from being out, drinking with the boys, he's run into Rita, and he's drunk enough that he wants to torture his wife with that news. The next day I took my kids fishing to the same lake I used to fish as a kid, only an algae bloom kept fouling our hooks. We pulled up lake muck and gunk, and I remembered the time when I was a teenager when they had to dredge the lake and they dumped all the fill behind the grocery store where I was working then. The fishing being lousy, I took the kids biking instead, on a recently developed trail that used to be a railbed. To get to the trailhead, I drove through what used to be marsh on the lake's southern end (towards a train trestle I used to fish off, too), only lining the road now on both sides was a subdivision comprised of

modest ranches. And I remembered what a friend once told me
about subdivisions built on marshes: they shouldn't be. Their base-
ments leaked, their foundations cracked and the sump pumps were
always going. That Morton and Lilly would have made that kind of
mistake—building a house where it didn't belong—seemed in keeping with their characters. Having them standing out there on their
crumbling deck that's sinking into the marsh seemed like a good
place to open the story, and it seemed natural, too, to talk about them
collectively first, in full omniscience, before the narrator zoomed into
the consciousness of first one, then the other. It also seemed right to try
to balance both their views, for the narrator (and the reader) to have
equal access. But as I was writing, it seemed that Lilly had the greater
grievance, so she ended up with more pages devoted to her point of
view. I tried balancing things, though, by giving Morton the first and
final point of view sections—his thoughts frame Lilly's. And it's
awhile before we get to Lilly—Lilly's point of view doesn't start until
after we've seen them both together, had a Morton section, then
gone back to full omniscience, the narrator looking at them both
together again, then shifting his attention to an external view of Lilly
before finally sliding into her point of view.

Once I had the setting and had figured out that the narration
would be omniscient, capable of being in both their points of view,
the two biggest technical difficulties were finding places where I
could shift from one point of view to the other naturally, and getting
them to actually start talking. It turned out these were related issues.
At first it was a matter of the camera panning from one to the other,
and letting the importance of the past, both recent (Morton's just
come from a run-in with Rita) and distant, surface in their thoughts.
It seemed to make sense for them not to talk to each other here, for
them to be silently stewing in those thoughts. It allowed me to get in
a lot of exposition while maintaining tension—when is this stuff
going to surface between them? Later in the story, once they finally
are talking (it doesn't happen till halfway through the story), it

seemed natural to shift the point of view with certain lines of dialogue. Since there are only the two of them, I could generally dispense with the "he said/she said" tags and give descriptions of them as they're talking, and those external descriptions were places where I could shift focus (just the name itself could be enough of a trigger) before shifting point of view. For the final switch I used a repetition of the phrase "Morton, her husband." The first time it occurs in Lilly's consciousness, essentially a quoted thought. The second time the narrator invokes it consciously, ironically, and pivots into Morton's perspective one final time. I was pleased I stumbled onto that repetition.

Some other things I discovered as I wrote: I needed something for Lilly to be doing. The needlepoint seemed like a natural thing—something fine and tiny done by a large woman. Ditto the dog, Muffy. The bug lights—I worked in a canning factory and I was always fascinated by those insects' deaths. I figured that if they were on a marsh it'd be practical for them to have one of those. The leprechaun, the lawn furniture, the childlessness, the climax and its aftermath (what Morton and Lilly would actually say to each other)—I had no idea about any of that as I began writing. I just kept trying to picture them there on that deck, and imagine what they were doing, what they were thinking, what they would say to each other. That's probably why the climactic scene is fairly intense—when I finally got there, there needed to be an explosion. I knew, given the mention a couple of times of Morton drinking, that something had to happen with one of those bottles at the end (especially after he wants to throw one or smash one and doesn't). And after I wrote the opening I knew that the marsh was enough of a presence, both physically and psychologically, that it needed to come back into play in some way at the end. I wanted things to feel cramped for them, the world—the past—pressing in on them, both in their minds and externally, and through the structure, the narration and the setting I worked to evoke that.

David Haynes

THAT'S RIGHT, YOU'RE NOT FROM TEXAS

HERE COME A couple of useless sentences: We couldn't make it work. We just weren't each other's types. Think if you will about the untold millions for whom such ideas are entirely outside their ken. Their parents trade a goat and a couple of pounds of cheese for some poor creature wrapped in a sheet, and for a lot of young men a positive outcome is one in which his future life partner has all her limbs intact and whose visible anatomy doesn't feature any giant hairy moles. Makes one ashamed, doesn't it, and perhaps a little embarrassed too about all those who jumped off our own hooks.

Yasmine and I, both recent transplants to a godforsaken urban wasteland known as Dallas, were headed to the Melrose Hotel bar for a quiet drink after seeing a student production of *Six Degrees of Separation*. We had been going out for three months, steering through the intellectual bona fides segment of dating. I'd sprung for the box seats at the Meyerson and she'd hauled me to the sorts of movies where everything is hazy and people talk in French for a couple of hours. To my mind the play had shared the curse of most school productions, that of forcing young adults to overreach toward emotions they'd not truly own for decades. This bothered Yasmine not one iota. Yasmine is a woman who finds much of life charming—run-of-the-mill greeting cards, spitting and obnoxious toddlers, Thursdays. And don't get me wrong. I've no problem with relentlessly sunny dispositions. Prior to Yasmine I had sustained a long-term relationship with a woman whose entire apartment had been decorated with crudely drawn cartoons of balloon-headed figures, reminding me at every turn what "love is." Generally speaking, we cranky types benefit from being around people like her. It's important to be reminded that the world is basically a good place, critical aesthetics notwithstanding. In response to Yasmine's generic critique of the play, I had offered my commentary on the lead actress, saying:

"There was something very 'nineteen' about that girl," remembering how she had been unable to abandon the annoying personal habit of tossing her hair over her shoulder after every line—a tic ill serving her middle-aged character and from evidence the only body language she could muster to support her clearly limited emotional range.

Yasmine breathed out a quiet, "Rodney," shorthand established early in our time together to be used when Rodney wasn't being very "nice."

She said, "I guess it's just that I feel so much empathy with those who are willing to take creative risks and put themselves out there for the rest of us." A typical Yasmine platitude. She no doubt lingered at shopping mall talent shows, dropped dollar bills into the greasy cap of the squawky saxophonist who frequented nightspots in Deep Ellum. I was saved from having to respond to her nonsense by something that went thump-thump-thumping beneath the wheels of the Camry.

A short side trip—to Europe, in fact—before I tell you my initial response to this disaster. My father—may God rest his soul—drove a gasoline tanker across German lines in Czechoslovakia. He adhered to the just-keep-the-vehicle-moving-forward school of life management, and I'd found that Dad's example served perfectly well in almost every circumstance I'd ever encountered. Furthermore, experience has taught us that there are two kinds of people in the world. Some are "come look what I found in the Dumpster, honey" kinds of people. You've seen them out behind your own apartment buildings, prodding with some sort of arm extender, eyes squinched together, genuinely curious these people are, they never allow anything to rest in peace. Others, people like you and me, we feel that whatever the hell is in there, we'd rather not know that such things existed on earth, thank you very much, close the lid, lose the stick and wash your hands before you handle the produce.

Yasmine, the moment the car went bumpety-bump, craned herself up and around like a fat guy looking for the meal cart on the plane. She grabbed my arm.

"I think you just ran over something," she announced, and I said, "Oh, really," as if it were news to me, and I kept rolling down Beverly Boulevard. We were driving through the Park Cities at the time. University Park or Highland Park; I can't tell them apart. The Park Cities would be the enclave of the unnecessarily wealthy, set into the heart of Dallas like a pearl in a pile of shit. Home of the likes of Ross Perot, Dick Cheney and the late cosmetics queen Mary Kay, I would be exaggerating if I told you that they had pictographic signs on the streets leading into town with a big red slash mark drawn through a pointedly ethnic face. This is Texas. No such signs are necessary. One look around and you just sort of knew that it was a good idea to get out of town by sunset.

It was well past sunset. I kept driving.

"Stop," she said, and this was nothing resembling a request. This was the Stop of the sun-weary border guard on the frontier between warring nations. This was the Stop of the curmudgeon physician, queried by the two-pack-a-day smoker for advice about his habit. This was the Stop of the soccer mom who, beyond hysteria, is one balled-up fist short of a date in family court. And like all hysterical mothers, Yasmine even put her hand across my chest as if to keep me from flying through the windshield when I jammed the brakes on.

Which, of course I did.

We, both of us, peered through the back windshield to discover what I had done. Alas, like tony communities across the globe, the Park Cities are tastefully underlit by gaslights, and all that stretched behind us was impenetrable darkness, interrupted here and there with quavering puddles of golden anemic lamplight.

Yasmine, as any second-rate disaster movie heroine worth her salt would have done, had concluded and then announced, "We'll have to go back." And we've all seen enough of these films to know the drill. Lava flows would be blocking the exits to the island even as I put the car in reverse. At any moment some unfortunate extra would be sucked into Mothra's gaping maw.

I backed down the street and eyeballed this woman sitting next to me. I gave her my what-the-hell-is-your-damn-problem-anyway look. This was another move I'd learned from my father. Mom would ask him—for the twenty-seventh time—if he wouldn't mind pretty please doing something like separating frozen pork chops or reaching down the double boiler from the top shelf of the pantry. Dad would slam that cleaver down into the meat, never, for not even one second diverting his curled-lip sneer from her direction, potential lost fingertips be damned. Ignoring his glare, her own face a vision of equanimity, Mom would shuck her peas, flinching now and again as the blade chopped through to the cutting board. "Supper in an hour," she'd chirp, gathering her hunks of hacked flesh into a baking dish. This was a broad who played to win and who knew how to savor a victory when she did.

I was a man who backed down dark and segregated streets at the whim of a woman I hadn't even made my mind up about yet. I rolled about as far back as I believed I'd rolled forward, announced, cleverly I thought, that there didn't seem to be anything there.

Undaunted, Yasmine bolted from the car to have a closer look at the situation.

"Ooooh," she sighed, that sound women make when they break a nail or when their stockings run or when the man they went to the bed-and-breakfast with finds ESPN on the cable lineup. "The poor, poor thing."

I warned her that I was pretty sure she wasn't supposed to be touching that. This is another thing one learns watching Monster-vision. Poking around strange animals always turns out badly. At any moment, whatever the hell that was would erect itself, extend its claws and eyes would be gouged from their sockets, almost certainly my own.

But Yasmine was way ahead of me on this one. Felix had already taken the express bus to kitty heaven. I must have gotten him real good—a two-tire job, at least, maybe I'd even dragged the bastard.

She asked me if I had something in the car to wrap him in, and I thought, okay, so we'll cover him up and leave him for the Mexicans to pick up in the morning. I agreed to sacrifice my tire emergency towel for the good of the order.

So peaceful he looked, curled up there against the curb, and I could imagine him reclined just so in the sunny spot at the foot of his former owner's bookcase. And as Yasmine approached him with the tire towel, I entertained a trashy fantasy that the moment she cradled him in cloth and lifted him into her arms, his little kitty-cat eyes would snap open and he would spring back to life. Santa Yasmina of Highland Park, patroness of mediocre actresses, restorer of lost house pets.

But that didn't happen, and instead she said, "We have to see if anyone around here is his people." And before I could protest, before I could remind her that it was nine-thirty at night and that we were in the Park Cities, a place that didn't cotton to door-to-door canvassing even in broad daylight; that we were two people of African decent in a part of town where people like us could not buy homes even if we could afford to; that what she snuggled there in her arms was most likely a stray, an animal that no one had ever wanted, a creature who perhaps, like us, had only been passing through this part of town on his way to the places where one could find actual food scraps in the street and where one could socialize with cats of a similar stripe; before I could say any of that, Yasmine was already making her way to the door of the house closest to where he had died.

It annoyed me, the fact that this woman seemed fairly nonplussed by the, frankly, icy reception she and I received from the good citizens of Highland Park. Perhaps her skin was thicker than elephant hide. Maybe the brittle disdain of the bourgeoisie meant no more to her than did the idle ravings of the homeless who lived beneath the flyovers of the Stemmons Expressway. Maybe she was just too dumb to notice. It was a blessing that many of the doors hadn't been answered at all.

"I guess a lot of folks must be out to dinner," she mused, passing me the corpse. Her tone betrayed just the slightest bit of annoyance; her ever so vague exasperation I heard as directed less toward the inhospitable residents of Beverly Drive than toward my having the bad judgment to run over a cat in the first place. I chose not to mention the flashes of faces I'd spied catching a quick eyeful of who'd dared ring their doorbells. I'd spent years selling candy bars door-to-door for the Midget Gunners football club, so I'd been trained to recognize the telltale signs of people pretending not to be home.

Yasmine rang on bravely up and down the block. More than a few of those chimes rang to the tune of "The Yellow Rose of Texas," a song which had ruined Emily Dickinson for me forever. In my arms, the dead cat seemed to have taken on weight. I hoped it wasn't seeping, hoped that the unpleasant dampness I felt was no more than the sweaty palms I remembered from working the cul-de-sacs of Breckenridge Hills with my winning smile and my carrying case of chocolate bars with almonds.

At the next house an actual bald person (as opposed to a fashionably bald person) opened his door but didn't say anything.

"Hi!" Yasmine enthused. A person would have thought she was from the Welcome Wagon or from the local high school pep squad. As I've already noted, this part of her personality was a big + for me. I'd grown tired of sullen, cool women, the sort you'd have to beg for a friendly word or a smile. And then when they did smile—those ice princesses—they did so with all the ersatz sincerity of the disembodied woman on the campus voice mail. Yasmine, she had this lovely way of popping her head off to the side when she greeted people. Her whole face would open up and she would clasp her arms behind her back. I loved this about her.

Bald guy, by contrast—he seemed unmoved.

Yasmine pressed on. She said:

"This unfortunate critter ran under our car, and we're trying to find his people." What an endearing way of putting it, I thought, although who knows what Baldy heard? From the expression on his face, we'd apparently just asked him for a donation to the Gay Communist Pro-Abortion League. He grunted—it was a Texan kind of noise—and then he shook his head. He closed the door, disappearing himself into the depths of his McMansion.

"Moving on," Yasmine suggested, though I sensed, however subtly, her veneer of optimism crumbling. Just like it did for the runners-up on the high school homecoming court, this being-a-good-sport business could really get a girl down. Even so, chin held high, she persisted, and five houses down, our heroine hit paydirt.

"Well, hi," the woman at that door said, her "hi" having somewhere in the neighborhood of seven syllables. Another mark of my character: I don't necessarily consider it a good sign to be greeted quite so eagerly at ten P.M. on a school night. Yasmine, however, had been buoyed by our reception.

"We're trying to find his owner," she told the woman, and she flourished a hand in the direction at my unfortunate cargo. Like some Renaissance Madonna, I tilted my bundle toward his viewer.

"Bless his heart, that's old Sammy-cat."

Yasmine extending a sympathetic hand, asked, "He's yours?"

"Lord, no. Old Sammy don't belong to anyone. He's a wild old tom what's lived around here for years. He's dead, is he?"

Directing this question toward his murderer, Yasmine looked over where I was standing, so I said, "He was run over by a car that had been being driven by me."

Which caused Yasmine to give me a look, which was then short-circuited by our homeowner, who said, "Y'all bring him right on in through here. Come on with him."

She showed us into her front parlor. She had filled the room, as had many of her neighbors, with the sorts of heavy hard furniture one imagines might have decorated medieval castles, assuming, of course, the lord of the manor had an account at the local Sears. Leather, hard edges, wrought iron, rough-hewn cedar-beamed boxes. A dog the size of a small horse pranced through the room, ignoring us. We were not introduced.

"That Sammy-cat's been living back in here for four or five years. He wouldn't stay anywhere and they never could catch him. Can I offer y'all something?"

Yasmine enthused over the hospitality, though she ultimately passed. What I wanted more than a drink was a place to unload my bundle of joy. Hoping that we didn't mind if she did, our hostess topped up her goblet with something brown from a lovely crystal decanter. Pioneers could have crossed the continent on her liquor cart.

"Do y'all live around here?" she asked. "I don't think I've seen you in the neighborhood."

And I thought, here we go, but charming Yasmine bit this conversational hook like a starving piranha, unlike myself detecting not the slightest ill intent in the query. She described my professorship and her own association with a prominent law firm in town. She confessed to her lifelong citizenship of North Texas, however recently new to the Metroplex.

"Rodney here lives right down the street, practically. Just down Douglas, over the city line."

I hefted the carcass in my arms by way of acknowledging my residence. The old tom had been a big mother. That had to be a good twenty pounds of dead cat meat I was holding, and in an uncomfortable position too, eschewing dead animal emissions from my immediate person.

"A professor!" the woman chirped. "I could tell you were a something." And then she took another big slug of the sauce.

Personally I'd about had it with Park Cities cocktail hour, so I asked, "Do you have a trash bin out back?" And I once again lofted the guest of honor for emphasis.

Well, you'd have thought I'd asked these women to peel off their panties and get down on all fours.

"What?" I asked. "Isn't that what you do with these things?" I honestly didn't know. When I was growing up, house pets on their last legs had a way of disappearing quietly sometime during the school day. They didn't make dads any cheaper than my father's edition, and I can't imagine him doing anything other than making a run to the nearest dump. I bet he didn't even slow down while tossing the bag from the car. We are not a sentimental people.

Apparently our other mourners were. The two women had reached their hands toward each other the way that women in the audience on Oprah do when Dr. Phil isn't making any headway with the bad husband of the day.

With her other hand Yasmine caressed the bundle in my arms. "Sammy here deserves something a little more dignified than that," so I said, "Fine." I might have mentioned the fact that this piece of work in my arms had no doubt crapped in every garden between here and Texas Stadium, crap no doubt composed largely of the remnants of dozens and dozens of songbirds, but I played the good boy.

Our homeowner rounded up an old fishing tackle box, property, she claimed, of her late husband (the introduction of whom provided another opportunity for the gals to bond). I was ordered to arrange my victim ("delicately, please") inside the case, which I did, and I then stepped aside so our funeral directors could fluff up the towel around him, make the old boy comfortable for the long night ahead. Then I was directed to a small washroom to remove the gore from my hands. Soaping and soaping some more and then some more, I remember having one of those moments of insight that, while on the surface are not necessarily profound, somehow resonate deeply, feel life-transforming.

I thought, This is *so* not me.

And for just a moment walking out of that washroom I thought that what I would do was run out to my car and drive away from these people and never look back. I did not, and again in my head there had been the image of Dad, a man who believed, if in nothing else, in the importance of staying the course. Sure the road up ahead may be mined, and without a doubt the woods around you are chock-full of Krauts with bazookas and grenades. You are inches from enough fuel to send you to the moon and back. What do you do? You stay the course. Later, maybe, you tell them what they can do with their f—ing silver star, but for now, you agreed to be here, so you stick it out.

I followed the women's voices to a tiny garden behind the house.

"That was one of Sammy's favorite spots," our hostess was announcing, adding the fact that her "boy," Jose, "fished turds out of there by the sackful." For just a moment I expected to be handed a shovel, but it quickly became apparent that it would be Jose's job to inter the remains beneath the azaleas. But I was not entirely off the hook.

"Perhaps the professor here will say a few words for us," and before

I could suggest that perhaps he wouldn't, hands had been joined, and there we stood, gathered over a tackle box full of dead cat and two citronella candles. Yasmine squeezed my hand in a way that had already come to indicate that Rodney should "behave." And so I did.

"Friends," I began, "we gather here on this lovely Texas evening to bid a fond farewell to our beloved neighborhood hooligan, Sammy-the-cat. A fixture in the Park Cities for almost a half decade, he was known for his irascible sense of humor and for his deep interest in all things culinary. Sam never met a stranger, and, good Texan that he was, he lived free till his dying day."

I actually believe that I heard both women sniffing back the tears. Just before she closed tackle box, I'm sure I saw Sammy's yellow fur emitting a warm glow. Yasmine intoned a quiet prayer and we blew out the candles, backing away solemnly from the picnic table-cum-bier. Following the women inside, I actually looked behind me, though what I expected to see, I couldn't tell you.

Later, in the car, Yasmine made it clear that my graveside service had pretty much made up for running over the cat in the first place.

"That was very sweet," she offered, but I had been miffed and couldn't even thank her for the compliment.

What I said was, "The old girl can tell her bridge club about the nice coloreds that stopped by with a dead cat the other night."

"Oh, come on," she sighed, assuring me that I had the situation all wrong.

I reminded her that the woman hadn't even bothered to tell us her name.

Yasmine clicked her tongue and pronounced our homeowner harmless. She started to lecture me about old southern white ladies, then stopped and, midsentence, nodded her head, said:

"I keep forgetting, you're not from Texas." And I may have mumbled something to the effect of Thank God almighty, but I don't really remember because, just then, she reached across the car and she caressed a hand that was still soft from when I'd washed away the dead cat stink. I loved that touch. It had been the perfect thing to do just then. It had said to me, "I get you." And, "It's okay." And it felt right and good. So good in fact that we skipped the drinks that night and went directly to my place and, as they say down in these parts, we had us a whole bunch of sex, a whole bunch of times.

And I imagine you're thinking how crass I am. But people hook up over much less every minute of every day. Neither of us had anything to be ashamed of.

We hung out for almost another half year after that night, Yasmine and me. Me, through all that time, denying to myself that we would not be each other's forever "it," because I really wanted her to be, or at least for a long time there I did. But it just sort of . . . ended after a time.

I ran into her just once since and we chatted for a while, and it was real friendly. I could tell that neither one of us bore the other the least amount of ill will, and that was comforting to see. It's unlikely we will cross paths again. There are four million souls in North Texas and nothing resembling a place where folks like us might meet. And, anyway, I will leave Texas soon. If there's a God in heaven, I will.

I think about her now and again. About the night in Highland Park, of course, but other things too. The time in Mazatlán and a Thanksgiving with my folks. I liked her and I'm sorry that we didn't fit. I'm two or three ladies down the line these days, and sadly, this current one doesn't feel like a keeper either. Call me picky, but this is supposed to be for the rest of one's life—Dad's rule, remember. A fellow just can't take any chances.

And I'd like to think that Yasmine thinks about me as well. She would still be unattached I'm pretty sure, and you just know that there's a group of girls around her age who she hangs with on the weekends and sometime after work. They go to that wine bar on McKinney or they drive up on Greenville and get the jumbo margaritas at the Blue Horse.

They are a self-sufficient lot, these friends. Each of the ladies has a good job and everyone pays her bills on time. And, no, not a one of them has a live one on the wire, or at least none of them has what she'd consider a keeper. Everyone is disappointed, but they are a cheerful and optimistic lot. They buy another round and talk about the big sale at Kohl's and a potential trip to Ocho Rios. Now and again the talk circles around to the dearth of good black men and all the might-have or should-have-beens.

Yasmine—she's the sweet one of the group—she wonders rhetorically whatever happened to good old Rodney. The girls have a good laugh at his silly name and they try to remember which one he could have been. Was he the brother with the BMW and the bad BO? Didn't he live down there in a loft in the West End? Doesn't his mama still send you a birthday card every year?

Yasmine, she'll giggle and shake her head. There's a place in her heart for every one of those men, and we all hold on to her as well. But she'll say, no, she'll say "Rodney. You remember Rodney. He's the one who ran over the cat."

A T   T H E   T I M E I sat down to begin working on this story I had been thinking a lot about boundaries and borders—an ongoing obsession of mine. I've come to believe that one of the characteristics of North Texas is that the lines between things—between men and women, rich and poor, progressive and reactionary, gay and straight, between and among all kinds of ethnic, religious and cultural groups—are more sharply drawn than they are in other parts of the country in which I've lived. These dichotomies exist in parallel with a denial that such boundaries are real or important. (At least at the level of public conversation this denial seems true.) I also believe that that which gives fiction its narrative energy are the frictions that exist at borders; this energy is also a by-product of the explanations, justifications, mythologies and lies people create in order to explain who they are as they come up against these boundaries from one day to the next. This story continues an exploration in my fiction of people on the borders and the fictions we make out of our lives.

There exists a natural tension between comic sensibility and the strictures of fiction. The wildness, silliness and absurdity that I relish push against the neatness and discretion we are taught to value. In creating my comic stories I find it is important to keep a keen eye on the secondary characters. If I find them becoming too much of a cartoon, then I know that the fiction is in trouble and just might get lost in the funhouse. The writer of comic fiction must also pay close attention to rhythm and sound. A misplaced beat can cause an otherwise funny line to fall flat. A good deal of the revision in this piece went into re-creating entire passages until the flow of the language achieved the exact effect I was looking for.

The story began with the place—Highland Park, Texas—a neighborhood I actually do drive through every day on my way to and from the university. There's nothing particularly unique about the apart-ness of this place—all metropolitan areas have their wealthy enclaves. But when you drive through such a place on a regular basis, you start to notice things. And those things start to annoy you. Or amuse you. It's interesting to me, for example, that people with three-car garages prefer to park their SUVs in their circular driveways out front; that the streets are unbelievably immaculately clean; that during the day the thoroughfares are clotted with construction vehicles— apparently any house older than thirty years must be bulldozed and another one constructed in its place. I knew I had to set a story there. I'd been writing a lot about mismatched couples, so that element of the story fell right into place. As for the cat, well, many years ago, yes, I did run over one late one evening, or at least I was told I had done so. Not by a passenger, but by another driver who followed me several miles down the street, pulled up beside me and pronounced me a cat mangler. And, yes, I did sort of feel that telltale thump-thumping, but this was St. Paul, Minnesota, and our street maintenance crews were nowhere near as diligent as the Mexicans who scour the byways of Highland Park, Texas—ergo crap went thump-thumping under the car on a regular basis. And, no, I didn't go back there and check, and, no, I didn't feel particularly guilty about it either. What I have always wondered is what exactly did that other driver expect me to have done. Or what he might have done to me. He was a very scary person, that guy in the other car. He had one of those bland, Middle America, serial-killer faces. His voice carried almost no affect, like someone who has been lobotomized or like a pod person. I think about him, actually, a lot more than I do about that poor cat.

Andrea Barrett

OUT HERE

ILANA KOESTLER KNEW Willy Michaels for a total of three weeks, split between a spring and the summer that followed. She spent two nights with him toward the end of the second week of their second time together; then she watched him drive out of the parking lot and disappear over the mountains. After he left for the second time, her life unraveled completely.

This was in Meltonville, off Route 76, five hours west of Philadelphia and a little north of Ohiopyle and the West Virginia border. The Youghiogheny River gorge was visible from the restaurant where Ilana worked, which was set on a small rise at the base of the Chestnut Ridge. The first time Willy walked in he ordered coffee, toast, and juice: hardly enough to keep a man alive.

"Scrapple?" Ilana asked him. "Pancakes? Eggs?"

Four cars piled with narrow bright boats and headed for the steepest stretch of the gorge had swooped into the parking lot that morning before Ilana had even finished making coffee. "The river's up," one of the paddlers had said, as she set a platter of food on the table.

"I heard the first set of rapids is washed out." Holes and rapids and giant waves, obstacles and how to conquer them—the things paddlers always talked about. Some years they also talked about who had drowned the year before, and Ilana had once seen a young man get up and lose his homefries and sausage on the hood of a car outside. No one she knew went down the gorge on purpose, and she had no respect for the strangers who tempted fate in their helmets and silly clothes. But Willy was no paddler, she could see that right away.

"Just toast," Willy said. He killed an hour reading through the Sunday issue of a paper he'd brought with him; then he left her a two-dollar tip and a smile she took to bed with her that night.

On Monday morning the restaurant was empty; all the weekend paddlers had gone back to wherever they lived. Nikos, who owned the restaurant, was in the kitchen cooking and arguing with his wife. Sharon, the other waitress on the early morning shift, was helping Ilana clip the mimeographed sheets of the day's specials onto the menus. She sighed and rose heavily when Willy walked in and chose a table near the window.

"Why don't you finish these?" Ilana asked her. "I'll take care of him."

Willy ordered coffee, toast, and juice again. This time he introduced himself when Ilana brought his order. "I'm visiting my brother," he said. "Half-brother, really—Dalton King. Maybe you know him."

"I don't think so," she said.

Dalton—what kind of a name was that? She would have remembered it, she was sure. She would have noticed if anyone who looked even a little like Willy had moved into town. Willy's face was as clear and smooth as a child's, complicated only by a curved and mobile mouth. She could not imagine how he fit a razor into the soft furrow between his nose and upper lip.

"Dalton and his wife started an organic farm out here a couple of years ago," Willy said. His hair was thick and glossy and almost as long as hers. "Biodynamic French-intensive raised beds, major compost, ladybugs imported from northern California. You know—the whole deal. They ship their stuff to snooty restaurants."

"Really?" Ilana said. That was nice, she thought, the way he said "the whole deal"—as if the two of them shared a set of assumptions about the world. She was used to strangers who acted as if she were entirely ignorant.

"It's a pretty peculiar place," Willy said. "May is always nuts for them—I had some extra vacation time, so I came out to help."

Out, he said. *Out here.* As if there were an *in* somewhere from which he'd ventured forth. She refilled Willy's cup and asked him where he lived.

"Oh," he said. "The city—Philadelphia. You know."

And there was that flattering assumption again. She had never been to Philadelphia; she'd only been to Pittsburgh twice. She learned, over the next few mornings, that Willy had four weeks of paid vacation every year. The fancy blue-and-white sneakers he wore came from the company where he worked; once, he said, he'd been mugged outside a Chinese-Cuban restaurant for the sake of a similar pair. He worked in market research: who bought what sneakers and when and why. He was twenty-six and drove a company car and lived in a tall apartment building overlooking the Delaware River. He liked to dance, he said. There was a club near his apartment where he went dancing almost every night.

WILLY CAME TO the restaurant for six days and then he disappeared. All through the next few months Ilana thought about him. His smooth hands and the way he rolled his cuffs so neatly; his nose, which was a little too short; the dent like a thumbprint below his bottom lip. She told herself it was not his looks that had captivated her but his easy, good-humored charm.

"Was it fun?" Willy had asked her, when she'd told him she'd grown up in Meltonville. Toward the end of his visit he'd spent most of each morning at the restaurant, reading his paper and talking to Ilana whenever she had a free minute. By then he'd told her a lot about himself but asked her hardly anything.

"Growing up out here, away from the McBurbs—it must have been great," he said. "It feels *real* here. You know?"

She'd laughed at him. "We have TVs," she'd said—although she had not, actually, had one for the last eighteen months. "We go to the movies. It's not like we don't know what we're missing."

"You're not missing anything," Willy assured her. "City living sucks."

But his newspapers told a different story. No one in town read the Philadelphia paper, but she learned that she could buy a Sunday issue if she ordered it a week ahead. In bed she spread out the folds of newsprint and imagined how Willy was living his life. The two cats her mother had left behind batted the sections around, and she read reviews of movies running in Philadelphia and imagined Willy watching them. She read articles about Italian restaurants famous for eggplants the size of tomatoes and beans as slender as string. Willy ate in restaurants like that, she knew. His teeth were strong and white and he had beautiful table manners. He had a haircut like the models in the clothing ads, but he was better-looking; the models lacked the heartbreaking dent in Willy's chin.

Willy's apartment, she imagined, hung over the city like a flying saucer. She liked to pretend that the stream running behind her house poured water into the same river that Willy's apartment over-looked. Her mother had told her, years ago, that their stream ran into the Youghiogheny, which ran into rivers that led to larger rivers that fed the Mississippi. That's where you would have ended up, her mother had told her, long after the incident that made Ilana briefly, locally famous. Your body would have floated to the Gulf of Mexico. But Ilana liked to think how a trickle split off from the main flow might run east through a gap in the mountains.

She pored over the Sunday papers and imagined telling Willy all he hadn't asked. How she, like almost everyone she knew, had meant to leave town but had stayed. How her high school boyfriend had dumped her and married someone else; how the plant where she'd had her only good job had closed; and how her parents had vanished. Willy had once asked her, casually, if she got along with her folks; his own, he said, were a pain in the ass, and he almost never saw them.

"Mine aren't around," she'd told him. "I've been on my own for a while." She hadn't said that her father was dead, and she'd glided over the fact that her mother had run off with Charlie Ione eighteen months ago.

"My mother moved south with her boyfriend," she'd told him. She'd smiled, she'd made a joke of it. She hadn't told Willy how her mother had said, "I'm sick of it here." Her mother had known Charlie for twenty years and Charlie's wife had left him. "And we're both sick of being alone," she'd said. "Charlie wants to take me someplace where it's warm." She had taken the TV, the blender, the blow-dryer, the iron, and every other appliance in the house. She'd left Ilana the house itself, signing over the deed as if she were giving Ilana a huge gift. "I want you to be all right," she'd said. "I want you to have something of your own." She hadn't told Ilana about the taxes, the utility bills, the endless list of needed repairs. And Ilana, slipping into the wry, lighthearted role in which Willy had cast her, had kept these facts to herself.

She was sorry, now, that she hadn't told Willy more of the truth. He liked Meltonville, he'd said. It felt authentic. He liked her and the restaurant and her uniform, and even the way Nikos came out of the kitchen and scowled when Ilana spent too much time idling near Willy's table. She thought that Willy might have admired her life had she been brave enough to tell him the details. He liked things gritty, he'd said. He admired grit.

Surely—she imagined telling Willy—surely what had happened to her was not her fault. She'd been resourceful, she thought. Clever.

Economical. No one wanted to buy her house, but after her first winter alone there she'd learned to cut down on the heat bills by moving her bed downstairs and sealing off everything but the kitchen and the living room. This had simplified housekeeping so much that she'd never moved her bed back or opened the sealed-off rooms. By a thousand small reductions she had made a life for herself, and somehow she believed that Willy might appreciate all the obstacles she'd overcome.

She didn't know then if she would ever see Willy again, but she believed that his brother would draw him back and that the story of her life she was rehearsing for him would someday find his ears.

IN JULY, SHORTLY after her twenty-fourth birthday, Ilana went to see Willy's half-brother's organic farm. She found Dalton's address in the telephone book, where it had been all along; after cursing herself for not thinking of this before, she drove out the Old Pike Road and right past the house that the Dubczeks had owned until the closing of the plant. Dalton had transformed it so completely that she drove another hundred yards before the address registered.

She turned her car around and parked in the Hoppelmanns' empty driveway. The Dubczeks' house had been sagging and faded and brush had grown up in the fields—it had looked like the Hoppelmanns' place, or the Meiers', or any one of a dozen abandoned farms along the road. Now it looked like a picture from a magazine. The faded clapboards had been painted morning-glory blue and a greenhouse extended over what had been the front porch. A taut web of strings sprouting tendrils and vines stretched from the glass walls to the second-floor windows. The front lawn was gone, replaced by rows of raised vegetable beds mulched with clean hay: peas, beans, Swiss chard, lettuce beginning to bolt. She saw fences in back, and a neat new shed, and a bulging chicken-wire container filled with clippings and leaves.

There was a woodstove in the kitchen, she remembered Willy saying—not a cookstove, like the one she'd grown up with, but something curved and polished and efficient, something Norwegian or Swedish. Bundles of herbs drying upside down, bins of whole-grain flour, a springhouse lined with smooth wooden shelves on which tiny round goat cheeses cured. She could see the goats in their pens out back, dainty and sleek and brown. A tractor as small and bright as a toy stood next to the huge shed.

She pulled out of the Hoppelmanns' driveway and drove slowly past Dalton's place, trying to sniff out the fierce, smug odor of virtue that Willy had described. Dalton and Amy didn't appreciate his help, Willy had said. They found him clumsy. He had held up his smooth white hands and smiled, and Ilana had tried to see him planting seedlings or pulling weeds. "They thought a week of clean living out here would straighten me up," he'd said. "Now they're disappointed."

"What's to straighten?" she'd asked.

By then she hadn't been able to see a single flaw in Willy. He was cheerful, he left her generous tips. When Nikos complained about the way he sat all morning over his spartan breakfasts, he ordered omelettes and then helped Ilana fill the catsup bottles. She'd thought his brother must be crazy not to appreciate him. She'd pictured Dalton in a worn house, struggling through the muddy fields, living like her neighbors. Envying Willy, she'd imagined. Too resentful to welcome Willy's help.

But now, looking at the fresh paint and the orderly vegetables, she remembered Willy's rueful comments. "I'm a little overextended," he'd said the day before he left. "Some money trouble. It drives Dalton crazy."

He'd won Nikos over and befriended Sharon by then; they'd let him make a home out of his window seat. He'd stretched his long legs out on the chairs and drunk enough coffee to float a ship. It was a good place, Willy had said. Meltonville; a real nice town. He liked that there was nothing around for him to buy.

ILANA'S MOTHER CALLED every three weeks during the months that Willy was gone, as she'd done since her own departure. She was trying to persuade Ilana to move south.

They were in New Orleans, her mother said. She and Charlie, near the mouth of the Mississippi. The weather was warm and the food was good and the people were very relaxed. "You could come as soon as you sell the house," her mother said. "Are you trying to sell the house?"

"Trying," Ilana said. "Sure am." Her mother knew nothing, she thought. Or everything. No one was ever going to buy her house, and her mother was either stupid or cruel. She had lost Ilana once, grown distracted and wandered off and completely failed to notice the danger Ilana was in. After her calls, Ilana often went out back and stood by the stream and watched the twigs spin and pulse on their way to the Youghiogheny.

"The shrimps are so delicious here," her mother said late in July. "Charlie and I are going to a potluck later, with some people we met." Ilana saw the tail end of a solitary kayak vanish around the bend in the stream like a piece of lemon-colored Tupperware.

AND THEN IT was August, and Willy was back. Ilana could hardly believe it when he walked into the restaurant. He was not as cheerful as he'd been before; his clothes were still impeccable, but he was quieter and his smile had dimmed. Where before he'd teased Ilana and told her jokes, now he stared out the restaurant window in a way that worried her. She wanted him to tell her everything.

"You're the only person who listens to me," Willy said one morning, after he'd finished telling her a story about his boss and the long-distance phone bills. "You're the only one who understands."

On the Wednesday night of Willy's second week in town they went out to dinner together. Ilana had Willy pick her up at the restaurant parking lot, so he wouldn't get lost trying to find her house. Then she took him to Shanahan's, a bar and grill that she seldom visited. As she'd hoped, the bar was almost empty and they got through dinner without anyone interrupting them.

She could have brought Willy to the White Horse, where she sometimes went after bowling, or to Burton's, where there was dancing on Saturday nights, but she had no desire to introduce Willy to her friends. Most of them were married; almost all of them had kids. None of them, she thought, could appreciate Willy or the way she felt about him. In the dim light of Shanahan's they drank beer and ate chicken wings and ignored the occasional curious glance.

Afterward they drove out the Old Pike Road and paused in front of Willy's brother's house just long enough for Ilana to wonder if Willy meant to take her in. Instead they drove to the end of the road and parked on a piece of abandoned land near the entrance to the gorge. Willy thought he'd discovered this place; he said he'd found it when he'd been driving around one day enjoying the scenery. Ilana didn't have the heart to tell him that anyone who'd gone to Meltonville High had been here more than once.

Hours later, Willy drove her back to the restaurant and said he had to get some sleep. He didn't come into the restaurant Thursday morning. All Thursday night Ilana lay awake, waiting to see if he'd show up on Friday. He did; he ordered a big breakfast and then asked her if she was free that night. On Friday night he took her back to the gorge, and from there they drove straight to the restaurant on Saturday morning. Ilana said goodbye to Willy in his car.

"I'll miss you," he said. "You take care of yourself."

He kissed her twice and apologized for the rasp of his unshaven cheek against her skin. The parking lot shimmered and danced before Ilana's eyes. Her shift started in ten minutes and she'd hardly slept all week; she could not imagine how she'd survive the day. Or the next week, the next month; Willy's vacation was over and he was going home again.

"I could write you," she said to Willy. "Is there someplace I could write you?" Her hands were shaking, she saw. They seemed to belong to someone else.

Willy looked over her shoulder at the long stretch of highway rising into the hills. "I'm moving," he said. "I'm right in the middle of looking for a new apartment." The skin beneath his eyes looked bruised. "But I'll be in touch," he said. "You're sweet."

He reached across her lap and opened her door. She moved her legs, set her feet on the pavement, and stood up shakily. Willy waited. She shut the door between them and watched him drive away.

FOUR MONTHS AFTER Willy left for the second time, Ilana was still tormenting herself with the thought that the squalor and discomfort of their nights by the river had offended Willy, depressed him, distressed him; kept him from writing to her. Where she remembered only pleasure, she feared Willy remembered insects and awkward postures and bruised elbows and knees. But still she could not imagine what else they might have done.

That Wednesday, as they'd been finishing dinner at Shanahan's, Willy had snaked his hand through the empty bottles between them and laid his fingers on hers. The surge of desire she'd felt then had almost been canceled out by the fear of bringing him home. She'd imagined his eyes on her house, seeing it the way she'd learned to see it after her drive past Dalton's: the sagging roof, sagging porch, broken steps, clogged gutters; the cluttered kitchen and the living room stuffed with her unmade bed; the cat hairs matted everywhere and the pale tongues of her laundry. Of course she couldn't bring him home, she couldn't bear for him to see how she lived. And at Dalton's place, where Willy had hesitated, she'd realized he couldn't bring her there. Later, Willy had said, "I wish I had enough money to bring you someplace nice."

It was fine, she longed to tell him. It was more than fine. Every day she expected a letter and every day was disappointed. Early in December, seized with the wild hope that Willy might visit his brother for Christmas, she decided to clean her house.

She scrubbed the kitchen floor and lugged bags of trash to the dump. She took down the living room curtains and washed them. She tried to open a few more rooms but was driven back by what lay beyond the doors: cobwebs, dampness, rank smells, mice. But she brought down a dresser from her parents' old room and stowed her clothes in there, and she aired an old comforter until the smell was gone and then draped it over her bed. She dusted and swept and arranged dried flowers in Mason jars, and when she was done she told herself she'd almost reproduced the look of a smart studio apartment in the city. If she ignored the outside of her house and pretended that the closed-off rooms did not exist, she could imagine that the tiny island of order she'd made was a place she might bring Willy.

Christmas came and went without him. She spent the day with her cousins, whom she had never liked; they had asked her for dinner late, out of pity, she knew, and only because she'd bumped into them in town. Just before dinner she accidentally dropped a Pyrex dish of sweet potatoes and then watched the silent glances the family exchanged.

"You look tired," her cousin's husband finally said. "Are you all right?"

AN EARLY THAW swept the valley that February, and then a blizzard so big that it earned a photograph in the Philadelphia paper. Ilana thought Willy would surely come then, to see if she, or at least Dalton and his family, had survived. When Willy didn't show up by the middle of March, she got in her car and drove to Dalton's house.

She would park on the side of the road, she thought. She'd walk up to the door and knock and then say that she used to know the previous owners; she'd introduce herself and compliment Dalton on all the improvements he'd made. Dalton would ask her in, she thought. He'd look nothing like Willy, they were only half-brothers, but he'd be pleasant; and when she found a way to drop Willy's name his mouth would open and he'd say, "But we're related!" After that it would be simple to act surprised and then say that Willy had left something in the restaurant, which she wanted to mail to him. Dalton would write Willy's address on a piece of paper so small she could hide it in her palm.

She was halfway up the path to the door before she understood that the house was vacant. A FOR SALE sign rose out of the tattered vegetable beds. The screen door hung loose and the strings along which the vines had climbed had snapped below the windows. Near the steps, the wind had knocked over a tower of red clay pots. The greenhouse was empty, the fields were blank. She drove back into Meltonville and walked into the real estate agency that had planted the sign in the lawn.

Her own house had been listed with this agency for almost two years, and Mindy Walinski, who ran the office, started apologizing as soon as Ilana walked in.

"I know," Mindy said. "I know, I know—it's been ages since we've shown your house, but the market's just collapsed out here . . ."

"What's going on with the Dubczeks' old house?" Ilana asked.

"Dubczek," Mindy said. "Dubczek, Dubczek—the Kings' house, you mean? The one out Old Pike Road?"

Ilana nodded.

"Beautiful place, isn't it?" Mindy said. "But a little outside your price range, if you don't mind my saying so. I mean, even if we *could* sell your place . . ."

"I know," Ilana said. "I was just curious. I sort of knew the Kings."

"Really?" Mindy said. "I didn't think they knew anyone. They sure did stick to themselves." Then she told Ilana a long and complicated story about a second mortgage. The money was supposed to go into new improvements, Mindy said: seed and fences and a special breed of sheep with multicolored wool. But someone in the family—"A nephew?" Mindy said. "Maybe it was a brother"—had borrowed the money from Dalton to pay off some debts of his own. A city person, Mindy said. Some bum of a kid who'd dug a hole for himself with a handful of credit cards. Then the kid—the bum, the nephew, the brother—had lost his job and skipped town with the rest of Dalton's money. Dalton hadn't been able to pay the bank and the bank had foreclosed on the house.

"Down the tubes," Mindy said ruefully. "Just like everyone else around here."

"You don't happen to know where they went," Ilana asked. "The Kings, I mean."

"No idea," Mindy said. "They didn't have a single friend in town."

OUT HERE, WILLY had said. What do you do out here? What's it like out here in the winter? As Ilana drove home from the real estate office, she could hear Willy's voice in her head.

At the gorge where Willy had parked his car, he had done most of the talking: his job, his family, his pleasures and small irritations. He had taken a blanket out of the trunk and spread it across the stone shelf overlooking the river. His arm had been draped around her shoulders but she hadn't been sure, then, that he meant to make love to her, and when he finally asked her to tell him about herself she hadn't known what to say. By then she'd realized that the version of her life she'd once imagined presenting was not what Willy was after.

Willy wanted something remarkable, she knew; something that would set her off like a unicorn and make what he wanted to do with her make sense to him. She told him how she'd fallen into the river when she was two.

"I was playing outside," she said. She couldn't remember this— what she knew came from her mother and the neighbors and the story the local paper ran. But she told her tale to Willy as if everything that had happened was still fresh. "I was out behind the house," she said. "A little stream runs behind us, the same one that runs behind Dalton's place and joins the river here."

She could hear the water from where they sat. Willy ran his fingers along her upper arm, back and forth, back and forth, so lightly she could feel her skin straining toward his hand. Slowly, quietly, she talked to him.

The rivers had been bulging from the heavy spring rains. She'd been playing in the backyard, near the trees and shrubs along the bank of the stream, and her mother had been doing something in the garden. It was very hot. She looked up one minute and saw her mother, then looked up again and her mother was gone. The phone, her mother told her later. The phone had rung, or the mailman had come, or a cat had streaked by with a bird in its mouth, and while she was distracted Ilana had crept through the trees, attracted by the babble of the water. Below her, near the base of the bank, an old wooden door was caught in a bush where the river had washed it up. She had crawled up on the edge of it, or maybe she'd rolled down the bank and landed on it, but her weight, however she'd landed there, had been enough to free the jammed edge from the bush. The door had slipped down the bank with her clinging to it, leaving a telltale track in the mud. When it hit the water the current swept it away.

"I floated for three miles," she told Willy. "Almost to the gorge here, before Anton Nicholson fished me out."

"Jesus," Willy said. "What did that *feel* like?"

"I don't know," she said. She remembered what people had told her—how her mother had said, again and again, "I only left you for a *minute*"; how Anton Nicholson had gone on and on about the heroics of his rescue. The paper had run a picture of her, pop-eyed and bedraggled. A few years later, when she'd started school, her teacher had introduced her to her classmates as the girl who'd been saved from drowning by a miracle.

"You can't remember?" Willy said. He sounded so disappointed that she lied. "I remember a little," she said: stammering, fishing for words. "It was . . . amazing. I was lying on my stomach at first, holding on to the doorknob. I wasn't frightened at all. The water was moving quickly, but it was so high that all the rocks were covered and all the rapids had washed out. The door went under the willow branches and when I leaned over I could see fish. When I looked up, the clouds were moving. I was laughing, I think. I loved it."

Willy drew her close to him. She had tricked him, she knew— what she remembered of her journey was nothing more than a black fog of terror and abandonment. She had presented herself as brave and strong and independent, a woman who loved an adventure. "You're terrific," Willy said. He kissed her and pressed her shoulders onto the stone shelf, fooled into thinking she was the kind of woman who could survive a river, and him.

IT HAD NEVER occurred to her, before her talk with Mindy, that Willy might also have presented himself as someone he was not. Something shifted in her when she learned that, and when she realized that he was never coming back. But by then the version of Willy she'd made for herself could not be dislodged by mere facts. She grew so inattentive at work that Nikos sat her down for two long talks, gave her a written warning, and finally fired her. He hated doing this, he said. He'd be glad to take her back when she could keep her mind on her work. Sharon gave her a potted fern and told her to keep in touch.

The rest slipped away so easily after she lost her job: nights out, movies, haircuts, visits, talking to anyone. Willy flowed through her heart like a big brown river, a Mississippi of longing and love that swept every scrap of her daily life away. She couldn't pay her utility bills and then she couldn't pay her taxes; the mail brought first notices, second notices, warnings, threats. She lost her phone and then her electricity. Years ago, she remembered, the lights had also gone out on her mother. She'd come home from school one day a few months after her father's funeral and found her mother sitting in a kitchen lit by candles.

I forgot, her mother had said then. I forgot to pay the bill. The lights had come back on the following day; perhaps her mother had been telling the truth. But now Ilana wondered if, had she been absent, her mother might not have sat all winter by candlelight. The flames cast shadows in which a missing man might hide.

And besides, it was June and the nights were short. Ilana bathed in the river and cooked outside, over a fire she made in a ring of stones. She had her mother's house, she thought, and her mother's cats and her mother's bills. She even had her mother's old candles. But she had nothing of Willy's, not a single relic by which to remember him. She puzzled over what to do about this until the day the river brought her a sodden sneaker the size and color of Willy's elegant footwear.

At first she didn't know what the sneaker signified. She hung it by its laces from a mock-orange bush on the riverbank, and a few days later she was moved to add two pairs of her old spike-heeled shoes to the branches. These looked so good against the fresh leaves and the flouncy white flowers that she suspended several hubcaps from a nearby willow. Willy wore running shoes, Willy's car had hubcaps. If Willy had taken her dancing she would have worn high heels; Willy was very tall. A storm window fell from the second floor and she wedged it into a beech; Willy had windows wherever he lived, Willy looked through glass. The river brought her a length of green garden hose and she wove that between a rhododendron and a sumac. Somewhere, she thought, Willy had used a hose; certainly he'd watered vegetables when he'd been visiting his brother.

She went through her old papers and magazines and snipped out pictures of men who had Willy's smile or his hair or his clothes. Then she brought the pictures to the hardware store and had them laminated between clear sheets of plastic. Wanda Noonan, who had known Ilana's parents, looked at Ilana oddly when she walked in.

"Are you all right?" she said. "I heard you were having some troubles."

Ilana held herself very straight. "I'm fine," she said. She didn't have enough money to pay for the laminations, but Wanda said she could pay her later that week.

"You have friends, you know," Wanda said as Ilana was leaving. "There are people around who'd help."

"I'm fine," Ilana said again.

After she trimmed the pictures and threaded bits of fishing line through holes in the corners, she was able to hang them from the branches of the dogwoods and striped maples springing up beneath the larger trees. In the wind the pictures fluttered and made a noise she could hear from the flat rock in the water at the base of the bank: *flip, flip, flip.* From the rock she could see that every piece of plastic bore an image of Willy's face. She hung a broken chair in the hemlock, because somewhere Willy was sitting, and she balanced a broom in the elderberry twigs so that Willy's troubles might be swept away. The weather was exceedingly wet for June, and after the third big storm the water rose over the flat rock and lapped at the foot of the trees.

The last storm brought Ilana another shoe, which she found perched like a spring hat upon a tuft of reeds. Although the shoe was black and quite small, she understood that it formed a pair with the sneaker she'd found and that the pair belonged to Willy. She hung the shoe near its mate in the mock-orange bush, and this seemed so clearly correct that she spent the night in the willow tree, wrapped in a blanket and guarding what she'd made.

Willy was near, he had always been near. The river rose all night, climbing the low bank until it was level with the willow's roots. Ilana watched the rising water and thought how a stranger, drifting by in a lemon-colored kayak, might look up and see the objects dangling in the trees. Later, after reaching the confluence with the Youghiogheny and then surviving the ride through the gorge, the stranger might stop at the restaurant for coffee and tell a fellow paddler what he'd seen. "Furniture," the stranger might say, having no idea that this was the shrine she'd made for Willy. "There was furniture in the trees."

A stranger would never understand the route she'd chosen. When the sun came up she walked stiffly back to her house and took her kitchen door off its hinges. She dragged the door across the yard and between a pair of dogwoods, and then she pushed it into the water, where it floated very satisfactorily. She could take the bus to Philadelphia, she thought, as she tested the door with her weight. But the bus ride was nothing, the ride was easy, anyone could do it. She stretched herself out on the door and pushed off from the bank, thinking *Willy, Willy, Willy,* knowing the water was the way to prove that she was who she said she was.

WHEN I STARTED "Out Here" I had three things: a setting (the Youghiogheny River, along which I'd often kayaked, and the tiny fringing towns where I'd sometimes stopped for food); an image (furniture dangling from the trees, courtesy of a neighbor in Rochester who turned his yard into a giant outdoor sculpture that included high-heeled shoes striding up the walls, a chair hanging from a spruce tree, and giant spheres made from woven vines); and a set of feelings (loss, confusion, despair: I was going through a rough patch).

What I didn't have were characters, a voice, a story, a plot, any sense of the underlying structure, a title, or the phrase "out here." The latter would, when I found it, ultimately deliver all the rest. That seems to me interesting: that it is through *language*—the rhythm, the syntax, the infolded meanings of a certain phrase—that so much else can be generated.

I had no model for Ilana; she arose from the language. I *did* have a vague model for Willy, but under the demands and the constraints of the language he became a completely different character from the one I'd meant to bring to the page. Once I heard him say "out here" for the first time, in a certain pleasant but condescending tone, I not only knew who he was but also something about why he was visiting his cousin Dalton and what Dalton did for work. I knew, too, something about the feel of the area. The diner, the high school, the trysting spot in the woods, Ilana's house—they could be only certain ways, in that place and time, for Willy to respond to them as he did.

Stories have their own logic; once the first few bones are laid down, the type and placement of the other bones, as well as the flesh that will clothe them later, become increasingly constrained. You cannot, generally, have a head that sprouts three legs and a finger, or a human pelvis connected to the spine of a snake. Ilana was alone, she had no money, she had no one to whom she could turn: those facts, which derived from Willy's attitudes and the way he spoke to her, virtually dictated that her mother would be ditzy in a certain way, that she would have fled before the story begins, that Ilana would be alone in that crumbling house. Structural demands dictated other elements—if a story has a great big rushing river in it, a river that appears in the first paragraphs and recurs obtrusively throughout— well, then that river must not only mean something but *do* something. It must, I saw in time, be directly connected to Ilana's life, something in her life must have shifted because of it—and that something must also be connected to Willy and, tangentially, to those passing boaters. Hence the near-drowning incident in her childhood, and the final scene with the floating door.

Here I will admit that when this sequence of events first occurred to me, I thought the Youghiogheny might flow into something that flowed toward Philadelphia and Willy; some swift readjustments had to be made once I consulted a map. So was I further constrained, and finally steered, by simple geographical fact.

"Dictated," I say. "Constrained." These words make it sound as if a writer has no choice in the writing, as if fiction appears from above, already made, and pours through the writer, who is a mere vessel. Some people believe this, or a version of this; I don't. What I mean to say is simply that fiction, which can appear to be formless when compared with, say, poetry, has its own rigors and hidden rules which guide the attentive writer along paths she might not otherwise have seen. That attention to the language, structure, patterns of imagery and metaphor in a growing piece often rewards us with richer characters, more interesting plots and stories, than we can generate ourselves in our first superficial attempts.

This is why we can't summarize good fiction, any more than we can summarize poetry. This is why we can't, usually, write well to an outline. And why, no matter what we *think* we mean to do with a certain piece, we are continually surprised and, if we are attentive and lucky, led to something more interesting than we knew we knew.

Something about the voice and tone of this story, and about wrestling with a complex chronology that shuttles back and forth in time and weaves together past and present, led me to new ground as a writer. While working on the final drafts of this I began the early drafts of "The Behavior of the Hawkweeds"—which, in turn, led me to the other stories gathered in *Ship Fever*. Much of what I work on now seems to hark back in some way to "Out Here," although the subject matter differs so sharply.

It's worth saying, perhaps, that although many people read Ilana's gesture as one of overt self-destruction, I never intended it that way. For me, that door is a boat and that mad journey is driven by a form of hope. If it ends badly that is not, I think, what Ilana consciously intends. But perhaps it is what the *story* intends.

Pablo Medina

~

MORTALITY

THREE WEEKS AGO I received a phone call at three in the morning informing me that Carlitos Bodeler had died. I had not seen Carlitos in thirty years, but mention of his name while the waters of my dreams slapped against the sides of my consciousness brought back memories in such profusion that I fell back in bed, overwhelmed by a kind of vertigo. I did not recognize the voice on the line, taut like a sinew, with a strange accent and an upward lilt to the intonation reminiscent of the speech of certain tribes in the desert regions of Chile. Before I could compose myself and ask why I, after such a lapse of time, should be called with this news, the caller was off the line.

I made myself some coffee and sat by the window to watch yet another snowfall blanketing the city and thought about him whom I had known so many years ago and who was now filling my room with the shadow of his presence. I met him my first day at the taxi stand in Caridad, a large man with an uncanny resemblance to Sidney Greenstreet, playing an instrument (I later discovered it was a *bandoneón*) which made the most plaintive and evocative of sounds. I became afraid. I felt like it was my heart he was squeezing, not his instrument. And he called my name before I said it. "Federico!" Just like that: "Federico!" and went on with his song, which I still to this day remember:

Perro azul y gato pardo,
esos son mis sentimientos,
hechos tierra con el tiempo
en el desierto de la traición.

I nodded to him then. He stared at me through his thick eyebrows, stopped playing, and stretched his hand, which I took in mine and felt an immediate and kindly warmth. By then Carlitos— it was a purposeful irony that led us to attach the diminutive to his name; diminutive he was not—no longer took customers. Instead he sat on his *taburete,* playing for us the tangos and milongas of his native Buenos Aires or else reciting the endless sagas he had learned in Reykjavik, where he had lived for some time. In fact, Carlitos had lived everywhere on this earth, and he spoke with familiarity and fondness of Benin and Saigon, Borneo and the Atacama. His songs, his poems, his commentaries kept me going through the busy times, when I was handling fifteen, twenty rides a day, and through the dead times as well, when time stopped and the midafternoon heat made us all sleep and dream of a prenatal nostalgia for snow.

Carlitos Bodeler was there always, drinking mojito, a tropical drink he much preferred over the heavy Argentinian wine that had made him fat and ruddy, floating comfortably in his lethargy and entertaining us—no, educating us—with his songs, his stories about eating human flesh in a feast of cannibals ("It tastes as only human flesh can taste—divine"), and the poems about Nordic savages and their penchant for death and unbridled rage. Before meeting him I had thought dimly my country and my city to be the center of the universe, but after listening to him, I was convinced.

I had no ambition to drink cow's blood with the Masai or share a repast of blubber with the Eskimos or a breakfast of raw reindeer liver with the Laplanders. It was enough that Carlitos had done these things and told me about them; that he had, for example, fallen in love with a prostitute in Kiev who had not bathed all winter—"Love is not only blind," he liked to say. "It is also odorless"; that he had been both a slave and a slave master in the markets of Tunis; that he had fallen under a spell of a santero in Santiago de Cuba and lost three years of his life; and many other experiences that I would be only too happy to relate were I not bound by my honor and my discretion. Why should I have felt any urge whatsoever to experience these things when Carlitos Bodeler had experienced them for me— absinthe, opium, even incest? "Mon enfant, ma soeur,/ Songe à la douceur/ D'aller là-bas vivre ensemble!/ Aimer à loisir,/ Aimer et mourir/ Au pays qui te ressemble!" he would recite with that faraway look that River Plateans get when thinking of their sisters.

To know Carlitos Bodeler was to know an encyclopedia. No, no, that is not right. His knowledge and experience could never be contained in a limited number of volumes. To know him was to know life. He told me of the devil's barbed penis and of the seven impenetrable veils that covered the Blessed Mother's womb. He sang of the cave of sorrows and the garden of delights. Bullets had entered his body, and he had a scar running from his temple to his chin where a cossack saber had landed. He had been on the other side of death as well, in the Ardennes, during the war, when he had killed twelve Austrian guards, cutting their throats with a stealth and precision that put him in high demand among the Allied forces in the trenches. "Their blood warmed my hands, and the moans escaping through their wounds turned my heart to ice." After telling that story, he sang a milonga and his bandoneón reached the deepest caverns of grief, lingering there for what seemed centuries. I wept with his sorrow. I wept as if I myself had heard the moans of those Austrian boys and spent twelve sleepless nights in hell with their blood burning my hands. Then I did something I had never done before nor would ever do again: I drank mojitos with Carlitos and became copiously drunk. Despite the fact that it was my busiest day of the week and I had many rides waiting for me, including several regular customers who were generous tippers; despite the risk of losing them to the other cabbies who roamed around my customers like sharks, I stayed with Carlitos that day weeping and drinking and singing too, my shy squeaky voice barely audible over the registers of his baritone and of his bandoneón, which, at that moment, gave off the attar of God.

Then the vertigo came, a maelstrom of emotion, intellect, and sense that sucked me to a place where everything whirled and collided and finally blended into blackness. I was not then nor have been since a drinker. Lights popped under my eyelids and my body turned inside out, then outside in, then inside out again. I remembered nothing and I remembered everything. I woke at night with my cheek to the pavement and an ache in my head like a stone must feel when it cracks. Manolo the constable was poking me with his stick, his flashlight square on my face.

"Hey, you, Federico!" he said. "Are you dead or alive?"

"Worse," I said, speaking the truth.

I raised myself off the ground with great difficulty and went home. I do not remember how I got there, but I fell in my bed and slept deeply through the night. The next day I did not feel any better but I was at the taxi stand promptly at my usual hour. Carlitos did not show up that day, but he was there the following one, drinking a coffee someone had bought for him. I avoided him from that time on. I did my job, driving people where they needed to go, and came home at night too tired to want anything else but sleep. When things got tough and the good money dried up, I left my country and came to this city where it is always cold and always dark.

Thirty years is a long time and much has happened. I could tell

Carlitos a story or two and he would listen. To be honest, there wasn't a day that I did not think about that man and relive his songs and his poems. I don't know why I was called. The phone call seemed an intrusion on my memories. Perhaps he was fonder of me than I thought and he wrote my name down somewhere where it could be found. That anonymous voice could have announced his death to me as it did to ten thousand others, and all of us may have felt the same sense of displacement, the same vertigo. I had known Carlitos Bodeler in life. Now I knew his death. As the last snowflake fell and the sky grew light, I felt revived and at peace, and I heard him calling my name. Carlitos was here. Carlitos was everywhere. Time stopped altogether and I came to understand what it was he waited thirty years to give me.

WHILE I WORKED on my book about Félix Nogara I came across a character by the name of Carlitos Bodeler whom Nogara first met at the famous Café los Cantos in Carenas, the capital of Barata. Bodeler claimed to be an Argentine who had traveled throughout the world, accumulating adventures the way most people accumulate loose change. He eventually settled in Barata, where he spent the rest of his days away from the endless political and economic troubles that afflicted his arrogant but hapless homeland since its independence from Spain. Some claim he was a Luddite, others that he was a renegade Marxist. All agreed that he was first and foremost a sybarite, wholly dedicated to the unencumbered pursuit of pleasure. Carlitos, a competent bandoneón player, soon became a legend on the streets of Carenas. It was said that Félix Nogara learned from him a number of milongas, one of which Nogara hummed repeatedly as he lay on his deathbed. Those who knew Nogara well, however, maintained that he and Carlitos would never have gotten along and that the idea of the Argentine teaching Nogara anything was simply preposterous. After studying the matter for some time I have concluded that Carlitos was not Argentinean but French and that his exploits, which so impressed his comrades in the taxi stand of Caridad, were the subterfuges, fabrications, and chimeras of an untrustworthy imagination. Had Nogara hummed any other song on his deathbed, I doubt that I would have written anything about a character as marginal as Carlitos Bodeler.

But write I did, disregarding point of view, characterization, structure, and other such things that seemed to occupy the minds of my fellow writers in those days. My principal concern was to highlight in as brief a space as possible (he was a minor character and, as such, deserved no more) the remarkable life of an unremarkable man. That Carlitos's tale came in the form of the reminiscences of an even lesser character was simply incidental. I gave myself eight hours in which to write this story before returning to more pressing concerns. By the time I was done, my companion was preparing afternoon tea. The sun had just dropped behind the trees bordering our property and the summer heat released its feral hold on the day. She called from the kitchen that the tea was ready, but before I responded, I phoned the man who made the story possible in order to release him from the purgatory of his life. It was the least I could have done for someone whose name I barely recall now and who had remained alive well beyond his time.

Susan Neville

NIGHT TRAIN

T THE TRIAL they said that Madge had been abducted. But there were little details that didn't fit: the doorman at the Claypool Hotel who saw her waiting in the car without an escort. She waved at him in the light from the gas lamps. He remembered her hair, so black it was almost blue, and the wet shine on the pavement, veined by the metal tracks from the trolley. He said the smell from coal dust was thick that night, he said he'd been washing down the beveled glass in the door to the hotel for hours.

Steve had a will larger than this city, the kind of will it's almost impossible to escape from. I've known men like him. All it takes is single-mindedness and narcissism and—what. Once I knew a cook who would put a speck of ground glass in the soup or cigarette ash in a sauce, just to know that he could. Not enough to hurt anyone, just so he would know it was there and he could watch an old man sip down bowls of chowder knowing there was that brittle bit of something that, if it were bigger, would begin to wear a hole inside large enough for his life to seep through.

This cook would look at the wet ground in the spring and watch the entire landscape loosen, unbuckle belts and fasteners and start to ooze around his feet, and he wanted to be the one who caused that loosening. Because he knew he could. He was a cook and when he looked at the world he saw it pressed into a fine string and woven through the bodies of people who knew in this world they would always be hungry. Once you know that, anything is possible.

That's how I see Stephenson and how I see Madge with him and that's how I think it happened. And I feel enormously guilty when I say that, going against the story of her abduction and rape by a man fully consciously evil. Who in this world ever sees himself as evil finally? No one. I think it was, instead, a loosening in the face of an enormous will, that she felt herself lifted into a whirlwind and then his voice, Steve's voice, saying *listen girl, believe me when I tell you to close your eyes and fly and believe me when I say my arms are larger than the state, larger than God's, so large I can hold you up here where nothing will touch us, and I absolutely will not let you fall.*

HE DIDN'T SAY he loved her, just that and the fact that it was a quick shot to Chicago, the straight humming rails with car after car all coupled in a chain like the cells of her body like all the human beings and animals and atoms in the world coupling, separating and reforming always with a kind of violence. And there she was, he said, maybe about to be left out of it or about to let go as she should, to take that freedom he was offering to her. I'm sure his argument had something to do with courage. I'm sure she heard heroic music playing. Otherwise where would she be? Straight rows of church pews, of moment following moment, of stitches in the hem of her good winter coat. The cemetery was filled with row after straight fixed row of sinking stones.

THEY DO SINK, you know, after awhile, like rocks to the bottom of a creek bed.

So Steve's driver took them to Union Station, and they walked into that huge vault of arches and stained glass and Madge felt something rise up in her as clear and high as that ceiling, a giddiness or expansion of her self, like a cathedral. You know I'm mad about you, he'd said, or something like that, and they were heading for the train to Chicago and some bit of work I'm sure he'd said they had to do there, so the whole thing was this heady mixture of passion and duty. She could picture all the rest of us, her sisters, sleeping in our dull beds in the dull midwestern night, the moon a fake mother-of-pearl with the plastic peeling off the surface, sleepwalking through our lives. When they, Madge and Steve, were in fact the ones sleepwalking. You know I'm mad about your body, he said, and in this much he was conscious: he knew he was seducing her.

I have to say this. The prosecuting attorneys painted her as wholly innocent. I believe she was. But not in the way they meant it. I do think that she started on this trip at least partially willingly, that there were times, even in Chicago, that she remained willingly. That doesn't make Steve less culpable. It just makes it more human, something you could see yourself being somehow sucked into. It's why it doesn't work to tell kids not to do something because they'll die. Then they're not prepared for the seduction, for how good it feels, how much they might want it, and when they find that out they think that everything they've been told has been a lie. So I think that a woman hearing the story of Madge dragged and bound in the middle of the night on a train to Chicago won't be prepared for anything. The dragged and bound kind of abduction—you can't see it coming, there's nothing you can do but work for some escape. But the kind that comes with power and charm, you think of it as a story outside and beyond you, not there in this particular smiling man. You know? Everyone loves him, even the governor. You feel so lucky that he turned to you. You! Madge Oberholtzer. A stenographer, working girl, with a life suddenly here in the dull center of the country like any New York flapper, the kind of life you read about in the magazines.

She had a beaded purse on her lap, with a handkerchief, some lipstick and powder, a pocket mirror. Why does that break my heart?

At one point on the train, maybe early on, maybe she felt the lens shift slightly from romance to something darker. And she laughed and said no to something he suggested, still living in that version of herself as the good Victorian girl with jazz-age courage, a difficult fiction to live behind as many girls like Madge discovered at that time, like a paper doll cut from paper made in two different centuries, the difficulty being that you have to find a man who isn't looking for the seam where the papers are joined, too flimsily, with makeshift glue. Madge and I were in the same sorority in college. I know what it was like then. The 1920s. We were born with the century. We really thought we'd invented sex. It's hard to believe now how innocent we were.

Why do I keep talking about innocence? Because this is a trial, and I have to come down on one side or another and I know that what I'm talking about is too human for that sort of certainty. Everyone has his own story, a story that's woven as tightly, that fits as warmly, as those footed pajamas that children wear.

Years ago I went tubing on the Little Pigeon River in Tenessee. It was a brilliant July day, not a cloud, everything shimmering like money. I was with a whole group of tubed people, bobbing around on the Little Pigeon in our orange lifesavers, a lot of chatting between tubes, a lot of falling and splashing in the water.

For a while I talked and then for a while listened and then finally, after an hour or so I just sat back in the tube and relaxed absolutely, letting the river take the tube and my thoughts without any direction from me—no paddling, no pushing against the shore, nothing—and after a half an hour there was this one moment when suddenly everything dissolved—the sky became the river, the river bled into the trees, I felt my body start to disintegrate into glittering pieces, or rather, I didn't feel my body as mine at all, what the Eskimos call kayak sickness, and I felt like I was falling into the sky. And suddenly there was this physical start, like the yank of a bridle, the bit in the corner of my mouth. That's up, that's down, this is upstream, that's downstream. These are the hard edges that separate one thing from another.

This has something to do with all of this, bear with me. I'm an old woman and allowed to wander.

My lover was with me on that trip, and that night when we came in from the tacky Carnival nightlife of Gatlinburg, the Little Pigeon outside the window of our room, I thought about the river and how there's a letting go that's terrifying. That if you could throw off the bridle, if you could trust that dissolution, if you trusted that your body was an especially strong and natural swimmer, then there would be this joy that might feel like drowning, like pain for a while but would eventually build this pressure and thrust you up through the endless water, or rather, through the brilliance of all the shimmering light, and you would rise up like the spouting foam of a great whale.

Or you could take something, a cup, and hold it in the fountain of that light, and drink it down, drain it into every cell.

I was madly in love, madly madly in love, and on that trip with my lover to the Smoky Mountains and the thundering river, I started noticing when the bit of fear pulled me back, said that's good but enough, and I consciously, in the middle of each wave let go even more, a greater and greater letting go, and I swear to you one night I just stayed there floating on top of this sea for an entire evening, and it was something like coming, but deeper.

You don't want to hear this about an old woman, do you, but there you have it.

And you may think I'm getting back to Madge and Steve and that I'm going to say that's what Steve wanted. But what I'm going to say is that it's what Madge wanted, what she sensed and couldn't articulate, and what, in her innocence, she thought had nothing at all to do with love, that love was in fact the binding cord, the bridle.

And what Steve wanted? Not this letting go at all, that's exactly what he was most terrified of, no matter what he said. If he felt someone like Madge taking him close he'd feel like he was floating on a raging river and right ahead, with no turning back, the endless, pounding falls. And that's when he sank his teeth into her, to pull himself back onto the shore. The autopsy showed them, on her breast. Puncture wounds caused by human teeth.

Did you know that at one time there were falls on the Ohio River? We domesticated them with locks.

I can't let go of the fact that she didn't tell her parents she was going to Chicago, that she didn't take anything with her for the trip. She left the house in her black wool coat, even though the day had been sunny and springlike, and she didn't take a hat. She'd been out dancing with a friend, had come into the house at ten. Her parents had both been ill for a week with the flu; despite the early spring weather, and the crocuses along the foundation of the house, they'd been closed in, the windows still sealed tight, and the house had that sickroom smell, and all week she'd noticed the dust in the cracks of the wood floors and the sticky film on the furniture. They were old, her parents, and she lived there with them, and when she shut the door on the night and felt the contrast between the gay dance she'd left and the closed-in house, and the flesh of her parents, and when her mother said that Steve's secretary had called for her, had said for her to call no matter what time she came in, Madge got on the phone and said she'd be right there. There was moonlight coming through the lace curtains in the entry hall, and the dim chandelier glowed like cool stars. He needs me right away, she told her mother, some papers I need to prepare. He's leaving later on the train for Chicago.

She didn't say anything about going with him. How could she?

Though maybe she was angry with them for some reason, maybe she told herself she would call them the next morning, and in fact she sent a telegram from a hotel in Hammond. Or maybe it was kidnapping, and everything else I've said applies to some other woman, not this particular one.

However it was, she was in the car outside the Claypool with no one watching, thinking to herself maybe that she shouldn't be doing this, that she would tell Steve that when he came back to the car, she would tell him and he would keep her on; they would still work on that project together, she'd still have the excitement of carrying messages for him, of being associated with the most powerful man in Indiana.

There was the yellow light from the inside of the hotel, all refracted into pieces like flower petals or gold glitter, and the light in the streetlamps and the headlights of cars, the light caught in the bracelet on her wrist, a ring on her right hand, some silver threads in her dress fabric. I wonder if she thought about crosses burning out in the country, the gangs of young men that Steve set in motion against Catholics, Jews, occasional black men, I wonder what or if she thought about those crosses, or if she even knew. She worked in the department of education, it's said she was compassionate, liberal, I wonder if she didn't know about the things the Klan was doing, or what it was Steve told her to stop her from worrying. Or if that was something she thought she might change in him, if it was part of their banter when they talked, something that attracted him to her— the fact that she had her own mind.

THE TRAIN STATION was busy, loud and dirty, even that late at night, and the train to Chicago was almost full. He got two private rooms, and for a while she thought that maybe it was going to be all right, but when they walked through the railroad car in the warm domestic light of the stopped train, and Shorty went into one room and Steve followed her to hers, and he came inside with her, and locked the door behind him, she knew that it wasn't going to be all right, but she realized she didn't care.

And then the roaring of the train on its bright rails, metal against metal like sharpened knives, and Steve came toward her in the dim light of the car. They were moving, and outside the window, all of Indiana was dark and somehow oceanic, unfixed, a wilderness of fields waiting for spring seeding. If she were outside, she knew, she could smell the mud from spring thawing, in the morning there would be the early sound of birds, it was March. She'd been waiting months for the feel of spring, for the damp ooze of spring, but here in the railroad car there was only speed and metal, and the hard oil-cloth seats and the thin mattress on what served as a bed, like the beds, she thought, that men slept on in prison.

I'm thirsty, she said, still feeling like a seduced one, which implies a moment of giving in, thinking she had a choice still, still not believing that she could be in any real danger. It was a *game* of danger they were playing, and at any moment she could say enough, let's stop this now, it was an adventure, but I want to go home, I want the feel of my own soft bed, the smell of clean sheets, my mother's voice and in the morning the bell of the phone and my girlfriends calling, and the story I could tell them of how much you wanted me.

He turned out the light in the car, and there was only the reflected light from the moon on his face, an ashen grayish light, and from then on there would be only the occasional light from a farmhouse or small town. His face was round as the moon in fact, floating above her, his lips were too full. He took a flask from his pocket and made her drink; he wouldn't ask the porter for any water. In the dim light he looked boyish with his pale blond hair, boyish and swollen, like someone's child. And she, Madge Oberholtzer, wasn't there at all for him, she could tell that right away, his boyish face, lost, his eyelids closing over the pale blue eyes, the half smile on his face as he touched her. She was something just ordered up on the table, a woman with wide hips and pink aureoles large as platters. That's all he saw, or, rather, all he felt. She believed she had an awkward face. It didn't matter. Maybe she should accept this as the adventure it was. But wasn't he at least supposed to say he loved her?

He had a baby face, dark shadows around his eyes, oval shadows like the slits in the white hoods of the Klansmen.

She hoped that he would grow to love her.

The last thing she remembered being excited by was his face, by the picture she had of herself as brave, by the romance of the long dark train thundering like a river through the country. She was a little bit scared, but that was part of it. If pushed to the wall, she'd have to say she still trusted him.

I SAW HER two days later, an hour or two after Steve's bodyguard brought her into her parents' house. There were scratches all over her body. She was barely breathing. She told the story, whispered it. For three days the lawyer had her tell the story slow. There was a stenographer who typed it up at night and read it back the next day. Madge's dying statement. She had to say she knew that she was dying before she signed it. I was a witness to her signature.

At one point, in Chicago, she'd found his gun lying on a table. She stood in front of a full-length mirror and lifted the gun to her head. She thought about her mother then, the disgrace this kind of suicide would bring, and somehow in her confusion, the lawyers said, decided on another way.

That's when she talked Steve into letting her go out with his assistant to buy the hat, and she went into the hat shop unescorted. This is another part of the story that never fit. And she tried hats on, several of them, looking for one that would cover the marks on her face, hoping to go back on the train maybe like any woman out for the day, not like the woman she felt she was at that point, with the sky as blue and absolutely flat as enamel, red buds coating all the trees and somewhere a metallic bell-like sound that seemed to rise up out of the day itself, like that sound you get when you run a wet finger around the top of a crystal goblet, that kind of sound. She looked at herself in the mirror at the hat store and she saw a Madge whose life would never be the same again. She felt nauseous and brittle, and there wasn't even the tiniest bit of magic in the hat. The mirror's glass was a yellow greenish gold. She looked like an old woman to herself, and she couldn't imagine living. This part is all conjecture. The lawyer only had the time and Madge the strength to gather facts.

She went into the pharmacy then, unescorted, by telling the bodyguard that she needed some female things, that she was bleeding. He'd been kind to her in the hotel room. He'd soaked white towels in warm water and applied them to the scratches and the bites, washing the towels out in the sink when they got too cool, the blood a pale pink. He was a kind man. He was clumsy with his nursing, embarrassed and slightly deferent, the way she imagined a husband might be, so different from Steve. All that was closed off to her now. Steve gets like this, he said, I'm so sorry, but it's just the way he is, you know. We all have our failings, and this is his. He might have called the police or a doctor, but he was also a weak man, she could tell, and he owed everything to Steve, and he was slightly afraid of him. And he probably told himself that Madge wasn't a whole woman anyhow, not one of the women the Klan was defending, she was one of the other kind, slightly less than a woman since this had happened to her, a good woman who'd allowed herself to become a whore.

But he let her go into the pharmacy alone. And there was clearly no thought of escape. She could have leaned over to whisper a word to the pharmacist, but she didn't.

If she'd lived, we agreed that no one else would ever hear a word of this story. It would have just meant shame for her. She knew shame.

Mercury chloride is the drug she bought in the pharmacy. Maybe she had been a virgin before that night; maybe she was terrified of pregnancy only, her mind so clouded at that point with the beating that the only real shame she could imagine was the one she was familiar with. The physical evidence, like some disease. Mercury chloride was used in those days to induce abortions.

Maybe Steve's story was partially right. Maybe the initial tragedy had been compounded by the beating. He was a man for whom beating women came naturally, it was part of what he did with women; it was the only way he could let go completely. There were parties at his house where he dressed like a satyr and beat women with whips. He paid them to ask for more. Like a little dog who takes hold of the female with his teeth and shakes and shakes her in between coming.

However it was, he didn't mean to have a dying woman on his hands, and suddenly he did. That's when he was fully conscious of the harm he'd done and he chose it again and again. Each minute he waited to get help for her, he was choosing to let her die.

How do I know all this?

When we were in our thirties, my lover married someone else, and I painted my apartment red. Not a rust color or a burgundy, this was the most fake food dye maraschino red that I could find. I painted it myself, spread the bright stain over the light switches, the vents, the electrical outlets, even the ceiling.

Only six months after his wedding, my lover started coming by again. I was a woman he would sleep with but not one he would marry. It hadn't of course seemed that way to me. It was the 1920s. I loved him.

It was different after. Sometimes we made love when I was bleeding. He would turn me over on my belly where we couldn't see each others' faces. I heard him groan, he could watch it all and he felt, he said, like an animal. You could forget you were human, he said, the blood, it was so good to watch. You see? What a relief it was to him, this man who thought too much. Face down on the bed, I would tilt my head and look for a mirror where I could catch a glimpse of his face. All I saw was red. He took a shower before he went back home to his wife; there was blood underneath his nails, smears of it on his thighs and arms. How could he have explained it? When he left, I made a smear over the red paint, and at first it blended in but in the morning there was a brownish stain.

I felt shame then, actually, and I couldn't wait for him to call the next day, to reassure me that he'd loved it. Me. Had I loved it? I'm a strong woman in most areas of my life, but it occurs to me now that I didn't ask myself that question. I asked myself very few questions when it came to him. I loved that he loved it. I'm ashamed of that as well. Or not ashamed. If I had it to do over, I'd do it the same way.

The red walls of my apartment would glow in the afternoon sun like the inside of a heart. The rhythm of his life brought him to that apartment over and over again. You see? The rhythm of *his* life.

I've been obsessed for years with what kind of hat it was. I wish the jurors had asked to see it, I wish I'd looked in Madge's closet. It didn't occur to me until the middle of the trial that it was the key to knowing why and how things happened. A large hat, veiled, would have meant something different than a straw hat with fruit. Was she still a woman with enough sense of a self that would continue to live and need a hat, or was she a woman who wanted to cover the bruises just long enough to buy the poison that would kill her?

Or maybe there was the tiniest bit of hope, and when the hat didn't do its work, that was the end of it.

Whatever hat it was, I feel like Madge has sent the memory of its spinning through the years to me, to any woman who would hear this story, and if I could only see it clearly, only latch on to the meaning of it, I would know how to get through my own grief, my own anger. She was a young woman then and had no idea what she was doing, but it was a gift somehow, her purchase of that hat. I would have read that hat for days to find its meaning. If it was the right hat, I thought, it would give me the courage I needed, a kind of hat I could use to demand things or to whisk him out the door.

In the end, Steve went to prison for his crime. Though it was clear from the trial that no one really cared about Madge. At that point he had become simply an embarrassment to everyone, even the Klan, and they had to get rid of him. In that sense, Madge was a martyr.

You know how, during the plague, they locked up the house when someone in the family became infected? And even after the infection was in the house, the people would do anything they could to escape that confinement, so there were guards at the doors who had to steel themselves to the screaming, the bribes, the tricks of those trapped inside? I'm not sure why I'm bringing this up, I'm old, but somehow I think that what they wanted to escape was not the house, but the disease, even after it was within them. There's always some disease we're trying to escape, and the night train is easy transportation. In my lover's case, it was the house of his body, its limits. He was desperately afraid of dying. In my case, it was the closed-in house of what I knew. I wanted mystery. And maybe in the end that was true of Madge as well.

A trial is just an attempt to make a story out of the facts. Both sides wedge their stories into the cracks in the other one, like scientific theories, like religion, like any stories. But maybe in the end the night train never makes sense in the light of day. It roars through the orderly towns and farms and graveyards and breaks them up like children's toys. We all wear masks at night. Maybe hers was a large-brimmed hat to cover the face that seemed unmasked and fragile in the light. Which face was the real one? Me, I rode that train for most of my adult life, no brakes on, the wind so harsh through the open windows. I rode the train and at the same time never left that room. Who am I now? There were Stephensons coming to power then all over Europe. Madge and I standing beside each other in our college yearbook. So innocent, we thought, so trusting. Hearts open, hands clutching the fare.

ARGUERITE YOUNG, AUTHOR of *Miss MacIntosh, My Darling* (the book that William Hurt packed in his suitcase in the film *The Accidental Tourist*) lived in a nursing home in Indianapolis for the last year of her life. I visited her often that year and listened to her stories, which were often brilliant, often extraordinary, often surreal, occasionally mad, but always, even in their occasional madness, fascinating. She talked about the footprint of the angel Gabriel that's imprinted in a stone above the Wabash River, about a whole town of people who went deaf from malaria and walked around with trumpets blooming from their ears, about a whale she saw once in a boxcar in the middle of an Indiana cornfield. And she talked about Theodore Roethke and about her years teaching in Iowa and about Anaïs Nin and Elizabeth Hardwick and about Indiana history.

It seemed we shared a fascination with a woman named Marjorie Oberholtzer, secretary to the Ku Klux Klan leader D. C. Stephenson. Madge, Marguerite said, was the only woman in history with the presence of mind to, in the middle of her extended rape and murder, go into a store and buy herself a hat.

I wanted to write about the mystery of that hat.

I write creative nonfiction as well as fiction, and I thought about writing a meditation on the hat, and even tried a draft, but it didn't work. I couldn't get as close to the material as I wanted. It's an intimate and terrifying story, and I wanted that intimacy. Third person didn't work for much the same reason. I tried writing a draft from Madge Oberholtzer's point of view, and that turned out to be too close. There were technical problems with first person as well. I wrote that draft in present tense, as it was happening, which meant that, since she ends up dead, I found myself beside a cliff as I reached the end. I knew I'd reach that cliff but thought I'd discover some use of white space that would allow me to leap over it. Most importantly, though, I discovered that Madge herself probably didn't know why she bought the hat, or rather, that the reason she would have given covered layers and layers of other reasons I couldn't begin to fathom.

I never thought about writing the story from Stephenson's point of view. I didn't want to listen to his excuses. I gave serious consideration to writing the story from his bodyguard's point of view, but discarded it. I thought about making the narrator a cousin or a sister or a mother or a father or the lawyer who took the statement or a juror at the trial. Nothing clicked. Sometimes the point of view problem had something to do with what I could know, what I couldn't, what I could get close to, and sometimes it had something to do with whether I could hear the voice.

AS IT TURNS out, Madge Oberholtzer had graduated from the university where I teach, as had Marguerite Young. So I went to the library and looked up old copies of the yearbook. I found their faces that afternoon. There were not that many years between them.

In the copy of the yearbook where I saw Madge's face, I chose, randomly, another face, someone who might have known Madge, who might have been, I thought, a friend or a sorority sister. She would be my narrator. Close enough to care about her but distant enough to have the same questions I had. When I was confused, my narrator could be confused. When I was angry, my narrator could be angry.

Once I had her face in front of me, the narrative came easily. In many ways my narrator was writing nonfiction, writing an essay about something she was trying to understand.

Of course what started to be the central mystery—the hat—turned out to be a vehicle once this narrator began speaking. Where did her own urgency come from, I wondered, and that's when I realized that it came from her own sexual trauma. For me, that was the first turn toward the unexpected in the writing of the story. The second came when I realized that Stephenson was rising to power in the same historical period as Hitler and Mussolini. Actually, I say that I realized it but it was a realization I reached only after the narrator fought through both Madge's story and her own to the mystery of the fascist's charisma and power over the individual body and finally the body of a community.

AND ONE MORE thing.

The reason William Hurt carries Marguerite's book in *The Accidental Tourist,* it turns out, is because Anne Tyler was reading *Miss MacIntosh, My Darling* for inspiration as she wrote the novel. Whenever she got stuck, she has said, she opened the book randomly and the sound of Young's narrator carried her back into the voice of her own novel.

I knew when the red room scene entered the story that it was Marguerite's Greenwich Village room I was describing. Her Indianapolis niece had gone to great lengths to paint a room in her own house that same shade of maraschino red, and I'd been inside it. It's a color not easily forgotten. But it wasn't until I finished "Night Train" and went back to visit Marguerite and heard her dreamlike voice again that I realized why the narrator's voice had finally come so easily. The leaps she makes, her age, her intensity, the honesty and urge toward confession. It was, of course, the cadence and passion of Marguerite's voice that allowed me to finally write this story.

Steven Schwartz

STRANGER

AFTER PACKING UP the apartment and helping her sister deal with their father's estate, Elaine was flying back to Denver. Her father had died peacefully in his sleep at the age of seventy-nine. He had been strong and healthy right up until the end. He walked a mile a day at a brisk pace; he drank celery and carrot juice, watched his weight, and kept his mind active with everything from crossword puzzles to practicing piano to the occasional nine holes of golf; and he played a sharp game of poker with the other "youngsters" at the Jewish Community Center in Philadelphia. His blood pressure and cholesterol count had been that of a teenager's and his doctor expected him to live another decade or two. On the dark side, as her father put it, he liked his cigars and his martinis. But he hadn't died of smoking or drinking; he'd gone out just as he said he would: "They'll take me when I'm not looking, without a fight." And they had; he'd died right in the middle of the seven hours he slept a night.

Elaine's Aunt Winnie, his father's sister and a spry seventy-seven herself, had walked across the hall from her condo and found him lying on his back, one hand across his stomach. "He looked like he'd just eaten a good meal," Aunt Winnie said. Elaine thought that everyone was trying to make his death appear so serene because her mother's had been so violent. She'd died at forty-eight in an automobile accident when Elaine was in her senior year of high school and her sister Janice was a sophomore in college.

Sitting in the waiting area now for her flight, she glanced at the Philadelphia newspaper and then heard the ticket agent's voice on the intercom. The news was not good. The plane had been delayed by bad weather in Chicago and would be at least an hour late landing in Philadelphia. She slumped in her seat. She just wanted to get back to Denver. Richard and Katy—or "Caidee," as she spelled it these days, their thirteen-year-old—had already flown home a week ago. As it was, Elaine would be coming in late at night. She'd made a reservation on the last possible flight of the day because she wanted to pack up as much of Dad's stuff as possible and not leave her sister Janice with the entire mess. Still, she would need to make another trip back anyway. There was too much to sort through, including all the clippings from the local theater productions he'd been in. She'd read each of them, going back to the forties, when her mother had been with him in *Oklahoma!* Elaine's expectation had been she'd race through all the old photographs, accounts, bills, medical and insurance records, and pave the way for Janice to finish. But she'd been painfully slow, and frankly, at the end of two weeks, she felt as if she'd failed to make meaning of the details that profaned death into tabulations and schedules, receipts and scribbled notes, worn shoes and dusty suits.

Her father had never remarried. Plenty of widows and divorcees had been after him, but he rejected their interest. "Marriage is for life," he told Elaine once, "and in my case, death." The gloomy sentiment drove Elaine crazy. He could have remarried and had a full life, even perhaps another family. Instead, for the past thirty-one years, he'd kept a shrine to his dead wife. Her pictures were everywhere in the condo. In his later years he became even worse, referring to "we" all the time, as though Elaine's mother were still alive. When Elaine and the family visited from Colorado and he had his only grandchild in front of him—Janice and her husband had never had children—he told stories not about when Elaine and Janice were young but about his life with Elaine's mother: the ballroom dancing they did so suavely (foxtrot champions), the husband-wife golf tournaments, the synagogue charity balls they organized. "We were quite the team," he boasted to Elaine in a phone call, just before he died. She held the phone through his reverie hoping for him to ask about Caidee, let alone her and Richard. But he didn't, and she could see now that he'd been bowing his head at death's door all this time waiting to knock.

ELAINE AWOKE TO the announcement that her flight would be delayed another hour. She'd fallen sound asleep; her head had lolled back on her left shoulder, her arm flung out as if she'd died in battle.

Reflexively, she touched her collar for any sign of drool; it had been that kind of sleep—deep and insular, from which you returned as if kidnapped. She sat up and started off to the bathroom. An older woman with white hair and thick tinted lenses in square frames stopped her.

"Your husband," the woman began, and gave Elaine's hand a friendly squeeze, "will be back in a moment."

"Pardon?"

The woman wore pink slacks and white sneakers and had a large straw bag that said *Grand Caymans*. Fragile, slight, about the same age her mother would have been if she'd lived, she squeezed Elaine's hand again. "He's coming right back. He had to take your wallet for a minute to buy some travel items."

Elaine immediately plunged her hand into her bag, then dumped the contents of the purse out on the floor, combing frantically through the items: keys, lipstick, sales slips—her checkbook!—but no wallet. "Who?" Elaine said. "Who took it?"

"I don't . . . I thought—"

"What did he look like?"

"He was tall, blond—"

"What was he wearing?"

"A dark suit and a blue tie, I think. My goodness, I thought—"

Elaine quickly scraped everything back into her bag. A suit and blue tie. Every businessman in the world fit the description. "What else?" she said, her voice shrill. But she couldn't control her impatience, directed now at this woman who shrank from her. How could she have just watched someone take her wallet?

"He was carrying an overcoat on his arm. I'm so sorry. I didn't even look which way he went. He was so nicely dressed, and he . . . I thought he must be your husband," the woman said, obviously distraught now. "He kissed you, after all."

"What?" Elaine asked. "*What* did you say?"

"He kissed you. Right there," and she pointed to Elaine's right cheek, close to her lips. She touched her cheek and felt incredulous that this had been done while she slept, a violation disguised as sweetness.

The elderly woman said she was going to Miami, a flight that was scheduled to board in ten minutes. There was no time to search the airport. The best thing would be to call Richard at work and have him start the process of canceling their credit cards. He was teaching today, so she'd have to leave a message for him on his phone, or with the department secretary, and how could she succinctly explain that a stranger had kissed her while stealing her wallet? She felt the burn on her cheek, his lips creeping toward the moist corner of her mouth.

A ticket agent came up to her. The elderly lady from Miami had brought him over while Elaine had been trying to remember her calling card number—that card gone too.

"I understand your wallet is lost, ma'am."

"Stolen."

The agent nodded noncommittally.

"I saw him take it," the older woman spoke up. Elaine felt grateful for the witnessed support.

"We can have security look into it."

"I have to make my flight. I know it's delayed but I don't want to miss it just to have . . ." She was about to say just to have nothing happen, because she knew nothing would. The airport police or whoever was in charge would get information from her about something she'd not even observed.

The woman who had seen it all, who had been an unwitting participant, searched nervously in her own handbag for something to write her name and address on, as directed by the ticket agent, so she could make the last boarding call of her flight. She gave Elaine a hug—it felt awkwardly inappropriate—and looked back over her shoulder once before she disappeared into the Jetway. Elaine summoned enough generosity to smile back at her, then sat down with her purse gutted of its wallet, her license, pictures of Caidee, credit cards from too many stores—she'd been meaning to consolidate—emergency phone numbers, her AAA, library, and insurance cards, a picture of her mother and her taken at a photo booth in Atlantic City when Elaine was eight years old and that she'd kept in her wallet all her life.

She looked for a tall man carrying an overcoat over his arm, dressed in a blue tie and a dark suit. Hundreds of them of course. A crowd of travelers safely on their way. That's all, nothing else.

THE AIRLINE GAVE her fifteen dollars in food vouchers and ten dollars in cash. "We're not required to do this," the woman at the customer service desk told her. "But we certainly understand and sympathize with your predicament." Of course her plane, coming by way of Chicago and held up by weather, was two hours delayed now, so the gesture was less altruism than an appeasement to the restless passengers, most of whom just continued sitting in the waiting area. Elaine had made her way to customer service, then to security, filled out papers, and said what she knew. Which was nothing. A man had taken her wallet from her purse. She'd been sleeping. The purse had been wedged next to her in the seat. He'd apparently kissed her— though she left this part out, because she didn't want to undermine her claim. She had talked to a round-shouldered man with an airport badge and she didn't want to see anything cross his face that would indicate he thought she was imagining or fantasizing the incident. The kiss was both the least relevant part of the robbery and of course the most. Long after today, she would remember it beyond any money gone or other inconvenience. For now, it was her own private piece of news, not quite a secret—that bestowed on it too much intrigue and hinted of pleasure—just a lone fact only she would know.

"We'll contact you as soon as we hear anything," the security officer had told her, then sent her back to customer service for further assistance—the vouchers. She thought the choice of "as soon as we hear anything" instead of "if we hear something" sounded much more positive, even if she didn't believe a word of it. It was all public relations at this point. She herself worked in the marketing department for a large software company in Denver, so she knew all about making a concept appealing. You sold the idea, not the thing.

NOW SHE SAT in a bar, using part of her courtesy money not for food but to have a glass of wine. She should buy some food to fill her stomach—her appetite had been off anyway ever since the funeral—but she was not hungry. The airline meal would be expectantly horrible, and she would pass and perhaps order another drink. The thought of doing so, of having another glass or two of wine with the chintzy little bag of pretzels, made her happy for a moment. Something to look forward to. She should also get off her stool and phone Richard. Who knew how many charges had been made to her credit cards? But she was feeling lazy, knowing she would not be responsible for unauthorized purchases and dreading having to explain the whole annoying mishap to Richard. She continued to sip her wine.

A tall man sat down next to her.

He had an overcoat over his arm. But he had brown curly hair, not blond, and he wore a herringbone sports coat, not a dark suit and blue tie. Nor was it a surprise that he'd have an overcoat; it was cold and damp outside, and this was Philadelphia where people dressed more formally than they did in Denver with parkas and ski jackets. Indeed, nothing about the man looked like the description of the thief. He was what her father would have called an ordinary Joe and after he ordered a Scotch from the bartender he turned to her and said, "Your flight delayed too?"

Elaine placed her wine back on the cocktail napkin. "Yes," she said, and left it at that. It had been a long time since anyone had tried to pick her up. She was forty-six and although she did not feel old, she didn't think men noticed her anymore, not in "that" way. Her figure was still good, trim. But it was her "figure," no longer her "body," and she was trim, not hot.

"I've been here since noon," the man said. "How about you?"

"A little after three."

The man—he had a strong, slightly hooked nose and his short curly hair was speckled with silver, about fifty, she guessed—checked his watch. "What I hate," he started to say, and then looked up at the TV. "Oh, Jesus, we're never going to get out of here now. Did you hear that? There's a blizzard in the Midwest." He shook his head and took a long sip of his Scotch. "So, anyway, I cut you off, what were you saying?"

Elaine laughed at this, and she did not know whether he laughed along with her because he understood that he had only cut himself off or because he had no clue. It was sometimes hard to tell with men like him. The good-natured salesman type, who rolled from one segue to another without noticing much in between. She could say anything to him, she supposed, and he would listen pleasantly and meaninglessly. "My purse was stolen," she told him.

"Oh, for Pete's sake," he said, an expression she hadn't heard for a while. "That's misery. When'd it happen?"

"About an hour ago. I fell asleep in my seat and a man took my purse." She paused a minute, to let him finish shaking his head. "He kissed me on the cheek."

Elaine waited to see his reaction. She would explain nothing further, a test of sorts.

"The kissing thief," he said. "Herman Grace," he added, extending his hand, and she wanted to laugh again—his last name. Was it real? She certainly wouldn't give a stranger her full name, but he was a man, after all, and on much safer ground here. "So anyhow," he was saying, "it takes all kinds, doesn't it? Next thing you know we'll have apologetic murderers and counseling prostitutes. What's the world coming to? Criminals bussing you on the cheek. That must be some sort of new age mugging."

"I don't think he meant it as a sensitive gesture."

"No," Herman Grace said, shaking his head. "You're quite right. There is nothing the least bit kind or caring about what was done to you. I've taken your comment about being robbed and kissed and made it into fodder for chitchat. I stand corrected."

At least he believed her.

The bartender came over and asked if she wanted another glass of wine. Reflexively, she checked the remaining cash in her hand. Always a good budgeter, Richard had said about her, and the thought of Richard made her unhappy with responsibility: she should be calling him to inform him of the theft, checking in about Caidee too.

"I'll have another," Herman said, holding his empty glass aloft.

"And for the lady too, whatever she pleases." He turned back to her, his mouth, it seemed, suddenly full of extra teeth. "You don't mind if I buy you a drink, do you?"

"I should really check on my flight."

"Me too," he said. "Me too," but neither of them made a move to go, and when their drinks arrived, he slipped the bartender a twenty-dollar bill and told him to keep the change—a conspicuous, even vulgar gesture meant to impress her, she decided. She checked her face in the mirror behind the bar. Her hair curled smartly at the neck. Her eyebrows were darkened, her cheeks lightly—very subtly, she thought—rouged. And her eyeliner modest, restrained compared to, for instance, the spook show of Caidee's eyes. No, she didn't look like someone waiting to be picked up, not in her black turtleneck and gray skirt, her unpolished nails and stylish if discounted camel-hair coat that she'd gotten at a factory outlet mall in Denver. She looked, she thought, like her mother did before she died, if she hadn't dyed her hair and had let the gray show through like Elaine. It would soon be all gray. "Where are you from, Herman?"

"L.A. Born and raised. And trapped there. You?"

"From Denver."

"Terrific skiing. We try to make a trip there every season."

So, he had a family. He was not wearing a wedding ring and there was no mark from where he might have slipped it off. Now she was curious. "Do you have children?"

"Grown," he said. "Two boys and a girl. My daughter, she's in Haaavaad."

"You must be very proud."

"I certainly am," he said, and took a swallow of his Scotch.

"And your wife? Is she back in L.A.?"

"Divorced." He drummed his fingers on the bar, smiled—defensively chipper?

"I'm sorry," she said.

"No need to be. We waited until the kids were grown, did our duty. Ten years of love, ten of stale bread." His eyebrows twisted a bit. "I'm not trying to pick you up, you know."

"Oh?" It was all she could manage.

"Am I insulting you?"

"Of course you are. I suspect you know that, though."

"You needn't worry about me. I'm harmless."

She considered him for a moment while he lit a cigarette, offering her one, which she refused. She never smoked. "What exactly *do* you want?"

"To talk. Just to talk."

She put her drink down half finished on the napkin. It was time to go.

"In which case I don't know anything about you," he said.

"Pardon?"

"You want to be anonymous. You would have told me something about yourself if you didn't."

She should leave instantly and decisively, but the wine made her legs feel as if they were kicking lazily through water at the bottom of the barstool. "If I'm not mistaken, you didn't ask."

"Because you weren't going to tell me. If you were, you would have told me your name when I told you mine."

"I must be out of practice. I don't make a habit of talking to strangers."

"I can see. Otherwise you would at least have given me an alias."

She looked at him for a long moment, then laughed. Alarmingly, she was finding herself less afraid of him. "What line of work did you say you were in?"

"I'm a private investigator."

"No, you're not."

"That's right, I'm not. I'm in the electronics industry. Semiconductors."

"Now I believe you, Mr. Grace."

"Is it Mr. Grace, now? We were on a first-name basis a minute ago, at least unilaterally."

"A minute ago you were asking if I wanted to be picked up."

"If memory serves"—he put his glass against his forehead to feign concentration—"I was saying the opposite."

"You were *thinking* it. Am I wrong?"

"I was thinking you are very attractive, sure of yourself, and guarded, as you should be. I was also thinking you wouldn't believe me if I told you I have never done this before."

"Done what?"

"Approached a woman at a bar."

"You're right. I wouldn't."

"Let me ask you a question or two," he said. "Is that permitted?"

"Yes."

"Your name?"

"Elaine."

"Elaine," he said, as though examining her name like a small, pleasing, striated rock. "What is it you do?"

"Marketing, software. But don't ask me anything too technical. I depend on R and D to give me the details and then I spin them into gold."

"I'm sure you do." He picked up a pretzel from the bowl of party mix the bartender had left them and slowly chewed, then took a long drink. "I want to tell you something, Elaine. You won't mind, will you?"

"That depends."

"That's the sensible answer. But you needn't be afraid. I won't offend you."

The bar had become noisier, almost six o'clock, and she could see by the crowd at her gate that her plane had still not arrived. She put her palm over her empty glass of wine, her second glass, to keep herself from ordering more. That was her limit usually, two glasses when she and Richard went out for the evening, but the idea of limits had suddenly become just that, an idea. She studied his hands; he had strong smooth fingers and clean nails. She appreciated a man who gave his fingernails attention. She stared at the white half moons of his cuticles, then raised her eyes and said, "Tell me. I'd like to hear."

"I'm not here on business. My children lured me here, perhaps that is the best word. They are fed up with me and have tried an intervention of sorts, to no avail. That's what I was doing in Philadelphia and that's why I am leaving alone. The intervention failed. They are furious with me. This is my fourth Scotch and my second pack of cigarettes in as many hours. Airport delays are unstructured, unhealthy time and I am as weak as I've ever been." He stared out the window a moment at the parked planes. "What nakedness would you like to tell me, Elaine?"

Names were being called over the paging system, Mr. Agler, Mrs. Hong, Ms. Lewis . . . Elaine heard them dimly along with the announcements of flights; the electronic beeping of courtesy carts going by; cranky children screaming at being dragged another inch through the miserable terminal with its delayed passengers. Right now the dirt of her father's grave would be running muddy from the rain, while a thief somewhere was picking through her assets, discarding credit cards, throwing her wallet with the photograph of her mother and her in Atlantic City into a filthy dumpster behind a warehouse. Her mother had hated the cold and damp, and on such mornings her father would warm her sweaters over the old steam radiators in their house on Belmont Street.

If her mother had remained alive Elaine might not have made certain mistakes—entered into a disastrous first marriage or cut off friends when she needed them most. She might have told her mother, as she never did her father, about the "struggle" with the boy in college—what would flatly be called date rape now. She might have drawn more comfort and courage for this second part of her life had her mother lived and had her father not expected her and her sister to handle everything on their own, because Mother's death was mostly his loss. And yet she had loved her father all the more desperately after her mother died, jumping to him, her only remaining oar.

"My father just died," Elaine said. She was thinking about Herman Grace's grown children surrounding him, pleading with him to save his life. The image had an exquisite pain, so much love and so much stubbornness, so much trouble and so much spilled hope.

"I'm a man who still carries a handkerchief. May I?" and she let him dab at her face—she had started to cry. He worked tenderly, as if his fingers themselves were gloved, touching her cheeks with the soft cotton cloth, fresh and clean as a white veil.

"Can I help you get somewhere?" Herman Grace asked, because he could see when she stood up she was slightly unsteady from her two glasses of wine.

"I'll be fine," she said, but then leaned into him anyway, and he put his arm around her shoulder. He smelled of aftershave, Scotch, and smoke, a not unpleasant combination at the moment, and she listened to his breathing—heard all the discordant sounds of his life commingling into a stand against oblivion.

They walked silently toward her plane. She held his arm for comfort more than support, and she felt safe next to him. At the gate, passengers were gathered around the ticket agent's desk.

They went over and listened. The flight had been canceled, stuck in Chicago. People were angry, asking why they hadn't been told sooner. "We got the information to you as soon as we received it," the ticket agent said, a thin man with droopy eyes. One other flight this evening was scheduled for Denver, but that was on a different airline and presently at full capacity, the ticket agent said, studying his monitor. "Everyone will be rebooked on flights tomorrow morning," he told them. "We can't control the weather. I'm very sorry, but if you need assistance with arrangements for staying overnight we can try to help."

" 'Try,' " Herman Grace said. "Key word. They're not obligated to do anything because it's weather-related."

She stared in disbelief at the moving red letters across the board that said *Flight Canceled*. "I can't believe this. I can't fucking believe this." Herman Grace looked away, quieted, she wondered, by her profanity. "You'd better check on yours," she told him, though she did not want him to leave her alone.

"I did," he said. "It's still canceled."

She stared at him. "Still? What do you mean?"

"It was canceled hours ago. I've been—how shall I put it?—*reluctant* to leave the airport. I didn't want to face my children, and I didn't want to go to an empty hotel room. And then I met you."

She knew now he was asking her to spend the night with him, and she was thinking that she could do it and live with the guilt or not do it and live with the relief and that the two choices didn't seem that far apart in consequence. She had assumed such parallel lines would never converge—and they never had for her. But, as Richard was fond of saying, she was in a state. All the more reason to behave badly and irresponsibly, not be accountable for her actions from the shock of her father's death, her stolen wallet, her canceled flight. . . .

None of this equaled the clarity of knowing that what she was about to do was wrong.

She could—*should*—take a cab to Janice's house and spend the night. Her sister would surely be glad to drive her the next morning to the airport, as she had done this afternoon. She could even sleep in her father's apartment, the bed where he died, a communion of sorts, maybe finding a macabre peace in his penultimate resting place. She certainly had resources, unlike Mr. Grace. "I need to make a phone call," she told him. "Where should I meet you?"

"Same old, same old." He pointed to the bar where they'd been. "Shall I order you anything?"

"Water, please."

"Me too," he said. "The healthy choice."

She went over to the pay phone and made a collect call to Richard, prepared to hang up if he didn't answer after three rings, long enough to fool herself into believing she tried.

"Hello?"

"Richard," Elaine said, and could feel herself saying his name as if she had just dropped all her heavy bags in front of him with utter relief.

"Where are you, Laine?"

"I'm still at the Philadelphia airport. My flight's been canceled. Oh, Richard, what a day it's been."

"I was just about to go out the door to pick up Caidee after her swim practice and go straight from there to the airport. What happened?"

"My wallet was stolen. I'm so sorry, I should have called earlier."

"Your wallet? Are you all right? Were you hurt?"

"No, no," she said, imagining his worried face. "I'm fine. I was sleeping. It was stupid. He took it from my bag by pretending . . ." She looked over at the bar. Herman Grace waved to her and she back at him.

"Laine? Are you going out on a later flight?"

"There are no others tonight. I'll have to fly back tomorrow morning."

"You'll stay at Janice's, right? Can we reach you there? I want to know you're safe. It will be good to be with your sister after such a miserable day."

"I think," she said, and fingered the coin return, letting it slam closed, "I think I'm going to stay near the airport. The flight leaves early."

There was a pause, and she thought that Richard didn't believe her, but he said, "That's a good idea perhaps." She nodded, as if she'd gotten a forged permission slip. "But what will you do for money?"

"What?" she asked, understanding clearly what he had said.

"Money for a hotel. Oh!" he interrupted himself. "They're paying for it, the airline. I get it."

"I'll call you in the morning, all right?"

"Are you sure you don't need anything? I hate to think of you there without a cent."

"I'll be fine. Give Caidee a kiss for me. I miss you both."

"I love you too. And, Laine, be good to yourself. Your father and all." She touched her cheek where the thief's lips had been and felt a bluish heat, ran her finger up near her earlobe where Richard liked to kiss her and felt Herman Grace's mouth there.

When she got off the phone, she didn't look over at Herman Grace at the bar; she didn't want to show anything on her face. She went into the bathroom and sat on the toilet and listened to more names being paged . . . Mr. Callahan, Ms. Wilkens, Mr. Pintauro . . . a dull drone of missing people. She looked at herself in the mirror for a long time after she brushed her hair: her brown eyes, such pretty, warm eyes her mother would always say, *like little poems.*

She walked out of the bathroom, joining the dwindling crowd—people on their way home or to hotels overnight or back to where they started. There were only two men sitting together at the bar, younger men. She stood in the middle of the concourse and watched both ways, and then kept her eyes on the men's bathroom for a moment. She went into the bar and sat down to wait; he was no doubt in the bathroom himself.

The bartender, the same one who had been here before, came over to her. "The gentleman said to give this to you." He handed her a business card. Elaine looked at it: Herman Grace, Tritronics Electrical Systems. She turned the card over: *Is it cowardly or honorable of me to leave? Try to think well of me. I always will of you. Love, Herman.*

The bartender had his back to her and was washing a glass. Elaine stared out at the terminal—the people passing through. When she'd been young, her whole family would watch the show *To Tell the Truth.* She'd sit with them on the couch with its rose-patterned brocade fabric, running her finger across the delicate petals, the sturdy stems, the sharp thorns, imagining the touch of a boy's spine. One night, while her parents held hands and she shared a pan of popcorn with her sister, the show's host had declared to the three contestants, *Will the real thief please stand up?*

Beside her was the bottled water Herman Grace had ordered for her—she'd only noticed it now—poured into a glass, with a slice of lemon. Elaine looked down and smiled to herself. Her sweet, gentle mother would have said, you're smiling from ear to ear, darling, why?

Behind the Story

H ERE'S THE STORY: a woman walks into an airport, checks her luggage, gets her boarding pass, and goes to her gate. While waiting for her flight to arrive, she falls asleep. When she wakes, an elderly lady tells her that her husband will be right back with her wallet—he went to buy something. And by the way, he kissed you on the cheek.

A friend told me this story ten years ago; the experience had happened to a friend of his. Unlike in my fictional version, the woman boarded her plane after all, realizing she could do nothing about the crime by staying behind at the airport. The elderly lady who had witnessed the theft was also a passenger on the flight. At the last moment, just as the door was about to close, a final passenger boarded. The elderly lady got up quickly from her seat to inform the woman that this was the thief who had robbed her. They decided to point him out to the flight attendant, but by this time the plane had been cleared for takeoff and the flight attendant insisted there wasn't anything that could be done until they landed again.

When the plane did land, the thief was escorted off and searched. Nothing was found. Not a shred of evidence that linked him to the crime. He was set free with an apology. Shortly afterward, however, the woman received a call from the airline. They had found her wallet with her credit cards but with no cash.

"Where did you find it?" she asked.

"Wedged between two seats on the plane," the airline official told her.

The problem with true stories is that they're often too good to write. "That would make a great story," people often say. Of course no such guarantee exists. At some point, while you're typing away, the air leaks out of the experience and you're left with a beached and deflated plastic whale.

My protagonist Elaine kept getting onto the plane only to be trapped there with the thief. What I couldn't let go of in the real story was the woman on the plane flying for several hours, knowing that the man who'd robbed and kissed her was sitting just two rows behind. A perfect situation, I thought. No escape. High tension. I wrote two, three . . . six drafts. Yet nothing budged. Elaine became isolated with her thoughts. To nudge along the story and get some interaction going, I had the thief sit down next to her (in a conveniently empty seat). Once, he even touched her hair while standing behind her. But my thief became smarmy, a stereotypical and predictable villain; Elaine, meanwhile, turned out to have a bird's nest of worries that I could do nothing interesting with. When was she going to make her big move? How was she going to get out of her predicament? Couldn't she at least get up to go to the bathroom instead of sitting there paralyzed with fear? Frankly, who cared? The Elaine I really cared about was back at the airport grieving over her father's death.

In the earliest version of the story Elaine was a character without a past. We never learned her name—I found it sufficient to cloak her in the pronoun "she." I'd tried to make the story one of those narratives where the character's history is implied and even determines the action but is never discussed, as in Earnest Hemingway's "The Killers": *Man walks into a diner* . . . Indeed, I was so keen on the strength of the original incident that I believed action in this case would define all we needed to know about character; anonymity would intensify the story's momentum. Unfortunately, unlike stories where effacement sometimes does work, I had a character without the deeper currents of a true purpose—good perhaps for a fascinating anecdote but decal-thin for a narrative. It was only after I wrote that her father had just died that "she" became Elaine.

I now had a character with a past and a voice that suited her, but I still didn't have that other crucial element: conflict. I had a *staged* conflict, one without any leavening ambivalence—not the kind that shakes a character up from the inside out. For all the suspense I tried to create—or milk by way of the original story—Elaine existed in a vacuum. The thief, to my surprise, was only a foil for Elaine's growing, if plodding, terror. Her emotions pinged off his static presence and shot back with the dimmest sonar. Besides that, I now had too much exposition, not to mention the story was front-heavy with background material. Elaine, tightly buckled into her seat, only burdened the story with more reflection.

Eventually, I had to let go. Elaine would not board the plane. I brought in Mr. Grace whose character emerged in one piece, hardly a word changed or added from my first writing of him. Of course, the last thing Elaine needed, after burying her father and being robbed at the airport, was for some guy to sit down and try to pick her up at a bar. But it's often the whispered dare deep in the writer's gut that makes for the right intuitive choice. Mr. Grace, with his sorrow, opened up the story for me. Elaine in all my previous drafts, despite putting her through the paces of facing a thief up in the skies, had stubbornly remained the same person from the beginning of the story to the end, lacking in complex motivation. Once Mr. Grace entered the story, their private and civilized conversation ironically had more engagement and uncertainty than any number of machinations I might have concocted for Elaine and the thief. Then too, Mr. Grace was all about loss. He had reason to be desperate. And much to my surprise, as a nonviewpoint character who could keep us in the dark as to his motives, he supplied the sexual tension I'd been looking for from the thief, who was too handsome for his own good when we first met him on the plane.

Writers frequently juxtapose their own stories with those they appropriate from the world, adding that bridging detail to make the connection personal, in this case, for me, a father who had just died.

At the time I heard this story my mother had been dead for two years and my father would die shortly after I began trying to write it. I'd dealt with the loss of my mother by becoming all the more clutching of my father's existence. It was only after he died that I felt truly bereft, alone as I'd ever been before, robbed and empty.

My original title, during my many drafts about Elaine and the thief trapped on the plane together, was "What She Left." It was meant to indicate something about loss and redemption. Unfortunately, as with many working titles that suggest a This-Space-For-Rent status, it referred more to what I wanted the story to be about than what I'd achieved. Eventually the story would come to fit its one-word title. Elaine's father, Mr. Grace, the thief . . . all would be the stranger, but most of all it would be Elaine who would, as I realized in the depth of my grief over my own parents, become a stranger to herself.

Kevin McIlvoy

THE PEOPLE WHO OWN PIANOS

for Rick

W E NEVER CAN FIND their fuckin houses.

We get a set of shit directions there, a different set of shit directions back. Okay, we've got an attitude about the goddamn load no matter what we're told it is—grand, baby, standup, damaged, used, good used, or good—fifth or first floor, basement, attic, narrow or wide staircase—the kit or the whole coffin—it's the same to A.D. Moving.

We carry it out into the light beyond the lighted, decorated, dimwit room we rearrange, rip, gouge, and nick all we want on our way out. Make way, we say, make way—words that give us rights greater any day than the owners', am I right?

Some are widows, widowers, divorcees or divorcers, retiring or retired. They are not as sensitive as you would think. We're hauling off something they wanted bad or still want, but they won't complain, it's like they can't. They stall out, clamp up, they stutter those fucked witty things we never get or ever got.

What makes us us and them not us? What makes them them and

346 • *Kevin McIlvoy*

us not them? They were politely chewing when we were swallowing hard. That's how they were, that's how they are. They learned putting together when we were learning pulling apart.

So fucking what? So, fucking what? So-fucking-what.

We amputate the legs, mummify the sound and the keyboards in blankets, rope and tape, and cart the thing to freedom, taking no educated guesses ever about how the damned load has gotten in there, how the fuck it will get out, how many hours we'll take making way and making way and making way. You do this job long enough you can't think of anything good to say about the people who own pianos, with their walk-in closets and their screened-in porches, their Eurostyle custom kitchens, wet bars, hot tubs, and blond Mexican tiles.

Everything we scar scars that bandaged monster we bump against the plaster or wallpaper. We make the walls drum, the floors groan. We strike the chandeliers and bronze standing lamps, strum the dumb leggy houseplants these people hang in jute from their ceilings.

Fuck yeah, they're the people who macramé and refurbish and antique—or would, or have that look like they might. They might, they might, they might, they say, and never have to speak it, do they? Whatever they want they only have to say they want it once.

I love them.

I love the people who own pianos decorated with some shredded piece of lace of crochet they want to tell you the story of. I hate their stories about some other piano in some foreign country someone fled for some reason that has to be recited, for some reason, and can't just be said. I hate their sad, ugly mugs, but I love them, and I tell them, Hey, A.D. loves you, you buttfucks, that's why I'm here—to ease your pain at Your Time of Loss. See, I brought my best crew of compassionate men. They love you too. They do. Right, guys? Hourly employees. Hourly they love you.

(Okay, all right, I don't say any of that to the people who own pianos. You can't say that shit to them.)

If they want, they can talk. God, they can talk. They can. You can listen. One time, this guy says to the crew—and the crew was all parked on his couch because he told us to—he made us—he was about to fuckin cry—he called us "boys,"—he said, "Boys, our dog has gone to prison, boys. For life."

A strange thing to hear from an old guy sitting alone at his worthless standup piano with no "our" in sight, one chair at his table, one empty glass at his place, who probably meant "our son," "our grandson," or "our minister" has gone to prison, but couldn't have meant the dog unless it was another dog than the haunted-looking, balding red hound dog cowering like a convict or ex-con against the piano pedals and gumming a rubber doll baby that kept its eyes and mouth shut, its arms and legs straight out.

"Boys," the old man said, "*I* was a piano mover," gray boogers floating in both his eyes, "Can you believe it?"

Fuck no, we thought. Fuck no, I said. Oh, hell no, I didn't really say it, I couldn't, but I must've almost-did because he made a snorting sound and said, "Fuck, yes."

The people who own pianos are never people who moved them. He couldn't've been the player. It couldn't've been his piano.

"Get off my bed," he growled. His bed? Hell. It might've been a foldout or something, how do you know, because their couches aren't always couches, and their groomed, good-looking dogs are more like blue or yellow budgies in sparkling wire cages. He couldn't've been the owner. It couldn't've been his dog.

"Our dog was the one who played," he said. Probably meant "our daughter," "our granddaughter," "our ghost," "our god" played this monster. We got up anyway. We petted his dog, named after that prick Judge Bork. It was on his tags. "Hey, get this," we said to the old guy who couldn't have got, owned it, named it. "Bork," we said. "Bork!" Bork never moved, never stretched, yawned, scratched, twitched. Just chewed on the doll's eight toes, and hummed and made the old man's same snoring sound. "Fetch," we said, and threw the old man's magazines and sheet music and sofa pillows and shit like that at Bork's head, with no results.

But the old man. The old man on his piano bench, flinched, bent, and all of a sudden he thumped the closed key cover, and said, like it meant something, "Piss on it." He meant on it all, the whole thing, piano, piano makers, buyers, sellers, players, movers, traders, and the entire damn unjust prison system, but at first we thought he wanted us to lift our legs and piss on his dog, and we looked at Bork like he was a fire hydrant, and he might've been he might've been, he was that red and that immovable and stupid.

He said, "Piss on it," again, which we didn't. He said, "Do you know who I am?" which we didn't. He said, "Of course not," and shook his head.

I guess that's when we decided to screw him over. Love is like that, you know.

We took the piano, took the couch, the table; took the one chair, the one glass, the magazines and sheet music. We took the rubber doll baby. The last thing we did was shovel Bork onto the piano cart and roll him out like the royal dog he was or the genie or dragon or troll who played the old man's piano really well before he did a life sentence and died and came back as a red dog. Make way, make way, we said. And the old man did.

Hell, we are different, to be honest. So-fucking-what. So fucking what? They never cuss. We cuss. They tell the truths that lie; we tell the lies that lie, and that's the truth. The people who own pianos never share the stories they are most ashamed to share, and that's no lie. That's how they are, that's how they were.

We are different, us and them, them and us. They were learning rest when we were learning restless. Oh, fuck yeah, sometimes we have to put the damned thing on the floor or the stairs. Or we get as far as the front yard, and lay it down there that loving way you lay down a tire you just busted off a rim. We rest our backs or heads on the hard pillow, the hard lost island of overambitious, undertalented piano bangers, the hard silent coffin you could fit three little Mozarts and their wigs inside. We slap the black giant on its ass or pet its smooth, hard chest, or we make a guess at middle C and play muffled "Chopsticks" through the ropes and tape and blankets. What? Did you think we never knew people who knew the people who played pianos?

Well, we did.

And all the people who own pianos stare at us through their clean front windows or lean out their solid walnut doors or stand on but not beyond the front edges of their long driveways and lawns. They don't like our cussing, laughing, or our doll we call "Sleeping Ugly" asleep on the dash, dreaming of an open mouth and open eyes; dreaming of two more toes, of chewing on the dog to show him what it's like; dreaming of some clothes, for God's sake, to cover her genitals, and some cash to cover her ass on the short fall into trouble and the long climb out of it; dreaming of a halfway house or a hospital room or a cardboard box on a steel steam grate; dreaming of toothaches and nosebleeds and rubber or—why not?—real scabs, and nails to pick the scabs; and dreaming of prescription drugs and sex toys and sleeplessness—fabulous fucking sleeplessness. And teeth. And a tongue—and the spit to go with it. And bile. And blockage and gas and life-size shit, and no bitchy sisters and no goddamn prince. Dreaming of leaving home with a mean red dog and criminal friends in a dangerous ride on the black vinyl prow of a speeding van.

(Okay, okay, she's not dreaming of any of that. Probably not. Probably not. So-fucking-what. So, fucking what? Soooooo fuuuuuucking what?)

They don't like us.

They don't like our dog's erotic dancing, and they hate the applause when we applaud ourselves. They don't like our need to know the kind of happiness they knew before they needed something else.

I HAD WORKED MANY hours, written many pages of "The people who own pianos," only following the narrator's voice wherever it led. My inefficient writing process stresses intuitive wandering in an effort to write from negative capability, from a "stance of wonder" (John Berryman).

In twenty-plus pages and thirty-plus hours of writing, I had not found a story. I had found a dynamic moment—beginning with "We never can find their fuckin houses"—in this profane and prayerful voice that I knew I could trust. It has been my practice to place my first trust in the human voice into which the streams of other voices (inflected by the rhythms of the setting and the textures of the culture) are poured; into which the poisons and blessings of life experience (particularly work experience) are trickled; and, most importantly, from which emerges both the selves and the true selves of characters. Until this piece, I had placed my first trust in the voice, but not my *absolute* trust.

I fully deserve the "Huh?" response I have received when I have disingenuously named as "novel" my record of an expansive voice, or as "novella" or "short story" my records of self-limiting voices. I revise extensively, not in order to find the circumscribing causalities and shapely structures of plot, but to further honor the alimentary elements and the many musics inside the music of a certain voice. I do not revise in order to discover how the voice behaves, but how it breathes. I admire, study, envy writers, real novelists and short story writers, whose work honors voice and story at once. To name a few: Herman Melville ("Bartleby, the Scrivener"), James Baldwin ("Sonny's Blues"), Katherine Anne Porter (*Pale Horse, Pale Rider*),

Miguel Torga (*Tales from the Mountain*), and Clarice Lispector (*The Passion According to G.H.*).

At the time I revised "The people who own pianos" I recognized that I was writing deeper and deeper into a blues voice, which doubles back on itself ("They don't like our need to know the kind of happiness/ they knew before they needed something else"), which has a moaning turnaround (a moment at which words won't serve, or in which the words only stand for moans: "So fucking what?/ So, fucking what?/ So-fucking-what"), and which reflects the rage and joy felt by this narrator who is caught up in the rhythm of his work ("We slap the black giant on its ass/ or pet its smooth, hard chest, or …"). I thought maybe I heard the Delta blues in the voice. And those blues, crudely and subtly carved on the frets by a bottleneck, are not part of a storytelling tradition; those blues are a cry from a field of laborers; they are the moan from a heart at last caving in or at the very first moment of recovering. As I put each draft more fully at the service of A.D.'s messy but rhythmic voice, my own controlling and self-censoring inclinations were undermined.

I resisted this story. I fought it. At a very important moment in my life as a writer, I lost. I lost the fight with "The people who own pianos," and I have never been the same.

Draft by draft, I observed the narrator's voice moving from an "I" voice to an "I/We" voice, and I believed that the drafts had uncovered some elemental truth about his crowded heart. I welcomed in more "We," putting aside my old superficial goal of consistency. I observed that the narrator was conflicted about the "They" for whom he and his crew move pianos; he hates them, and he loves them, and he hates loving them, and loves hating them. I welcomed in more "They," and, as a result, I discovered that his monologue was both interior and dramatic; and, with each draft, I learned a new authorial generosity that would allow the narrator to address them all: the "I" and "We" and "They" and the inextricable "We-I-They."

I found that I understood the narrator less definitely but knew him more generously; that is, I knew more about his ways of being, and I understood less about his ways of becoming (plot); less about how his piano-moving memories mattered (theme).

If such a tiny work of fiction—barely five pages in its final form—defeated me in this way, I must have been ready to have all my presumptions about storytelling defeated. Without knowing it, I was indeed ready. I wish for all the writers I know, especially all those I presume to teach, to always be on the brink of such ignominious defeat.

The first time I read this story in public, a good and dear and mercilessly honest friend said to me, "You really don't understand that it is a story about class, do you?"

· I didn't. But I gave no answer. Dishonest of me. A big part of me was ashamed that, after thirty years of writing, I had not developed into a storyteller. I knew that "The people who own pianos" was a kind of *song* that owed no absolute allegiance to *story* however it might vaguely resemble one. I now believe that this good song (in which others, looking, wishing, might find story) has worth as a reading experience.

I am more honest with myself now, though I am not less dishonest with others about how I name my work as "short story" or "novella" or "novel." What does it say about me that "The people who own pianos" appears in a "story collection"? That I have submitted this essay for an anthology entitled *The Story Behind the Story*?

I have so much to learn.

Debra Spark

MARIA ELENA

T HIS IS THE story of how I met and won the recalcitrant heart of one Sandrofo Cordero Lucero, astute student of the mechanics of work habits and—well, to tell the truth—of not much else. It's a fairy tale of sorts, so I always tell the girls to pay attention. They might learn something for the future. Lesson number one, I tell them, is some clichés are true. There is such a thing as love at first sight. How do you think a cliché got to be a cliché in the first place? The truth was repeated till it got boring. But no one wants to think the truth is boring. Listen up, girls, I say, and believe. It's not interesting, but that doesn't matter; opposites *do* attract. Who would have put me, Maria Elena, onetime anarchist, crazy person attached to a fire-engine mouth, with the silent, conservative baker? No one, of course. No one but fate.

I WAS THIRTY-FIVE then, a believer in signs and omens, past lives and future ones. The tarot. The patterns of seashells. Advice in the horoscopes of supermarket magazines. I was democratic when it came to other worlds. I still believe today, but at that point, the right words hadn't come my way. I'll confess to being despairing. I was a hen among many hens and only a handful of roosters. You see what I mean. In that age, in this place, it wasn't easy. I'd had the questionable benefits of the sexual revolution. I am talking about years of live-in lovers and only the oldest of old folks disapproving. But where had that got me? On the day I met Sandrofo, I was thirty-five and alone. My parents were dead. My sister, Sisa—whom I had loved desperately—was dead. A heart attack related to her diabetes. I suffered from the disease myself, but I had things more under control. Still, years earlier, I had been in the loony bin, almost dead of grief myself, staring at the rabbit-shaped water stains in the ceiling and crying about my sister. All through my twenties when I dreamed of good times, I dreamed of return visits to the bin. What is this but tragic?

Of course, I had been out of the loony bin too, had been working in a museum and then at a gallery on Calle del Cristo in old San Juan. I was a convert to beauty that year, the middle of my fourth decade of life. The job helped. I tool real care with my appearance and with keeping the floor of the gallery clean. I liked the cocktail parties before an exhibit opened. I liked how I held my elbow just so when I poured out wine. I took beauty home with me, started thinking of "wearable art" instead of jewelry. I imagined hanging Japanese silk tapestries in the living room. Needless to say, *dinero,* cash, scratch . . . it was all a problem. And I was still sad all the time. Yes, yes, yes, I'd argue with myself, it was better than the hospital. My neighbors weren't in four-point restraints. But, but, but . . . there was this sadness, this weariness. People know the feeling, or they don't. It's no use trying to explain.

That day, the one when I met my betrothed, started out ordinary enough. Unremarkable weather. The bus didn't break down on my way to work. No terrorists threatened to blow up the governor's bedroom. We were five weeks into an exhibit at the gallery. We were showing that famous series of illustrations to the child's tale "The Emperor's New Clothes." Predictably enough, gallery traffic had slowed to include only tourists and the occasional passerby.

Even though there wasn't much to do that day, I delayed going to lunch. I'd been doing this for weeks. Lucia, who minds the gallery with me, said later she thought it was a way to deny that I was sick. I would have agreed, but it wasn't true. I knew I had diabetes, and I was playing with things. How close could I get to going too far and still pull back? I don't say this was conscious. It was something I puzzled out later.

Anyway, this one day, the game served me well. It was sugar that got me a husband. Sugar got me a sugar, I say in English. A sudden drop in my sugar level that sent me out of the gallery to look for food. I was dizzy for the better part of the noon hour, but I ignored the feeling and set to retyping a smudged price list. It wasn't until I found myself daydreaming about making tiny construction-paper clothes for the Emperor Who Had None that I said, "Lucia, I'm off to lunch."

I stepped out of the cool, air-conditioned gallery into the hot street and felt a bit crazier with every step I took. I had the real feeling that the watercolor paint of the sky had been mixed with too much water and was now running down over the buildings and puddling on the gray-blue ballasts of the street. I knew enough to head for an ice cream vendor in the plaza just at the end of the street.

When I crossed over the street into the plaza, I saw that the vendor who normally operated out of the northwest corner of the square was gone. Ordinarily, I'd have thought, "Well, it's time for some juice," but ordinarily I'm avoiding sugar, not looking for it, and I couldn't think where, in the whole of the old city, I could find what I needed. Just thinking about it made me feel terribly hot. In my mind, I went down one street after another, but I could only see greasy *empanadas* and plump flies under heat lamps. Of course, anyone else would have also seen the bright orange bottles of *parcha,* which are, invariably, lined up by the heat lamps, but my mind wasn't right. In my head, I saw some fried cheese. It made me reel just to picture it. I wiped my forehead with the back of my hand. I could have washed my hair in the water from the sweat at my temples, so I made my way to the center of the plaza to dip my fingers in the fountain and cool off. As I stood at the fountain and bathed my neck, I felt I was about to faint.

"Excuse me," I said to a woman who was standing next to me. She was short haired, stoutly built and rough complected. Clearly, a cold-climate woman, and I wondered what she was doing here. I couldn't really gather much else about her, because the world was turning into a cheap black-and-white TV set with bad reception. "Excuse me," I heard myself say again. "I'm about to faint."

"Oh," the woman said, and it sounded as if she said it with real pleasure. She took my right hand firmly in hers. Presumptuous, I thought, but did feel steadied by the press of her fingers against my own. "It's so good you *told* me. I'm a healer. Lie right down. Right down here."

Mother of God, I thought, I've got a crackpot. Still, I did as she said and put my back on the stones of the plaza. I had enough sense to worry about pigeon droppings and to put my purse under my head. I could feel the sharp clasp of my wallet just below my crown. A pen stuck up into my ear. Why had no one ever invented a cloth writing utensil? I wondered. My best thoughts always came to me when I was depleted of sugar.

I looked up and then turned my head so I wouldn't be staring at the brightness of the sky. The woman was still holding my hand. "Diabetes," I said and shook my medical-alert bracelet. Wearable art and practical too, I said to myself in the voice of a radio announcer. So buy some before midnight tonight. My inner voice pitched and squealed in such an odd way that I wondered if I'd spoken aloud.

"Just breath in deep," the woman told me. I sucked in air. "And out." I blew hair away from my eyes. "In and out. In. Out. Now," she said in that hypnotic voice people use when they want to make sure you're going to follow their instructions, "what I'm going to do is press very hard in the center of your hand. This is called a pressure point, and I'm going to press hard, so you can release the tension in the rest of your body."

I shook my wrist once again to indicate that I had a genuine medical problem.

She said, "Now just let the tension flow down your legs and out of your toes."

She pushed her thumb into the center of my palm. The pressure was so strong and so painful that I thought, for a moment, it would be possible for her to push her thumb right through my hand. Still, it felt weirdly pleasant, like rolling backward slowly into the warmest, gentlest of oceans. I closed my eyes. I opened them. A crowd had gathered above me.

The woman said to me, "My name is Iriamne. Who are you?"

"Maria Elena," I said, but the way my voice came out it sounded like a needle scraping a record, a fingernail scratching a blackboard.

"Well, Maria Elena," she said, as if I were an idiot, "we think it would be a good idea to take you into the bakery. It's cool in there, and we can get you a little something to eat. How do you feel about going to La Madeleine?"

La Madeleine. Why hadn't I thought of it when my mind was wandering the streets?

"Does that sound OK?" Iriamne asked. She went on without waiting for a reply. "We're going to let these men here carry you." *What* men, I thought, though I knew she was referring to some people behind her. "And some other people are going to get an ambulance. Now, can you hold your hands like this?" She rearranged my arms so that I hugged my sides.

"Yes," I said. "I think I can handle that." I counted on the fact that my voice had, of its own accord, risen two octaves to conceal my sarcasm.

I felt her twist my long hair into a single dark rope and tuck it into the collar of my shirt. Then I was aloft. I'm not a heavy woman. I pride myself on my figure. Slim. Nice breasts, I've been told. (That's a side point, I guess, about the breasts. It doesn't directly relate to my tale.) I closed my eyes. (They're brown.) I didn't want to be embarrassed by the faces that were lifting me. Soon enough, I thought, you'll be hiding your eyes when you meet these people on the street. Hands were pushed under my back, and I was in the air. I felt Iriamne tuck my skirt up between my legs so everything was proper. And then the hands kept lifting. This was strange, I thought. They carried me—I felt six, flat palms in all—as if I were a gigantic tray at a fancy restaurant. Their arms must have been nearly outstretched, for instead of holding me at chest level, they had me up in the air. Seven, maybe eight, feet.

I opened my eyes. What a strange way to see the city. I closed my eyes again and then opened them quickly. It was like being dead, I suddenly thought, being carried at this height, out of the plaza and past cornices that, from my vantage point, needed painting. The TV screen flickered again. It went dark, then light, and the words "funeral bier" inserted themselves in my brain like an unwelcome mantra. I panicked and started to shout, "Let me down, let me down, let me down." Then, we were there, and I was being lowered through the door of the bakery. I smelled confectionery sugar and saw the pressed metal of a ceiling that had been painted an ugly yellow. I saw two ceiling fans and six flies. I heard the scrape of chairs being pulled back and people clearing the way. A girl cried, "No, not the floor. It's filthy. Not the floor. Not the floor." Then I was being laid out on the linoleum counter of the coffee shop.

A different voice, male, deep and commanding, approached. "Stand back. Stand back," it said. "Let the lady have some air." Things faded, and then this same voice said, "OK. Tata, Beatriz, push it over here.

Lift the wheels over that thing in the floor. OK. I've got it. Good. Now, give her some room."

Even when I am not thinking straight, I am a curious person. I wanted to know what the man was talking about. Wheel *what* over *what* bump *where*? That's just the way my mind works, so I tried very hard to open my eyes and focus on what was going on around me. I saw a fork with a piece of cake looming above my nose. Behind that, things were blurry.

I did my share of drugs in the sixties, and I can honestly say that, as altered states go, I preferred just about everything to what I was feeling at that moment. Still, I could not bring myself to put that bit of cake in my mouth. Now, what happened next takes some time to describe, though it happened in the space of a few seconds. I squinted and focused my eyes on the prongs of the fork. I looked at that piece of cake for what seemed like hours. It was white, and there was a dab of blue icing, smeared like a wayward bit of toothpaste, on part of it. I stared so hard at that cake that it came apart in my mind. I thought about crumbs and how many crumbs make up a single bite of cake. My depth of field was narrow. I saw one end of that bite of cake in perfect focus, but the far end was out of focus and in no way related to the very interesting crumbs on the near side. Then I looked farther, past that fork to a hand. One of the fingers of the hand was deformed, turned, so the knuckle faced the palm. I looked even farther to a face. The cake went blurry. A handsome man was holding the fork. Well, this got my attention, as a handsome man is bound to do.

"Have a bite of this?" the man said. He was dark, clean shaven. I saw a long nose and blue eyes. There was brown hair and a single section in the front that was too long and flopped in his eyes. He pushed it back, and I could see he was Spanish, but I guessed right away that he had other blood in him, for he was too pale to be from the island, even if both of his parents had been "white" Puerto Rican. He had a good, an intelligent look about him, but what I noticed was something else: he looked like a man who was used to serious concern about others.

I said to him, "Señor." Again, my voice screeched out of my mouth and sounded nothing like my own. I propped myself up on my elbows. "Señor," I repeated. Later, when I knew him, he confessed it looked as if I were leering at him. "Señor," I said a third time. And here is where the TV set of my vision clicked off. I only remember bits of the rest. Like a child, I have to appropriate the memory of others and claim it as my own.

I said, "Señor, isn't matter funny? Last night, a cake could have killed me. Today, it saves my life."

"Yes," the man replied, almost as if he were talking to himself, "the way the world twists and turns, twists and turns again." Then, apparently, I had a mouse-size nibble of cake. I looked at the handsome man in a funny way. My head was cocked like a perplexed puppy dog's.

"It's good. Right?" the man asked. "It's a wedding cake, but the wedding was called off. I knew it wouldn't go to waste." His tone was friendly, matter-of-fact. This was business, getting the patient to eat. "Have some more," he offered.

"No," I said. People say I sounded flirtatious when I said this.

"Christ," the man said. He turned his head and said something to someone behind him.

"You're very handsome," I said. Again, this is only hearsay, and I can tell you that I don't just up and say something this forward on an average day.

"Just force-feed her," someone suggested.

The man turned back to me and started to stroke the top of my left arm in the slow, rhythmic way a mother pats the back of a child who is throwing up. "Just one bite," he said.

I started to stutter my replies to him. "I just . . . wait . . . I just . . . what did you say? Before? Before the cake?"

"Come on. One bite," he repeated.

"No, you . . . just, you . . . you're . . . it's . . . before the cake?"

"What do you say we have some of this cake?"

"I've got to tell you this one thing, Señor."

A voice again shouted out a suggestion. "Just push it in her mouth. She's not going to spit it up on that silk dress."

I said, "I've just got to tell you this one thing, Señor. Because I'm thinking, but you're saying."

Someone pushed the handsome man's arm closer to my mouth, but he jerked his hand back.

"What?" he said. "What did you say?"

"You're saying what I'm thinking. I think the words, but you say them." I gave him a smile. This, it seemed, was all I had to say, and having said it, I began to eat forkful after forkful of cake.

And here I stop again to do what no storyteller can honestly do. I tell you what the handsome man—but, of course, he was Sandrofo—thought when I said all of this. He told me—much later, to be sure—but he told me. He said the idea so fascinated him—that I was seeing him speak my thoughts—that he didn't mind hesitating a second to hear me say it again. In retrospect, he felt ashamed of the desire. I was sick, and for a brief moment, his curiosity got the better of him, and he forgot that what was important was that I eat the cake, not that I make myself understood, not that he understand me.

But he paused, almost reflexively. It was a real desire. *What* had I said? Sandrofo wasn't a man, by all accounts, of many desires. Even his three daughters by his dead wife—Beatriz, Melone and Tata—confirmed this. Birthdays were impossible; there was nothing the man wanted. But he was curious about what I had said and then . . . Well, you know how it is. Recognize one desire, even a small one, and the rest come tumbling out, demanding attention.

Red lights flashed over the ceiling and down the far wall of the bakery. I confess to having a memory of this. I remember it because the yellow wallpaper was patterned with brown pen-and-ink drawings of an Italianate city. I remember I thought of the red lights as they fell down the wall as so many sunsets, burning themselves out hysterically over the cities. As I watched, days and days, and then years, whole lifetimes, seemed to pass. It was like one of those calendars in an old movie, one where the pages tear off with frightening speed in the wind. Meanwhile, cheery music plays in the background, so the audience won't notice how horrifying the image they are looking at really is.

The cake must have had its effect, because I started to feel more normal. I turned and saw Sandrofo smiling at me. "It's just the blood," he said. "Soon you'll be fine."

"Yes," I said. Softly, I think, in something more like my own voice. "Thank you."

I imagined that I was in bed and making love to this man. As I moved, there was a moment when my breasts were brushing his chest, and then I didn't experience my body as separate at all from his. Together, I thought, we were one creature. Four-armed, four-legged, I could cartwheel through life with this man to whom I was meant to be attached.

The ambulance was still at the door. I said, "Wedding cake," and Sandrofo used his fingers to put another piece in my mouth. I tasted the dirty salt of his skin underneath the frosting. The sirens started up again, and I said, "Wedding bells."

Some hands lifted me again, and I was carried out. Someone else carried out the wedding cake and put it in the middle of the road, in case I would still accept a forkful of the sweet stuff. Sandrofo remained by my side. "Maybe we'll get married," I said in that joking voice you use when you're frightened about how someone will respond if they take you seriously.

"Maybe," Sandrofo allowed. Then, he said, as if he were musing on the possibility, "The baker's wife."

An IV went into my left arm. The technician said, "We're going to stabilize you here. I'm going to tape this down." White tape went over the crook of my left arm. The technician strapped me to the linen of the ambulance stretcher. For no reason, I felt like crying. Such bad things had happened to me up till that day. Sandrofo's face was still just above me. I thought, I am a loaf of bread. I am ready to rise. And that thought was mine and mine alone. I never, to be honest, heard Sandrofo speak it.

THIS STORY CAME to me easily once I had the voice of Maria Elena. She's a version of a charming but loony woman I met years ago, a woman who had a self-justifying self-regard that might have been feminism or too-much-therapy. I couldn't quite pin it down. Certainly, she was nothing like me. She wasn't self-conscious or self-deprecating. She was actually a little full of herself, but in a way (because she'd had her troubles) with which I sympathized. But my character Maria Elena wasn't simply a fictional version of this woman. She was also a believer, and I wanted to write about such a character, I suppose, because I'm a skeptic who is nonetheless interested in systems of belief, about what it means to believe.

I often quote Virginia Woolf—"There must be great freedom from reality"—to my writing students. After all, that is part of what made writing "Maria Elena" so fun; she wasn't me. Not that I'm usually an autobiographical writer, but it's hard not to agree with Don Lee, the editor of *Ploughshares,* when he says that all writing is "emotionally" autobiographical. I think in this regard of a bit from the old *Seinfeld* TV show. Jerry, delighted to have met the woman of his dreams, a comedian with his exact sense of humor, exults, "Now I know what I was looking for all these years. Me!" In the next episode, Jerry says something like, "I don't know why I thought I'd like dating her. She's just like me. I hate me!"

But there were other things that made this story easy to write, and they're connected to the fact that I was writing this story (though not consciously) long before the actual hours during which I sat before my computer. For example, even before I had a sense of a narrative, I knew where I wanted the story to take place—in the few blocks between an imaginary San Juan art gallery and an imaginary San Juan bakery, streets separated by a real plaza which had impressed me when I was last in Puerto Rico. And even before I started writing, I knew all the minor characters of the story, for the story (though I mean for it to work *as* a story) was imagined as part of a novel. Actually, it was the story that helped me reconceive the novel, which (though it largely centers on Maria Elena in its published version) didn't even have Maria Elena as a character in the first draft. The failed novel helped me write the story, and the story then turned around and helped me redo the novel.

On some level, I suppose I'd been rehearsing parts of "Maria Elena" out loud for years. Like a lot of people, I have a handful of anecdotes that I retell in social situations, stories that have (on past telling) proved successful. (Which is to say, I get laughs where I expect laughs.) I have a photographer-friend who finds her writer-husband's tendency to retell such anecdotes so irritating that when he launches into an oft-told tale, she'll announce, "That's two." He's only allowed to tell an anecdote three times and then he has to retire it. How poorly I'd function under such restrictions! At any rate, as I was writing this story, I saw I had a chance to get some of my old chestnuts (about the time I fainted in a health food store, about the time I fainted on the evening news) into my fiction. I changed the details, of course, but otherwise (since I knew the basic arc of those mini-narratives) wrote those bits of "Maria Elena" on automatic pilot.

Around the time I wrote this story, I was also trying to write a completely unrelated story. Although to say I was trying to write another story is a lie, since I was mostly angst-ing about a story I couldn't even begin. What happened is that I'd been following a radio program on NPR in which several different writers were given the same image (a wedding cake in the middle of the road) and asked to write a short short story using that image. I liked this game and decided I'd give it a try. Only I couldn't come up with a good idea.

I'd gotten as far as imagining a person dressed up as a wedding cake (why? for a parade float? some stage set?) pausing (while crossing a Manhattan street) to object to something her companion (friend? lover?) was saying to her. All in all, a rather ridiculous setup, and I had a low level of irritation at myself for not managing to alight on something better. Toward the end of the few hours that I spent writing the first draft of "Maria Elena," I thought—with about as much pleasure as I've ever thought of anything—"Good Lord, I can get a cake in the middle of the road here!" Something of the pleasure of that realization seems to have floated into my character's self-satisfaction at the story's close. And my own, I confess, as I raced to finish the story and print it out. (I was done! I was done!) Like my character, I was ready to rise too. At least from my chair, and then, since metaphors and baked products were on my mind, I went into the kitchen to make some French bread.

The sad (but true) coda to this story is that mid-knead I got a phone call with some disastrous news. I tossed the bread dough into the trash, so I could drive to the hospital. I still think of the sound of dough hitting a plastic trash liner as apocalyptic. A decade passed before I tried to make bread again. Free yourself from reality and you'll come back to it nonetheless. I was superstitious; I had my own irrational belief systems, after all.

Chuck Wachtel

THE ANNUNCIATION

> ... thus, I do not want my opposition to the anti-abortion movement to be construed as an opposition to the people who are its members, but rather to the two erroneous assumptions repeatedly put forth in their names: the first resides in the seeming refusal to comprehend the word *choice*; the second, utterly inhumane in its lack of truth, is that it is an easy choice to make.
>
> —ÉMMA SAINT-REAL

THE DRIVER OF the car that had approached him from behind, then pulled close to the sidewalk and slowed to the pace of his walk, was a bear. It was as tall as a human, but plumper around the torso and neck; not made of flesh, or any weighted, three-dimensional substance, but of light and color, like characters in animated cartoons. It was purple, except for its ears, nose, and hands, which were red, kept its eyes on the street directly ahead, and maintained the same slow speed just long enough for him to catch a partial glimpse of the only other passenger: a little girl in a yellow dress, her legs extending to a point just beyond the edge of the back seat, her toes up, one foot turned slightly inward. She was wearing sneakers, blue and white high-tops: the colors were bright and clean, and because she was too young to walk on them, they hadn't a trace of wear. When the car suddenly sped up and turned at the corner, he became angry and frightened. He woke then, with Nan's hand on his chest.

"You all right?" she asked him. "You said something, kind of, and you were rocking back and forth."

"What did I say?"

"It was like a whole sentence, but it didn't really have words, just sounds."

I T   H A D   B E E N   six days since the morning he sat beside Nan, lying on an examination table, and watched, on the screen of a sonogram monitor, as a thin tube entered her belly, then came so close to the fetus that the small hand actually reached toward it. "They do that," Dr. Gisse said, as he affixed a syringe to the end of the tube and withdrew a sample of amniotic fluid. A moment before that the sonographer had been impatient with Nan, who'd begun to shiver and cry. It was the kind of casually dramatic impatience meant to communicate that the person it is aimed at has made your day harder.

"What's your fucking problem?" he said to the sonographer.

"Johnny," Nan said, as if the man weren't there. "Look." She nodded toward the monitor.

Before Johnny turned away, he pointed at the sonographer's stubbly, unshaven cheeks. "And why don't you fucking shave?" He then followed Nan's gaze toward the screen, and focused on the small, curved body made of shadow and light.

"They've been through this once before," Dr. Gisse said to the man, who looked back at Johnny, but not at Nan—having understood: the last time the news was bad—and gave a nod that constituted an apology.

A nurse came in, labeled the vial of amniotic fluid, and held it up to Nan. "You identify this as your name?" The question was part of the same litigation-prevention protocol they'd gone through the last time. Nan took her time and the nurse looked at Johnny for help. Johnny lifted his gaze to the red-lit exit sign. Two of the four screws that held the plate with the letters to the frame of the fixture were missing and it tilted a degree or two downward on the right side, revealing thin dashes of white light over the red *I* and *T,* that reminded him of the lines that tell you a vowel is pronounced as it is spoken when not inside a word.

"My last name is Wilk," Nan said. She'd kept her own name when they got married.

"But on the chart it says Rizzotti," the nurse said.

To Johnny the two missing screws seemed cognate with the sonographer's lack of manners and unshaven cheeks.

"We use my husband's plan."

The nurse pulled a strip of labels from the pocket of her smock.

"The post office," Nan said, then paused as she watched the nurse write her name on a label, peel it off the strip, and wrap it around the vial, covering the top portion of the label already there, so that all the information, other than the first version of her name, was still visible.

"The post office?" the nurse asked her.

"The post office?" Nan asked her back.

"I work there," Johnny said.

"And it has the best medical plan," Nan said, "in the whole damn country."

THE DAY AFTER Dr. Gisse's assistant called with the results— normal, a girl—they discussed how they'd announce the good news to their friends and relatives whom they hadn't told about the pregnancy. Nearly all family members, on both sides, lived at a distance, and Johnny and Nan had laid low during the last weeks prior to the amniocentesis, at which time she'd begun to show. The few friends and neighbors and coworkers who'd figured it out were sworn to secrecy. Two years ago, when they'd learned Nan was pregnant the first time, they told everyone, even strangers, and the most difficult part was untelling them, undoing what the world immediately around them was still expecting to happen.

Since the day the at-home EPT test affirmed their second pregnancy Nan kept the test wand in a Ziploc bag in her sock and underwear drawer, and the next afternoon, before she got home from work—she was a professor of art history at City University—Johnny set their huge volume of the works of Leonardo da Vinci on the living room floor, opened to the *Annunciation* they had seen at the Uffizi Gallery while on their honeymoon in Florence, and laid the wand across the space between the hand of the Archangel Gabriel, with two fingers gently raised, and the serene yet startled eyes of the Virgin. Johnny then knelt over it with his thirty-five-millimeter camera, and from various angles and distances, and at slightly different foci, shot two rolls of color film.

Eight years before, when Nan led Johnny across the huge, echoey, marble-walled room to the painting, she had said, improvising on an ad for Kentucky Fried Chicken, "When it comes to angels, nobody does wings like da Vinci." This composition, reproduced as a postcard, would make a unique announcement, a revelation of the knowledge they had kept to themselves for more than four months.

The next day, on his lunch hour, Johnny picked up the two rolls at the 1-Hour developing counter at the Rite Aid Drugstore. He opened the envelopes before leaving the store and by the time he'd flipped halfway through the second stack of photos his anticipation had eroded to disappointment: the collage he constructed had looked perfectly clear through the camera lens, but was unrecognizable in the images he held before him. The flash had bounced off the page where it curved above the spine like a wave of parted hair, spilling a wide oval of white light across half the photograph, and leaving the other half too dark to identify anything.

Later that afternoon, before Nan came home from school, he'd shot another roll from different angles in the consistent, nonviolent light of the overhead lamp.

Although the next batch didn't come out much better, there were three shots in which all the component parts were identifiable. If you knew what an annunciation was, you would know this was one; the implausible object lying across the composition was recognizable as an EPT wand and, most importantly, the red line that bisected the positive box was clearly defined. It was time to show them to Nan, who had much more experience photographing art, and get her advice for the final shoot. He left the three best ones face-up on the kitchen table to see how she'd react when she saw them.

During the last two days they'd been granting entry to feelings they'd held at abeyance for months. They'd reached the top of a mountain so steep that the labor of climbing had kept them from taking notice of the scenery. Now they'd stroll down the other side, enjoy everything, let gravity do the work. "Even so," Nan had said thoughtfully, "innocence lost is never regained. And guess what?" She began to laugh. "I could give a shit less."

On the morning he would bring in the second roll of film, he woke to find Nan sitting up, leaning against the wall on her side of the bed, watching him sleep. "You know what I just realized?" she said, as if he had not been asleep, but engaged in an ongoing conversation with her. "We've been pregnant more than nine months combined, and now, finally, we're in control." Her exhilaration and certainty frightened him, but he was much too happy to be worried about anything. "Now we're in control," she repeated. "*We* control the horizontal. *Do do do do* . . ." She sang the first four notes of the theme from *Twilight Zone*.

"That's the wrong show," he said. "It's *Outer Limits* where they control the horizontal."

She slid her hand under the blanket, gripped his penis. "And we certainly control the vertical."

After they made love—the fifth time in two days—Nan laid the back of her head on Johnny's stomach and slid her feet up the wall. "I'm telling you right now, there'll be none of that textbook-sentimental-story-to-tell-later crap. No cravings for ice cream or shrimp dumplings, no belly-hiding muumuus, no sudden mood swings, no sentimental platitudes, no storks on the birth announcement . . . No fucking storks anywhere."

JOHNNY WAS SITTING in the living room, trying to read the paper, when he heard the door to their apartment open, the sound of Nan's footsteps crossing the kitchen and the clunk of her shoes, one after the other, hitting the floor. Then the *whoom* of the bathroom door being pulled shut, followed by the clack of the door-hook striking wood.

He walked into the kitchen. Her briefcase was on one of the chairs and a take-out bag, with a Bamboo Pavilion menu stapled at the top, a widening grease blotch on its side, was sitting on top of the photos. Johnny moved the bag across the table, and slid the photos to the side she would approach it from. The toilet-flushing was followed by the sound of the tank refilling itself, and when she opened the door, it grew louder.

"Not a spot," she said. "Not a spot all day."

Nan had been spotting since the fifth week of the pregnancy, and though they had reached the middle of the second trimester, it still hadn't stopped. Dr. Gisse told them it probably wasn't anything to be concerned about. He told them they worried too much about everything, "But don't worry about *worrying.* That's not unusual after what happened the last time." *The last time,* when the call came, they were sitting in front of the TV, watching *Jeopardy,* eating dinner. How could anything real happen at such a moment? The genetics counselor told them he always waited until evening to make calls with such news, so that both partners would be at home: *trisomy 21:* Down's syndrome: three of the twenty-first chromosome instead of two, forty-seven in total instead of forty-six: *odd,* two parents, two of everything: odd numbers are bad news in genetics. It would have been a boy.

They had not yet reached the point in this pregnancy at which they had aborted the last one. In the nearly two years since then, they had never stopped being surprised by the ever-present substance of loss.

Johnny took Nan's briefcase off the chair and motioned, like a maître d', for her to sit. "What do you think?" he asked, when she looked down at the three photographs. She picked one of them up but still said nothing.

He could no longer wait. "Da Vinci's Annunciation. And that's *our* EPT test."

"I get it," she said, "but I didn't get it fast enough."

"I thought we could take a better shot, then make a postcard. *Nan and Johnny have an announcement . . .*"

"At first, I thought it was some kind of weird submarine," Nan said.

"Not in a better photograph. That's where you come in."

Nan started laughing. "I like it. I like that you want to tell everybody. I do too."

"I think it's a work of art," Johnny said.

Nan opened the take-out bag and began setting the take-out containers on the table. "I'm starved," she said. "Although the Virgin conceived in a very different manner than I did, I know this: As her belly got bigger, her appetite got bigger."

"Maybe it's a good thing," Johnny said, "that it slowly reveals itself. I mean, that's how art works, no?"

NAN HAD BEEN right about this pregnancy not being ordinary. Although they felt the anxieties of people becoming parents for the first time, they felt, even after entering the unexplored territory of the last trimester, that they would not experience the sensation of newness, the constant surprise, that they remembered.

Once the news was out, Johnny's mother, who lived in a senior housing apartment in Florida, called often, usually to talk to Nan, and when she called on the morning of Johnny's birthday, near the end of the second trimester, he was in the shower.

"We talk while I wait for him," she told Nan, in her Italian accent. "And I tell you about forty-five years ago today when I *didn't* have to wait. He was in such a rush I still had my shoes on."

In the last weeks Nan had grown tired of her mother-in-law's voice over the phone, annoyed at the endless child-bearing stories from three generations of Johnny's family told as if they were instructions for how to conduct her own pregnancy. So before she got started Nan tried to head her off with the condensed version: "I know the story: Johnny's father was at work . . . your brother Gianfranco drove you to the hospital . . . Johnny was born five minutes after you arrived."

"Did I tell you that Johnny was named for my brother?"

"More times than I can remember."

"Did I tell you about the *baccalà*?"

"The what?"

"The codfish."

"The codfish?"

"That's where the real story begins. On the way to the hospital we had to pass through the old neighborhood in Brooklyn and when he stops the car in front of Sal's Fish Market I know what he has in mind.

"'I'll be quick,' he says. 'You wait in the car and we don't get a ticket.' What am I gonna say? Since he never got married *baccalà* was all he ever thought about.

"Then we get to the hospital. Like a gentleman now, he opens the car door and as soon as I stand up, it's Niagara Falls under my dress. Forty-five years ago today. I tell the doctor I can't stand up my back is hurting so bad, and when they put me on the rolling thing I tell him, No, no, I can't lay down neither. The doctor examines me right there, we're not even in the room yet, and he says, 'Why'd you wait till now?'

"In a car out front," I tell him, "there's five pounds of dried codfish that'll answer your question."

"That's something," Nan told her. "Wow."

"Every year on his birthday the first thing I remember is getting out of that car. That's when it hurt, I can't tell you how much. That's when I say to myself, He's gonna get born—even then I knew he was a boy—even if I'm gonna die."

"Oh, he's dressed," Nan said, waving Johnny into the room, "and he's about to leave for work."

"That's all right," her mother-in-law said. "You just tell him for me. Tell him happy birthday."

TWO MONTHS HAD passed since Johnny showed Nan the photos for the *Annunciation*/EPT wand announcement, and they still hadn't pursued the idea. By this time the few people who hadn't been told had gotten word from those who had. At first there was an influx of notes and cards and phone messages, then baby gifts had begun to arrive.

One evening Nan walked in looking pale and exhausted. Their plan was for her to take the next semester off, but there were still four weeks left in this one.

"You're working so hard," Johnny told her. "I wish there was a way you could just stop now. Couldn't they get a substitute or something?"

"How dare you," she said, anger flashing in her tired eyes.

"What?"

"How dare you accuse me of being lazy?"

"You got it all wrong."

"*You're* the one who got it wrong, buddy."

Johnny walked into the living room, sat on the couch, picked up the remote, and turned on the TV. He stared at the Weather Channel, listened to a few bars of the soft jingly music that accompanied the five-day local forecast, then got up and walked back to the kitchen.

"Does your mother ever sleep?" Nan asked. There were tears in her eyes now.

He remained standing in the entryway. He would not attempt to answer her question until he had some idea of why she had asked it.

"Last night some movie star told David Letterman that she had the uncontrollable urge to eat flowers while she was pregnant. Daisies especially. Eight o'clock in the morning your mother calls because she has to tell me this. Plus she keeps suggesting names. This morning it was Ricardia, *her* mother's name. 'Doesn't Ricki sound nice?' she said. How many times do I have to tell her we're not discussing names yet? Especially not with her."

"That movie star, did she eat them?"

"I can't get enough sleep."

"I'm sorry," Johnny said. "Next time let the machine answer."

"You are such a gaping asshole."

He walked back into the living room, turned off the TV, and lay down on the couch.

Five minutes later Nan came in. He lifted his legs as she sat down, then lowered them onto the arm of the couch so they crossed the space above her lap like the safety bar on a Ferris wheel seat.

"And you can tell your mother that we're not doing to *our* daughter what Italians do to little girls."

Johnny laughed at this, though not too much, since there had been no acknowledgment that the fight was over. She was referring to an argument they'd had during the last pregnancy—during the wait for amnio results—something they had not spoken of since. The sonogram image had given some evidence that it was a boy. If the results confirmed that, Nan wanted him to be circumcised. Johnny did not.

"He'll automatically be Jewish since you are," Johnny said. "It's matrilineal. You told me that."

"I did."

"So can't he be Jewish without having his little dick whacked?"

"Anatomically, he should look like his father," Nan argued. Johnny had been circumcised in the hospital, as had most male babies of his generation, and had never given it a thought. However, the idea of having it done to his son had caused him to imagine the pain for the first time: it would be as if it were happening to him all over again. He began to envision the cutting of the foreskin as an ongoing, constantly repeated process, like Prometheus's liver being eaten by an eagle, only to grow back again overnight, then to be eaten, once again, by the same eagle.

"And what about the thing Italians do to girls?" Nan had said, smiling, but tired of his persistence.

"What do they do to girls?"

"You know what I'm talking about."

"I have no idea what you're talking about."

"Prenatal ear-piercing?"

Nan slid Johnny's legs off her, turned so she could lay her head on the side of the couch, then laid her feet on his lap. She grunted, slipped her hand under her back, pulled out the remote, turned the TV back on, and began channel-surfing. She stopped at the image of Roadrunner racing up the side of a mountain leaving a wake of pink dust, then flipped back to a man and a woman aboard matching exercise machines, then flipped back again to a screen filled with beautifully pure blue sky, which held only for a second before the camera dropped and found two teenagers, a boy and a girl, leaning against the fender of a car. They were contemporary teenagers, but the car was a vintage, late-sixties Corvette convertible, bright red. They appeared tired; they were sad and a little bored, yet sexy in an adult way.

"You were *with* her," the girl said, energized by her anger, though sleepy-eyed.

The boy turned his head away.

The girl, wearing dark red lipstick, looked briefly at the camera, pouting, then slowly lowered her gaze.

The boy turned and directed his eyes downward, toward whatever the girl was looking at.

"I bet it's going to be Pepsi," Nan said.

"I was just . . ." the boy said, then paused. "I was just . . . *there.*"

The camera slid down their slender bodies. They were both wearing jeans. One of the knees on the boy's was ripped, showing the pale skin beneath.

"The Gap," Johnny says. "Five bucks says it's the Gap."

Nan, still holding the remote, turned off the TV before they found out.

THREE WEEKS BEFORE their due date, Johnny woke to the sound of Nan crying. He reached toward her before he even opened his eyes, found her side of the bed empty. She was sitting in a chair across the room, leaning over, her elbows on her knees. "Nan," he said, then, "What?" He was afraid something had gone wrong, or that she'd gone into labor early, but he knew, in the first instant of full wakefulness, that it would be best if he didn't appear as frightened as he actually was. He responded as if the loud sobbing that had penetrated his sleep were a question he hadn't fully heard or understood. "What?" he said again, softly.

"It's four-thirty in the morning," she said. Her breaths were sudden and shallow, her voice faint.

"I thought your idea for a pregnancy announcement was terrific," she said. "It *was* a work of art. I'm sorry we never made the postcards."

"Who cares? Nan, are you all right?"

"I need something," she said. She seemed angry now. "Why did your mother tell me about that stupid fucking movie star?"

"What do you need, baby?"

She started crying again, harder.

"Nan?"

"Flowers." She said this between gasps, in a whisper.

"What?"

She covered her eyes and shook her head. Johnny helped her back into bed, then held her in his arms. "You want flowers?"

"Marigolds," she said. "I keep thinking of the thick part in the middle." Her breathing was slower now. It seemed she might even be falling back to sleep.

He slid out from under her weight, then stood beside the bed. He pulled the blanket over her, leaned down, kissed her hair.

Just north of Houston Street, he found a greengrocer that was still open but there were no marigolds, only blue daisies that looked like they'd been watered with dye, ordinary yellow daisies, and roses that looked morbid and inedible. Before he headed toward the twenty-four-hour greengrocer on Avenue A, he bought the yellow daisies, just in case he couldn't do better. According to the thermometer on the Emigrant Savings Bank it was nineteen degrees Fahrenheit, minus seven Celsius.

He had met Nan in his first and only year of graduate school. She was a student in the freshman composition course he taught. At the end of that year, an enormous cut in federal funds had forced nearly all teaching assistants at CCNY to be laid off. Johnny, along with several other graduate students, quit school in what was both a statement of protest and an act of necessity: he could not afford to continue without the teaching assistantship that had paid his tuition. The first job he found was at the post office. He saw it as temporary and still does. One afternoon, more than eight years later, a woman who turned out to be Nan handed him a yellow slip at the parcel pickup and information window.

"Mr. Rizzotti?"

He didn't recognize her. He assumed she saw the name on his ID tag. "You gave me an A. My first in college. I never thanked you."

In his entire adult life he had never felt anything like what he was feeling now, walking east through the predawn morning. He'd carried mail for four years, and drove a mail pickup route for three more before becoming a supervisor. You could see the city in a million ways: during his workday, he saw it as a complex chain of mailboxes, with the rest—the buildings, the cars and trucks and people—slightly out of focus. Now he saw this neighborhood, the one where their daughter's first home would be, as a constellation of twenty-four-hour greengrocers: their lights glowing like stars. He did not feel the cold. His only sense of his body was as the vehicle that gracefully carried him to each location on this particular, complex errand. He was elated. They'd passed through all the danger zones, now all they had to worry about was dating and college tuition. He couldn't wait to meet his daughter. He couldn't wait.

When he walked in, Nan was sitting at the kitchen table. She had a pencil in her hand and appeared to be reading a typed essay by one of her students.

"Since I was up," she said, emphatically casual, "I thought I'd get some work done."

He set an array of cone-shaped bouquets, wrapped in gift paper or clear plastic, before her, covering the entire tabletop, including the paper she'd been reading. Among them were two batches of marigolds. He'd got the second batch at the last place he went to because their tops were bigger than the ones he'd already bought.

"Is it cold?" she asked, no trace of what she was feeling in her voice or eyes.

He began unwrapping each cone of flowers. When he laid them back down, the bouquets had lost their shapes. It was as if the yield of an entire flower garden was amassed on the table before her. "See anything you like?"

She picked up three of the bigger marigolds—the soft, orange centers inside the dense corollas of small petals were as big as marshmallows—and held them out to him. "You first."

"No," he said. "You."

She moved the flowers closer.

He shrugged, slowly leaned forward, and took the head of the largest one in his mouth.

She suddenly began to cry.

"Nan," he said.

"This is crazy," she said, anger filling her voice.

He did not know how he knew, but he knew what had happened. "That was the one you wanted," he said. "Wasn't it?"

"Shit," she said. "How dare you?"

"Was it?"

"You don't understand."

"Was it?"

"You're a man. A *mail*-man. How could *you* fucking understand?"

He was furious, but knew he was still happy underneath. "Tell me, Professor. What the hell is wrong?"

"I married an idiot," she said. "That's what's wrong."

WHEN THE BABY was six days late, Dr. Gisse sent Nan to the hospital for a nonstress test. Unfortunately, it was done in the same clinic as their second amniocentesis.

As soon as they entered the ultrasound examination room, Johnny's eyes found the exit sign. He was relieved to find that the missing screws had not been replaced: changing anything in that room might indicate a change in their fate, perhaps for the worse.

Though they had a hard time recognizing the parts of her anatomy, the baby appeared fine. At one point, the sonographer—a different one, a woman—told them that the baby had just moved a foot and a hand to her mouth, and pointed with a little plus-sign-shaped cursor to where it was happening.

"Does that mean she's hungry?" Johnny asked.

"It could," the woman said.

"Oh, Hannah," Nan said. Trying out the name they had chosen, softly curving the second syllable downward.

"What an appetite," Johnny said, shaking his hand Italian style, then began to weep.

Everything looked fine, but nothing would be certain until they got the results of the second test, which involved Nan sitting in a room with other beyond-due-date mothers, each with a fetal monitor strapped to her belly, while various electronic bleeps recorded the baby's movements and vital signs and her own mild contractions, most of which could not even be felt. Partners were not permitted to be present for this one.

Two days before the last pregnancy had been terminated, the doctor they'd been referred to had inserted a branch-segment of laminaria, a kind of seaweed, into Nan's cervix, to dilate her in preparation for the abortion. Once that was done there was no reversing the process. The following day he would remove the insert and replace it with two branch-segments, widening the cervix further. Those two days, during which Nan experienced the symptoms of early labor, were even darker than the previous two weeks, when they had lived each day with the news. They'd had to make a decision, as parents, as nonparents, and perhaps the most difficult part was accepting that the decision had already been made, and that it resided inside them, always had, and would continue to, long after the pregnancy was terminated.

On the first of those two visits, the doctor told them there was a possibility, though an unlikely one, that they would encounter anti-abortion activists on the morning of the procedure. Legally, they're not permitted to approach anyone, he said, not even be on the same side of the street, but anyone can walk into the waiting room, and there's no telling who someone could turn out to be. Records are confidential, but they have ways of finding out when second-trimester abortions are scheduled.

"They know," Nan told the doctor. "I think they knew before we did."

Less than a week after getting the amnio results, a pamphlet had arrived in the mail with a photo of Down's children sitting in a circle around a teacher, smiling and clapping their hands. Though the envelope carried a post office box as a return address, they thought, at first, it was the information they'd asked the genetics counselor to send. The tone of the pamphlet's introduction was sympathetic; it offered hope in the form of knowledge. The persuasion didn't assert itself until the second page, which began with the words *Search and Destroy,* an anti-abortion catchphrase for amniocentesis.

In the remaining two days that Nan would be pregnant, Johnny would have fantasies so real they lifted him entirely out of the moment, out of the abrasive, fast-slow dream of time: On the street, or in a hospital corridor, a crowd of strangers would approach him and Nan, and even before they spoke he would know they were the people who had sent that pamphlet. He would lunge into them shouting and throwing punches. He would not stop until he had hurt them all.

During that first visit they had also been told that in second-trimester abortions there are remains, and that now might be a good time to think about how they wanted to handle them. The hospital could take care of it; forms would have to be signed. Or they could choose cremation, even burial. Dr. Gisse implied that it would be best to not make too big a deal of this part, to begin leaving the past behind as quickly as possible.

On the morning of the procedure they avoided the waiting room entirely. After helping Nan into her hospital gown, Johnny waited in the hall outside the recovery room, along with two Orthodox Jewish women who stood facing the wall that separated them from the ward in which their loved one would awaken and rest, once whatever was being done to her had been done. One of the women opened a small book and held it between them. They began to rock gently, chanting softly in Hebrew: the rhythm of their praying was the only thing that enabled the minutes to pass. They continued to pray when Dr. Gisse came through the door from the recovery room, his green surgical mask hanging loosely from his neck, and approached Johnny. Everything had gone smoothly, he said. Nan would be awake in a minute or two. He handed Johnny a clip-on tag that granted permission to enter.

It was as if the weighted matter within his own body, relentlessly subject to the pull of gravity, had been removed. For a breath's time it was over, but Johnny knew that the next moment would begin a process of unbearable mourning. The doctor stepped into the elevator. The two women had now stopped praying, and before Johnny walked through the door into the ward he told them that he hoped the patient they were praying for would have a full and speedy recovery.

A WEEK LATER, when their taxi arrived at the Upper West Side funeral parlor where they were to pick up the ashes, they had to wait while the three limos ahead of them discharged their passengers. It wasn't until they had stepped out onto the sidewalk that they noticed the police barricades holding in a crowd of onlookers on both sides of the street, and the network news trucks with telescopic antennae on top parked at the corner.

Johnny took Nan's hand, and they walked at a quick, deliberate pace. He had no idea what was going on, and as they approached the entrance he imagined the things he'd shout at a police officer if one tried to stop them. He half hoped one would, but no one approached them. They were walking through a different dimension: no one even noticed they were there.

The rotunda was filled with people, most of them standing in groups, talking, and when Johnny reached the middle of the room he realized that Nan wasn't beside him. He spun around and caught a glimpse of her walking into the office. At that moment he realized that the invisibility they had shared came from entirely different

sources: Nan was never more in the world than when she was pregnant, yet her grief had caused her to withdraw from it to such an
extent an onlooker's casual gaze could not detect her presence; he, a
father who lacked the ability to protect his child and his wife from
danger, was cloaked in his own helpless anger.

The most direct route to the office Nan had just entered took him
between two men that were facing each other, perhaps two feet
apart, talking. They looked familiar, and as they stepped back to allow
him to pass, he was certain he recognized them both.

When he walked into the office, the man behind the desk rose
and, without introducing himself, motioned Johnny to one of the
two seats facing his desk. "Your wife is in the rest room," he said. The
man apologized for the crowd, pressed the fingertips of both hands
together, looked down at the desktop, and said nothing more.

On the cab ride back downtown Nan examined the white cardboard canister, the same size and shape as a container of Quaker Oats.
There wasn't a word or number to identify what it contained.

"How do they know it's ours?" she asked, then said, "Give me your
keys."

With the penknife on his key chain she cut the tape encircling the
middle. She then tried to open the canister but couldn't get her nails
into the small space between the two parts.

"Let's wait till we get home," Johnny said.

Nan turned, looked out the window, and said impatiently, "We're
only at Sixty-eighth Street?" and then, as if it were part of the same
thought: "It sounds crazy, but I think I saw Phyllis Diller coming out
of the bathroom in the funeral parlor."

Suddenly Johnny realized that the two men he had walked
between, less than fifteen minutes ago, were the ex-mayor David
Dinkins and the comedian Alan King. There had been no room
inside of Johnny for curiosity, no interest in looking through the
window it opens on the proximate world. The enormous crowd, the
police, the news trucks, were just there. "I bet it was her," Johnny

said, but by now Nan, still looking out the window, had lost the thought.

A few blocks later she tried to open the canister again, and this time handed it to Johnny. He held the bottom, and with both hands she loosened the top. Inside was a small plastic bag that contained less than a handful of pebble-hard gray ashes, and a scorched metal ring, perhaps an inch in diameter, with the number five stamped on it.

Nan closed it again, embraced it, and stroked the smooth cardboard.

When they got home Nan fell asleep on the couch and remained asleep for the rest of the afternoon. After sunset Johnny went out to buy soup for their dinner and on the way back noticed, on the front page of a *Daily News* on the top of a stack at a newsstand, a picture of the front of the funeral parlor and the headline: NEW YORK'S BEST, BRIGHTEST AND FUNNIEST SAY FAREWELL TO HENNY YOUNGMAN.

A LITTLE GIRL, sitting on the carpet in the waiting room, had set up in front of her a collection of plastic dinosaurs of different sizes and colors, along with a Barbie doll in a hula skirt, and a small stuffed bear. The bear was purple and red and reminded Johnny of the chauffeur bear in his dream, which he did not remember as one remembers a dream, but as something that actually happened, though a long time ago. The girl's mother, who was pregnant, was seated on one of the row of chairs across from Johnny, holding a smaller child asleep on her lap.

A copy of *People* magazine lay face-up on the seat beside Johnny with a cover photograph of Vanna White in a strapless, floor-length evening gown. The little girl held up the hula Barbie and moved its arm to wave hello. Johnny smiled and waved back. She was a beautiful child, no more than five years old. She wore thick glasses and had a yellow Band-Aid on her forearm covered with stars and planets.

The elevator door opened, and both he and the girl watched as a man wearing a business suit and yellow tie stepped out, crossed the room, picked up the *People* magazine, and sat down beside Johnny.

"It's raining," he said. His damp suit jacket smelled like cigarette smoke. "Your wife in there?" he asked Johnny, who nodded.

"Mine too. This your first?" Without waiting for an answer he said, "I already have a six-year-old boy." He lifted his feet, one at a time, and inspected his shoes, top and bottom. "She was two weeks late with him. I hope we don't have to wait that long for this one."

The man opened the magazine. Johnny looked at the girl, who had arranged the dinosaurs in rows as if they were an audience facing the bear and the biggest dinosaur, a brontosaurus.

"You know what I hate about *Wheel of Fortune*?" the man was saying to Johnny. He was holding up the magazine, pointing to the picture of Vanna White. "I hate it that some really nice person, someone smart and nice, can get all the letters except like maybe one or two, and then they go bankrupt." He shook his head. He seemed genuinely angry. "And then some idiot dip shit who can barely read gets the answer. Ever see that happen?"

Johnny shook his head.

"That's what happened last night."

"Last night?"

"The clue was *Theater complex of New York and home of the Metropolitan Opera.* Know what it is?"

"I don't think so."

"Lincoln Center. The dip shit wanted to buy a vowel but they were all filled in already. You could see him moving his lips as he sounded it out. The only letter not there was the *r* and I swear, at one point I thought he was going to say Lincoln Continental. He got it just as the buzzer went off and this sweet, smart young lady goes home with the parting gifts. You know, like carving knives and tickets to some shitty musical and dinner for two at a restaurant where the food's so bad they have to give it away."

Just then a very pregnant woman passed through the doorway leading out of the examination rooms. She smiled at the man beside Johnny and gave him a thumbs-up.

"All raaaaiight!" he said, then got up from his chair, met his wife as she crossed the room, leaned over, and kissed her belly.

"And of course he didn't win the bonus round," the man said to Johnny as he was helping his wife into her coat. "The dip shits never do."

THE HULA BARBIE waved at Johnny again, and this time he got up, walked over to the girl, and sat on the carpet beside her.

"It's a wedding," she said. He now understood the arrangement. The guests were the smaller dinosaurs. The bride and groom were the brontosaurus and the bear. She pulled off her Band-Aid and pressed it onto the back of Johnny's hand. "I don't need it," she said. "I was just wearing it because it's pretty."

He thanked her and looked admiringly at it. Up close he could see that the stars and planets had little faces. Johnny wanted to ask her mother, who was smiling at them, if he could pick the girl up, if he could hold her in his arms.

"They're going to have a baby," the girl said, pointing at the newly married couple, at the bear's fat little belly.

"The baby will be half bear and half dinosaur," Johnny said.

"No, no, no." She shook her head. "It's a girl."

"A beautiful one, I bet," Johnny said.

The girl stretched, held herself upright, but remained kneeling.

"They just had a checkup," she said, then picked up the hula Barbie and held it out toward him. "This is the doctor."

"I hope everything's okay," Johnny said to the doctor.

The girl rose to her feet, looked at him impatiently, held the doctor so close the hard small face was touching his ear, and whispered, "Of course it is."

I N T H E S U M M E R of 1999 my wife and I were told a story. It goes like this: A pregnant woman asks her husband to bring her flowers. Why? he asks her. Because I have an overwhelming urge to eat them, she says. When he presents her with a bouquet she hesitates, then says, You first. After he has chewed and swallowed one of the blossoms, she begins to cry, and when he asks her why she is crying she tells him, That was the one *I* wanted. At the time my wife, Jocelyn Lieu (henceforth Joce) was three months pregnant. We were in San Antonio, teaching for a week at the Gemini Ink Writers' Conference. The story's narrator, Nan Cuba, a fiction writer herself and the conference's director, offered a preface before telling us the story: it had been told to her by her grandfather, a physician, and, according to him, it was true. This story's gently comic outcome and anecdotal shape—though I didn't know it then—would provide a first idea, and a shape, for the story that would become "The Annunciation."

Another source lies in personal experience. Joce had been pregnant before, more than two years earlier, and, at the midpoint of that pregnancy, we found ourselves facing the same difficult decision as the characters in "The Annunciation," and elected to make the same choice. I'd had no intention of writing about our experience. It felt too close, still painful, and complex in the ways—not all of which I could articulate—the memory of it had gotten tangled in the current pregnancy.

(I want to say here that I distrust the term "autobiographical fiction." Facts are never where the action is. A work of fiction, however much its subject might approximate the life experience of its author, reveals little, if anything, of that person's personal history. However, fiction can open a much wider window on our inner lives than auto-biography or memoir, in that it reveals what we can imagine.)

The following January, just before Joce's due date, her parents came to stay with us in New York. As it turned out, our daughter did not choose to join us until thirteen days after her ETA. During that time my wife followed the advice of friends: go to movies, museums, galleries; do all the things you'll soon have little chance to do. Her parents accompanied her on these excursions. I was on winter break, and had been spending my time doing renovations in our apartment, painting and repainting the handed-down bassinet and crib, and going over galleys of a book that would be published the following fall. I did not expect to be writing at this time, beyond scribbling in my pocket notebook. On the afternoon of the tenth day beyond due date, alone in the apartment, the galleys and most of my nesting projects done, I began to write down the story of the flower eaters Nan had told us. Before I realized I was doing so, I found myself setting it in a familiar and more specific world. That night I had a dream that disturbed me to an extent far beyond my ability to interpret it. When I woke I remembered this much of it: a car drives up behind me, passes slowly by—a small child in the back seat—speeds up, then disappears around a corner. The next morning, I added that dream to the story, and made the car's driver a stuffed bear (Florence) that would soon belong to our daughter. The dream became the opening scene, followed by the story of the flower eaters, though I had no idea as to how the space between would be filled. That dream became a doorway that opened onto my own personal experience, and the act of writing it down, in changed form, began the process of walking through it. By lunchtime I'd invented the main characters, Nan and Johnny, who were sufficiently unlike my wife and me for me to gain the distance from the experience I needed.

That afternoon, Joce and I went to the doctor's office, where she underwent a nonstress test: a two-part examination that monitors the condition of the fetus, often done when pregnancies run longer than expected. The following day she and her parents went out to lunch, and then to a movie. While they were out, the *Annunciation*/pregnancy-test-wand photo project entered the story (it was something I'd tried during the first pregnancy, with even less success than Johnny), and the nonstress test wedged itself in after the flower-eating scene. By the end of that day, I had twenty pages that had begun to find a shape that, to some extent, resembled the form it's in now. (To better understand what I mean by the phrase "to some extent," I ask you to imagine the mass of shapes that can appear on an undeveloped Polaroid: when they achieve a more realized clarity, and have become either a mountain range or four family members, in winter coats, huddled close together, the general outline will remain the same.)

When Joce and her parents came home with take-out dinner, I told them I'd begun writing a new story. For some reason this fact was not as interesting to them as the movie they'd just seen, *Magnolia,* and as we ate, all they talked about were the possible meanings of frogs raining from the sky. After dinner my wife fell asleep, my father-in-law looked through a copy of the Bible for references to plagues of frogs, and my mother-in-law read the biography of Jane Austen we'd given her for Christmas. I went back to my desk.

Compelled by the thrill of being able to transform this difficult material into subject matter, and by my awareness that this period of free time would soon come to an end, I wrote steadily until just after two A.M., when Joce came out of the bathroom and, with sleepy, though surprising calmness, announced that she'd just expelled her mucus plug. This event usually begins the final countdown. One of fate's hands is generous, and I felt, with fear and with gratitude, that we were now being held in that one. Before turning off my computer, I was able to press the *Save* key on a version of the story that felt close to finished.

I didn't return to the story for many months. But I thought of it often, kept telling it to myself, imagined new bits of narration, and made notes for a number of small changes. When I finally sat down with it the following summer, I found it wasn't a story at all, but rather twenty-something pages of fictional narration that presented the reader with a loosely connected cluster of stars that could not yet be seen as a recognizable constellation. The various stories within the story needed a greater center of gravity, a more purposeful reason for being contained within the same larger vehicle. The events, whatever their sources, had organized themselves the way memory does, with its own mysterious priorities and no respect for chronology, or narrative structure, or the possibility that the rememberer might wish to assemble them into some kind of communicable form. A reader would not yet see what I saw: the subject (I paraphrase André Breton) had not yet become an object.

Rather than force a more dramatically purposeful time line on the narrative fragments, I strengthened the outer story—until this point I hadn't quite realized it *was* the outer story—of the second pregnancy. What I tried to do was to strengthen the implication that the second pregnancy, the second half of it, to be exact, occurred on what physicists call *the chronometric plane*: the span of moments we were actually crossing, the layer of time where each step taken was a new one. When I returned to this time frame after a visit elsewhere, I tried to give it a greater sense of immediacy, both in terms of physical location and in the main character's anticipation of what fate had in store.

In his essay "Philosophy and the Form of Fiction," William H. Gass wrote, "The story must be told and the act of telling it is a record of the choices, inadvertent and deliberate, the author has made from the possibilities of language." What I have talked about, thus far, are the "deliberate" choices. By clarifying and, thus, strengthening the outer shape of the container, I'd hoped to allow myself greater freedom, while working inside it, in making the "inadvertent" ones.

Some stories, for me, have come quickly, but this was not to be one of them. My daughter is now two and a half years old, and her age measures the amount of time I have held this story in my possession. During those thirty-plus months, while taking time out for other projects, working on a novel, teaching full-time, and experiencing the great pleasures, distracting busy-ness, and the recurrent state of exhaustion of being a new yet already middle-aged father, I'd periodically take the story out and revise the whole thing. I'd rewrite it as I did in the not-so-old days prior to word processors, by retyping each word and sentence off the page rather than working within a file I'd summoned to the monitor's screen. (I usually do this with early drafts and, as it turned out, this story was to have many more early drafts than most.) This, for me, is another way of helping along the "inadvertent" part: I could enter the story as if reading it, and often get closer to the thoughts and sensations that occurred within the trajectory that carried me through earlier versions, reentering, from a somewhat different stance, that process of reaching a certain step while simultaneously imagining what the next one would be. In this way time also became part of the process. And in time, what I hope has happened is that the story's parts have come together, or merged, or even interpenetrated each other, like the animals in cave paintings. Rewriting in this manner also gives language that isn't working as well as it should a better chance to reveal its weakness, not just by reading the sentences again, which helps, but only to a certain point, but also by visiting the frame of mind of an earlier moment in which I chose to fill the silence with those particular words.

I do not consider this story done. History might contribute, in part, to its completion: if the debate over abortion ever disentangles itself from the web of political issues in which it has been trapped, the charged environment within which this story was written and will be read would have to change. I can't imagine that that change would not, in some way, participate in the reader's experience of the story. Also, at this point—completing this prolegomenon marks the moment at which I will send my story to the world—I begin to miss all the things that had to be left out in order to shape the narrative to best perform the job of telling itself with some degree of cohesion and a reasonable smoothness. A character in Nabokov's story "The Passenger," a writer himself, bemoans the limitations of the job: "We cut from Life's untrammeled novels our neat little tales for the use of school children." Unlike this character, I cannot speak in such operatic and articulate declarations, and, unlike his creator, I cannot blame the limitations of fiction for my own.

All that said, this version of "The Annunciation" has reached the point at which my instincts tell me it is at least fit for human consumption; all that said, the reader will read this story as we read most stories, in ways largely independent of the things we have to say about them.

Michael Martone

THE MOON OVER WAPAKONETA

1.

There is the moon, full, over Wapakoneta, Ohio. Everybody I know has a sister or a brother, a cousin or an uncle living up there now. The moon is studded green in splotches, spots where the new atmospheres have stuck, mold on a marble.

2.

I'm drunk. I'm always drunk. Sitting in the dust of a field outside Wapakoneta, Ohio, I look up at the moon. The moon, obscured for a moment by a passing flock of migratory satellites flowing south in a dense black stream, has a halo pasted behind it. That meant something once, didn't it?

3.

When the moon is like it is now, hanging over Ohio, I come over to Wapakoneta from Indiana where I am from. I am legal in Ohio, and the near beer they can sell to minors is so near to the real thing it is the real thing. I told you I was drunk. The foam head of this beer glows white in the dull light like the white rubble of the moon bearing down from above. Over there, somewhere, is Indiana, a stone's throw away.

4.

Everybody I know has a brother or cousin or whoever on the moon, and I am using this pilsner for a telescope. Where is everybody? The old craters are percolating. They've been busy as bees up there. Every night a new green explosion, another detonation of air. This is where I make myself belch.

5.

The reflection of the moon over Wapakoneta sinks into each flat black solar panel of this field where I sit, a stone swallowed by a pond. In the fields, the collectors pivot slowly, tracking even the paler light of the moon across the black sky. There's this buzz. Cicada? Crickets? No. Voltage chirps, generated as the moon's weak light licks the sheets of glass.

6.

Let's power up my personal downlink. Where am I?—I ask by nudging the ergonomic toggle. Above me, but beneath the moon over Ohio, a satellite, then, perhaps, another peels away from its flock to answer my call. Let's leave it on. More satellites will cock their heads above my head, triangulating till the cows come home. But soft, the first report is in. Ohio, the dots spell out, Wapakoneta.

7.

What part of the moon is the backwater part? Maybe there, that green expanse inches from the edge where they are doing battle with the airless void generating atmosphere from some wrangling of biomass. Yeah, back there under the swirl of those new clouds, some kid after a hard day of—what?—making cheese, lies on his back and has a smoke consuming a mole of precious oxygen. He looks up at the earth through the whiffs of cloud and smoke and imagines some Podunk place where the slack-jawed inhabitants can't begin to imagine being pioneers, being heroes. There it is, Ohio.

8.

A pod of jalopies takes off from the pad of Mr. Entertainer's parking lot, racing back to Indiana where it's an hour earlier. The road is lined with Styrofoam crosses, white in the moonlight, and plastic flowers oxidized by the sunlight. X marks the spot where some hopped-up Hoosier goes airborne for a sec and then in a stupor remembers gravity and noses over into the ditch next to a field outside of Wapakoneta on the trailing edge of Ohio.

9.

They are launching their own satellites from the moon; a couple of dozen a day, the paper says. Cheap in the negative gees. Gee. I look hard at the moon. I want to see the moons of the moon. The moon and its moons mooning me. In Ohio, I pull my pants down and moon the moon and its moons mooning me back. And then, I piss. I piss on the ground, my piss falling, falling to earth, falling to the earth lit up by the moon, my piss falling at the speed of light to the ground.

10.

I am on the move. I am moving. Drawn by the gravitational pull of Mr. Entertainer with its rings of neon, I am steering a course by the stars. Better check in. More of the little buzz bombs have taken up station above my head. Surprise! I am in Wapakoneta. I am in Wapakoneta, but I am moving. I am moving within the limits of Wapakoneta. I like to make all the numbers dance, the dots on the screen rearranging. X, Y, and Z, each axis scrolling, like snow in a snow dome. The solar panels in the field around me slowly track the moon as it moves through the night sky.

11.

Over there in Indiana, it's an hour earlier. Don't ask me why. You cross a road, State Line Road, and you step back in time. It can be done. Heading home, I get this gift, an extra hour to waste. But wait! I lost one someplace coming here. I shed it when I crossed the street, like sloughing skin. It must be somewhere, here at my feet. This pebble I nudge with my toe. Just what time is it? I consult my other wrist where the watch burbles, all its dials spinning, glowing softly, little moon. The laser beam it emits ricochets off my belt buckle, noses up to find its own string of satellites, bouncing around a bit, kicking the can, homing for home, an atomic clock on a mountaintop out West to check in on each millisecond of the passing parade, then, in a blink, it finds its way back to me here, makes a little beep. Beep! Here's the report: Closing Time.

12.

Mr. Entertainer is not very entertaining. It's powering down before my eyes, each neon sign flickers, sputters in each dark window. The whole advertised universe collapsing in on the extinguished constellation of letters. How the hell did that happen? I had my eye on things, and the moon over Wapakoneta hasn't moved as far as I can tell. The rubble of the bar is illuminated now by that soft indifferent dusty light diffused through the dust kicked up by the departed cars. The slabs of its walls fall into blue shadow, its edges, then, drift into a nebulous fuzz, a cloud floating just above the ground.

13.

What time is it on the moon? It's noon there now. It's noon on the moon. From the stoop of the extinct bar, I consider the moon's midday that lasts for days, lunch everlasting, amen. They must get drunk on the light. They must drink it up. They must have plenty to spare. The excess is spilling on me, pouring on me down here in Ohio, enough light for me, a heavenly body, to cast a shadow on the studded gravel galaxy of the empty parking lot, a kind of timepiece myself, the armature of an impromptu moon dial, the time ticking off as my celestial outline creeps from one cold stone to the next.

14.

Cars on the road are racing back to Indiana. I hear them dribbling the sound of their horns in front of them, leaking a smear of radio static in the exhaust. I am looking for my clunker. It's around here someplace. According to my uplink, I am still in Wapakoneta. A slow night for the satellites, they have been lining up to affirm that consensus, a baker's dozen have been cooking up coordinates. I punch a button on my car key, releasing the ultrasonic hounds hot on the magnetic signature of my piece of shit. The nearby solar panels pivot toward me, sensing the valence of my reflection, hunger for the light I am emitting. Hark! Somewhere in the vast relative dark the yodel of a treed automobile. I must calculate the vectors for my approach.

15.

Later, in Indiana, which is now earlier, I will remember back to this time, this time that is happening now, as I navigate by means of sonic boom to the bleat of my Mother Ship supposedly fastened to the edge of some solar panel field out there somewhere in the dark. But the sound is reverberating, gone Doppler, bouncing off the copse of antennae to the right, the bank of blooming TV dishes to the left. The night air has become acoustic, dampening the reports. I am getting mixed signals, and it seems my car is moving around me. That may be the case. Perhaps I left it in autopilot. It's nosing toward home this very minute, sniffing the buried wire, or perhaps it's just playing games with me, its own guidance system on some feedback loop, as it

orbits under the influence of an ancient cruising pattern pro-
grammed long ago for the high school drag in Fort Wayne. My
guardian satellites, whispering to each other, hover above my head,
shaking theirs, "Lost, poor soul, in Ohio, in the holy city of
Wapakoneta."

16.

Everybody I know has a sister or a brother, a mom or a dad setting
up housekeeping in some low-rent crater of the moon. I intercept
postcards—low-gain transmissions of the half earth in the black sky
and a digital tweet eeping "Wish You Were Here!"—when I eavesdrop on the neighborhood's mail. On nights like this, with the moon
radiating a whole spectrum of sunny missives, I want to broadcast a
wide band of my own billet-doux banged out with a stick on any
handy piece of corrugated steel in the ancient language of killing
time.

17.

I fall into the ditch or what I think is the ditch. Flat on my back, I
stare up at the moon, canvas, sailing above this pleasant seat, my bish-
opric, and find myself thinking of my kith and kin again and again.
The starlight scope is in the car, I hear its honk still, a goose somewhere in the marsh night asking the tower for permission to land. If I
had the goggles now, I could see where I've landed but would, more
likely, be blinded by this moonlight boosted by the sensitive optics.
Night would be day, and the moon over Wapakoneta would be more
like the sun over Wapakoneta. I might see some real sun soon if I just
close my unaided eyes for a bit and let the whole Ptolemaic contrap-
tion overhead wheel and deal.

18.

But the watch I wear is still turned on and on the lookout for pulses
of light angling back this way from the fibrillating isotopes atop Pikes

Peak. The watch's microprinted works synthesize a "bleep" a second, a steady erosion to my will to doze. At the top of each hour, it drops a drip, and this absence more than the regular tolling pricks me to a semiconducted alertness. The solar panels at the lip of the ditch chirp their chirp, Wapakoneta's moon a dilated pupil centered in each dark iris. And there's the car's snarled sound still hoping to be found. So much for silent night, holy night. Lo, a rocket off yonder rips the raw cloth of night.

19.

At that moment I open my eyes, and in the ditch with me is the big ol' moon its ownself half buried in the mud. Hold on there! There is the moon, the moon over Wapakoneta. It's there up above, where it should be. It's there over this other moon mired in the mud of Wapakoneta. My eyes adjust to the light. O! I'm not in the ditch but on the berm below the old moon museum, the building's geodesic concrete dome, teed up on a dimple in a hummock in Ohio, mocking the moon overhead. The real moon rises above the arching horizon of this fallen fake.

20.

Armstrong hailed from these Wapakonetish parts. Got drunk here on near beer, I suppose. Contemplated the strobing codes of lightning bugs down by the river. The river caught the moon's pale and silent reflection. Pitched a little woo too. Looked up at the moon, very same moon I spy with my little eye. First guy to go there. Got a pile of rocks marking the spot there. I've seen pictures. "Wish you were here!" Down here, they keep the moon rocks he brought back under glass in the hollowed-out moon building before me. The schoolkids, on field trips, herd by the cases of rocks. The little rocks. The big rocks Big deal! The kids have got a brother or sister, uncles and aunts, sweeping the dust together into neat piles upstairs. Here's to the first man on the moon from the last person on earth.

21.

The earth is slowing down. Friction as it twirls. When the moon untucks the oceans, makes the tides bulge, it's like holding your hand out the car window as you race toward Indiana, a drag against the cool night air, skidding to a halt. Long time coming. Every once in a while, they throw in a leap second or two to bring the world back up to speed. Another cipher of silence at the top of the hour to keep the whole thing in tune. One day the earth will creep to a crawl, and one side will always be facing the face of the moon always facing me. A slow spinning dance around the sun. My watch skips a beat. The silence stretches on and on.

22.

At twelve o'clock high, a huge flock of satellites floats in formation, veiling the moon. They are migrating north. The swallows returning to Capistrano. A new season? Reconnoitering to be done by morning? Who knows? My own orbiting dovecote coos to me still, homing, homing. You are in Ohio, in Wapakoneta, in Ohio. I release them just like that. The blank LCD goes white in the moonlight. They disperse, disappear, kids playing hide and seek in the dark.

23.

At my feet are rocks painted blue by the moon's light. I pick one up out of the dust and launch it into space at the moon hanging over Ohio. I lose sight of it, swallowed up in the intense glare I am aiming at. Sure thing! I've chucked it beyond the bounds of earth. It's slipped into space on the grease of its own inertia. But I hear its reentry, splashing into the ocean of solar panels yards away, the light we've all been staring at turning solid. I heave another sputnik into orbit, hoping to even up the gross mass of the planets which is all out of whack in this binary system. I'm a run-of-the-mill vandal, my slight buzz waning. But soft! A frog jumps into a pond. It makes that sound a frog makes when it jumps into a pond.

24.

Didn't I tell you? It is an hour earlier in Indiana. The moon over Wapakoneta is gaining on me here as I race along the section roads toward home, all of its imaginable phases caught by the thousands and thousands of black reflections in their tropic glass panels. The moon waxes on all the mirrored surfaces, silent, a skipping stone skipping. Yes, I'll catch it tonight as it sets, embrace it, a burned-out pebble, in my empty backyard.

I WRITE ABOUT INDIANA. I consider myself a regionalist. "The Moon Over Wapakoneta" is from a new book of short fiction called *Planet Indiana*. It is my attempt to remain true to my regional subject matter while combining it with a new, for me, genre. In this case, that would be science fiction. Science Fiction Regionalism, then, is where this contribution aspires to be catalogued.

My basic take on this particular hybrid fiction is that, in the future, Indiana will be pretty much the same as it is in the present. My Indiana is a pleasant, unexciting place where nothing significant happens and from which its natives hope to one day escape. In the future, I suspect that not much happens in Indiana as well. It was the case when I was in high school that underage kids would go over to nearby Ohio border towns to drink 3.2 beer. I suppose that in the future this practice will continue but that the accoutrements of travel and navigation for even those short distances will be somewhat upgraded. Yes, a crop of solar collectors will replace the corn in the fields. The basic poignancy, however, for a narrator, for me, of such a journey through those fields would also remain consistent over time. Both in the present and future, the sense that one is in the middle of nowhere strikes the dominant chord. In the future version this might be accentuated by the possibility that the moon itself would be in the process of being settled and that would amplify the backwater, provincial feeling of the original place. The future and fiction that contemplates it is often about change and the dynamic of change. I am able, given this setting, to speculate on the dynamic of stasis and static.

So what does happen? A kid in the future gets drunk, looks at the moon, and goes home. Same as it ever was. Thus my particular problem was animating this sparse movement. I hoped to do it with the language of this drunken monologue, as the words of the narrator are the only thing percolating on that particular night and in this particular fiction. Fortunately for me, Wapakoneta, Ohio, one of those border towns Hoosier youth visit, was the birthplace of Neil Armstrong, the first human on the moon. The setting sets up the moon as the focus of the narrator's howling for the evening. What form that howling would take presented itself to me as the classic Japanese haiku with a particular fondness for Basho's frog jumping into the pond and his drunk attempting to hug the moon's reflection in the same or similar body of water. Also, I had to find a way to play with time in the form of the story. Time, it seemed to me, is theme, subject, motif as much as place. Or, put another way, time is a kind of place, a locale. I decided to push the technique of repetition, repeating the words "moon," "Ohio," and "Wapakoneta" as many times as I could. I wished that the story would itself, through this incantation, set up a kind of gravitational field as well, mirroring the inescapable force of gravity present that night to this particular narrator. Though this is a monologue, the other players in the drama, for me, continued to be time and gravity and the equilibrium of those forces, now and in the future, to strongly attract and repel and, thereby, keep the narrator and the reader both in flight and perfectly still.

Jim Shepard

LOVE AND HYDROGEN

MAGINE FIVE OR six city blocks could lift, with a bump, and float away. The impression the 804-foot-long *Hindenburg* gives on the ground is that of an airship built by giants and excessive even to their purposes. The fabric hull and mainframe curve upward sixteen stories high.

Meinert and Gnüss are out on the gangway ladder down to the starboard #1 engine car. They're helping out the machinists, in a pinch. Gnüss is afraid of heights, which amuses everyone. It's an open aluminum ladder with a single handrail extending eighteen feet down into the car's hatchway. They're at 2,000 feet. The clouds below strand by and dissipate. It's early in a mild May in 1937.

Their leather caps are buckled around their chins, but they have no goggles. The air buffets by at eighty-five miles per hour. Meinert shows him how to hook his arm around the leading edge of the ladder to keep from being blown off as he leaves the hull. Even through the sheepskin gloves the metal is shockingly cold from the slip-stream. The outer suede of the grip doesn't provide quite the purchase they would wish when hanging their keister out over the open Atlantic. Every raised foot is wrenched from the rung and flung into space.

Servicing the engines inside the cupola, they're out of the blast, but not the cold. Raising a head out of the shielded area is like being cuffed by a bear. It's a pusher arrangement, thank God. The back end of the cupolas are open to facilitate maintenance on the blocks and engine mounts. The engines are eleven hundred horse-power diesels four feet high. The propellers are twenty-two feet long. When they're down on their hands and knees adjusting the vibration dampers, those props are a foot and a half away. The sound is like God losing his temper, kettledrums in the sinuses, fists in the face.

MEINERT AND GNÜSS are both Regensburgers. Meinert was in his twenties and Gnüss a child during the absolute worst years of the inflation. They lived on mustard sandwiches, boiled kale, and turnip mash. Gnüss' most cherished toy for a year and a half was a clothespin on which his father had painted a face. They're ecstatic to have found positions like this. Their work fills them with elation, and the kind of spuriously proprietary pride that mortal tour guides might feel on Olympus. Meals that seem giddily baronial—plates crowded with sausages, tureens of soups, platters of venison or trout or buttered potatoes—appear daily, once the passengers have been served, cour-tesy of Luftschiffbau Zeppelin. Their sleeping berths, aboard and ashore, are more luxurious than any other place they've previously laid their heads.

Meinert and Gnüss are in love. This complicates just about every-thing. They steal moments when they can—on the last Frankfurt-to-Rio run, they exchanged an intense and acrobatic series of caresses a hundred and thirty-five feet up inside the superstructure, when Meinert was supposed to have been checking a seam on one of the gasbags for wear, their glue pots clacking and clocking together—but mostly their ardor is channeled so smoothly into underground streams that even their siblings, watching them work, would be satisfied with their rectitude.

Meinert loves Gnüss' fussiness with detail, his loving solicitude with all schedules and plans, the way he seems to husband good feeling and pass it around among his shipmates. He loves the celebratory delight Gnüss takes in all meals, and watches him with the anticipatory excitement that an enthusiast might bring to a sublime stretch of *Aïda*. Gnüss has a shy and diffident sense of humor that's particularly effective in groups. At the base of his neck so it's hidden by a collar he has a tattoo of a figure-eight of rope: an infinity sign. He's exceedingly well proportioned.

Gnüss loves Meinert's shoulders, his way of making every physical act worthy of a Johnny Weissmuller, and the way he can play the irresponsible daredevil and still erode others' disapproval or righteous indignation. He's openmouthed at the way Meinert flaunts the sort of insidious and disreputable charm that all mothers warn against. In his bunk at night, Gnüss sometimes thinks *I refuse to list all his other qualities,* for fear of agitating himself too completely. He calls Meinert *Old Shatterhand.* They joke about the age difference.

It goes without saying that the penalty for exposed homosexuality in this case would begin at the loss of one's position. Captain Pruss, a fair man and an excellent captain, a month ago remarked in Gnüss' presence that he'd throw any fairy he came across bodily out of the control car.

Meinert bunks with Egk; Gnüss with Thoolen. It couldn't be helped. Gnüss had wanted to petition for their reassignment as bunkmates—what was so untoward about friends wanting to spend more time together?—but Meinert the daredevil had refused to risk it. Each night Meinert lies in his bunk wishing they'd risked it. As a consolation, he passed along to Gnüss his grandfather's antique silver pocket watch. It had already been engraved *To My Dearest Boy.*

Egk is a fat little man with boils. Meinert considers him to have been well named. He whistles the same thirteen-note motif each night before lights out.

How much happiness is someone entitled to? This is the question that Gnüss turns this way and that in his aluminum bunk in the darkness. The ship betrays no tremor or sense of movement as it slips through the sky like a fish.

He is proud of his feelings for Meinert. He can count on one hand the number of people he's known he believes to be capable of feelings as exalted as his.

Meinert, meanwhile, has developed a flirtation with one of the passengers: perhaps the only relationship possible that would be more forbidden than his relationship with Gnüss. The flirtation alternately irritates and frightens Gnüss.

The passenger is one of those languid teenagers who own the world. She has a boy's haircut. She has a boy's chest. She paints her lips but otherwise wears no makeup. Her parents are briskly polite with the crew, and clearly excited by their first adventure on an airship; she is not. She has an Eastern name: Tereska.

Gnüss had to endure their exchange of looks when the girl's family first came aboard. Passengers had formed a docile line at the base of the main gangway. Gnüss and Meinert had been shanghaied to help the chief steward inspect luggage and personal valises for matches, lighters, camera flashbulbs, flashlights, even a child's sparking toy pistol: anything which might mix apocalyptically with their ship's seven million cubic feet of hydrogen. Two hundred stevedores in the ground crew were arrayed every ten feet or so around their perimeter, dragging slightly back and forth on their ropes with each shift in the wind. Meinert made a joke about drones pulling a queen. The late afternoon was blue with rain and fog. A small, soaked Hitler Youth contingent with two bedraggled Party pennants stood at attention to see them off.

Meinert was handed Tereska's valise, and Tereska wrestled it back, rummaging through it shoulder to shoulder with him. They'd given one another playful bumps.

The two friends finished their inspections and waited at attention until all the passengers were up the gangway. "Isn't she the charming little rogue," Gnüss remarked. "Don't scold, Auntie," Meinert answered.

The first signal bell sounded. Loved ones who came to see the travelers off waved and shouted. A passenger unbuckled his wristwatch and tossed it from one of the observation windows as a farewell present. Meinert and Gnüss were the last ones aboard and secured the gangway. Two thousand pounds of water ballast was dropped. The splash routed the ranks of the Hitler Youth contingent. At 150 feet the signal bells of the engine telegraphs jangled, and the engines one by one roared to life. At 300 feet the bells rang again, calling for higher revolutions.

On the way to their subsequent duties, the two friends took a moment at a free spot at an observation window, watching the ground recede. The passengers were oohing and aahing the mountains of Switzerland and Austria as they fell away to the south, inverted in the mirrorlike expanse of the lake. The ship lifted with the smoothness of planetary motion.

Aloft, their lives had really become a pair of stupefying narratives. Frankfurt to Rio in three and a half days. Frankfurt to New York in two. The twenty-five passenger cabins on A deck slept two in stateroom comfort and featured feather-light and whisper-quiet sliding doors. On B deck passengers could lather up in the world's first airborne shower. The smoking room, off the bar and double-sealed all the way round, stayed open until the last guests said goodnight. The fabric-covered walls in the lounge and public areas were decorated with hand-painted artwork. Each room had its own theme: the main salon, a map of the world crosshatched by the routes of famous explorers; the reading room, scenes of the history of postal delivery. An aluminum bust of General von Hindenburg sat in a halo of light on an ebony base in a niche at the top of the main gangway. A place setting for two for dinner involved fifty-eight pieces of Dresden china and silver. The butter knives' handles were themselves mini-zeppelins. Complimentary sleeping caps were bordered with the legend *An Bord Des Luftschiffes Hindenburg*. Luggage tags were stamped *Im Zeppelin Über Den Ozean* and featured an image of the *Hindenburg* bearing down, midocean, on what looked like the Santa Maria.

WHEN HE CAN put Tereska out of his head, Gnüss is giddy with the danger and improbability of it all. The axial catwalk is ten inches wide at its base and 782 feet long and 110 feet above the passenger and crew compartments below. Crew members require the nimble-ness of structural steelworkers. The top of the gas cells can only be inspected from the top of the vertical ringed ladders running along the inflation pipes: sixteen stories up into the radial and spiraling bracing wires and mainframe. Up that high, the airship's interior seems to have its own weather. Mists form. The vast cell walls holding the seven million cubic feet of hydrogen billow and flex.

At the very top of Ladder #4 on the second morning out, Meinert hangs from one hand. He spins slowly above Gnüss, down below with the glue pots, like a high-wire act seen at such a distance that all the spectacle is gone. He sings one of his songs from the war, when as a seventeen-year-old he served on the LZ-98 and bombed London when the winds let them reach it. His voice is a floating echo from above:

> *In Paris people shake all over*
> *In terror as they wait.*
> *The Count prefers to come at night,*
> *Expect us at half-past eight!*

Gnüss nestles in and listens. On either side of the catwalk, great tanks carry 143,000 pounds of diesel oil and water. Alongside the tanks, bays hold food supplies, freight, and mail. This is one of his favorite places to steal time. They sometimes linger here for the privacy and the ready excuses—inspection or errands—which all this storage space affords.

Good news: Meinert signals that he's located a worn patch, necessitating help. Gnüss climbs to him with another glue pot and a pot of the gelatine latex used to render the heavy-duty sailmaker's cotton gas-tight. His erection grows as he climbs.

THEIR REPAIRS COMPLETE, they're both strapped in on the ladder near the top, mostly hidden in the gloom and curtaining folds of the gas cell. Gnüss, in a reverie after their lovemaking, asks Meinert if he can locate the most ecstatic feeling he's ever experienced. Meinert can. It was when he'd served as an observer on a night attack on Calais.

Gnüss still has Meinert's warm sex in his hand. This had been the LZ-98, captained by Lehmann, Meinert reminds him. They'd gotten nowhere on a hunt for fogbound targets in England, but conditions over Calais had been ideal for the observation basket: thick cloud at 4,000 feet, but the air beneath crystalline. The big airships were much safer when operating above cloud. But then: how to see their targets?

The solution was exhilarating: on their approach they throttled the motors as far back as they could while retaining the power to maneuver. The zeppelin was leveled out at 500 feet above the cloud layer, and then, with a winch and a cable, Meinert, as air observer, was lowered nearly 2,000 feet in the observation basket, a hollow metal capsule scalloped open at the top. He had a clear view downward, and his gondola, so relatively tiny, was invisible from the ground.

Dropping into space in that little bucket had been the most frightening and electric thing he'd ever done. He'd been swept along alone under the cloud ceiling and over the lights of the city, like the messenger of the gods.

The garrison of the fort had heard the sound of their motors, and all the light artillery had begun firing in that direction. But only once had a salvo come close enough to have startled him with its crash.

His cable extended up above his head into the darkness and murk. It bowed forward. The capsule canted from the pull. The wind streamed past him. The lights rolled by below. From his wicker seat he directed the immense invisible ship above by telephone, and set and reset their courses by eye and by compass. He crisscrossed them over the fort for forty-five minutes, signaling when to drop their small bombs and phosphorus incendiaries. The experience was that of a magician's, or a sorcerer's, hurling thunderbolts on his own. That night he'd been a regular Regensburg Zeus. The bombs and incendiaries detonated on the railroad station, the warehouses, and the munitions dumps. When they fell they spiraled silently out of the darkness above and plummeted past his capsule, the explosions always carried away behind him. Every so often luminous ovals from the fort's searchlights rippled the bottoms of the clouds like a hand lamp beneath a tablecloth.

Gnüss, still hanging in his harness, is disconcerted by the story. He tucks Meinert's sex back into the opened pants.

"That feeling comes back to me in memory when I'm my happiest: hiking or alone," Meinert muses. "And when I'm with you, as well," he adds, after having seen Gnüss' face.

Gnüss buckles his own pants, unhooks his harnesses, and begins his careful descent. "I don't think I make you feel like Zeus," he says, a little sadly.

"Well, like Pan, anyway," Meinert calls out from above him.

THAT EVENING DARKNESS falls on the ocean below while the sun is still a glare on the frames of the observation windows. Meinert and Gnüss have their evening duties, as waiters. Their stations are across the room from one another. The dining room is the very picture of a fine hotel restaurant, without the candles. After dinner, they continue to ferry drinks from the bar on B deck to thirsty guests in the lounge and reading rooms. Through the windows the upper surfaces of the clouds in the moonlight are as brilliant as breaking surf. Tereska is nowhere to be found.

Upon retiring, passengers leave their shoes in the corridor, as on shipboard. Newspaper correspondents stay up late in the salon, typing bulletins to send by wireless ahead to America. In the darkness and quiet before they themselves turn in, Gnüss leads Meinert halfway up Ladder #4 yet again, to reward him for having had no contact whatsoever with that teenager. Their continuing recklessness feels like love itself.

Like their airship, their new home when not flying is Friedrichshafen, beside the flatly placid Lake Constance. The company's presence has transformed the little town. In gratitude the Town Fathers have erected a zeppelin fountain in the courtyard of the Rathaus, the centerpiece of which is the count bestride a globe, holding a log-sized airship in his arms.

Friedrichshafen is on the north side of the lake, with the Swiss mountains across the water to the south, including the snowcapped Säntis, rising some 8,000 feet. Meinert has tutored Gnüss in mountain hiking, and Gnüss has tutored Meinert in oral sex above the tree line. They've taken chances as though cultivating a death wish: in a lift in the famous Insel Hotel, in rented rooms in the woodcarving town of Überlingen, and in Meersburg, with its old castle dating back to the seventh century. In vineyards on the southern exposures of hillsides. Even, once, in a lavatory in the Maybach engine plant, near the gear manufacturing works.

When not perversely risking everything they had for no real reason, they lived like the locals, with their coffee and cake on Sunday afternoon and their raw smoked ham as the ubiquitous appetizer for every meal. They maintained their privacy as weekend hikers, and developed the southerner's endless capacity for arguing the merits of various mountain trails. By their third year in Friedrichshafen their motto was "A mountain each weekend." They spent nights in mountain huts, and in winters they might go whole days skiing without seeing other adventurers. If Meinert had asked his friend which experience had been the most ecstatic of *his* young life, Gnüss would have cited the week they spent alone in a hut over one Christmas holiday.

NEITHER HAS BEEN back to Regensburg for years. Gnüss' most vivid memory of it, for reasons he can't locate, is of the scrape and desolation of his dentist's tooth-cleaning instruments one rainy March morning. Meinert usually refers to their hometown as Vitality's Graveyard. His younger brother still writes to him twice a week. Gnüss still sends a portion of his pay home to his parents and sisters.

Gnüss knows that he's being the young and foolish one but nevertheless can't resist comparing the invincible intensity of his feelings for Meinert with his pride at serving on this airship—this machine that conquers two oceans at once, the one above and the one below—this machine that brought their country supremacy in passenger, mail, and freight service to the North and South American continents only seventeen years after the Treaty of Versailles.

Even calm, cold, practical minds that worked on logarithms or carburetors felt the strange joy, the uncanny fascination, the radiance of atmospheric and gravitational freedom. They'd watched the *Graf Zeppelin,* their sister ship, take off one beautiful morning, the sun dazzling on its aluminum dope as if it were levitating on light, and it was like watching Juggernaut float free of the earth. One night they'd gone down almost to touch the waves and scared the crew of a fishing boat in the fog, and had joked afterwards about what the crew must have experienced: looking back to see a great dark, whirring, chugging thing rise like a monster upon them out of the murky air.

They're both Party members. They were over Aachen during the national referendum on the annexation of the Rhineland, and helped the chief steward rig up a polling booth on the port promenade deck. The Yes vote had carried among the passengers and crew by a count of 103 to 1.

MEALS IN FLIGHT are so relaxed that some guests arrive for breakfast in their pajamas. Tereska is one such guest, and Gnüss from his station watches Meinert chatting and flirting with her. *She's only an annoyance,* he reminds himself, but his brain seizes and charges around enough to make him dizzy.

The great mass of the airship, though patrolled by crew members, is off limits to passengers except for those on guided tours. Soon after the breakfast service is cleared, Meinert informs him, with insufficient contrition, that Tereska's family has requested him as their guide. An hour later, when it's time for the tour to begin, there's Tereska alone, in her boyish shirt and sailor pants. She jokes with Meinert, and lays a hand on his forearm. He jokes with her.

Gnüss, beside himself, contrives to approach her parents, sunning themselves by a port observation window. He asks if they'd missed the tour. It transpires that the bitch has forewarned them that it would be a lot of uncomfortable climbing and claustrophobic poking about.

He stumbles about belowdecks, only half remembering his current task. What's happened to his autonomy? What's happened to his ability to generate pleasure or contentment for himself independent of Meinert's behavior? Before all this he saw himself in the long term as first officer, or at least chief sailmaker: a solitary and much-admired figure of cool judgments and sober self-mastery. Instead now he feels overheated and coursed through with kineticism, like an agitated and kenneled dog.

He delivers the status report on the ongoing inspection of the gas cells. "Why are you *weeping*?" Sauter, the chief engineer, asks.

RESPONSIBILITY HAS FLOWN out the window. He takes to carrying Meinert's grandfather's watch inside his pants. His briefs barely hold the weight. It bumps and sidles against his genitals. Does it show? Who cares?

HE SEES MEINERT only once all afternoon, and then from a distance. He searches for him as much as he dares during free moments. During lunch the chief steward slaps him on the back of the head for gathering wool.

Three hours are spent in a solitary and melancholy inspection of the rearmost gas cell. In the end he can't say for sure what he's seen. If the cell had disappeared entirely it's not clear he would have noticed.

RHINE SALMON FOR the final dinner. Fresh trout from the Black Forest. There's an all-night party among the passengers to celebrate their arrival in America. At the bar the man who'd thrown away his wristwatch on departure amuses himself by balancing a fountain pen on its flat end.

They continue to be separated for most of the evening, which creeps along glacially. Gnüss sorts glassware for storage upon landing, and Meinert lends a hand back at the engine gondolas, helping record fuel consumption. The time seems out of joint, and Gnüss finally figures out why: a prankster has set the clock in the bar back, to extend the length of the celebration.

On third watch he takes a break. He goes below and stops by the crew's quarters. No luck. He listens in on a discussion of suitable first names for children conceived aloft in a zeppelin. The consensus favors Shelium, if a girl.

Someone asks if he's seen Meinert. Startled, he eyes the questioner. Apparently the captain's looking for him. Two machinists exchange looks.

Has Gnüss seen him or not? the questioner wants to know. He realizes he hasn't answered. The whole room has taken note of his paralysis. He says he hasn't, and excuses himself.

He finds Meinert on the catwalk heading aft. Relief and anger and frustration swarm the cockleshell of his head. It feels like his frontal lobe is in tumult. Before he can speak Meinert tells him to keep his voice down, and that the party may be over. What does *that* mean? Gnüss wants to know. His friend doesn't answer.

They go hunting for privacy without success. A crossbrace near the bottom of the tail supports a card game.

On the way back forward, they're confronted by their two roommates, Egk and Thoolen, who block the catwalk as though they've formed an alliance. Perhaps they feel neglected. "Do you two *ever* separate?" Egk asks. "Night and day I see you together." Thoolen nods unpleasantly. One is Hamburg at its most insolent, the other Bremerhaven at its foggiest. "Shut up, you fat bellhop," Meinert says.

They roughly squeeze past, and Egk and Thoolen watch them go. "*I'm so in love!*" Egk sings out. Thoolen laughs.

Gnüss follows his friend in silence until they reach the ladder down to B deck. It's a busy hub. Crew members come and go briskly. Meinert hesitates. He seems absorbed in a recessed light fixture. It breaks Gnüss' heart to see that much sadness in the contours of his preoccupation.

"What do you mean, the party may be over?" Gnüss demands quietly.

"Pruss wants to see me. He says for disciplinary matters. After that, you know as much as I," Meinert says.

The radio officer and the ship's doctor pass through the corridor at the bottom of the stairs, glancing up as they go, without stopping their quiet conversation.

When Gnüss is unable to respond, Meinert adds, "Maybe he just wants me to police up my uniform."

At a loss, Gnüss finally puts a hand on Meinert's arm. Meinert smiles, and whispers, "*You are the most important thing in the world right now.*"

The unexpectedness of it brings tears to Gnüss' eyes. Meinert murmurs that he needs to get into his dining room whites. It's nearly time to serve the third breakfast. They've served two luncheons, two dinners, and now three breakfasts.

They descend the stairs together. Gnüss is already dressed and so gives his friend another squeeze on the arm and tells him not to worry, and then goes straight to the galley. His eyes still bleary with tears, he loads linen napkins into the dumbwaiter. Anxiety is like a whirling pillar in his chest. He remembers another of Meinert's war stories, one whispered to him in the early morning after they'd first spent the night together. They'd soaked each other and the bed linens with love and then had collapsed. He woke to words in his ear, and at first thought his bedmate was talking in his sleep. The story concerned Meinert's captain after a disastrous raid one moonless night over the Channel. Meinert had been at his post in the control car. The captain had started talking to himself. He'd said that both radios were smashed, not that it mattered, both radiomen being dead. And that both outboard engines were beyond repair, not that *that* mattered, since they had no fuel.

AROUND FOUR A.M., the passengers start exclaiming at the lights of Long Island. The all-night party has petered out into knots of people waiting and chatting along the promenade. Gnüss and Meinert set out the china, sick with worry. Once the place settings are all correct, they allow themselves a look out an open window. They see below that they've overtaken the liner *Staatendam,* coming into New York Harbor. She salutes them with blasts of her siren. Passengers crowd her decks waving handkerchiefs.

They're diverted north to avoid a front of thunderstorms. All morning, they drift over New England, gradually working their way back to Long Island Sound.

At lunch Captain Pruss appears in the doorway for a moment, and then is gone. They bus tables. The passengers all abandon their seats to look out on New York City. From the exclamations they make it's apparently some sight. Steam whistles sound from boats on the Hudson and East Rivers. Someone at the window points out the *Bremen* just before it bellows a greeting. The *Hindenburg*'s passengers wave back with a kind of patriotic madness.

The tables cleared, the waiters drift back to the windows. Gnüss puts an arm around Meinert's shoulders, despair making him courageous. Through patchy cloud they can see shoal water, or tide-rips, beneath them.

Pelicans flock in their wake. What looks like a whale races to keep pace with their shadow.

In New Jersey they circle over miles of stunted pines and bogs, their shadow running along the ground like a big fish on the surface.

It's time for them to take their landing stations.

Sauter passes them on their way to the catwalk and says that they should give the bracing wires near Ladder #4 another quick check and that he'd noticed a little bit of hum.

By the time they reach the base of #4, it's more than a little bit of a hum. Gnüss volunteers to go, anxious to do something concrete for his disconsolate beloved. He wipes his eyes and climbs swiftly while Meinert waits below on the catwalk.

Meinert's grandfather's pocket watch bumps and tumbles about his testicles while he climbs. Once or twice he has to stop to rearrange himself. The hum is up near the top, hard to locate. At their favorite perch, he stops and hooks on his harness. His weight supported, he turns his head slightly to try and make his ears direction-finders. The hum is hard to locate. He runs a thumb and forefinger along nearby cables to test for vibration. The cables are covered in graphite to suppress sparks. The slickness seems sexual to him. He's dismayed by his single-mindedness.

On impulse, he takes the watch, pleasingly warm, from his pants. He loops it around one of the cable bolts just so he can look at it. The short chain keeps slipping from the weight. He wraps it once around the nut on the other side of the beam. The nut feels loose to him. He removes and pockets the watch, finds the adjustable wrench on his tool belt, fits it snugly over the nut, and tightens it, and then, uncertain, tightens it again. There's a short, high-pitched sound of metal under stress or tearing.

BELOW HIM, HIS lover, tremendously resourceful in all sorts of chameleonlike self-renovations, and suffused with what he understands to be an unprecedented feeling for his young young boy, has been thinking, *Imagine instead that you were perfectly happy.* Shivering, with his coat collar turned up as though he were sitting around a big cold aerodrome, he leans against a cradle of wires and stays and reexperiences unimaginable views, unearthly lightness, the hull starlit at altitude, electrical storms and the incandescence of clouds, and Gnüss' lips on his throat. He remembers his younger brother's iridescent fingers after having blown soap bubbles as a child.

Below the ship, frightened horses spook like flying fish discharged from seas of yellow grass. Miles away, necklaces of lightning drop and fork.

Inside the hangarlike hull, they can feel the gravitational forces as Captain Pruss brings the ship up to the docking mast in a tight turn. The sharpness of the turn overstresses the after-hull structure, and the bracing wire bolt that Gnüss overtightened snaps like a rifle shot. The recoiling wire slashes open the gas cell opposite. Seven or eight feet above Gnüss' alarmed head, the escaping hydrogen encounters the prevailing St. Elmo's fire playing atop the ship.

From the ground, in Lakehurst, New Jersey, the *Hindenburg* malingers in a last wide circle, uneasy in the uneasy air.

The fireball explodes outwards and upwards, annihilating Gnüss at its center. More than a hundred feet below on the axial catwalk, as the blinding light envelops everything below it, Meinert knows that whatever time has come is theirs, and won't be like anything else.

Four hundred and eighty feet away, loitering on the windblown and sandy flats weedy with dune grass, Gerhard Fichte, chief American representative of Luftschiffbau Zeppelin and senior liaison to Goodyear, hears a sound like surf in a cavern and sees the hull interior blooming orange, lit from within like a Japanese lantern, and understands the catastrophe to his company even before the ship fully explodes. He thinks: *Life, motion, everything was untrammeled and without limitation, pathless, ours.*

"LOVE AND HYDROGEN" began when I was stuck for somewhat longer than I wanted to be in the children's book section of my local bookstore. I'd been trailing back and forth through it in the company of my four-year-old son, and he'd been not much interested in his father's conceptions of what constituted adequate browsing time. The afternoon came and went. Sometimes he wanted to show me what he'd found; sometimes he wanted to poke through discoveries on his own. During one of the latter periods I came across a children's book about the *Hindenburg*. The oversized illustrations seemed startlingly evocative, though evocative of what, I wasn't sure. I was struck by the immensity of the ship's scale, which I'd known about intellectually but hadn't experienced viscerally. A sense of the hubris of the thing—building a lighter-than-air machine *that* immense, and then filling it with *hydrogen*—and then building into its belly a *smoking* room—touched off in me a sense of the apocalyptic, which, it's been recently pointed out, has been a long-standing fascination of mine in my fiction.

So I did what I always do in such situations: I started researching, and hoped that all of that reading would start setting off bells somewhere, would generate that vaguely excited feeling of a possible story beginning to coalesce. I forged through books with titles like *The Complete History of Lighter-Than-Air Aircraft*. (My bookshelf is often studded with spines that seem stunningly dull or nerdy.)

All that research hugely enlarged my sense of just how bizarrely compelling that now-lost world of zeppelins was. All sorts of wonderful and evocative details began to accrue.

The crucial step, though, was still to follow. Arcana without some sort of emotional stake in the arcana was just trivia. I still needed something to lift the project beyond your average small boy's absorption with big things that blew up. And that something was provided when, surprising myself, I wrote, a page or so after having introduced my two protagonists, "Meinert and Gnüss are in love. This complicates just about everything." Which, I discovered happily, turned out to be the case.

In one quasi-intuitive stroke, I'd provided myself with a way of thinking in more individual and personal terms about the apocalyptic hubris involved in building and flying a sixteen-story-high aircraft filled with explosively inflammable hydrogen. Now one relationship would illuminate the other; one would instruct me about the other. The personal and the political would again begin their usual intricate interpenetration.

Had this been a departure from other stories I'd been working on? Yes and no. "Love and Hydrogen" was produced in the middle of that rarest thing, at least for me—a creative roll—during which I'd generated a series of stories all of which had necessitated a lot of research, and then some hard thinking about why these subjects had fascinated me in the first place: one about the movie monster the Creature from the Black Lagoon; one about a young couple who found themselves in the middle of the Charge of the Light Brigade; one about the rock group The Who; one about John Ashcroft's early days as a politician; one about cryptozoologists and one of their obsessions: *Carcharodon megalodon*, the prehistoric precursor to the great white shark. And so on. The librarian at my college library finally looked up from one of the piles I'd lugged to her station and said, "Can I ask: what *is* your field, anyway?" It's a question my parents and relatives have wondered about more than once, as well.

426 • *Jim Shepard*

Where do these stories come from? They come from fascinations I've cultivated; obsessions I might have had; intrigued curiosities I've allowed myself the luxury of pursuing. In all such ways and others, I've tried to expand that horrifyingly narrow bandwidth we call autobiographical experience, while still engaging those issues and emotions which most matter to me.

Peter Turchi

NIGHT, TRUCK, TWO LIGHTS BURNING

L ATE NIGHT IN early winter. The last hour of the long drive home. I tend to the thermostat, keeping the car warm enough for my sleeping family, but not so warm that my focus turns dull. Beyond the chilled glass to my left, green dashboard lights angle up toward the stars.

Distance defines our relations. My wife's parents live five hundred miles away, what we have come to think of as a day's drive.

When we arrive, she will hoist our son high against her chest and take him, murmuring his dreams, into the house. I will carry our long-legged daughter from our car to her room, where I will lay her gently on the bed we have made for her.

I REMEMBER BEING proud that I hadn't fallen asleep.

"You go ahead and rest," my father told me. "I'll let you know when we get there."

But I had promised my mother I would help him stay awake, so sat straight and hugged my pillow, to keep warm. The truck's heater wasn't working. A good thing, according to my father; it would have only made us drowsy. This was November, sometime between my birthday—which we had celebrated in an empty house, amid packed boxes—and Thanksgiving. Under my father's influence, the past Christmas Eve, I had seen a reindeer's red nose from my bedroom window; with the same power of persuasion, he had convinced me, at least, that our move from Maryland to North Carolina—a place so far off it might as well have been wholly imaginary—was a great adventure.

When we finally left the highway, he said, "Home at last." There at our exit were three big hotels and a restaurant called the Kountry Kitchen and another called Noah's and a go-cart track. My attention lingered on the go-cart track, which was closed. It was after midnight, the latest I had ever been out in my life.

My father stopped the rental truck at a traffic light, looking down at a piece of paper he had drawn from his shirt pocket. We turned left, and then right, and then there were no more hotels, no more restaurants—nothing but a curving road. The farther we went down that road, the more I worried about what my mother would think. She had made no secret of her opposition to the move; rather, she had expressed this so strongly that I harbored the unspoken fear that she might not follow us. She was very much in my mind as we passed a small house with a chain-link fence strung with Christmas lights that somehow looked as if they hadn't been taken down the winter before, and a collapsing larger house, with covered porches on three sides, and beside it a field populated by broken school buses and eyeless shells of trucks. (To be honest: I'm not sure how many of those things I took in that first night; but they were there the next morning, when the overall impression of neglect and decay hardened the fear in my stomach.) I had just started to think that if we went far enough we'd get away from this kind of place, we'd reach another road with bright lights and hotels and restaurants, when my father slowed down, then stopped, then backed up.

"Here we are," he said. "Camelot." He had told me his version of the legend of King Arthur on the ride. We had sung songs, and told riddles, and played games using the letters on billboards. My father could always be depended on to think of something interesting to do. On the edge of a field across from the entrance to the Natural Bridge, in Virginia (which we did not see, as there was an admission charge), we ate sandwiches my mother had packed, and played a game he invented using two sticks and a crabapple. Later, while we drove, my father wedged a paper cup between the dash and the windshield and had me take shots with a crumpled cigarette package, narrating like a commentator on TV. We were football fans, my father and I, but we would play any game that presented itself.

Rule number one, he liked to say: Keep your options open.

MY MOTHER ARRIVED two days later, in my father's pickup truck. We had made a sign for the door—Welcome Home—but that didn't appear to register. Even before she went inside, I understood that the pizza we had watched the pizza man spin almost to the ceiling, the cupcakes for dessert, and the grocery store flowers my father had arranged in a beer bottle on the tiny countertop would not be sufficient to create, for my mother, a mood of celebration.

THE TRAILER PARK was not a park, as I had imagined, but a series of crude terraces cut into the side of a steep clay hill, with a gravel road up the middle and a security light at the top of a telephone pole. There were twelve trailers, six on each side, and the way they were placed on the hill, one above the other, meant nearly everyone could look down into someone else's kitchen, living room, and bedroom. The most desirable spots were the two at the top, which were relatively private—though none of the trailers could have been more than twenty feet from its neighbor—and had the best view of the woods across the road. Our trailer was at the very bottom, which meant, my mother said as she stood in the doorway, not unbuttoning her coat, Everyone could see in. A modest woman, she sewed our curtains closed.

I WOKE TO a strange sound. Not a dog, not a cat . . . There had been talk of bears, and I hoped to see one in exactly those circumstances: from under the covers, safe inside our trailer. When I heard the sound again, and understood what I heard, it became a glowing ember, a warm promise.

My parents, laughing. Not my father alone, which I was used to, or my mother's polite acknowledgment of a joke, but the two of them, together.

The laughter was followed by other sounds, and an exchange I either heard through the thin wall or imagined. The result of my father's insistence, my mother's reluctance, was my father rolling from the bed, then shuffling out to where I sensed I should pretend still to sleep.

Did she know what he meant to do? I doubt it. My father believed in asking for forgiveness, not permission.

He slid one strong arm under my knees, another behind my shoulders, and lifted. I fought to suppress a smile of anticipation, expecting to be carried in to share with them the wonderful discovery they had made, the cause of their laughter. I felt my rear end sag, my father's knee rise to prop me up. My feet, then my head, bumped against the wall of the trailer, and then the door was open, cool air reached under my blanket. In two long strides we were at the door of his truck, I heard the click of the latch, and he fed me in. When my feet reached the far door, I understood this wasn't the start of a late-night drive. I heard my father's heavy step into the trailer, heard him return, and the passenger door opened once more. My head rose, then was lowered onto my pillow. Reaching under the blanket, he set in my hand the stuffed creature I slept with.

"Sweet dreams," my father said, and shut the door.

THE FIRST TIME I told this story, without a moment's fore-thought, was ten years later. She had confided something about her own parents, and we were, after all, in the dark, in the back of her mother's car. Her reaction surprised me, to the extent that I stored the memory in a room at the end of one of the long, turning hall-ways of the mind.

THE MOMENT WE confine memories to words, images are obscured by the language, the understanding, we have now. To be as true as possible to what I can still see, I would write:

One-eyed kitten—white, stuffed, red stitches where a right eye would have been—on the open glove compartment door. (My stage, where the kitten performed with a tire gauge and magnetic St. Christopher.)

Dark shadows cast by the bright security light.

Some nights, loud adult voices from a trailer up the hill. Others, the long, low rumble of a freight train.

I TRIED TO explain to that young woman, in her mother's car, how it was that I didn't feel abandoned, or cast aside, but elated. My parents were happy; I was playing my role, never opening my eyes when my father carried me out to the truck, or back to my room. But then I woke one dawn with the windows frosted over. The blanket had slipped, exposing my back to a chilled seatbelt buckle.

Huddled on the vinyl seat, wrapped as tight as I could get, I waited for my father to push open the trailer door. My clouded breath reminded me of the numbness of my ears and nose. Unable to deny my need, I made a plan: open the door silently, take long, barefoot strides across the gravel, use the bathroom, and return. But the instant I entered the trailer my mother awoke, began shrieking accusations at my father. Bundling me close to her chest, she carried me to their warm bed.

She intended comfort, but I felt crushing disappointment. If only I had sneaked back in. If only I had held out a little longer, my father would have been spared my mother's anger, my mother spared her shame.

I CAN ONLY guess how much time passed. My parents returned to their familiar relationship: my father exuberant, loud, ("Let's all go dancing," "Let's go down to the field and set off some fireworks"); my mother quieter, more steady. She mended our clothes, and fed us, and took me for long walks along the river, and made friends with a nearby farmer so I could pet the horses and stare back at the new-born calves and take warm eggs from under his hens. She taught me songs like "Red Sails on the Sunset" and "King of the Road." Each time we went to the grocery store, she gave me a coin to use either on the noisy rides out front or on the clear-globed machines filled with worthless trinkets just inside the doors. My desire for those trinkets was as urgent as it was irrational; I dreamed about the rides, the horse and ambulance and the blinking spaceship that rose, as one rode, until it angled toward the sky. Yet some days I dropped the coin into my pocket, remembering rule number one.

What I mean to say is, my mother was kind and generous and attentive. But my father shone with the brilliance of a sun.

HE STOCKED VENDING machines with candy and crackers. It seemed to me the most marvelous job a father could have. Once we drove his route together, me on the (filthy, my mother said) floor of the panel truck, him telling stories about people he had met. My father knew everyone in the world, and introduced me to them, one by one. "I've got the boss with me today," he'd tell his customers.

His plan was to own and manage a fleet of sandwich wagons. It may not sound like much of an ambition, but my father had the charm of a scene-stealing actor, and convinced people he was going places. My mother must have thought so, because she married him young, against her parents' advice. She was independent, and serious, and had, I imagine, plans of her own.

ONE DAY, AN envelope arrived which gave her so much pleasure she said we could do whatever I wanted—which was to make cheese sandwiches and have a picnic on the large flat rock in the middle of the river we sometimes walked to, which we did. The envelope, she confided, contained a check for a large sum of money, designated by the sender to be used by my mother to buy a car. The gift was a great mystery to me. Adding to the intrigue was the fact that, while she had known the envelope was coming, my father did not. That night, the news of the check and its intended use was the cause of prolonged debate. My mother did not cry, or curse—I never heard her curse. Rather, she grew quietly, darkly resolved.

I was a beneficiary of her insistence. In her yellow car we drove to the local branch library, and to the enormous central library, where my mother looked up one thing or another while I sat in a corner, happily lost in picture books and early readers. I never thought to ask what she was looking for. We also drove to the grocery store, where the women at the bakery gave me a tea cookie whether we bought anything from them or not, and took long rides on the Blue Ridge Parkway, where we hunted blackberries and wild blueberries, and my mother sat on a boulder and read while I tested the seaworthiness of leaves and sticks in a narrow stream.

She bought a magnet with my name on it, which she fixed to the dashboard directly ahead of the passenger seat. The letters were raised, in script, and as we drove I traced my name again and again.

BEDTIME CAME, AND I said I wanted to sleep in the truck.

I remember planning my announcement, and thinking the gesture heroic; I remember its silent reception.

Finally, my mother asked me why.

Because it was fun to sleep in the truck. (This was not entirely a lie; I had come to think of the vinyl bench seat, with its warm smell of my father, as more truly mine than any part of the trailer.)

My mother suggested that sleeping in the truck was not a good idea.

I must have responded badly. My memory is of getting my way, and an extra blanket, and realizing, somehow, that my offer had not had its intended effect.

MY MOTHER WAS not an extravagant woman, but in the spring we washed her car every week. She would vacuum and clean the trailer, then together we would haul the vacuum cleaner and sponges and a bucket of hot, soapy water outside. I wore shorts. I had never owned a bathing suit, and my mother did not approve of children of any age "running around without a stitch." Some days she wore her old housecleaning clothes, but other times she wore a one-piece bathing suit, an outfit that made her fair game for both of us. For me, it meant that she wouldn't be angry if I accidentally turned the hose in her direction. She would shriek, and grab the nozzle from my hand and aim it at me, and we would take turns exclaiming at the cold water and hosing the other down. For my father, the bathing suit seemed to guarantee that he would pick her up, and call her Daisy Mae in a preposterously exaggerated version of the accent of our neighbors. It made her laugh, but my father's arrival almost always meant an end to our fun.

I NEVER WONDERED what the neighbors thought when they heard my father going out to his truck in the middle of the night. I don't know that any of them ever saw me inside.

IN MY MEMORY, during the months we lived there, it was nearly always night. Some nights he collected me in his arms hardly waiting for me to scoop up my blanket and pillow. Other nights he stood in the space between the open truck door and the cab, or better yet, held me aloft, and talked a beery cloud. One night he turned his back to the security light and the rental trailers on concrete blocks stacked on the clay and we stared up at a reddish dot in the night. "Mars," he said. "You might live there one day." For a moment we both imagined such a thing. At least, I did. And while on that grocery store ride a journey through space had always seemed like an observed heroic adventure, all rockets and thrusters and urgently shouted commands, that night I imagined life on Mars to be a quiet, solitary enterprise.

"Near the moon," I said, silently equating moon with mother.

"That's right," he said.

Long after an introductory astronomy text set the record straight, the sense of the night that held sway over me was the one I gathered in my father's arms.

THE ARGUMENT OVER my mother's car may have seemed worse than it was, as I imagined myself in the middle of it. I don't recall the expression on either of their faces, which suggests I was either standing outside, listening, or staring at the floor. She wanted to take the car to a service station; my father wanted to do the work himself. It was a waste of money, he insisted. She claimed he would get distracted, or have to find a part at the junkyard, and the car would sit, neglected, for weeks. My father's tendency to stop short of finishing his projects was indisputable.

Nevertheless, he disputed it, said he'd be damned if he'd pay some high school dropout to do a half-assed job (a remark meant to cut deep, as my mother had not graduated from high school). She said she'd pay for it herself, and if he didn't want to follow her she'd hitchhike home, she wouldn't have any trouble finding a man who would give her a ride, and something about that must have convinced my father there was no stopping her, because he relented.

I rode with him, absorbed in a book from the library. I opened the crisp cover wide and put my nose close to the pages, inhaling the scents of ink and paper and the hands of boys before me. I turned the pages carefully, admiring the bold lettering of the title. I couldn't have been more than a page into the story when my father cursed, quickly shifted, and jumped out of the truck.

The scene in front of me remains perfectly clear. On the left side of the intersection, headed right, a blue pickup. On the right, a man in a straw hat getting out of a white sedan. And in the middle of the intersection, my mother's car, with a horrible impression the width of the pickup truck's bumper running from just ahead of the driver's door to just behind it. Even before my father roared I saw, at the top of the door panel, a bright streak of red on the yellow paint.

ANY NUMBER OF people said it was a good thing I had gone in the truck. But the thought that pulsed through me for days, years, was that I should have been with my mother. It would have been such a small favor, to have ridden beside her.

In my dreams, she held out her hand. Night after night, I told her, "I'm right here."

MY FATHER AND I were not together much longer. You can imagine the conversations with relatives, my father's grief. We insisted on going it alone, and lasted perhaps a month. There was an excruciating drive back to Maryland, where we said what we both claimed, maybe even believed, were temporary goodbyes. Over the next few years there were regular visits, a much-anticipated trip to the beach.

I should admit here that I came to resent some of my father's decisions, and let him know it. Every so often he would burst onto the scene, trying in a weekend to make up for months without a phone call. There was another wife, and a child. Then a third wife, and two children. Those choices soured some people's impression of him.

I don't believe my father is a bad or shallow man. He was young, and heartbroken, and committed to the belief that life should be lived as if every day were a great adventure. That attitude can be terribly appealing.

SOME PEOPLE BELIEVED, and on one or two occasions even expressed, that my "new family" was the preferable one: a settled, loving couple, with energetic and companionable children. My mother's brother, an amateur historian, encouraged intellectual curiosity in whatever form it took, bookish or less orthodox. My aunt is an industrious woman who believes boys should be able to replace a button and cook a decent meal, and girls had better be prepared to change a tire. The home they made was demanding, in the best sense, and supportive, and I mean for nothing I write here to imply a word of criticism of them, or anything but the deepest gratitude for all they have done for me.

And yet, inevitably, I have wondered what would have become of me if that other life, the one three of us began, had been allowed to continue. There might very well have been a different painful separation, other difficult times. I might have found my way into that same second household, under different circumstances. I realize I am indulging a deep streak of romanticism when I imagine that my mother and father might have clung together, discovering solutions to their apparently contradictory desires and sacrifices, and that I might have completed my childhood in the family that made me, gone on to live the life I was meant to live.

For a long time I believed that if my mother's accident had been avoided, if my foundation had been more solid, everything that followed would have felt more certain. But every foundation is, eventually, shaken. My grandparents are gone now. As is my uncle. More and more, I find my nights, and my days, illuminated by the light of dying stars.

Soon our daughter will be too big for me to carry.

IMAGINATION, ABHORRING A vacuum, insists on filling gaps; assumptions made years later insinuate themselves as fact. If these memories I have tried so carefully to record are not, strictly, true, what is this that I've made?

O, my mother.

O, father.

We put our children to bed, and then we tell ourselves the stories that will carry us to sleep.

"NIGHT, TRUCK, TWO Lights Burning" is an unusual story, for me, because I wrote it in response to a technical challenge. The story I had written previously ("Black Eye," published in the *Colorado Review* in spring 2001) was something of a departure. I tend to write long, and to fill in all the blanks; "Black Eye" was composed as a series of distinct short sections which, in my mind, formed a whole the way individual stones form a wall: by fitting snugly together, with the courses staggered for strength. Those short sections seemed to call for a terse voice, but after I finished it I began to wonder if a similar structural technique could be applied to a story with a more meditative voice. (Of course, I don't mean I wondered whether such a thing could be done; rather, I wondered if I could do it.)

I imagined a story beginning with an elderly man lying in bed, having just taken medicine and, in the moment of euphoria that comes from the easing of pain, remembering the similar weightlessness he felt as a child, when he was carried by his father from the car to his bedroom. Stories often begin, for me, in images. Not far from where I live there are several trailer parks, large and small, and another resonant image was of a pickup truck backing into the steep road of one of the smaller parks. Why that image took root, I have no idea.

Around the same time, I was introduced to the work of visual artist Charles Ritchie. One of Ritchie's pieces, "Night in Three Panels," depicts a row of modest houses, at night, in a wooded suburb. The house in the middle is dark. The house on the left is also dark, with the exception of a breezeway light someone has left on. (By mistake? For security? For someone expected to arrive after everyone was asleep?) Of the house on the far right, only one window and a bit of the porch are visible, but a light is on inside, implying that someone in that house is awake. For some reason, I imagine that person to be alone. I imagine that person to be writing.

While Ritchie's image didn't provide the actual setting for the story, it did suggest a tone, and later it offered those two metaphorical lights, the one implying a presence, the other an absence.

Marrying the narrator's voice with the short sections wasn't as difficult as I had anticipated; the brevity of the sections actually created a useful tension, as they constrained his expansiveness. There were other surprises. The notion of the narrator being elderly and sick in bed never made it to the page; the first draft began as the final story begins, with a middle-aged man driving his family home. In that first draft the narrator recalled a time in his past when he lived in a trailer, which was news to me. A simple reversal of my original notion led the narrator to recall being carried from the trailer to the truck, which seemed more interesting. But most surprising, and most troublesome, was the fact that his mother died in a car accident. I had never intended for anyone to die in the story—I always wish my characters full and productive lives—but the narrator's mother died. This was, as I've said, troublesome, as killing off a narrator's mother in a very short story is a little like loading a cast iron safe into a canoe. The new challenge, then, was to record the mother's death in a way that seemed true to the narrator's sensibility, but also from a distance, so that the story didn't switch focus to the mother. (For what it's worth, the story, to my mind, is not about a woman's untimely death, or about a boy losing his mother, but about the inevitable awareness of compounding losses.) In early drafts I had a scene or two leading up to the mother's death, and the accident itself was a larger scene; all of that required heavy pruning.

The danger of sentimentality was strong. A few writer friends were good enough to point out, in later drafts, where I had fallen short. Sentimentality is a tricky charge since, like humor, it is in part a matter of perception. When someone tells a joke, we may or may not find it funny, but in either case we learn something about the teller's sensibility. Likewise when someone tells us a story he finds "moving."

As the story evolved, it became increasingly appealing to move away from a mere chronological recounting of a time in the narrator's past. The leap to his recalling the first time he told the story, to an old girlfriend, encouraged other leaps, and encouraged me to keep cutting away at the primary narrative, to include only the sketchlike images that might flit through his mind as he recalled them once again. Somehow that combination of leaps and cuts allowed me to end the story with a combination of unarticulated lament and articulated observation, the sort of insight that comes to us in the middle of the night. To prepare the reader for the juxtapositions, I tightened the opening section, deliberately offering no transition to "Distance defines our relations," which became a precedent for the story's final lines. In the last few drafts I worked to tighten the imagery, which included putting a noisy toy rocket in front of the grocery store, a rocket that aims backward, to the story's fourth sentence, and forward, to Mars and the light of dying stars.

The story concludes with a series of abstract assertions. In general, that may be a flawed strategy. Narratives are built from detail. But narratives must also transcend their details, and a first person narrator often has some notion of the import of his story beyond its particulars. Late at night, a man is driving, his wife and children asleep around him, and his thoughts lead him to a sobering moment. He is, after all, essentially alone, and thinking of a place in mind we call home.

Robert Boswell

A WALK IN WINTER

NOW WEIGHTED THE limbs of trees. Mounds of snow lined the shoulders of the county road and cloaked the adjacent fields. Snow lathered the air. Snow brought Conrad home.

"You have to like the cold if you want to live up here," Sheriff Mallon said. He slipped a hand from the steering wheel and removed his hat, dusted his shoulders, the finger of his glove erasing a dozen years from his eyebrows. The official vehicle, a huge Suburban, was forest green, inside and out.

Conrad positioned his hands before the heater vents. He had left his gloves on the plane. The township of Chapman, South Dakota, had no airport. In this weather, the drive could take four hours. "I never liked the cold," Conrad said. "Not when I was a child, not now." A pier of electronic apparatus separated him from the sheriff. A queue of red lights flashed on the slender face of a police radio. Saddled to the radio was a louvered microphone and cochleate cord. A second screen displayed digital numbers shifting from 00 to 05.

"That's the radar," Sheriff Mallon said. "The trees are growing at five miles an hour." He indicated with a nod the plastic trumpet on the dash. Without his hat, he looked like a boy. "It sounds slow, but if they really did grow that fast, a seedling in the a.m. would be taller than Everest by nightfall."

Conrad tucked his hands inside his jacket and under his armpits. "You must spend a lot of time alone." He was a chemist and spent a lot of time alone himself.

The Suburban gyrated slightly on the ice. "I should have chained the tires," Sheriff Mallon said. "You have to drive so slow with chains, I didn't want to bother."

The road wound through a broad valley. The river that dictated the road's curves had vanished, turned to ice and laminated with snow, as solid now as any other piece of the frozen world. Beyond this rolling esplanade, on either side, lay forest. Conrad had learned of his mother's disappearance in such a landscape. He had been ten years old. The farmhouse in which he had lived had a handmade ladder that led to the unfinished second story, the walls framed but only the exterior covered. Conrad had leapt over straw insulation from one joist to the next. Frost made the lumber slick. Twice he fell. The noise, he feared, would alert his father.

Beginning with the south window, he searched for his mother's path through the snow. No one could walk on snow without leaving a trail, he reasoned, not his mother, not even Christ. Beyond their farm stood the forest, as dense and dispiriting as a roar. The only clear footpath led to the chicken coop and had been made by his father's boots. Their tractor, the one functional vehicle they owned, had a heap of snow on its black seat, the great tires buried. Not that it could have gone far in this weather. Conrad could not even see evidence of the road that led to their house. The only possible paths were two runnels in the snow that curled out to the forest. The wind

444 • *Robert Boswell*

could have softened their appearance, and new fall disguised them. Or they could have been made by animals, a funnel of wind, a trick of the geography beneath the snow.

If she did the smart thing, she cut through the woods to their nearest neighbor. Conrad ran to the next window, stumbling again, the straw slapping his cheek. He couldn't seem to catch his breath, yet it fogged the window. There was no sign of a trail, but he resolved to hike to the neighboring farm anyway and search for her.

His father waited at the bottom of the ladder. He took Conrad's head in his hands to examine it. "Straw," he said, pulling loose a golden twig. Gripping the waist of Conrad's pants and the collar of Conrad's shirt, he carried him down the hall and locked him in his room. The drift beyond the bedroom window reached almost to the top of the glass. Conrad threw himself on his bed and wept.

"SNOW HAS ALWAYS been a civilizing factor in history," Sheriff Mallon said. "Compare the north to the south, Scandinavia to the tropics." He pointed the gloved finger at the landscape, but Conrad saw only the rumpled white blanket of winter. His window held a cornea of ice. "Deer," the sheriff said.

As he spoke, the deer materialized by the side of the road, a startled doe racing alongside the Suburban. The sheriff lifted his foot from the accelerator. "They do the damnedest things." The deer cocked her head toward the vehicle, and the sheriff braked. The vehicle began to skate, turning to one side, sliding forward at an angle, the running deer suddenly framed by the windshield. As the front of the Suburban crossed the centrifugal line, the engine's weight whipped the vehicle around. At the same moment, the doe made her crossing, darting in front of them, the swinging rear of the truck gliding magnetically alongside her body. But the trailer hitch caught the deer's back leg and upended her, sent her skidding into the high white bank left by a state snowplow. She flew into the mound headfirst and snow collapsed over her. She vanished.

The Suburban rolled backwards to a stop, all four tires on the road. The sheriff eased the vehicle forward. "Be careful with her," he said.

The outside air, brittle glass, splintered in Conrad's lungs. He nudged his door shut, afraid to touch the metal with his bare hands. On the other side of the truck, the sheriff paused at his door to flip a switch. The flashing lights on the roof shone blue and white. Appropriate colors for the cold world, Conrad thought. They had not encountered another vehicle since leaving the city, but he supposed this was a wise precaution.

Conrad reached the snowbank first. He shoved aside loose fall, cursing himself again for losing his gloves. A furred flank appeared. Conrad touched the leg, hesitantly at first, then gripped it and pulled, his feet sliding. The animal was larger and heavier than she had looked. The sheriff uncovered another leg. Together they freed her.

"She's not breathing," Sheriff Mallon said. "Watch her." He began making his way back to the Suburban.

Conrad thought they might gut this deer and lash it to the metal rack on the truck's long roof. His father had been a hunter. Conrad had eaten a lot of game as a boy.

The sheriff carried a metal box from the vehicle. The open lid revealed columns of switches and dials. Sheriff Mallon lifted two disks from the box, each with a black cord and plug like those on headphones. Velcro straps were affixed to each disk. Mallon plugged in the cords and slid the straps over his hands. "When I tell you to, hit that green button," he said and knelt over the deer. He worked an elbow beneath one leg, and leaned forward to roll the doe onto her back. He positioned the disks on the doe's chest. "Now!" he yelled, as if Conrad were far away.

Conrad punched the green button. The disks sent a shock through the doe's body. Her four legs kicked. She raised her head, back from the dead. Suddenly she was on her knees in the snow staring at Conrad, her face inches from his. Her look was questioning but calm. For an absurd moment, Conrad thought she might speak. Then she got to her feet and began running.

Conrad's laugh caused him to teeter on the ice and drop from his squat onto his butt. He rose quickly to one knee to follow the doe's prance through the high snow. He was speechless with delight until he saw blood on the sheriff's face.

"She kicked me," Mallon said. The right side of his face was split open.

CONRAD DROVE THE Suburban in the direction from which they had come. There was not even a clinic in Chapman. Sheriff Mallon lay moaning in the wayback. The snowfall grew heavy. Conrad kept his eyes on the yellow line dividing the road when it was discernible, or on the slope of snow that marked the shoulder. He'd had only one accident behind the wheel, five years earlier, before he had moved to St. Louis. No one had been hurt, but it had changed his life. He had been driving his girlfriend's son to daycare. The boy was buckled into his safety seat in the back of the Taurus. They were talking, as they did daily. The boy said, "Remember that dream we had about those guys and those animals?"

It should have made Conrad smile, and perhaps he tried to. He recalled looking for the boy in the rearview mirror. He meant to smile and ask him to describe the dream. But he could not complete the gesture. His stomach cramped and his hands trembled. This is fear, Conrad thought. He had to name it to understand what was happening.

Fear made Conrad double over. He threw his arms around the steering wheel and leaned against it. Tilting his body, he directed the car off the road, onto the shoulder. He failed to find the brake in time, and ran into a chainlink fence. The poles of the fence remained upright, but wires holding the links snapped, and the fence recoiled into itself as if it were a living creature.

He cut the engine, pushed open his door, and tumbled from the car. "I'm all right," Conrad shouted because the boy was calling for him, but he did not sound all right, even to himself. The child cried and flailed in his safety seat. Conrad climbed to his feet. He leaned against the car and walked hand-over-hand to the open door. The cramping began to ease. "I'm all right," he said again. Lifting his knees to dust them, he expected to find snow, but he lived in Arizona and it was September.

He seated himself behind the wheel and tried to calm the boy, but the boy kept crying. For the moment, Conrad let him cry. It was not that Conrad had recalled something he had forgotten. He would never forget the walk he took with his father. He did not like to think about it, but he had not forgotten it. He had suffered a moment of terror from the walk. Something had brought it back. He caught the boy's eye in the rearview mirror. "*Snap* goes the fence," he said, but the boy was inconsolable.

Conrad did not trust himself to drive. He lifted the boy from his seat and carried him to a parts store across the street. Conrad called his girlfriend. A *breakdown,* she labeled it. She picked them up at the auto parts store, and she spoke as if the breakdown were merely vehicular, as if the suspension in the Taurus had given out.

Conrad checked the gauges on the Suburban. He did not believe he would have another breakdown. He had managed his life more carefully since the accident. Ahead, he saw white and blue flashes. *The northern lights,* he thought. He couldn't see the car until he was almost even with it. Sheriff Mallon had radioed ahead. The window on the cruiser lowered. "Follow me," said a young man in a ski mask. His siren sounded. Conrad felt a funny thrill, driving the Suburban, following the police car, the few vehicles on the plowed city streets pulling off to let them by—all the moving things in the world scurrying to get out of their way.

———

THE FIRST DECADE of his life Conrad spent on a small farm outside Chapman. By the time he was old enough to have memories of the place, his father had quit raising cash crops. They had a vegetable garden each summer, pickled vegetables for winter, and his father hunted game in the neighboring woods. They had no money, except the monthly envelope his aunt would send. She lived in St. Paul, Minnesota, where she cleaned the houses of the wealthy. Eventually, Conrad would go to live with her and help her clean those houses. One of her clients, a professor at Macalester College, took an interest in Conrad. When Conrad graduated high school, the professor came to their house with a present—a tuition waiver to the college. The life that Conrad lived he owed to that professor and to his aunt, but not to them alone. He owed his mother, who had protected him from his father. And he owed his father, who had saved his life.

His aunt liked to say that his parents had not been well suited for each other. To others, she said horrible things about his father. Conrad's mother had a few slight deformities—her nose was asymmetrical and one of her eyelids drooped. In profile, her right side showed a disfigured woman, while her left side revealed a beauty. Her teeth, too, were a mess, the bottom row listing like a stand of trees maligned by prevailing winds. It might have been her teeth that made her speech funny, or there could have been something wrong with her tongue.

Conrad's father was no taller than his mother and almost as slight, but he was dark while she was light, and handsome while she was ugly. He had gone to St. Paul looking for a wife. His parents had died the winter before. He needed help on the farm. He was marginally educated and nervous among people, but he was healthy and good-looking, and Conrad's mother, who had been a cashier at a grocery, had been happy to give him directions about town and flattered to find him waiting in the parking lot when she finished her shift. He owned land and the farmhouse. At that time, he'd had a few cows and pigs. He likely told her about the animals and especially the house, how it looked complete from the outside, but the rooms upstairs were skeletal.

Conrad had no memory of animals on the farm, except for the ragged hens in their stinking coop and the creatures his father would kill and drag home—rabbits, quail, deer, elk, a neighbor's dog or goat, prairie dogs, ducks, fox, house cats, mice. He presented the gutted creatures to his wife with a kind of magisterial silence. He spoke little and expected to be obeyed. He hadn't always been a harsh man. A bad crop of corn the summer Conrad was three had changed him. The pigs and cattle didn't survive the winter. They needed grain he couldn't provide. Conrad's mother spoke often of the winter their lives turned grim, as well as the time before, when she had held out some hope. Conrad was returning to Chapman to identify his mother's frozen remains.

"WE GOT A ROOM for you at the Motel 8," the policewoman said. She had a boxy head, a square smile. OFFICER PATTY, her tag read. Her police cap had flattened a recent perm, making it stick out on the sides. She looked deranged. She had purchased him gloves and handed them over, along with the receipt and his change.

Conrad thanked her. They stood in the hospital cafeteria drinking coffee. The room smelled powerfully of gravy. Everyone had taken a table near a window to watch the blizzard grow near. The snow had let up, as if in anticipation of the storm, while the sky turned solid, a thick metallic lid the color of pewter. Conrad asked about the sheriff.

"He'll live," Officer Patty said and finger-waved to someone seated nearby.

One of the nurses had flirted with Conrad, a young blonde with straight white teeth and a full chest. She somehow thought of him as heroic, although she had heard the details of the afternoon. Nonetheless, he had driven up under the flicker of constabulary lights and delivered an injured officer to people who could care for him. She had hinted about dinner. Conrad had politely ignored her.

"I know your aunt," Officer Patty said. "Most of the people in law enforcement hereabouts know her. Quite a determined lady."

"She's a force of nature," Conrad said.

"You'd think, after twenty years, she'd give up. Finally we have something on our plate. I hope this'll put an end to her grief." She touched her hair. "Oh, flatty Patty."

"Can you give me a lift to the motel?" Conrad asked her.

"In the job description," she said, fluffing her hair. "Protect and serve. Around here, it's mostly serve."

She, too, drove a Suburban, a pair of foam dice swinging from the mirror. A hula dancer wiggled on the dash. She drove slowly. Wind lifted fresh fall from the drifts, but the impending storm still lingered outside the city. A peculiar light resulted, a solemn gray illumination that lent the drab buildings a dignity they didn't deserve. Officer Patty said, "Your aunt thinks maybe you spoke with your father back five or so years ago."

"She never said that to me," Conrad replied. His aunt wanted to find her little sister. She wanted justice when there could be none.

"Something in your behavior tipped her off."

"My aunt is a peculiar kind of conspiracy nut," he said. A single flake landed on the windshield, followed by another, and then a dozen more. "She believes every detail of my behavior has its roots in a single bed. But the world is full of unpleasant catalysts."

The wipers made a sweep across the glass, clearing it. "She's always putting two and two together," Officer Patty acknowledged, "and sometimes gets five. Or seven. Still, she says you suddenly went into a shell."

"I had an accident in a car. That's all. I haven't seen my father since I left the farm."

"*Seen* is a tricky word," Officer Patty said. "*Contact* might be the better word. Any contact whatsoever?"

"None," Conrad said.

"It may all seem like ancient history, but if this turns out how we expect," Officer Patty continued, "talking with him and not telling us, that could be interpreted as 'accessory after the fact.'"

Conrad said nothing in response to this, but he shook his head contemptuously.

"I'd just hate to see that happen to you," she said.

At Motel 8 he said, "I appreciate the gloves."

SHERIFF MALLON APPEARED at Conrad's motel room at nine the following morning. A white square of gauze covered one side of his face. White tape held it in place. "You're gonna have to drive," he said. "I'm taking Percodan."

"You look like a deer kicked you in the face," Conrad replied.

Mallon offered a quick smile.

They had to take alleys to the edge of town. The chains on the tires would gouge the asphalt, Mallon explained. "Policy is twenty miles an hour max with chains." He shook his head. "I may lose vision in the eye."

"I can get someone else to take me," Conrad said.

The sheriff began to shake his head, then stopped himself. "I'm supposed to keep my head still. Had to pay a kid twenty bucks to put the chains on. My doctor will be in Chapman on Thursday, anyway. No point staying here."

At the highway, Conrad kept the vehicle on the shoulder until they came upon a stalled snowplow, a man in a fat coat examining its smoking engine. Sheriff Mallon studied the scene as they passed. "This is an idiotic place to live," he said.

Once they had the chains on the appropriate terrain, the men rode in clanking silence. After a while, the sheriff said, "You know what I kept thinking the whole time they messed with my face? They didn't put me under. I wish to god they had. I kept thinking about that deer. She's out there wondering what the hell is going on. Pain's got to be a different experience if you don't know what it is, you know what I mean?"

"No," Conrad said, "I don't know what you mean."

"Maybe it's the Percodan talking, but it seems to me humans must feel pain differently because we can point to the source of it. A deer gets hit by a truck and it hurts. Fine. She knows the source of the pain—that great green metal monster that tried to eat her. That's what she'd think." He gestured with his hand, the open palm hesitating in the air like a command to stop. "But then, she gets up and runs away, sleeps through the night. Now it's morning, and she wakes up feeling real bad. What's the deal now, she wonders. There's no green metal monster—well, she wouldn't know what *metal* meant—there's no roaring green monster here to bash my leg. Why do I feel this pain? Me, I know why and I know what can happen. I can wind up needing cosmetic surgery, which my insurance won't cover. I can wind up blind in one eye, which'd mean I'd have to quit sheriffing. Depth perception and all. Hell, I'm not even sure this will be taken as an 'in the line of duty' injury. In which case, I'll owe the hospital a fortune. But that's not the point. What was I was talking about?"

"The deer."

"She's got to be thinking there's something inside her, like a rat—not that she'd know what a rat is. A forest animal, a squirrel or something. Maybe she'd think that her thigh is frozen. That's my point. She can't know. It's like lightning striking when you don't even have a word for the sky."

"How many Percodan did you take?"

"Several. This thing hurts like hell. I just was trying to tell you what I thought was this profound thing. How a deer can't know what we know."

"Do you think deer have a concept of death?"

"Sure, they do," Sheriff Mallon said. It began to snow. "Not the way it really is, but they know there's something that happens to the others—the deer they run with. The ones that die. They know that a body asleep and a dead body are two whole different things. I don't imagine they guess it could ever happen to them personally." He grew quiet again. The snow fell lazily like the snow in dreams. "I have a friend used to work in a slaughterhouse down in Iowa. Cows marched along this ramp to the killing floor where it was my friend's job to shoot them in the head with a rifle. Says those cows knew. They were scared as hell. Lowing like all get-out. Christ, I hate to think about it." He started to shake his head again, but put his hand to his chin to hold his head in place. "Iowa's an awful place. My buddy is my age, but you'd think he was fifty. How old are you?"

"Thirty-two," Conrad said.

"I shouldn't have revived that deer." The patch on his face made him appear unfinished, missing a piece. "It's out there somewhere in pain. There's a kind of code about this. You don't leave an animal to suffer."

"Relax," Conrad said.

"I'm supposed to keep my head still." The Suburban descended into the valley they had visited the day before, the white fields and hazy defoliated forest. "I shouldn't be laying all this on you. You've got your own burden. Your mother found after all these years." He unbuckled his shoulder belt and shifted in the seat to lay the good side of his head against the headrest. "Had to clean out the freezer to store her parts. Everybody at the station took home venison. We don't get much actual crime. Graffiti. If it's summer, Mrs. Morrison's likely to run up the street in her nightie. But murder . . ."

"It was a long time ago."

"People remember your dad," he said. "No one has heard from him since he left. Not till we found this body did people think he literally killed her, just that he made her run out into the cold where she froze. A man matching his description in Saskatchewan operates a diner. Had a run-in with local authorities. They faxed a photo, but after twenty years, who could say? I *will* ask you to take a look." He settled his head back and shut his good eye. "Nobody much recalls your mother. I hope there's enough that you can I.D. her." He remained silent for several minutes. "That poor creature," he said. "Out there in the cold. In pain. And not a clue."

BEGINNING AT THE age of six, Conrad accompanied his father hunting. Once he was tall enough, he carried his father's rifle and lugged home small game. He attended school rarely. His father had no interest in it, and his mother liked having him at the farm. She taught him to read and write, to add, subtract, multiply, and divide. Occasionally she would decide he needed to be with other children, and she would hike with him into Chapman, drop him off at the schoolhouse. He never attended more than a few consecutive days. The road was not passable much of winter, in any case.

The sheriff began to snore. Conrad noted the place where the deer had been hit. The emergency gear still rested on the shoulder, covered now in snow. He did not consider stopping to retrieve it. As for the deer, Conrad believed she likely knew as much about death as he did. He would be able to identify his mother if they had the lower jaw. Her slanting teeth—two of them missing—would make the identification concrete. She claimed his father hadn't hit her until after the winter the animals died. Before that he might have slapped her, an openhanded swat at her cheek or her rump, but nothing more. She had given Conrad her solemn oath that his father hadn't always been a brutal man.

The idea that his father might run a diner amused Conrad. His father had cooked for him exactly once. His parents had fought the night before. His mother hadn't come to Conrad's room afterwards. When Conrad stepped into the kitchen the following morning, he found his father frying an egg. "Your mother run off," his father said. He put the egg on a plate and handed it to Conrad. "From now on, cook for yourself."

"Is she coming back?" Conrad asked him.

His father had said all he was going to. The morning air was white. The temperature would not reach zero all day. Conrad ate the egg, fearing his father would beat him if he didn't. His father had never actually hit him, nothing more than a cuff or slap, but his mother had always been there to intervene, to put her body between the man and the boy. Conrad ate the egg and ran to his parents' bedroom. Her coat was gone. He climbed the ladder to the second floor to look for her, but he never saw his mother again.

CONRAD RECOGNIZED ALMOST nothing about Chapman, yet the general contours of the town were still somehow familiar. The school had been remodeled, but he could make out the old shape hiding beneath the stucco. The county sheriff's office took up a corner of a strip mall.

"Oh, my heavens," the secretary said. She put her hands on her face, as if she wanted Conrad to count the painted nails. She was a vaguely pretty woman. It might have been just her concern that made her attractive. She reached out to Sheriff Mallon but pulled her hands back. Blood had soaked through the bandage, and the sheriff's cheek was swollen. "I've got to get him home," she said to Conrad, and then she introduced herself. Abigail. About to turn forty, Conrad guessed. Her fingernails were the pink of salmon. "Could you hold down the ship for me?" she asked. "There's only the two of us, and a deputy who's been on duty since Sheriff Mallon left. Everybody and his dog has slid off the road. He's got his hands full with vehicular. I won't be more than an hour."

Minutes after arriving, Conrad found himself alone in the sheriff's office. He seated himself at the sheriff's desk and went through the sheriff's drawers. None of the reports he found related to the body. One drawer held a Polaroid of the sheriff with two people who might be his parents. They had chalky skin and prim smiles.

Conrad tried the smaller desk of the deputy's. The drawers held almost nothing—loose paper clips and cellophane-wrapped Post-its, a can of soup, a motorcycle magazine. The cover of the magazine showed a woman wearing a bikini on a chopper. The photo centered on her buttocks, her bathing suit the same chrome as on the motorcycle.

Conrad found the file on the unidentified remains in Abigail's desk. She also had the most comfortable chair. Blanched photographs showed a stand of trees, the yellow ribbon of official business, and a vague shape on the ground, which must have been a piece of the body. It had been found by a farmer's son, the report said. Conrad already knew this. The boy's dog had brought in a bone with a scrap of clothing chewed into the marrow. The boy followed the dog's tracks through the snow to a wooded ravine where other bones lay scattered.

The sheriff had found shot in the splintered pelvis. "The unidentified victim appears to have been blown in half by the discharge of a shotgun at very close range. Or animals may have separated the body after the shooting." The report was full of pen scribbles—someone, likely Abigail, making grammatical suggestions, revising for clarity. The county coroner had attempted to reach Chapman but had been stopped by the weather. By the coroner's name, Abigail had written *prima donna!* State investigators would arrive at week's end, weather permitting. A fax explained to what extent *presumed relatives* could examine the remains in order to identify the body.

Conrad closed the file. He found the freezer in the hall, long and white, large enough to hold an intact body. The lid of the freezer had a lock with the key in it. Conrad raised the freezer's hood. Frost covered the Tupperware containers. The first he lifted contained a bone shard, as did the second. The third had discolored skin and gray gristle attached to the bone. As he snapped the lid back on, he spotted a label and wiped frost from it. BONE, it read. Conrad laughed, and the laughter continued long enough to make him nervous. He squatted with his back against the freezer and slowed his breathing. What amateurs these people were. Yet he liked them. The cold air from the open lid slipped over the side of the appliance and chilled the back of his neck.

He took the containers from the freezer and stacked them on the floor. They were as tall as a person. He wiped frost from the labels, working his way down the stack until he found one that said JAW-BONE. He pried off the plastic lid. The bone was in three pieces, but the angle of the teeth was clear enough. This was not his mother's body.

Conrad returned the containers to the freezer. He closed the freezer and settled himself at Abigail's desk. He felt neither elated nor discouraged, merely fatigued. He lowered his head onto the desk and fell asleep.

"IT'S NOT GOOD coffee," Abigail said, "but it warms you up."

She had wakened him. He looked at his watch. He had slept almost two hours. True to her word, the coffee was terrible but it felt good in his throat and warmed his stomach. Abigail had changed clothes. Conrad was certain of this, although he couldn't recall what she had worn before. She had on a dress and black leggings. Earrings. Makeup. She looked ready for a date. "I'd let you sleep longer," she said, "but it's time for me to lock up."

"The sheriff's office shuts down?"

"We have call forwarding," she said. The part of her lips revealed teeth as white as the snow. "Where are you staying? It's almost dark."

"Is there a motel?" Conrad asked.

"In Chapman? Are you serious? Have you made eating arrangements?"

"Can I sleep here?"

"There's only the cot in the cell, and that's just too ghastly." She sighed. "I suppose you're my guest."

"You have plans. You're all dressed."

"This is nothing," she said. Because he still hesitated, she added, "I'd have to lock you in." She rolled her eyes. "*Rules.*"

In her car, navigating the frozen parking lot, she revealed that the deputy had turned up another bit of evidence. "You should have seen the sheriff when I told him. He hates anything happening while he's gone." Her coat seemed to be made of bubble-wrap.

"I looked in the freezer," Conrad said. "It's not my mother."

"Well," Abigail said, deflated. Snow pelted the windshield. She slowed for a pedestrian standing at an intersection. He was bundled in black—shoes, pants, parka, woolen hat. Only his scarf had any color, a red like the lipstick from old advertisements. Abigail brought her car to a full stop and waited while the pedestrian crossed the road. "I guess I shouldn't be disappointed. You can still have hope that she's alive somewhere."

"No," said Conrad. "I don't have any hope of that."

"Who could this be?" The car slowly accelerated. Abigail put her fingers to her mouth and tapped a tune on her teeth, pausing to say, "We just don't have people unaccounted for."

Conrad thought he could make out the tune she tapped: "Happy Days Are Here Again." He asked, "What's the new evidence?"

The tapping ended. Her hand returned to the wheel. "The murder weapon. We think. A gun—rifle. Right there with the bones. The handle was chewed up some, like an animal had dragged it about."

Conrad took a deep breath. He felt a specific, small elation, like being the first at a party to get the joke. "It was a sawed-off shotgun," he said.

Abigail slowed the car and looked at him.

"It's my father you've found." He crossed his arms against a shiver in his chest. "You can show me tomorrow, but I'm certain."

"Who would have killed your father?"

"He himself," Conrad said.

Her gaze made her face naked. She stared so long that he had to reach over and correct the wheel. "There's no traffic," she said softly. "There's the silver lining."

Her house was small and painted red, nestled among larger houses, hardly more than a cottage, but warm inside. She boiled spaghetti and heated sauce from a jar. Conrad told her a few things.

After his mother disappeared, his father gave up language almost completely. He became edgy with Conrad, pushing him roughly from behind to make him fetch wood or shovel the steps. Conrad would have to guess correctly what his father wanted or he would get shoved again. In the past, he and his father had never been alone in the house—only in the vegetable garden or in the woods hunting for game. "I know it sounds unbelievable," he said to Abigail, "to people raised in a house with a television and stereo, whose home was in a neighborhood, whose parents held jobs, but it's the truth. My mother never left me alone in the same room with my father for more than a matter of seconds. When she went to the bathroom, she took me with her."

"Unbelievable," Abigail said. Then, "I believe you."

Conrad and Abigail slept that night in the same bed. The shared bed was not about sex. The electricity in the house died shortly after dinner. They built a fire and lit candles. They kept each other warm. "I'm tempted to entertain myself with your body," Abigail told him, her painted nails touching his neck. Her husband was six years dead. A burst vessel in an important place. "But I shouldn't while you're here on official business."

Conrad recognized his disappointment in this dismissal. He hardly knew her, but he felt uncommonly alive in her bed. She fell asleep, the warm air from her nostrils ruffling the slight, bleached hair on her upper lip, her eyes moving beneath their thin sheathing.

He was too agitated to sleep. He ran a finger over the textured chambers of Abigail's insulated shirt. He traced a nipple, and it changed shape beneath the material, but she did not wake. He thought of the emergency equipment left by the side of the road. He placed his hands on her chest just where the disks would go. She stirred but did not wake. The memory that had been summoning him for years blew against the dark windows. Conrad did not try to resist it now.

Conrad had been building a fire in the stove. His father came into the kitchen and said, "Leave it." He made a gesture with his shotgun, the buttstock pointing to the door.

It was midday, and a dim sun lit the snow on the ground, the sky cloudy and cold, wind lifting the skirt of recent snow up and into the freezing air. Conrad carried the shotgun. His mother had told him that a dog had made the teeth marks in the gun's buttstock. He ran his fingers over the indentations. A month had passed since his mother disappeared.

The neighbor's livestock seemed their most likely prey, but they did not head in that direction. His father said nothing. The teeth of the cold air gnawed at the soft places on Conrad's face. He had to take two steps to his father's one, but he felt a pathetic surge of glee. He had been terribly lonely without his mother, and the only time he felt comfortable with his father was when they were hunting.

At the edge of the wood, they stopped. Conrad needed to pee but it was his custom to wait, out of modesty, until they were in the woods, even though there was no one within miles to see. It had begun to snow. His father asked for the shotgun. Beyond his father lay the house. It seemed to have a hole of light in it. It took Conrad a moment to understand that the front door was open and the lamp within had been left burning. He shifted his gaze to his father's face. His father appeared to be studying him.

He said, "You know what that word means?"

Conrad had spoken no word and neither had his father. His father seemed to think Conrad was privy to his thoughts. Conrad opened his mouth but only breathed. The cold air found his tongue, and he could taste winter. His father turned quickly, looking over his shoulder at their house. The barrel of the shotgun swung around. It would have hit Conrad had he not moved. He stumbled and fell, but got up quickly and dusted snow off his knees.

His father said, "It's what you do to a woman." He breathed heavily, the exhaust of his nostrils white and furious. "And there's no pleasure in it." He pointed to a tree stump covered in snow. "Over there." He wanted Conrad to sit on the stump. His father evidently had more to tell him. When they reached the stump, Conrad shoved the snow off. A thin layer of ice covered the wood. Conrad sat anyway. He looked up to his father, who gestured for him to turn, to face the other way.

Snow animated the sky and painted the world about him. He heard the shotgun crack open behind him, heard his father load one shell and then the other. It was then that he understood. The frozen world paused for him, the woods still and orderly under their white quilt. Even the snow coming from the heavens became stationary in midair, a white organism Conrad had never before seen whole, but only in its million parts.

The shotgun reunited with a snap. Conrad sensed creatures in the forest going about their lives, refusing to be his witness. The fabric of his father's coat made a little cry as he raised his arms. Conrad lost control of himself. Urine soaked through his pants and ran out onto the stump. It made a spirit of steam.

"You wet yourself," his father said, his words startling and heavy. "Get up or you'll freeze to the stump." He lowered the shotgun. "You'd best hurry."

The urine began to ice Conrad's legs as they retraced their steps. Conrad tried to run. His pants froze to the fine hairs on his legs, and each step pulled the hair. He stumbled and continued. He fell to his knees, got up, and fell again into the crusted snow, which embraced him, held him as his mother had, a comfort and protection. Conrad tried, but he could not get back to his feet. The snow was no longer cold but warm, and the warmth began to spread throughout his body.

His father lifted him by the waist of his pants and hefted him into his arms. He carried Conrad the final distance home. When they crossed the threshold, his father shut the door that had been left open. He put Conrad before the stove in the kitchen and rekindled the fire.

Conrad sat before the blazing stove in a kitchen chair, his feet on a second chair. His father stood nearby, his back against the wall, his hands behind him, the shotgun at his side. He thought to bring the boy a blanket and then resumed his position. He did not speak. As Conrad remembered it, his father did not move. But he stayed there, watching while his son thawed.

Conrad was sent to bed. He heard the front door open and shut. His father did not come back until after dark, stamping snow from his boots, walking heavily to the bedroom door. The boy's heart beat so hard that he imagined he could make it out beneath his flesh, hidden but present. His father spoke through the closed door. "Pig you have to cook clean through."

In the morning Conrad discovered that his father had stolen a neighbor's pig, a small thing that he had gutted in his arms while he held it like a baby. Conrad found his father's clothes on the porch, blood frozen into the fabric, and he reconstructed the butchering. His father himself was gone. Conrad would not see him alive again.

It occurred to Conrad, while he lay sleepless in Abigail's bed, to wonder about the boy who had been riding in his safety seat when Conrad crashed into the chainlink fence. How had that accident become one of the stones on which the boy's character was built? The boy by now would be ten himself. He would no longer think another person might share his nocturnal dreams. Conrad understood that he had loved the boy.

ELECTRICITY RETURNED TO Chapman before dawn. Abigail made coffee. Conrad had slept little, but his head was clear. The coffee was strong and gratifying. He told Abigail about the walk in winter with his father. "I feel better about it now," he said.

"Why?" she asked him. "Why on earth would you? Because you know he's dead? Because he can't harm you now?"

This would be what his aunt would think, what his therapist would think. "It's more specific than that," he said. His father had meant all along to include himself. Conrad understood that now. He tried to explain. "It makes it less personal."

Outside, the morning snow fell onto the snow that had fallen through the night.

Behind the Story

I GREW UP ON a tobacco farm on a county road that ran along a wooded ridge in western Kentucky. In winter, when the trees dropped their interference, we could catch glimpses of the Mississippi River from our car windows. Our town lay a few miles south of the farm, just below the confluence of the Mississippi and Ohio Rivers. It would have been the first town Huck and Jim passed after missing their turn that foggy night. In our neck of the river, the breadth of the Mississippi exceeded a mile. It was a wide, moody, muddy deity. "Everything makes its way to the river," my father often said—once, I recall, on the occasion of our peeing together on the slope behind our shed.

My best friend lived on the same blacktop road. His name was Brady. He and I played together in the woods: cowboys and Indians, pirates and captains, the War Between the States—anything with a narrative. We had decided we would be writers when we grew up and we played in chapters, narrating in the third person, pausing to invent a new chapter heading whenever we reached a suitably mysterious moment. In the woods behind Brady's house, we stomped out a network of paths and constructed a tree house that overlooked a creek. Brady suggested we ought to one day follow the creek all the way to the river. We agreed that it would make a beautiful story, but the woods were dense with brush and briars. We never hiked very far beyond the beaten paths.

Snow came every winter, but the winter Brady and I were in third grade it arrived early and was followed by a hard freeze. The creek became solid, its gray surface resembling marble more than glass. Brady opened a chapter with "At last they had a clear path to the river," and we were off. Our narrative made us brave and neither of us was terribly bright. We set out on the ice for the great wide waters of the Mississippi.

We didn't tell anyone our plan. It wasn't part of the story.

Hiking on the frozen creek was unlike any of our other adventures. It was thrilling to be walking on water. It was also slippery, cold, and slow-going. The ice made noises, as did the trees, and things beyond the trees we could not name. I did not at that time own sneakers. My school shoes had slick cardboard soles. I could slide long distances on the ice, but my feet were cold and I fell at regular intervals, as if to punctuate the stream's winding passage.

The creek meandered so much that the hike of a few miles became an odyssey. Walking kept off the chill, except about our faces and ears, where we felt the sting. After awhile it began to snow, a frail and hesitant fall. The gray sky turned to pearl as it approached dusk, hedging into darkness. As the air cooled, the forest sounds grew sharper. The wincing of overhanging limbs became ominous. If the adults who endured our disappearance that afternoon are to be believed, we hiked for four hours.

It seemed to us much longer.

Our story faltered now and again, but we did not let it slip away. I began to wonder what we would do when we reached the Mississippi. In my mind, the center of the river rose up higher than the frozen banks and was rounded on top like a great unsheathed vein. I imagined standing before that vast expanse of ice and water, snow and sky. My legs—or perhaps it was my character's legs—wobbled at the thought. We were engaged with something enormous, I understood. I didn't have the right word to express what it was, but I felt it.

The dark gathered density while we walked along, cheerful and exalted and on the brink of terror. I do not remember much of our storyline, but I do remember that Brady identified a flaw in our body of work. We never had any girls in our stories.

"It just isn't realistic," he noted.

I reluctantly concurred.

By this time we had no chance of getting home before the dark became as solid as the ice. We had not brought a flashlight or matches. Our parents would have realized by now that we had disappeared. Still, we kept walking and telling our tale. There was very little pretend left in it. We announced our progress to ourselves. We speculated on the comely woods. Our breath shimmered in the evening air, the little clouds that stories make.

We knew we were going to be in a lot of trouble with our parents. We thought too much of ourselves to believe we might get *spanked,* and we thought too much of our parents to believe we would be *beaten.* We would get *whupped.* We could not even deny that we had it coming. It might have been a comfort to consider the whupping we would get. It kept us from thinking we might die.

My father knew the woods in a way I never would. He had grown up on the same county road during the Great Depression. As a teenager, he had hunted in the bottomland to provide for his family. "We ate a lot of squirrel," he liked to say. Invariably, he would add, "It's good eating." His schooling was interrupted by war. He served in Italy and North Africa. When he returned, he married my mother and finished his degree. They tried living in Missouri and California, but my father kept returning to Kentucky. He would spend the latter part of his life in Arizona—a move dictated by the health of a child—but he would only ever know one place.

Luckily for Brady and me, we chose the right place to lose ourselves.

His voice seemed to descend from the heavens. "That's far enough, boys." I think it was my father who said it. He and Brady's father stood on the creek bank beside poplar trees, each with his arms folded into the tucks of his jacket.

A wild topple of emotions brought a sudden pressure to my eyes. I felt relieved and deflated, rescued and arrested, fearful of punishment and angry at being caught, ashamed that I had made my father look for me and proud that we had covered such a distance. More than anything, though, I was amazed. We had told no one where we were going, and yet there were our fathers. Mine seemed to me something like omniscient. He had on his reversible hunting cap, the red plaid turned inside, showing only at the earflaps, a sift of snow on the bill.

Brady and I exchanged a look, but we said nothing as we tramped up the creek bank and through the trees. The men had come in separate cars, driving over a backroad that had taken them within a dozen yards of the stream. Brady's father had a pickup. We owned a new Impala. It was not made for such roads, and I felt responsible for the muddy slush on its grill. Brady and I did not even wave goodbye, but trudged like convicts to our separate vehicles. Our winter story would remain unfinished.

Now and again, I find myself writing a story that revisits that illicit walk. None yet is precisely about those two boys and their fathers, but I often discover that the walk on the frozen creek has one way or another informed the plot, the setting, the characters, or even the structure of a story. I do not set out to re-create the walk, but it introduced me to a new quality of fascination and that fascination feeds my work.

I have grown to understand narrative as a form of contemplation, a complex and contradictory way of thinking. I come to know my stories by writing my way into them. I focus on the characters without trying to attach significance to their actions. I do not look for symbols. For as long as I can, I remain purposefully blind to the machinery of the story and only partially cognizant of the world the story creates. I work from a kind of half-knowledge.

In the drafts that follow, I listen to what has made it to the page. Invariably, things have arrived that I did not invite, and they are often the most interesting things in the story. By refusing to fully know the world, I hope to discover unusual formations in the landscape, and strange desires in the characters. By declining to analyze the story, I hope to keep it open to surprise. Each new draft revises the world but does not explain or define it. I work through many drafts, progressively abandoning the familiar. What I can see is always dwarfed by what I cannot know. What the characters come to understand never surpasses that which they cannot grasp. The world remains half-known. In such a world, insight is only valuable if it produces an equal share of mystery.

Writing fiction, for me, is the practice of remaining in the dark.

My father and I sat in the dark of the idling car. He motioned for Brady's father to go first. We would take longer to get out of the woods. My father wanted to navigate the Impala down the icy road slowly, inching over the camelbacks and through the muddy sumps. The Impala had been a demonstrator, and my father had gotten a good deal. It had the chrome package and still smelled of new car. He adjusted the heating vents, which made my feet ache, and said nothing, waiting for the taillights of the truck to disappear entirely into the woods. People who grow up in the country have their own ideas of privacy.

Finally, he pulled the knob for the headlamps. "This was a stupid stunt," he said.

"Yes, sir," I said, choking up but also understanding that he was not really angry. *Stupid stunt* was a favorite phrase of his, and I suppose I spent a lifetime giving him opportunities to use it. *Going off half-cocked* was another one he liked. I got to hear it that night, as well. But he did not swat me or restrict me or even make me go to bed early. He did not punish me in any way.

Brady was not so lucky. He got a whupping. I was not invited to his house for some weeks. When we finally got to play together, shame kept us from talking about our punishments. He was ashamed that he had been spanked, and I was ashamed that he had been disciplined while I got off scot-free. The topic of the walk became off-limits.

On that long drive home, while my father corkscrewed the car down the road, the windshield wipers slapping away the snow, he and

I talked. He was stern enough at first but he couldn't keep it up. Like other men of his generation, he desired to see some of his passions alive in his son. Men still have this wish, but I think there was something different about it for that generation. Immense forces of history had taken liberties with their lives, and they needed to believe particular things they loved would endure. My father was happy that I had shown some interest in the woods and the river. He disguised his pleasure, but he could not contain it.

Of course, I failed him. I don't hunt. I don't fish. I don't know any landscape the way he knew the river bottom. All I can claim is that some power lures me out again and again to that creek, to the walk as I remember it, the woods dark and lovely and deep, the snow as white as a page. Did I mention that Brady and I had a rifle? We may have had one. It would have been a .22 or a BB gun. We would have taken turns carrying it. We likely had peanut butter sandwiches in our pockets, wrapped in wax paper. We would have had some in the tree house. Did we remember to eat them?

It had not occurred to me that "A Walk in Winter" had its origins in this memory until I wrote this essay. Although the connections seem obvious to me now, I did not recognize them even in the early drafts of this essay. In "The Art of Fiction," Henry James advises writers: "Try to be one of the people on whom nothing is lost." I work by the opposite means. I resist knowing until the story finally rubs my nose in it.

Writing this essay has also reminded me of one other moment that I had forgotten—or chosen not to remember.

Before Brady's father drove off with his son, he walked over to our car. My father lowered his window. The other man stuck his head inside and eyed me. He said, "This was Brady's idea, wasn't it?"

I understood the ramifications of the question immediately, how it might help my case if I said yes and how it might get Brady beaten. How my saying no might save his hide. Our characters were fiercely loyal, sacrificing themselves each for the other without a thought.

There was no question what my character would do. But I felt another, complicating tug. The walk had begun with Brady's chapter. I didn't know the word *plagiarism,* but I felt the terrible weight of it. I did not want to betray my friend and I did not want to take too much credit for our magnificent, flawed story.

"Tell the truth," my father said.

Which truth? I might have thought.

Ultimately, I nodded and let my friend take his beating.

CONTRIBUTORS' BIOGRAPHIES

Wilton Barnhardt was born and raised in North Carolina, and has recently returned there to teach full-time in the Creative Writing faculty of North Carolina State University in Raleigh. A former *Sports Illustrated* reporter and Oxford graduate, he is the author of three novels, *Emma Who Saved My Life, Gospel,* and *Show World.* He is at work on a large saga of the Mexican-American West.

Andrea Barrett is the author of five novels, most recently *The Voyage of the Narwhal,* and two collections of short fiction, *Ship Fever,* which received the 1996 National Book Award, and *Servants of the Map.* She lives with her husband in Rochester, New York. She has been a Fellow at the Center for Scholars and Writers at the New York Public Library. In 2001, Barrett was awarded a MacArthur fellowship. In 2003 she received an Award in Literature from the American Academy of Arts and Letters.

Charles Baxter is the author of *The Feast of Love,* which was a finalist for the National Book Award, and, most recently, *Saul and Patsy.* He has published two other novels, *First Light* and *Shadow Play,* and four books of stories, including *Believers.* He has also published essays on fiction collected in *Burning Down the House,* and has edited or coedited two books of essays,

The Business of Memory and *Bringing the Devil to His Knees*. He also edited *Best New American Voices 2001*. He has received the Award in Literature from the American Academy of Arts and Letters. His work has been widely anthologized and has been translated into ten languages.

Robert Boswell is the author of five novels (*Century's Son, American Owned Love, Mystery Ride, The Geography of Desire*, and *Crooked Hearts*), two story collections (*Dancing in the Movies* and *Living to Be 100*), and a play (*Tongues*). His stories have appeared in *Best American Short Stories, O. Henry Prize Stories, Best Stories from the South, Pushcart Prize Stories, The New Yorker, Esquire, Ploughshares, Harvard Review, Colorado Review, Epoch, Hayden's Ferry Review,* and many other magazines. He is married to the writer Antonya Nelson. Their children are Noah and Jade.

Karen Brennan is the author of a collection of poems, *Here on Earth* (Wesleyan University Press); a collection of stories, *Wild Desire* (University of Massachusetts Press), which won the AWP award in fiction; and, most recently, *Being with Rachel,* a memoir from Norton. She is a professor at the University of Utah, where she teaches in the graduate creative writing program.

Robert Cohen is the author of three novels, *The Organ Builder, The Here and Now,* and *Inspired Sleep,* and a collection of stories, *The Varieties of Romantic Experience*. His awards include a Whiting Writers Award, a Lila Wallace Writers Award, and a Pushcart Prize. He teaches at Middlebury College.

Tracy Daugherty is the author of three novels and two short story collections, including *What Falls Away* and *It Takes a Worried Man*. He has also published a book of personal essays, *Five Shades of Shadow*. His latest novel, *Axeman's Jazz,* is forthcoming. He directs the MFA Program in Creative Writing at Oregon State University.

Stephen Dobyns has published eleven books of poetry and twenty novels, including ten mystery novels set in Saratoga Springs. His collection of essays on poetry, *Best Words, Best Order,* appeared in 1996. His first book of poems, *Concurring Beasts,* was the Lamont Poetry Selection for 1972 of the Academy of American Poets. *Black Dog, Red Dog* was a winner in the National Poetry Series. *Cemetery Nights* won the Poetry Society of America's Melville Cane Award in 1987. Dobyns has received a Guggenheim and three fellowships from the National Endowment for the Arts. His most recent book of poetry is *The Porcupine's Kisses* (2002). He has also published a collection of short stories, *Eating Naked* (2000). Dobyns lives near Boston. He teaches in the MFA program at Sarah Lawrence College.

Judith Grossman is the author of a book of stories, *How Aliens Think,* and a novel, *Her Own Terms.* A former director of the MFA fiction program at the University of California-Irvine, she has held fellowships from the National Endowment for the Humanities and the Fine Arts Work Center, Provincetown, and won the Cohen Award for Fiction from *Ploughshares* in 2000.

Ehud Havazelet is the author of two story collections, *What Is It Then Between Us?* (Scribner, 1988) which won the California and Bay Area Book Reviewers Awards, and *Like Never Before* (Farrar, Straus & Giroux, 1998), which won the Oregon Book Award. His work has appeared in many periodicals, most recently in the *Southern Review* and *New England Review.* He has been a Stegner Fellow at Stanford and was awarded fellowships from the Whiting, Rockefeller, and Guggenheim Foundations. He teaches in the Creative Writing Program at the University of Oregon.

David Haynes is the author of seven novels for adults and five books for children. His books include *All American Dream Dolls, Live at Five,* and *Somebody Else's Mama.* He was selected in 1996 by the British literary magazine *Granta* as one of twenty of the best young novelists in America. He is also currently on the faculty of Southern Methodist University in Dallas, Texas.

C. J. Hribal is the author of *The Clouds in Memphis,* which won the AWP (Associated Writing Programs) Award in Short Fiction. He is also the author of *Matty's Heart,* a collection of short fiction, *American Beauty,* a novel, and the editor of *The Boundaries of Twilight: Czecho-Slovak Writing from the New World.* He is currently completing a new novel, *The Company Car.* The recipient of fellowships from the National Endowment for the Arts, the Bush Foundation, and the Guggenheim Foundation, he is a professor of English at Marquette University. He lives with his wife and three children in Milwaukee.

Margot Livesey grew up in Scotland and now lives mostly in Boston, where she is a writer-in-residence at Emerson College. She is the author of a collection of stories and four novels, most recently, *Eva Moves the Furniture.*

Michael Martone's *The Blue Guide to Indiana* was published in 2001 by FC2. His book of essays, *The Flatness and Other Landscapes,* winner of the AWP Award for Nonfiction, was published in 2000 by the University of Georgia Press. With Lex Williford, he edited *The Scribner Anthology of Contemporary Short Fiction* in 1999. He is the author of five books of short fiction, including *Seeing Eye, Pensées: The Thoughts of Dan Quayle,* and *Fort Wayne Is Seventh on Hitler's List.* He lives in Tuscaloosa with the poet Theresa Pappas and their two sons Sam and Nick.

Christopher McIlroy's story collection *All My Relations* won the 1992 Flannery O'Connor Award. He is a founder of ArtsReach, which conducts writing programs for Native American students in southern Arizona.

Kevin McIlvoy is Regents Professor in the MFA Creative Writing Program at New Mexico State University, where he has been editor in chief of *Puerto del Sol* magazine for twenty-two years. In 2005 Graywolf Press will publish his newest story collection. His other published works include *Hyssop, Little Peg, The Fifth Station,* and *A Waltz.*

Cuban-born **Pablo Medina** is the author of several works of poetry and prose, most recently *Puntos de apoyo* (poems in Spanish, 2002), *The Return of Felix Nogara* (novel, 2000; paper, 2002), and *The Floating Island* (poems, 1999). His work has appeared in numerous periodicals and anthologies in the United States and abroad, and he has lectured and read throughout the United States, Latin America, and the Middle East. He has received several awards for his work and has taught at George Washington University, American University, Hunter College, and Juniata College. Currently, he teaches at New School University in Manhattan.

Antonya Nelson is the author of three novels and four short story collections. She shares, with her husband Robert Boswell, the Cullen Chair in Creative Writing at the University of Houston.

Susan Neville is the author of two story collections, *In the House of Blue Lights* and *Invention of Flight,* as well as two collections of creative nonfiction. Her fiction has received the Flannery O'Connor Award, the Richard Sullivan Prize, and a Pushcart Prize. She lives in Indianapolis with her husband and two children.

Steven Schwartz is the author of four books, including the novels *Therapy* (Harcourt Brace) and *A Good Doctor's Son* (William Morrow). His writing has received the 1999 Colorado Book Award, the Nelson Algren Award, a National Endowment for the Arts Fellowship, and two O. Henry Awards. He directs the creative writing program at Colorado State University.

Jim Shepard is the author of six novels—*Flights, Paper Doll, Lights Out in the Reptile House, Kiss of the Wolf, Nosferatu,* and the forthcoming *Project X*— and two collections of short stories: *Batting Against Castro* and the forthcoming *Love and Hydrogen.* His short fiction has appeared, among other places, in *The New Yorker, Harper's, The Atlantic Monthly, Esquire, The Paris Review, Tri-Quarterly, DoubleTake,* and *Tin House.* He teaches at Williams College.

David Shields is the author of two novels, *Dead Languages* and *Heroes*; a collection of linked stories, *A Handbook for Drowning*; and four books of nonfiction, *Black Planet* (a finalist for the National Book Critics Circle Award), *Remote* (winner of the PEN/Revson Foundation Fellowship), *Enough About You,* and *"Baseball Is Just Baseball": The Understated Ichiro.* His essays and stories have appeared in dozens of publications, including the *New York Times Magazine, Harper's, Yale Review, Village Voice, Salon, Slate,* and *McSweeney's.*

Joan Silber is the author of a story collection, *In My Other Life,* and three novels, *Lucky Us, In the City,* and *Household Words,* winner of a PEN/Hemingway Award. Her stories have appeared in *The New Yorker, Ploughshares,* and *The Pushcart Prize XXV.* She has received awards from the Guggenheim Foundation, the NEA, and the New York Foundation on the Arts, and she teaches at Sarah Lawrence College.

Debra Spark is the author of the novels *Coconuts for the Saint* and *The Ghost of Bridgetown* and editor of the anthology *Twenty Under Thirty.* She teaches at Colby College in Maine.

Peter Turchi is the author of a novel, a collection of stories, and two books of nonfiction, including the forthcoming *Maps of the Imagination: The Writer as Cartographer.* He coedited, with Charles Baxter, *Bringing the Devil to His Knees: The Craft of Fiction and the Writing Life.* The recipient of North Carolina's Sir Walter Raleigh Award and an NEA Fellowship, he has taught in and directed the Warren Wilson College MFA Program for Writers since 1993.

Chuck Wachtel's books include *Because We Are Here: Stories and Novellas*; the novels *The Gates* and *Joe the Engineer*; and two collections of poems and short prose: *The Coriolis Effect* and *What Happens to Me*. His short fiction, poetry, essays, and translations have appeared in numerous magazines and anthologies both here and abroad. A new novel, *River of Stars,* is forthcoming. He teaches in the Graduate Program in Creative Writing at New York University.

PERMISSIONS